IN THE FLESH

My Story

Michael Gabriele

And the Word became flesh,
and dwelt among us.

John 1:14

Contents

1

And So It Begins

THE SCATTERING CLOUDS set free the full moon, lighting my steps from the house into the small courtyard that had served as our workshop. I stood still, as still as the mild air, and gazed up at the moon's circular luminescence.

I was so very small.

I listened. I waited. I wanted to hear something but heard nothing—not so much as a distant goat cry or dog bark. Nazareth was asleep, as were the heavens. But still I listened and waited.

Silence.

A gentle breeze hushed through the palm trees and swept over the stone wall, caressing my face with the all-too familiar scent of wood shavings. My eyes closed. Never before had such a simple aroma given rise to such competing emotions. That slight hint of sawdust on the air instantly took me to a simpler time—learning the trade with my father and how proud he was when my skill developed to rival his own craftsmanship. I longed for those days, which is why that pleasant whiff of wood also brought the pain of great loss.

I missed dad.

I sauntered along the wall, lingered to replace a mallet from the carpenter's bench to its proper hook and sighed deeply. It was time. These tools that had practically become extensions of my own hands would never be part of my life again. How many tables, benches, chests, doors, ladders and shelves had we crafted together right here for much of Nazareth, Cana and Sephoris during the last fifteen years? So many long, challenging, physically taxing, wonderful hours of work with my father.

As I fiddled with the lathe handle, it became apparent. With the passing of my earthly father, it was now time to begin the work of my heavenly Father. There was nothing vague or uncertain about what I was here to do. A divine will had grown within me and was ready to overcome human limitations and guide my destiny here on earth. That isn't to say I wasn't confused. I *was* human after all. The feelings, emotions and sensations of mankind were all mine—all present to help and hinder me. Yet it was clear from the start that the divinity of God's own son rested within my soul. My flesh and blood were mysteriously divine, but the gray matter between my ears was completely limited by human nature. So yes, I was very disconcerted. Where do I start? How do I start? How will my Father in heaven and the Spirit accompany me on this journey?

Confusion also fed fear. But the real anxiety rooted itself in what was hardly ambiguous to me—the culmination of this undertaking. It was fully transparent and always had been. But I now possessed a sacred love that made achieving it possible. Indeed, even human love can strengthen men and women to endure peril, pain and even death to save their children. And that was surely my mission as well—my children's salvation.

I was so preoccupied with what lay before me that I hardly heard my mother enter the courtyard. It was not until she stood at my side that I finally noticed her and turned. Her face, peeking from under a neatly wrapped head covering, betrayed a look no mother can disguise—concern for a pensive son or daughter. The moonlight left little shadow on her face, and we beheld each other peacefully for a moment. Her eyes finally acquiesced to an inquisitive squint as her head tilted to speak, soft and genuine. "Dare I ponder what is on your mind tonight, Jesus?"

I forced a smile that swiftly faded, unable to articulate my thoughts. I glanced down and intuitively rearranged some chisels on the work bench. It was not necessary to verbalize my contemplations. "You know where my thoughts are, mother."

I looked up.

Her eyes expressed expected awareness.

"The time has come, hasn't it?" she asked, not needing an answer. She navigated my eyes just as fluently. "I knew this day would arrive," she offered even softer. "Ever since your father and I found you with the scribes in the temple all those years ago, I knew it was only a matter of time."

I turned to face her. She embraced me as if I were already leaving. I held her tightly and kissed the top of her head. "This is why I came into the world. You know that."

"I do," hardly a whisper. "For thirty years I have contemplated this day."

I drew back enough to raise her eyes to mine. They were wet with tears. "I will take with me the perseverance you taught me, the love you showered upon me and the will to please God that you demonstrated every day."

"Jesus ..." Her words stalled behind the emotion caught in her throat.

I took her fingers tenderly in mine and moved her hand over to my heart. "You and I are bonded here, remember? That will never change."

She smiled despite a tear escaping down her cheek, then kissed my knuckles and held my fingers to her face. "Come, my son. I have something for you."

I followed her into the house where a single oil lamp burned on the table. She had me sit, then took it to an alcove to search for something. She returned shortly and placed the lamp back in front of me. Beside it, she placed a wooden chest the size of a bread loaf. I looked at her inquisitively. Before I could speak, she nodded, "Open it. It is yours."

I furrowed my brow at the old, timeworn box. "Mine?"

Although the wood showed obvious signs of age, the ornate metal clasps and hinges gleamed as new. It was truly an alluring keepsake of some kind. But what could possibly be inside?

I again looked at my mother who coaxed me with an eager nudge. So I carefully lifted the front clasp and slowly raised the lid. It squeaked just a little as the top tilted open. I was not prepared for what I saw.

"Where—where did you get this?" I whispered.

She pulled a stool beside me and sat down. "It was a gift ... given to you the week you were born."

"Who would have given me such a thing?" My eyes remained riveted to what flickered and danced in the oil lamp's waning light. Inside the box, nearly filling it, were sparkling gold coins. I tried recalling if I had ever seen a single gold coin, let alone several handfuls.

"You remember the star I told you about, the one that moved across the night sky just before you were born?"

"Yes."

"Well, with it came several astrologers from the East. They had been following the star for months. They followed it to you, convinced it was heralding the coming of a great king."

I finally released my gaze to her.

"They were right," she breathed.

I glanced back at the gold. Even in the dim glimmer of the lamp the coins glowed from the chest. "I can't take these."

"They are yours, Jesus. You will need them."

"You, mother. You should have them. I will rely on—"

"I have family. So much of this province is kin; I will be well taken care of, you know that. And your father forged so many lasting friendships that consider me family as well. It is you I worry about."

She sincerely wished my acceptance, and seeing her candor, there seemed little sense continuing the discussion. But my thoughts turned away from the gold to something else she mentioned … *family*.

"John," I whispered.

She smiled and squeezed my hand. "The Spirit guides him. He has been preaching and preparing your way for months now. Go to him. How happy he will be to see you."

"I heard he was baptizing on the Jordan. In the desert outside Jericho."

"Yes."

"A far journey," I thought out loud.

Mother closed the box's lid and slid it to the table's edge. "Go."

2

Baptized

AFTER A WEEK OF WALKING, I reached Jericho at last. It had been a long, tiring, uneventful journey, and thankfully so. Anyone making this trip alone risked exposure to bandits and thieves who often preyed upon solitary travelers along the Jordan pass. So on the occasion I could find others heading south, I traveled with them. There is safety in numbers and even the company of strangers helped pass the time.

Jericho was an old but bustling hub, a welcome sight after such a long a trek through virtually nothing. An ancient city, it unfurled its cluster of stone dwellings from the desert—a labyrinth of over-crowded markets with overzealous merchants guarded by a majestic row of columns outside the wall, spaced like granite soldiers leading to the valley below. While many of the people roaming the streets were like me, simply passing through, the vendors, dealers and camel traders who called this place home made a decent living off the multitudes whose ultimate destination lay beyond the hills to the west.

The long hike from Galilee reminded me of pilgrimages to the great city of Jerusalem as a youngster—always a difficult journey—

parched, precarious and prolonged, but family and friends somehow made it an adventure. Finding myself in Jericho again, I paused to look from my position by the outer wall down to the road leading west toward the holy city. I remembered the excitement as a boy knowing we were close upon reaching this very fork in the road.

So long ago.

I now squinted off into those same distant hills sheltering Jerusalem. An uneasy tingle crept up my neck. Just over that horizon, my ultimate journey would come to an end. And the new promise for life would begin.

So much to do before then. The world was hungry, eager for spiritual deliverance, but would the people of this day recognize the truth despite their preconceived interpretations and self-serving connotations? I shielded my eyes from the unrelenting sun and became lost in its glare. Yes, I decided; those who held a genuine desire for my good news would surely hear my voice. And those who did not? Well, they would simply do everything in their power to silence me.

I shifted my gaze east toward the Jordan river and finally smiled with a deep breath. I had a very bold and courageous cousin already captivating those thirsting for so much more than water.

My mother's nephew John was only a few months older than me but had always been more outspoken and opinionated. Even as children, when we siblings needed an ambassador to persuade an adult for special permissions, we always looked to John to state our case. He would present his position and rationale so wholeheartedly and with such fervor, his ability to influence and convince most any listener amazed all. I remembered hearing that John's father Zechariah had a vision, an angel who foretold his son was destined to turn many from their sins and prepare Israel for my coming.

Now, the throng of people heading east out of Jericho numbered just as many as those traveling west toward Jerusalem. I marveled at how persuasive my cousin must be. After all, the path east from Jericho, if one could call it a path at all, winded haplessly through desert thickets and jagged rocks. But it now resembled a key artery for a rather determined parade of people. And I was among them, on a pilgrimage to be baptized by my cousin.

*　　*　　*

As usual with John, I heard him before I could see him. The embankment which sloped to the river concealed the water from view on the other side. Mingled with a small group, I ascended the hill as John's voice bellowed from below. I smiled at the prospect of seeing my kin while carefully sidestepping loose stones and desert brush. My sandals, coated with thick sand and dust, clung to feet in dire need of some rest. But I finally made it to the top.

I gently pulled back the cloth mantle from my head and wiped the hair from my forehead. Several hundred people blanketed the riverside dune, some standing, others sitting, all riveted to my cousin. John stood alone in the Jordan, up to his knees in the murky water. From this distance, I hardly recognized him with his tangled hair and unkempt beard. But it was John all right. A long animal skin draped over his left shoulder. It was tan, most likely camel hide, and was cinched at his waist with a leather band. A wide pottery flask dangled from this crude belt, bobbing back and forth with any movement from his leg.

The dusty bank of the river lay silent. Every ear hung on the words that boomed from this zealous hermit of the wilderness. "The time to repent is now!" he shouted. "You have not come here simply to confess your sins; you have come to demonstrate repentance! Why? Why have you recognized the need to wash your spirits clean?"

Only his echo answered off the hillside.

"I will tell you why!" he continued. "Because the kingdom of heaven is at hand!"

At this, I began weaving among the groups of onlookers, gradually descending the slope toward the water's edge.

John's words were irreproachable. They were precise and perfect. They pulled me even more eagerly through the crowd.

"And since the kingdom of heaven is upon us, you must act now!" he exclaimed, raising his arms to the sky. "For the Almighty has his winnowing fan in hand and is ready to gather his wheat into the barn! I tell you that claiming Abraham as your ancestor will not be enough! God can make children of Abraham from the very stones upon which you stand! He calls you to act! He will not reward your intentions; no, he will only recognize the action of your repentance! That is why you have come to the Jordan today, to be baptized in repentance!"

Not a soul on the bank moved, their hearts and minds captivated and inspired by the vehement voice rising from the water. And that is how John spotted me. I was simply the only one moving, albeit languidly down the slope, finding breaks in the bodies to wind my way closer to where the desert met the river.

His voice suddenly fell silent. He watched, not sure at first who I was as I meandered along before finally coming to a standstill directly across from where he stood.

I was still too far to discernibly see his face, especially with that knotted mess of hair, but my name softly escaped his lips, carried clearly on the calm air blanketing the Jordan. "Jesus?"

I couldn't help but grin from ear-to-ear. I raised my hand to him and called, "John."

He tried rushing toward me so quickly that he lost footing and almost splashed face down in the water. As he steadied himself, I started into the river to meet him halfway. The calm, shallow water was like tepid soup but felt so good on my fatigued feet and legs. John reached me and threw his arms around my shoulders. I could now finally see his eyes, filled with tears of joy. As were mine.

The murmur of the crowd behind us rose like the drone of bees in wonderment of what was happening. John didn't let them wonder long. With his strong arm still tightly wrapped around my body, he turned me around and introduced me to his followers. "Rejoice my brothers and sisters!" he cried, even louder than before. "Behold the lamb of God! Behold him who comes to take away the sins of the world!"

Gasps of amazement clamored from the riverbank at this startling revelation. But John pressed on, presenting me with a gentle shake. "This is he, the one I spoke of! I have baptized you with water, but he who comes after me will baptize you with fire and the Holy Spirit!"

The crowd could contain itself no longer, and many were already venturing into the water. I turned to speak with John, but the intensity in his eyes held me silent. He then uttered what he probably had already proclaimed to the masses, but now sincerely confessed privately, gazing into my eyes. "He is mightier than I and existed before I did. I am not even worthy to untie his sandals."

I grabbed him by the back of the neck and held his head before me in a friendly embrace. "It is time, John. Time to fulfill the prophecy."

He then said something that caught me completely off guard. I would hear it many times in the coming years, but this was the first time hearing myself addressed in this way. "Yes, Lord. What shall I do?"

By now scores of people had come to within several paces of us, wading into the water to more closely examine the man their great prophet held in such high esteem and honor. I looked at them, struck by how anxious they all were for a sign and how deeply they yearned for spiritual direction. So I turned back to John, who also seemed equally expectant to hear some guidance or command from me. My few words surprised him more than I anticipated. "Baptize me, John."

His lips moved, but no sound came forth.

"Now. Here. Baptize me."

He slowly shook his head. "I—I should be baptized by you, and yet you come to me?"

"You have paved a way for me," I answered. "I shall set an example by honoring the way which you have prepared it, so that many may receive me and my message of life."

John still looked perplexed.

The people waded closer, practically on top of us now.

I bent down and eased myself into the water until my knees came to rest on the river bed silt. "Allow this now, John. It is fitting for us to fulfill all righteousness."

Still dumbfounded, he fumbled to untie the flask that hung at his belt. As he submerged and filled it to the brim, I lowered my head. An excited chatter arose from the crowd, but they quickly quieted as John's robust voice returned. "You are all witnesses! Today you see that I baptize the one who always was ... who is today ..." his voice fell slightly, the words resonating from his heart, "and who always will be."

He raised the flask and poured the water in lavish waves over my entire head. It cascaded through my thick hair and trickled refreshingly through my beard, invigorating me both physically and spiritually. John had not realized how much I needed this moment as my own signature that I was officially washing any reluctance or hesitation away to fully accept and begin my mission at hand.

As the final streams of water dripped from my face, a crack of thunder split the air as if during the strongest of storms. My human reflexes flinched. Those around us recoiled in sudden panic, startled and frightened by thunder out of a clear blue sky. And that's when I heard it—a loud voice—but was it really a sound or just some intonation echoing within my head? A deep, benevolent voice spoke, *'This is my beloved son with whom I am well pleased.'*

Did I alone hear this acclamation?

John, and even the multitude around us, reacted with acute expressions of awe directed at the heavens. I suddenly knew the message was intended for all. Not even the bright sun kept the stunned crowd from searching above for the sound source.

Despite the arid surroundings, a perfect white dove appeared from the sky and glided gracefully down to me. It landed effortlessly on my shoulder, and a permeating sense of peace and well-being washed over me. Those disquieting thoughts that had troubled me a week before, wondering how I would fulfill my purpose on earth without my heavenly Father or the Spirit present, were now set at ease.

They were here. I was not alone.

3

Tempted

SURRENDER IS RARELY WISE. Giving up or yielding to an adversary is a sure sign of defeat. That is of course, unless you are surrendering yourself to the will of God and the call of the Holy Spirit. Submitting yourself fully and completely in this way brings a harmony and respite to the soul that cannot be equaled. After my baptism in the Jordan, I was convinced I should take a step back and submit myself entirely, my full instinct and intellect, to the supernatural presence of God. Being human in every way, I habitually tried reasoning things out on my own. By abandoning this self-reliance, I opened myself more fully to hear my Father's voice and remove the burdensome delusion of having all of the answers all of the time.

So it was with more than a little perplexity that I found the Spirit of God leading me north from Jericho, west of the Jordan pass into the barren hills and valleys of the desert. With no animal to carry provisions, no road to mark my passage and just barely enough water to keep me hydrated, I disappeared into the dunes and canyons where not even camels dared tread too far. A testament to my surrendering trust in God, I confidently embarked on what otherwise would surely seem a suicide mission. During the heat of the day I only walked for short periods, retreating often to rest in the shade of the dunes. They protected me from the sun that baked the arid bluffs and blurred them in wavy ripples of parched air. At night, the chill kept me curled in a fetal position for hours. These drastic conditions, coupled with my lack of food and dwindling water supply, taxed me to my limit.

There was a reason I was here though. There had to be. To build strength? To cleanse my mind? I was losing both with each passing day.

I prayed for the protecting presence of my Father and nourished myself with the care of our Spirit. Drawing on his strength was the only thing that kept me going to see another day.

The extreme temperature swings and near constant hunger pangs were not my worst afflictions. As I wandered alone and lonely, thoughts invaded my mind beyond personal temptation. Urges crept in and forced my consideration of escape—to slip away, abandon who I was, disregard my calling and mission and find a way to retreat fully into humanity. Human comforts and pleasures were seductive and beguiling. Impulses to disappear into the flesh both lured and persecuted me. How easy it would be to just withdraw—abdicate everything except the flesh and blood of my life. Stake a claim, start a family; I had already mastered a trade that would keep me clothed and sheltered for life … why not?

It was Satan. The great tempter and consummate liar beckoned me with desires too hard to resist alone in this wasteland. I clenched my eyes tight. Please, Father, I prayed; keep me from running. Keep me from succumbing. Keep me from a path that now seems so clear, so easy and so satisfying, but one I know is the serpent's lie.

There had to be a reason, some rationale for allowing me to be so disturbed by this cowardly traitor's enticement of desertion. I tried focusing on the premise behind these emotions and less on their effects on me, and it soon became clear. This was preparation. The Spirit led me into this physical suffering, beset with temptations to flee, to develop and fortify my human character. It was preparing me for an ordeal with torments a thousand times more horrifying and the impulse to escape unyielding. I realized I wasn't in this desert simply to follow the will of my Father and the direction of our Spirit. I was strengthening myself for what was to come—building and sharpening my human will and resolve to endure at all costs.

With renewed determination, I staggered to the crest of the next hill and fell prostrate to the gritty gravel. There, through the stinging sweat that blurred my vision, was the outline of Jericho in the distance. I was close to finally making it back to civilization and out of this dreadful region. But for now I just lay motionless, too exhausted and weak to move.

A dull hum suddenly grew out of nowhere, steadily building around me. I noticed an approaching black swarm, like a thousand fat gnats, flying in erratic swirls across my line of sight. But they weren't buzzing haphazardly about the hill in the typical, chaotic zigzagging of insects. This was a thick, organized swarm moving back and forth in unison, like a flock of birds somehow synchronized. And then the odor hit me—a pungent stench of decay. Each time the cyclone of pests zoomed by my head, the smell of death gagged me. My empty stomach, however, eliminated any need to retch.

I turned my face to the abrasive ground, intentionally moving my gaze away—nothing but dry soil and rocks beside me, large and small, all dusty and wind-polished smooth. My body ached for nourishment. If only these scattered stones were loaves of bread, I could simply reach out and—

"Do it," the swarm somehow whispered within my mind, seemingly louder than its actual whirring from above.

I closed my eyes and breathed through my mouth to avoid the revolting smell settling down upon me.

"Only you have the power," the living cloud hissed at my brain. "Warm bread. Just reach out your hand and command it. Eat and you shall be well."

Fearing I might succumb if I opened my eyes, I kept them closed. My hunger had weakened me, exposing me to the very temptation of Adam—*take and eat; you shall be delivered.*

"One does not live by bread alone!" I finally hurled back. "But by every word that comes forth from the mouth of God."

The droning stopped.

My eyes cautiously opened to nothing but sand and silence.

I took my chance, summoned what little strength I had and scurried the last few paces to the crest of the slope. My fingers reached the rim and I peered over, my heart skipping a beat. It was not a gradual dune or hillside beneath me but a steep cliff—a dizzying canyon. A few pebbles cascaded into the chasm and echoed soft cracks on the rocks far below.

As I gazed into the abyss, the swarm returned out of nowhere and sped over me, carrying its rancid breeze along with it. "So you're the son of God?" it cackled inside my ears. "Jump ... For is it not written that angels will come to your aid to ensure that not even your feet are hurt on the stones?"

I had mentioned the word of God, and now this thing was bold enough to quote it. But in this, the liar was right. I could make this leap and instantly deliver divine power for my human safety. I hesitated. Could such a display of my sanctity bring renewed assurances? The enticement released adrenaline through me—a quick high. I then shuddered, recognizing this as Satan's perverted twist of the ninety-first Psalm. The demon knew scripture well and how to abuse it.

I slowly knelt, staggered to my feet and started the longer way around the precipice. The dark, buzzing swarm swooped in, and I turned to cry, "It is also written that you shall not put the Lord your God to the test!"

The infernal presence suddenly became disoriented, drifted over the edge of the cliff and disappeared into the canyon depths.

Just stay focused, I told myself. Get to Jericho and this will all be over. I glanced left to make sure I could still see the contours of the desert city on the horizon. What I saw instead stopped me so abruptly that my feet slipped on the loose earth, nearly sending me to the ground. In the distance, where I had just moments ago seen the colorless, drab silhouette of Jericho, was a much different sky-line. In its place, through a lifting haze, an expansive kingdom of unimaginable opulence beckoned me from across a short valley. The stone walls surrounding the city were massive in structure. Towers, buildings and monuments rose majestically higher above its fortifi-cations. Even at a distance they were imposing and impressive, ob-viously designed with engineering proficiency and constructed by masons of meticulous skill. The domed capitols and pointed spires glimmered as if forged from precious metals, flickering glints of gold or emerald back into the desert sun. The royal palmetto trees that lined the perimeter stood perfectly tall, each equal in their soar-ing height, trimming the idyllic city with a lush fringe of grandeur.

I had never seen, nor could I have imagined such a palatial place to ever exist here on earth. I stood marveling at the city's splendor, wondering if it was really there or just a figment of my exhausted, heat-oppressed senses. The raspy sound of shallow breathing inter-rupted my daze, soon followed by the now familiar hiss of the black swarm.

"Does a mirage have such detail?" it taunted. "No. This magnif-icent nation is real, and I have many other such kingdoms. I can give you complete and full dominion over all of them." As it dribbled these tantalizing possibilities into my head, the great iron gates of the fortification opened, revealing a serene path and reflecting pool that welcomed my eyes further into the entrancing city. "All this will be yours," the promise echoed. "All this and more, if you just turn and worship me once. Just once."

The evil one, as always, was most persuasive, but now desperate. He knew who I was. He understood that my mission would finally offer mankind a way out of his grasp. Having seen my humanity, he now tried luring me into the same wicked, self-serving mistrust and disobedience of God that he had once used to successfully deceive, defile and damage my people. He had seduced them in the desert to turn from God and worship him instead. Now he was indeed desperate enough to try the same with me.

How impudent.

I spun and shouted my command, "Away from me, Satan!" My authority bellowed. "It is written that you shall worship the Lord your God, and he alone shall you serve!"

As if blown apart by a strong gust of wind, the swarm instantly scattered into the invisible. One by one, the tiny black flecks fizzled into the dry air until there was nothing but silence and sand once again. I stood there listening to and savoring the stillness, almost afraid to turn around. But I did.

The great kingdom was gone. Now only the faint, windswept outline of Jericho rose wearisomely from the desert's horizon. While the missed opportunity of a temporary, easy escape left my human appetites and desires deprived and unsatisfied, I was consoled at having prevailed over that lying rebel. The confidence from my victory in this barren wasteland and my fidelity to the tasks for which I was made flesh, filled me with the strength I needed to make it to that horizon.

I was prepared.

I was primed.

Through prayer I had triumphed. I had come through the winepress.

I was ready to take on the world. And save it.

4

My First Disciples

I RETURNED TO JOHN and stayed for a few weeks. We traveled north up the Jordan with his disciples. I began teaching the crowds about what John meant by the coming of the kingdom of heaven and how important a role he played in heralding it.

"Did you all come to this wilderness to hear a great prophet?" I asked. "Yes, and one who is more than a prophet! John has given you a voice to hear and words to teach that the kingdom of heaven is in your midst, so listen!" I motioned to my cousin while addressing the group. "Rejoice all of you, because I tell you that no greater man has ever lived than John the Baptist, and yet even the least in the kingdom of heaven is greater than he!" I paused and looked at the many faces before me. They were waiting, hoping for some definitive guidance or instruction they could easily understand, cling to and remember. "So listen if you have ears," I urged. "For when the word of God appears, you will need more than ears and eyes to recognize it. You will need your hearts to be fully open."

Those who traveled to hear these messages inspired me in many ways. Their longing for change and fulfillment was truly refreshing, but I marveled too at their diversity. Young and old, Jews and gentiles, Levites and Samaritans, even Roman citizens stood peppered among the pilgrims. My heavenly Father was right. Now most certainly was the time to provide the possibility of eternal life to all mankind—the time to unite all nations through me.

The following day, we reached the tributary where the Jabbok river emptied into the Jordan. It was here my cousin and I would finally part ways. Only John's closest disciples were with us as I held him tightly with the foreboding that I would never see him again while on earth.

"Continue to baptize, John," I said. "I am forever grateful for all you have accomplished. You have indeed made the crooked path straight and the rough way smooth."

He quietly confided, "It is your voice that speaks the words of everlasting life. Now, you must increase while I decrease."

I bid farewell to his group and resumed my journey north, following the meandering Jordan toward Galilee. I hadn't departed for more than an hour when I sensed I was being watched. I turned to see a man quietly tracing my path about fifty paces behind. I stopped and allowed him to advance toward me. He continued closer until decreasing our distance to about half. I wasn't sure how to react to his stealthy shadowing until I recognized him as one of John's ardent followers.

"You're one of John's," I called.

He hesitated. "Yes. My name is Andrew."

I stared off into the distance, then back at him. "What are you looking for?"

He fidgeted before answering, "Where are you headed, teacher?"

I leaned on my walking stick and gestured with a wide smile, "There's only one way to find out."

The relief on his face was noticeable even at this range. He quickened his pace to catch up, but upon reaching me, was unsure what to say. Abandoning his group and following me, however, explained his desire more than any words. He just wanted to be with me. This indeed was my Father's purpose—*for those desiring us can be with us by following me.* Hopefully many generations would also follow my way as Andrew now was.

This sudden meeting moved me more than I might have expected. My first disciple—a true apostle who could not fully comprehend who I was—was overjoyed just to be walking with me. My Father blessed him with a hunger to learn more about me by being with me.

Andrew had hope.

"Are you ready for a journey that will change your life, Andrew?"

This time there was no hesitation. "I am."

I grabbed his shoulder with a look of assurance. "Good."

Together Andrew and I traversed the banks of the Jordan and arrived that evening at the town of Bethabara. We replenished our pouches with food and water, and after a much-needed sheltered night's sleep, we visited the local synagogue on the way out of town. Following a reading from the Torah, a discussion ensued that sparked several conflicting views. When a lull finally descended upon the group, I stood among them and began to speak. I calmly addressed each of their points, tying their worthy ideas back to the scripture passage, as well as why and where they had missed the mark. The room remained quiet. Andrew too, seated at my feet, hung on every word.

When I finished, all heads turned back to the rabbi, anxious for his response to my impromptu lesson.

He cleared his throat nervously. "Who are you, rabbi?"

I did not contradict his assumption. "I am Jesus of Nazareth."

"And you are just—"

"Passing through," I confirmed.

"That is a shame," he said. "Your words, they are unlike any we have ever heard."

I looked about the small congregation, so intent to learn more. Part of me wanted to stay for days, but I had an important agenda. "I will return. Until then, keep your minds open as you hear the word of God. For what the prophets foretold has come to pass."

Andrew and I set off. We headed east toward Nain, then made the short trip north to Nazareth. I was anxious to see my mother and tell her all that had happened. As always, she listened closely and held dear to her heart everything I had to say. It was good to be home—so very good to sleep in familiar surroundings.

I blew out the lamp and was nearly asleep when Andrew's voice cut through the darkness, pulling me from drowsiness. "I have a brother I would like you to meet, teacher."

"It is late, Andrew," I replied groggily. "I will meet your brother."

"He is a good man, but can be a bit intense at times."

"Intensity has its benefits."

"I say this because I know he will like you once he hears your words. He's a very passionate man."

I smiled at my new friend, even through the dark room. "And what is your brother's name?"

There was a moment's hesitation, as if he now considered his sibling's reaction to me. "Simon."

"Where does Simon live?"

"Capernaum. He's a fisherman."

I reclosed my eyes. "Very well. Tomorrow we shall head up that way to see your brother."

"Excellent." There was a long pause. "And even if your first impression is—"

"Andrew?"

"Yes."

"Go to sleep."

Another pause. "Good night, teacher."

"Good night." I chuckled silently. It seemed I was in store to meet quite a character in Andrew's kin. His uncertainty as to how I might react to him made me like him already.

*   *   *

I had forgotten how much I enjoyed Capernaum. Nestled on the Sea of Galilee's north shore, expansive vistas of the lake could be savored from most any rooftop. This massive body of fresh water was indeed a sea in all respects, often stretching from horizon to horizon and providing livelihoods for countless fishermen who trawled its depths day and night from dozens of ports.

It was early morning. Andrew and I walked by the stone wall along the seashore, gazing out at the scattering of boats dotting the water. With few ripples disrupting the surface, the rising sun lit up a wide corridor of water, bathing Capernaum in a brightening glow.

I stopped and turned toward the great lake, leaned my elbows on top of the wall, closed my eyes and breathed a deep breath of freshwater air.

I could live here.

"What are you doing, teacher?" asked Andrew.

"A beautiful morning, is it not?"

He nodded, though somewhat impatiently. "Yes, quite nice."

I turned my face again to the warm caress of dawn radiating off the water.

Andrew persisted politely, "My brother's boat should be getting in about now."

I acknowledged with a relenting grin, "Lead the way, my friend."

Sun at our sides now, we strolled farther from the main concentration of Capernaum's buildings down to where the receding shore sheltered several crudely constructed docks. Several fishing vessels had already returned and were tied to their moorings with men busy hauling nets, crates and other sailing gear to shore.

A robust man with a thick black beard instantly caught my attention. He wrestled with lowering and stowing a sail while barking orders to his crew. Despite this radiantly resplendent and calm morning, he did not seem to be in the best of moods. I glanced at Andrew. His expression told me all I needed to know. We had found his brother Simon.

The big man grabbed a linen sack, disembarked and started down the dock toward us. As he neared, he caught sight of Andrew and stopped. He threw the bag to the ground and held out his arms. "Brother!" He cried, his voice as robust as his shoulders.

We approached. Simon embraced his brother vigorously, but upon releasing him, promptly scolded, "Where have you been? Four or five weeks I think you'll be gone chasing the Baptist. But no, you go missing five times that long. This boat doesn't sail itself you know."

His brother's indignation did not phase Andrew. He was too anxious to change the subject. "His prophecy has come to pass, Simon."

Simon cocked his head and scowled. "What prophecy?"

"Has the sea waterlogged your memory? The revelation you and I have waited for since childhood."

Simon's mouth curled in skepticism. "The one?"

Andrew slowly motioned his head toward me.

Simon's eyes followed. "Who? Him?"

I forced a smile. Apparently Simon was not as socially adept as his brother.

"This is Jesus of Nazareth. He is the one—the one proclaimed by John the Baptist." Andrew beamed as he introduced me.

Simon was not impressed. He looked me up and down before turning critically back to Andrew. He tersely and derisively summarized his assessment. "You've been duped." He bent over to grab his bag.

"Simon, son of Jonah."

He straightened back up, somewhat startled by my direct address.

I continued, "You are a fisherman, no?"

He stroked his beard and eyed me inquisitively. "On a good day," he sarcastically answered. "But not last night … or this morning. No one here was a fisherman."

"No catch?" asked Andrew.

"Nothing," his brother confirmed. "Not even ones too small to keep."

"Take me out," I said and nodded to his boat. "Maybe we should try again."

Simon was visibly confounded. "I don't think you understand. There aren't any fish out there right now. None. Plus, we just folded our nets and are heading—"

"Take me out," I calmly but confidently suggested again.

Simon looked at Andrew as if to ask, *Who is this guy?*

"Do what he says, Simon," his brother coaxed. "I will help with the gear."

Simon swelled his chest to project a protest, but after engaging my eyes, he reluctantly exhaled, swiped up his sack, turned and headed back toward the dock. "Let's go then! You want to waste all of our time, fine by me." He then called to the two fishermen in the adjoining boat, "James, John, don't even bother tying up! Andrew's returned with a stranger in tow and they insist on going out to fish!"

The two men on the other side of the dock seemed just as baffled. "Nothing's out there!" one said.

Simon motioned back at us. "Tell them that!"

We got to the boat where Simon instructed his hired crew to leave the nets and go home. With me and Andrew on board, he didn't want to pay anyone for what would surely be an unprofitable excursion.

Simon sporadically muttered under his breath as we got the vessel ready to return toward the open water. He was not a happy sailor. Casting off, he spewed another complaint, "We have practically no wind. Even if there were any fish to catch, it will take forever to get out there."

I tried calming the tension as we hoisted the sail. "Look, it's a beautiful morning. A bit calm, yes, but have faith. Don't always assume your predictions to be inevitable. Surrender yourself and trust in God."

For the first time since meeting him, Simon relaxed a bit. "I guess I'm just tired," he said, securing the sail. "This is not an easy or predictable trade. Over time, one would hope to learn the waters and find the catch, but it's always hit or miss."

Andrew looked out to sea, lost in contemplation, then turned to his brother. "Sell the boat, Simon. Come with us."

"Come with you?" he asked incredulously. "Come with you where?"

"With the teacher." His eyes pointed to me. "Follow him."

"Yes, Simon," I agreed. "Join us."

He held steady to the mast despite the boat drifting listlessly. "You two must be insane. I have a livelihood here." He gathered his thoughts by speaking them in my direction. "Don't get me wrong, Andrew can attest that I have knelt in that synagogue year after year, imploring God to send his Anointed one to deliver Israel, and to send him sooner than later. Nobody hopes and prays to see that day more than I, but please. No disrespect to the Baptist, but as lousy as this profession can be, I need more than even my brother's word to drop everything and follow a stranger from Nazareth."

I beheld his eyes closely until I knew I had his full attention. "Today is that day, Simon."

"Huh?"

"Cast out your nets."

The abrupt, concise request startled him. A bewildered smile crossed his mouth. "Here? We're not even close to any fishing areas yet."

I nodded, fully aware we were far from where any fish were likely. "You will learn to have faith, Simon."

"Faith to do what, blindly throw my nets overboard in these shallows?"

"You've cast them all night with no luck," I reminded. "Can you do any worse by casting them here?"

He had no answer. All he wanted now was to prove me of unsound mind so we could head back to shore. He maneuvered to the other side of the boat. "Andrew, grab that section of the net and make sure it's tethered to the side."

His brother moved quickly, grabbed the bundle of mesh and hoisted it to the deck rail. They both inspected the weave, ensuring it was fastened tightly to the side.

Simon glanced over his shoulder to see if I might change my mind before we all really looked ridiculous. Seeing no reaction from me, he turned to Andrew and sighed, "At the count of three, we throw it as far as we can."

"I'm ready," Andrew affirmed.

"One …"

I closed my eyes. Heavenly Father, I prayed, I thank you for bringing me to this solid soul named Simon. I see great potential in him. If it is your will, let him see the fruits of faith—the blessings of hard work done in your name.

"Two …"

I opened my eyes and grabbed hold of a cleat to keep me steady even though the boat was perfectly balanced. Knowing my loving Father and our powerful Spirit, I seized a taught rope with my other hand and held tight.

"Three!" The two fishermen flung the large net out from the boat, arching it high in the air. The small lead weights hit the water first with staccato splashes. Then the net itself slapped into the sea.

Immediately the surface surged on our port side as if a whale had passed with great speed, turning our boat. The once dead-calm water suddenly sprang to life. It erupted into a frenzy of tiny, violent splashes as thousands of fish raced impulsively toward us. The immense school cut a swath in the water that left a rapidly expanding wake, all heading directly into the widening net. Their force stretched its mesh to the limit and rocked the boat turbulently to port. Andrew nearly fell overboard, and Simon lost his balance, finding himself on his rear.

"Pull it back in!" he roared excitedly with a hint of understandable fear.

Despite Simon's strength and Andrew's agility, the two of them hoisting with all their might could not retrieve the net. In fact, it was now pulling the boat dangerously over on its side. I held tightly to the rigging and planted my sandals firmly on the deck to secure my stance.

"What do we do?" Andrew shouted.

Simon yelled to the fishing vessel approaching aft, "James! Get over here and help!"

James and John, the other two fishermen in the boat sailing by, masterfully maneuvered it along our starboard side, which was rising still higher. They lashed their vessel to ours and scampered aboard. As they slid across the deck, I joined them, and soon there were five men tugging at the net overflowing with wriggling life.

Simon bellowed over the maelstrom thrashing before us, "Heave! Heave together—all together!"

Somehow we were able to pull the near-side of the net alongside the hull, trapping the huge school. Their weight and frantic efforts to regain freedom stressed the fibrous cords to breaking. The boat now listed so far to port, we tried rolling the swollen net right into the craft. Lifting it would be impossible. We all reached out and together gradually dragged the colossal catch on board. The net, packed with large carp, struck the deck with a loud thud. The ship lurched back to a more even keel and almost sent Andrew over the side again. Our deck rails were now so critically low from the weight of the catch, we were close to taking on water. Several wide tears split down the net, gushing fish to every side of us until we were all either standing or kneeling in fins and gills.

"Throw some into our boat, lest we sink!" cried James.

We scrambled to grab armfuls of fish and hurl them into the adjoining boat.

When our vessel was no longer in jeopardy, everyone lay silent for a few moments, exhaustion mixing with awe.

I managed to climb my way over to Simon who crouched against the side of the boat, shaking.

"Not a bad catch," I mused.

He peered up at me—his hardened visage gone, replaced by humility and reverence.

"Please … do not look upon me," he tiredly breathed before glancing away. "I am a sinful man."

"Simon," I answered quietly, "do not fear. From now on you will be a fisher of men."

5

Expanding My Numbers

I LAY ON THE ROOF of Peter's small house and gazed up at the night sky. Thin wisps of cloud hardly hindered the massive firmament showering its beauty upon me. Amidst the perfect stillness of that glorious dome, a shooting star suddenly rifled across, flickering above the clouds like an archer's flaming arrow. Watching this unexpected spectacle arc through the heavens, I realized that my all-powerful divinity did not rob my human naiveté of the awe and joy I now felt.

The more I experienced the wonderful night, the more bizarre it all seemed. The Father had not merely sent me; I was of the Father, and thus participated in the creation of everything around me. Through me—space, time and all things in them had been established, set in motion and kept in existence. And yet here I lay, amazed by the moon and stars, pondering in wonder at them and their stunning effect on me. By humbling myself to be human in every way, I chose to be subjected to the bewildering existence of human life.

Except of course where my heavenly Father provided a connection to discernible visions and voices of our Spirit. Yes, growing up

I had studied the scriptures and learned from the rabbis, but my current awareness and understanding of the word of God stemmed not from study and schooling. My divinity enlightened me. While I might gaze at the moon for hours with no understanding of why or how it gradually drifts across the sky, I immediately understood with all the lucidity of actual experience, the wonderfully mystical and transcendental realities of heaven. I truly perceived the eternal experience of God's pervading presence—so uniquely perfect, it defies human description. The paradise that mankind had disinherited as a consequence of original mistrust and disobedience was now something my Father wished to give back and share its abundance forever. My love was willing to endure the entire burden of sin so that the world could again be reconciled with God. *That was why I was here*—why I had begun to gather followers who would carry my mission forward once I was no longer visibly present as a man.

Only four fishermen had joined me so far—Andrew, Simon, and their two colleagues James and John, both brothers as well. After docking the boats from our miraculous fishing trip, James and John bid their father, who owned their fishing vessel, goodbye. Their immediate allegiance to me, leaving behind all they valued, proved that these relatively uneducated and unsophisticated fishermen were fit for my mission to gather the nations. They willingly abandoned everything. They left the familiar and the comfortable in their lives to follow me.

Their sacrifice would surely be great, as would their reward.

John hadn't waited to stay in Capernaum another night. He set off for Bethsaida, several hours northeast, anxious to tell two more friends about me—Philip and Bartholomew. Although having known John only a few hours, I was confident nonetheless he would plant the right seeds. Barely twenty years old, John possessed an eagerness to seek the truth that was matched only by his energy to find it. How glad I was he had been out on the water with us today. In fishermen's terms, John was *a keeper*.

But when he returned the following morning, Philip alone was by his side. Bartholomew had chosen to remain in Bethsaida.

I shook Philip's hand and embraced him. "Welcome, Philip."

It took a moment for him to digest the way I spoke his name as if I had known him forever, which in a way I had. But his words finally found their course. "I have never seen John so excited in all my life. He is young, but his heart is the purest I know. I had no choice but to come."

"Sorry, teacher," said John, ashamed he had only half succeeded on his recruiting mission. "Bartholomew did not feel the same way, I'm afraid."

"Not your fault, John," Simon quipped. "He is as bullheaded as I am. His loss."

I tended to somewhat agree with Simon. After all, I couldn't force anyone to join our group. As Philip had just expressed, it had to come from the heart. But my love for Bartholomew wanted the best for him, and as I stood wishing his presence among us, one of those visions from my Father entered my mind—the image of a man sitting under a broad fig tree deep in prayer.

"Philip," I said, not meaning to sound as firm as I did.

"Yes," he replied.

"Is there a fig tree near Bartholomew's home?"

The man audibly gasped. "Yes. There is. The largest one I've ever seen."

I looked at them all and nodded. "We must go to him."

*　　*　　*

The northern tip of the Sea of Galilee was just a short journey from the outskirts of Capernaum. From there, the serene walk over the hills to Bethsaida finished all too quickly. Knolls of deep green grass welcomed us, occasionally interrupted by glades of wildflowers swaying lazily in the morning breeze. Nearing Bartholomew's village, we were all so caught up in the beauty of the morning and in our own personal reflections of recent days that we almost missed him. In a field not far off to our right, he walked with a shepherd and his flock.

Luckily John noticed him. "Look! It's Bartholomew!"

We all turned, our reveries returning to reality.

"It sure is," said Simon.

Philip waved to get his attention. "Bartholomew!"

The tall, rugged man with a tightly wrapped crimson head scarf glanced over and saw us. He bid his shepherd companion farewell and started in our direction. I knew as soon as he came closer that this was a genuine man. My reaction sprang from natural human intuition, formed simply by the way he carried himself—confident but not presuming.

Philip and Bartholomew grabbed elbows and shook each other as if it had been much longer than a day since their last meeting.

"Philip," he said, pleasantly surprised to see his comrade. "I thought you were off with John to follow some prophet. What brings you both back toward Bethsaida?"

Philip glanced at me, hoping I wasn't offended by his friend's remark. I stepped in before he could attempt an answer.

"Hello, Bartholomew," I said with a straightforward salutation. "I am he, the one Philip has chosen to follow."

He looked at me in disbelief, then at the others for confirmation. The five of them concurred by remaining silent.

"This is Jesus," John finally said, moving beside me. "From Nazareth. The one we believe has come to guide Israel."

By now I was used to scrutiny, but Bartholomew's was overtly critical. He turned to the others and delivered his negative assessment. "Nazareth? What good can honestly come from Nazareth?"

Simon responded before I could. "What difference does it make where he—"

"No, wait," I said and raised a hand to politely quiet him. "I am intrigued to hear Bartholomew's thoughts. Tell me, why such an impression of Nazareth?"

"No impression," he answered. "Other than it being a scant, off-the-trail-borough filled with yokels who cater and coddle the Romans."

Before my small entourage could react, I burst out laughing. It was an honest laugh that quickly eased the tension. "Behold," I exclaimed, turning to the others and nodding at Bartholomew. "Here is a true Israelite in whom there is no deceit."

He chuckled himself. "I'm amused that you think you know me."

My laughter stopped, and my abrupt look of compassion silenced him. "I do know you. For I have seen you under the fig tree. I know you seek the truth. I know that you have taken comfort under that tree many times, praying to find it."

My words struck him with the force of a physical blow. His eyelids quivered as he struggled to come to grips with what he had heard.

"Today I call you, Bartholomew. Follow me."

He didn't speak. Only the hush of air rustling the trees on the ridge kept the hill from silence.

Philip finally stepped forward, a gesture of support for his friend. "Bartholomew, we—"

He was interrupted as Bartholomew found his voice, speaking deliberately and directly to me. "You are indeed the king of Israel."

My smile returned. "You say this because I mentioned seeing you under the fig tree and perceiving your prayers. Truly, you will see greater things than this."

Bartholomew turned to the others and opened his arms as if to welcome them as brothers. He then placed his hand on the back of John's neck and said to him, "My sincere apologies for not trusting your judgment yesterday. How foolish I feel."

Simon snickered, "You should have seen how Jesus overcame

my stubbornness. Nearly drowned me!"

Watching my new group of friends laughing, I silently thanked my Father. Six Galileans … Six men who had no clue what tomorrow would bring but trusted me enough to take them there. These were righteous people—men who held a good relationship with God. Six salt-of-the-earth individuals willing to do more than just change their lives. They were surrendering themselves to start new ones. Six lambs who I would ultimately send out among wolves.

My contingent was now halfway complete.

6

Welcoming A Tax Collector

AS USUAL ON A SABBATH, the synagogue in Capernaum was standing room only. In addition to the Jews that called this lakeside village home, visiting travelers often swelled the worshipers to the room's capacity. Many sat on the floor that stretched between two rows of columns, while others stood beneath their arches or peered into the main hall from the side aisles. A dozen Pharisees and scribes sat prominently at the front, overlooking the grand room. I took the center of the floor and addressed the congregation. The local synagogue officials were especially anxious to hear the teaching of this new, "contemporary" rabbi. Naturally quizzical and cautiously hesitant, they still appeared eager for a fresh voice to read and interpret scripture.

My apostles, grouped by one of the pillars, were curious how this familiar assembly would react to my words. Although these six men had been with me only a few days, we had already enjoyed many spiritual conversations about God's plan and a new hope for mankind.

But now I wasn't just speaking to a few devotees. I had the floor of a crowded synagogue on the Sabbath. And no one—not my disciples under the arch, not the Pharisees in their honored seats, nor any of the more than a hundred devout Jews before me—could expect what I was going to say. Once I did speak, I spoke for almost an hour, holding their rapt attention. My message was different from their normal Sabbath teachings. I did not preach to them about the Law. I did not emphasize doctrine or ritual practices. I did not substantially invoke the prophets. I spoke from my own heart about love, hope and the kingdom of God. Most importantly, I was talking to them about *them*.

"You ... each and every one of you is the light of the world," I said, addressing the entire room yet speaking to each soul individually. "Does anyone light a lamp and put it under a bowl or cover it with a basket? No. They put it high on a stand so that it can give light to everyone in the house. You must do the same. Let your light shine. Your good works must reveal the love in your heart to all, and thus give glory to God."

I looked about. Their silent, focused attention encouraged me. "So what can you do to make your light shine brighter?" I challenged. "You may have heard in the past to love your neighbor and hate your enemy. But I say to you ... love your enemies as yourself and pray for those who persecute you. For if you love only those who love you, what reward does that deserve? Even the pagans do as much. Love *everyone*, the righteous *and* the unrighteous. Care for and help those who do *not* deserve your good deeds, as well as those who do. Do this, and your Father in heaven will reward you with his care and love ... whether or not *you* deserve it."

I cannot put into words the joyful optimism that radiated from the faces in that room. When finished, my apostles and I left the temple. Nearly half the synagogue followed, including many of the Pharisees who scurried to keep pace and ask a myriad of questions. I was about to tell them that I planned on being in Capernaum often and would speak again at the synagogue, when we turned a corner and ran right into Matthew.

As soon as I saw him, I knew I had found my seventh. All it took was one sudden, cursory glance. I felt that I knew every facet of this startled stranger standing before me. Smart, resourceful and clever, with a sincere heart for God ... but one too burdened by guilt to dare seek his call. He stood at his post in front of the tax repository, clutching a Roman money box under his arm and glaring at us as prey might when suddenly caught in the open by hunters.

Simon struck first. "On the Sabbath, Matthew? You can't plunder enough during the week; you have to collect on the Sabbath?"

Matthew kept his eyes from the religious leaders behind us. "I'm not collecting," he muttered, unsuccessfully trying to conceal the money box under his garments. "I had appointments. That's all. I accommodate circumstances as best I can, and am not the robber you think."

James scoffed, "You're a tax collector for Rome. What do you call coercing hard-earned money from your countrymen to profit an oppressive foreign occupier?"

Matthew wasn't sure how to respond and didn't wish to further expose himself to the pious procession crowding the narrow street. As he turned to duck away, I grabbed his arm. He swung back and looked at me, visibly uncomfortable in this openly hostile company. Years of guilt pressed upon him behind a weary stare. I eased his angst with consoling eyes and two simple words, "Follow me."

"Teacher ..." warned James.

"Follow me, Matthew," I said again before James could express his doubts.

Matthew relented a bit but remained puzzled. "I can tell that you are a holy man. Of this I am certain." His voice was thin. "What could you possibly want with the likes of me?"

An incredible rush of the Spirit almost took my breath away as my Father sent a wave of insights to me. "You are planning a dinner tonight for friends," I said.

He nodded once with a limp jaw, stunned by my intuition.

"May we join you?"

He hesitated only a moment, then slowly lowered his eyes. "While I would very much enjoy that, sir, those who will be attending are—"

"I know who they are," I said. "And I would be pleased to dine with you and your guests, in your house this evening."

Matthew's reluctant smile disclosed joyous disbelief. He nodded again, tentatively at first but then more assuredly. "Then I must go. There is much to prepare." He regarded the other six. "Simon, you and Andrew, James and John—all of you. You must come as well. I beg you."

I looked at John who simply conceded to the town's chief tax collector with a shrug, "Wherever our teacher goes, we go."

Matthew took a few steps back, suddenly no longer ashamed to be in sight of the synagogue's convoy of people. He offered me a reverent bow, then turned and hurried up the street.

Simon sighed and managed a smile. "So, it appears we suddenly have a bookkeeper in our group."

I grabbed him playfully by the neck with my elbow. "Trust me, Simon. You and Matthew will get along famously."

One of the Pharisees pulled back his priestly head covering and approached us more closely. While he spoke with a tone of respect, it did little to mask his disdain. "Rabbi, your words today clearly show you possess a blessed gift for inspiration, but do you not realize you just agreed to eat a Sabbath meal in the house of a sinner? A house full of tax collectors and miscreants?"

I removed my arm from Simon's shoulder and addressed this accusation. "Tell me, does a physician go to the homes of those who are well or those who are sick?"

He furrowed his brow and answered obviously, "The sick."

"Exactly," I said, peering back up the road where Matthew had gone. "I do not call the righteous, but the sinners to repentance."

One of his fellow scribes chimed in. "Yes, but rabbi, consider the appearances. You will give scandal by associating with—"

"Appearances!" I uttered with clear contempt. "Everyone is so obsessed with appearances. Did you not listen to my words?" I turned to the full group of Pharisees and the throng of followers with them. "Stop judging, and you will not be judged. Stop condemning, and you will not be condemned. Forgive, and you will be forgiven. How is it everyone can see the splinter in his brother's eye so easily, but can never quite notice the log caught in his own eye? Hypocrites! Remove the wooden beam from your own eye first. Then you will see more clearly and can help your brother remove the splinter from his eye."

They all looked at one another.

Were they taken aback by my admonishment? Certainly. Were they somewhat offended? Naturally. But none of them pressed the issue further.

The meal shared at Matthew's house that night was both wonderful and fruitful. There was great rejoicing in the kingdom of heaven as even this small handful of transgressors turned to me for hope and fulfillment.

And Matthew, a man misunderstood for so long—a soul that had buckled to the breaking point by the daily self-reproach of shallow greed—repented. He gave his full commission, all of his Roman payoffs to the local synagogue's poor box ... and joined our group.

I was unaware as I welcomed him with a proud embrace, that this man who was once so hated for exploiting the Jews, would ultimately write my life's story for them.

7

My First Miracle

AS THE *WORD MADE FLESH*, words would convey my message and drive my mission. Opportunities for physical signs would surely present themselves, but faith based solely on signs and wonders is shallow superstition—and just as easily lost as found. My words are what carried my Father's authority. I was building and strengthening a foundation of fellowship. The mutual care and support among my disciples would grow through my teachings of faith and love that I had come to proclaim. This groundwork would then support the great miracles that were to come.

And so every chance I had, I spoke. And not just on the Sabbath, but every day. In the streets and in the fields, on the market steps and inside homes—wherever I could garner an audience, I preached the Gospel of salvation, the good news of repentance, the promise of God's kingdom.

It was a welcome message, and the good news traveled fast. First in Capernaum, where my daily walks grew from a handful of companions to crowds that rivaled those at temple on Sabbath. Soon accounts began to spread throughout all of Galilee about this new teacher who spoke like no other and offered hope to those struggling with life's trials. The poor and marginalized, the outcasts and crip-pled—all those who had no way to triumph in this world suddenly found a way. My words inspired.

Of course, many of the politically religious felt threatened. They themselves had never seen such numbers pack the synagogues. Their jealousy and fear of losing influence and power kept them aloof and secretly hostile to my thoughts and ideas. But since their temple taxes and tithes were increasing to record levels, they muttered their dissent quietly.

I began hearing questions and comments among the people as they speculated who I was, where I came from, and if I was the one to lead Israel from the throes of Roman captivity. And that's how I rounded out my twelve apostles—by allowing those searching hardest for the answers to come forward. Large crowds flocked to hear my message, but at the end of the day, they dispersed, returning home to resume their daily lives. But a few did not return home. These few would remain, conspicuously alone where once there were hundreds. Often they decided to keep my company with nothing more than the clothes on their backs and perhaps a good walking stick. "Teacher," they would say, "I want to hear more from you."

"I want to go where you go."

"I want to learn more of the kingdom of God."

"Please, let me follow you."

How could I ignore away such faith, bravery and devotion? How could I not respond to it with my own personal devotion and allegiance?

I couldn't, and I didn't.

There was Thomas, a great example of personal integrity who meant what he said, said what he meant and did what he said. Thomas was a reliable man you could definitely trust and count on.

Then came Thaddeus, a humble and gentle soul who knew the text and the spirit of scripture very well. His innate intelligence asked the critical questions that quickly got to the heart of the matter.

After the others fell asleep, Thaddeus and I often stayed up together reciting our favorite Psalm or passage from the Torah.

A second James joined our group, younger than John's older brother, so we referred to him as 'James the less.' He didn't seem to mind.

Another Simon came into our fold as well, a former member of the Zealots. Although he wished not to be known by his prior affiliation with the radical Jewish freedom movement, we often called him 'Simon the Zealot' nonetheless. It fit him well now for a different reason—his passion for leading others to hear my voice and my message of God's love for them.

And finally there was Judas from the town of Kerioth, in Hebrew, Iscariot. His public professions of loyalty to me and my mission were truly ardent. He, like Matthew, was well educated, and since Matthew had no desire to manage money anymore, we placed Judas in charge of our finances.

And so, my closest circle was complete. What may have outwardly appeared a ramshackle assembly of personal supporters, they were in truth, my army. God had always worked through the most ordinary people to achieve the most meaningful and blessed goals throughout the ages. Now that I actually walked the earth, I would continue to work through common men and women to gather the nations and reestablish the kingdom of God.

This union, starting here, would develop and grow my Church. I knew that after I was gone from this physical world, my Father and I would send our Spirit to inspire and sanctify that Church. But for now, it was equally clear that the heart of my work was essentially up to me and my band of twelve. And while not one of them carried a sword, javelin or even a Roman shield ... they were indeed soldiers. Spiritual warfare would be their battlefield, fighting for the hearts and minds of many.

As with any new brigade, however, this one required discipline and training. Only I could give them those essentials. Only I could adequately prepare them. Only I could motivate their complete self-surrender to our mission … and only by my own complete self-surrender to it as well. I must teach, prepare and confide in them—show them things nobody ever had, or ever would, witness with their own eyes.

Now that I had recruited my company, it was time for their training to begin.

But first, we received word of a celebration—an affair that would provide some much-needed fellowship, allowing us to decompress a bit and refresh ourselves before starting our public journey together. It was the perfect occasion to take some time off and just relax, have fun, enjoy the companionship of friends and family, eat and drink well.

The news came from my mother. Old friends of ours had a daughter getting married in Cana, just north of Nazareth. Knowing the family, the wedding feast would be a grand time indeed. I found myself looking forward to sharing in the joy of the couple, but also in unwinding and living a much quieter, private life for a few days.

*   *   *

Nestled in the rolling hills of Galilee, Cana hid itself from travelers until they were practically upon it. Most of the dwellings lay clustered along the edge of a wide valley with neat, well-maintained vineyards and orchards separating them from the bluffs beyond. A scattering of homes crept up the eastern slope, allowing spectacular sunsets to bathe their terra cotta porches.

Upon one of these porches, on a large stone terrace with breathtaking views of the Canaanite valley, a wedding feast was well under way. It was late afternoon, but the reception honoring the newlyweds had been in full swing for hours. A half dozen long tables stretched from the edge of the wide veranda all the way to the arches leading to the house and servants' quarters. Family members and friends sat shoulder-to-shoulder—some having journeyed no farther than from right down the hill, others from as far as the coastal territories of Tyre and Sidon. Dancers and musicians performed festively near the bride and groom's canopied table, sparking laughter and applause from much of the terrace. My twelve and I, however, sat at the farthest corner from the happy couple, closest to where the servants had been carrying trays of food and jugs of wine in and out all day.

Our position at this outermost guest table was perfectly fine by us. Relaxed but not tired, I enjoyed the company of my apostles and the others seated around us.

Through all the activity, I could see my mother at a nearby table. She occasionally glanced up and caught my eye, smiling contentedly, knowing I was there.

The day so far had proven a welcome change for me. My disciples did most of the talking. I said little and took it all in, satisfied to just listen to the stories of their lives, their struggles and the humorous anecdotes that seemed funny in retrospect.

The sun had only begun casting long shadows across the valley when a small commotion escalated among some of the servants under the portico. Their indiscernible bickering didn't last long, so I quickly dismissed it. I was more interested in a story at our table about the groom a few years ago. While I listened, I glimpsed over to my mother's table. She was no longer there. I paid this little mind since she knew many of the guests and had probably gotten up to make her social rounds.

Although muffled by the music from across the deck, the sudden urgency in her call startled me. "Jesus." It came from where the servants had been quibbling under the portico.

My head turned, unsure if I had really heard my name or simply imagined it. But there my mother was, standing under the first arch, motioning intently for me to join her. I leaned forward to better see her through the other guests.

Her expression did not imply urgency, but conveyed a situation beyond her ability to handle. I had seen this look often over the years, mostly when my father Joseph was determined to exercise his considerable woodworking expertise in a home-improvement project of dubious merit and even less necessity. My mother would gesture for me to help delay, distract and ultimately talk him out of it.

I tapped Simon and Andrew sitting beside me. "Come with me a moment. It appears my mother needs help with something."

We left our seats, and Andrew immediately noticed we were heading toward the servants' area. "Maybe they need help with more cinnamon bread," he said hopefully.

Upon reaching the archway, my mother's dismay indicated a challenge greater than needing extra servers for sweet rolls. She asked us to follow her inside.

We moved into a large chamber, and I glanced back to see my other apostles had now left the table to join us. Hopefully this issue would not require all thirteen of us!

Inside, four or five rather perplexed servants spoke excitedly among themselves. They stopped upon noticing our presence.

"What seems to be the trouble?" I asked.

My mother nodded to the head servant. "Amiel?"

The man nervously fiddled with his towel before apologetically stammering a few words that said it all. "We have run out of wine."

"No more wine?" asked Bartholomew as if someone had mentioned the word drought. Wine at weddings was as essential as water for crops.

"Already?" Matthew inquired.

"I don't think they were expecting this many people," Amiel responded, continuing to contritely explain, "especially all the guests who traveled so far to get here."

"It's not your fault," my mother consoled. "You all have done a wonderful job keeping the carafes full; how were you to know?"

I spoke to no one in particular, "The day is waning. Is there even a vineyard in the valley who could accommodate on such short notice?"

Amiel shook his head, confirming this was not possible.

My mother lowered her voice and confided her anxiety to me. "I really don't know what to do, Jesus. Daniel will be devastated if his daughter's celebration ends like this."

I couldn't help but admire her compassion for our hosts and their guests. But really, what was she expecting from me? I cushioned my response as softly as I could. "What can I do?"

She glanced at the floor, wishing she could speak to me without an audience, but simply reiterated the simple fact, "They are out of wine."

I looked to my apostles for any suggestions. They too seemed stumped, and in their silence, I turned back to my mom. She knew about these men. She knew I had chosen them as my colleagues, direct participants in my ministry. She understood and appreciated the importance of what I was to disclose to them and how.

I tried sounding sympathetic but asked directly, "What does this have to do with us?"

Rather than speak, she simply lifted her face and communicated her eyes clearly and powerfully to mine—*Son, help them.*

I certainly wanted to. I loved my mother dearly and truly commiserated with her good friends' predicament. But this was hardly the time or place for …

"My hour has not yet come," I whispered.

Her eyes indicated she understood. She calmly stepped over and gently kissed my cheek, revealing a discreet grin as she moved back. She then turned to the servants and issued the terse directive that she continues to echo to all God's children through the millennia. "Do whatever he tells you."

She touched beneath my chin with a familiar loving caress and left the room.

What is it about mothers? How mysterious is their innate mastery of subtle yet compelling influence over their sons and daughters? I stood there dumbfounded. I had to revere and cherish the trust in me and the empathy of others in that woman, that handmaid of the Lord. If I can but influence and persuade others as well as she, my call to conversion will surely succeed.

I sighed.

I then crossed the room to where six large stone jars, all about waist high, stood in a row against the wall. I spoke to the servants while admiring the smooth contours of the massive containers, each used for ritual washing in accordance with Hebrew Law. "These jugs, they are for purification purposes?"

"Yes, sir," confirmed Amiel.

I paused, contemplating what I was about to do. I closed my eyes and took a deep breath, exhaling slowly to completely relax. "Fill them with water."

"Fill them all?" asked one of the servants. "Why would we—"

"Do as he says," reprimanded Amiel. "Remember?"

The servant nodded, and they promptly set to the arduous task of drawing water from the well and filling the six capacious canisters. I left them to their work and stood under the arch, gazing over the wedding celebration. My disciples approached for an explanation. Although no one could hope to fully understand the ways of God, it was a great blessing for them to strive for the understanding intended for them.

John spoke the minds of all. "Teacher, why did you tell them to draw water? They ran out of wine."

I continued peering over the joyous crowd. "You have all learned much from me over the last few weeks. Continue to watch and learn."

Amiel finally approached from behind. "Sir," he said, "the jars are all filled."

"Completely?" I asked without turning around.

"To the brim," he answered.

I waited a moment and closed my eyes again. I directed my mind completely to my Father and soon felt my heart quicken, flutter even. I was greatly reassured that our Spirit was flowing through me. I opened my eyes and turned to face Amiel. "Bring the man in charge of the entire feast."

"That would be the headwaiter," he informed.

"Good. Please ask him to join us."

To spur Amiel along in summoning his superior, I reinforced my words with a definitive nod.

I sensed his reluctance, but he remembered my mother's advice and did not question me. As he left through the crowd, I returned to the privacy of the servants' room and explained the fundamentals of divine virtues to my apostles. "Faith is not the same thing as hope, but both depend on love. Faith is our response to God's love, while hope is our hunger for it. And love requires trust—trusting that God will provide."

Thaddeus beautifully declared, "We have put our trust in you, teacher. You have given us hope."

"Always remember," I urged them, "trust in the Lord with all your heart and do not rely on your own understanding. Depending on God *is* his will for you."

Amiel suddenly returned with a stout man bustling into the chamber. "What is the meaning of this?" he clamored. "Who are all these people?"

I motioned to Amiel. "Draw a sample from the container. Have him taste it."

Again he hesitated, not sure what to do. He lowered his head. Then, pursing his lips, he turned to his companion by one of the jars and nodded nervously.

The servant at the container stuttered, "But ... these are all just filled with—"

"Offer him a drink," I interrupted. "Please."

He looked at his fellow servants, obviously annoyed it had fallen on him to offer the headwaiter a scoop of well water to taste. He nevertheless dipped the wooden ladle into the jar and drew a large cupful. He then brought it to the portly, impatient supervisor. As he raised the spoon for him to sip, a few drops dripped onto the servant's white apron. His eyes widened, noticing deep, burgundy spots on the cloth. Before he could utter a gasp, the headwaiter swallowed, and a voice suddenly startled us from behind.

"What is going on in here?"

We all turned to see Daniel, the bride's father, standing in the archway. "Is there a problem?" he asked, focusing on the man now finishing the ladle's contents.

"Sir," exclaimed the headwaiter, "I am impressed, yet a bit bewildered."

Daniel entered the room curiously. "Bewildered how?"

"Well ... with all due respect, sir," he said wiping his lips, "hosts usually serve their good wine first and bring out a more common vintage later, after the guests have been drinking freely. But you ... you have saved this premium wine for later in the day."

Another servant quickly grabbed a goblet from the shelf and with shaking hands scooped some of the liquid from the surface of the jug. He brought the cup to his nose and glanced over at me in fearful shock. He then walked briskly over to Daniel. Too overwhelmed to speak, he simply offered the chalice to his host.

Daniel drank. When he lowered the cup, his eyes closed, savoring the robust, full-bodied taste of the wine. He then addressed the headwaiter. "Where did you get this?"

The headwaiter couldn't answer—undoubtedly wondering the same thing.

He was saved by another question. "Do you have enough for everyone?"

Amiel stared at the six massive stone jars and in a trancelike daze confidently predicted, "I believe we have enough."

With this issue resolved, I quietly turned and slipped out under the arch and back into the soft evening sun. My apostles surrounded me, just as astonished as the servants inside.

Simon spoke first, referring to me suddenly no longer as teacher. "Master," he breathed, "you turned the water into wine. How?"

"Faith," I answered to all of them. "I tell you the truth, if you have the faith of even a small mustard seed, you can say to this hill, 'uproot yourself and plant yourself in the sea,' and it will obey you."

James the less replied eagerly, "Give us this faith."

"Faith is not something for me to give. You must find it within yourself." I grabbed the shoulders of the two by my sides, symbolically grabbing them all in a friendly huddle. "Keep a thankful heart toward God in everything … surrender to his will every day … and you will find faith."

"A miracle is what you just did, Master," said Thomas, adopting Simon's new epithet for me. "We witnessed a miracle before our very own eyes."

"Listen, all of you," I imparted. "Today you have seen water converted into wine. In the days ahead, you shall see the lame walk, the blind see … and the dead raised to life."

Young John could contain himself no more. He sobbed excitedly with joy.

The others chuckled to console him, but tears of gladness were welling up in all of their eyes.

I glanced over their heads and caught my mother standing by the terrace. She smiled at me, knowingly.

I smiled back … in a way, thanking her.

8

A Day With Nicodemus

TRAVELING AROUND THE SEA OF GALILEE provided frequent scenic spots for rest between towns. Using Capernaum as our home base, we visited the surrounding villages mostly by foot—sometimes by boat if crossing the vast lake presented a more direct route. We spent our days spreading the good news of God's kingdom. When lucky, twilight found us within the dwellings of some welcoming villagers who accepted both our message and our bodies into their homes. On many occasions, however, we simply retreated to the hills, seeking a night's rest and refuge on a soft cushion of grass under a tree canopy. Sleeping under the stars never bothered me. A quiet, natural surrounding allowed me to more clearly thank my heavenly Father for the day, and mentally prepare myself for the next.

As the weeks progressed, it became apparent that more than preaching alone drew the masses to the towns we visited. Reports spread fast, reaching north past Caesarea and south to the outskirts of Judea, that the sick were being cured. Some were simply rumors spread through the grapevine, while other more descriptive accounts came from trusted sources. But whatever the source, the stories all shared the same revelation—this Jesus of Nazareth had the power to heal.

It was midweek, and I sat in the open gateway to a Pharisee's property just outside Capernaum. His name was Nicodemus, a leader of the local religious sect, but one who welcomed my methods and teachings more readily than other Pharisees. Nicodemus possessed what many of them lacked—an open and inquiring mind … probing and generally skeptical, but open nonetheless.

Nicodemus had a large yard outside the high wall surrounding his residence. It included a small olive grove. On this day, the wall presented only a minor potential obstacle to the throng assembled at its gate. So many people filled the grounds that many sat on each other's laps. A smaller stone rampart wrapped the full property where listeners perched elbow-to-elbow like living finials on a fence. My apostles and a group of Pharisees, including Nicodemus, stood behind me. There was literally nowhere for them to stand outside the wall.

Despite the closely-packed crowd covering the expansive yard, I did not have to shout to be heard. Hordes of people clustered before me, and yet I could plainly hear a fly buzzing about my head.

"So, how shall I describe the kingdom of heaven?" I asked my attentive audience. "It is like a dragnet cast into the sea, gathering fish of every kind." I looked over at Simon and gave him a quick wink. The fishermen would understand and appreciate this parable. "When the net is full, they draw it up on the beach and sit down to divide the fish. The good fish they collect into containers to keep; the bad ones they discard." I paused momentarily before continuing, "And so it will be at the end of the age. Angels will come forth and gather the righteous into the heavenly kingdom, while the wicked will be thrown away into the fire."

I allowed the analogy to sink in. "But being righteous is not something you should flaunt or use to bring attention. For example, when you give to the poor, do not make a spectacle of it, announcing your good deed to everyone around you for the recognition of others. Those who do this have already received their reward. Instead, do not even let your left hand know what your right one is doing, so that your alms-giving will be done in secret. Then, your heavenly Father who sees what you do in secret, will reward you."

A scattering of supporting nods indicated they were getting the message.

"And when you pray," I continued, "do not be like the hypocrites who love to stand in public and offer lengthy prayers for others to see and acknowledge. Truly they have already received their recognition." I could almost feel the Pharisees listening disquietly from behind me, but this point was critically essential. "When you pray, retire to your own room and close the door. Pray genuinely and earnestly to God in secret, and your heavenly Father who sees what you do in secret, will reward you."

Murmurs escaped the crowd as many exchanged comments and sought one another's opinions. Someone only a few paces from me promptly shouted, "How should we pray, teacher?"

I turned my head toward the inquiry, but before I could locate who had boldly asked it, another voice rang out, "What should we ask of the Almighty?"

These questions broke my heart. The most meaningful, significant way to experience the presence of God, and these people did not know how to open their hearts and communicate on a personal level with their Creator. Although many had undoubtedly memorized countless 'prayers' handed down by generations, few truly knew how to approach my Father and savor his presence.

I lowered my head, momentarily distracted by this spiritual void in their lives. Suddenly, a hand rested on my shoulder. It was John's. As the young often do, he saw this need not as an obstacle, but as an opportunity for himself and the others. "Teach us to pray, Lord," he urged quietly.

I stared back at the restless faces before me and wanted to gather them all in like a mother hen gathers her chicks. "Listen, all of you," I called. "Prayer is not a meaningless repetition of words you have stored in your head. You must release your own thoughts and feelings from your heart. You are all sons and daughters of the Most-High, and you should be honored and overjoyed that he invites you to come to him as his children. So do not hesitate to approach him just as you are. He knows what you need even before you ask, so there is no shame in fully baring your mind and heart to him. Call to him reverently and gladly—saying, 'Father; you who are in heaven, hallowed is your name. Your kingdom shall come. Your will shall be done, here on earth, as it is in heaven. Provide for us this day the daily bread we need. And forgive us our sins, as we forgive those who have sinned against us. Protect us from temptation and deliver us from all evil. For yours is the kingdom, and the power, and the glory. Now and forever.'"

Before I could draw a breath, a woman shouted through the silence, "Blessed is the woman who bore and nursed you!"

I countered just as quickly, "Blessed is anyone who hears the word of God and obeys it!"

"Come out to us, Jesus!" a voice cried from near the wall.

Another shout, "Over here, Jesus!"

The crowd began springing to its feet, moving and pushing toward me, oblivious that they were knocking into or stepping over others. I grabbed a few of the closest outstretched hands as the throng surged forward. Many started falling over in a rapid collapse of the front tiers like a single crack in a levy releasing a cascading torrent … and I was in its path.

Simon impulsively grabbed me from behind and pulled me back next to him. Nicodemus' servant slammed the large wooden gate and latched it before anyone else could press through. Shouts and cries now carried over the wall. "Jesus!"

"Touch us, Jesus!"

"Heal me, Jesus!"

"Where are you, Jesus?"

"Jesus, show yourself!"

"Tell us more, Jesus!"

One of the Pharisees motioned to a spot where arms were reaching over the stone barrier, people obviously climbing atop others. "They are crazy, teacher. You have stirred them into a frenzy."

"They were in darkness and have found a light," I said. "I must go to them."

Simon shot an anxious stare, listening to them bellow and bang the heavy gate. "I don't know, Lord. I fear for your safety. You remember last week in Tiberias."

Judas agreed. "Simon's right. We were in the open there and nearly got crushed. Here we're in closed quarters."

"We should retreat further into the house," another Pharisee recommended.

The latch on the gate started to jiggle, affirming their decision. They hustled me inside and secured the door.

Hardly a minute later, grinding from above, like brick scraping against brick, lifted our heads. Two large sections of roof tile slid back, sending a small shower of dust and grit upon us.

"My roof!" bemoaned Nicodemus.

I grabbed his arm reassuringly. "Do not fret, Nicodemus. We shall fix it later."

"Who do these people think they are?" scoffed a Pharisee.

"There are not many up there, I can assure you." My voice remained calm. "Just a few decisive souls."

"Decisively berserk," muttered the priest.

We all watched as the two men who had removed the tiles now carefully positioned a crippled man on a crude stretcher over the opening. They held tightly to ropes fastened around the front and back slats of the cot and gradually released more slack to slowly lower the stretcher in a steady descent into the room.

"What are you doing to this poor man?" Nicodemus implored to the hole in his roof as they now risked further injury to their brother's already lame body.

There was no response—only the continued, vigilant lowering of this paralytic.

For the moment, we had no alternative but to stand and admire such fortitude and determination. When the dusty, worn canvas came within our grasp, a few of us reached out to steady it. The ropes were released from above, and we gently brought the man to the ground. His arms and upper torso seemed normal, but his legs were spindly and frail, a sign he had been paralyzed from the waist down for many years.

His hands shook—perhaps from excitement, possibly from fear—probably a little of both.

"My son, you have great faith," I consoled, bending to one knee and stroking the top of his matted hair.

His voice trembled as much as his hands. "Jesus, I told them I must see you at all costs."

My smile finally warmed him, and he stopped shivering. "Take courage," I said. "Your sins are forgiven."

He reached out his free arm, grabbed my hand and pulled it to his face.

As I relished the power springing forth from this broken man's trust in me, I heard a scribe murmur scornfully from behind, "He is blaspheming. Who can forgive sins but God alone?"

The comment was not meant for my ears, but I spoke directly to it without turning my head. "Which is easier ... to say 'your sins are forgiven' ... or to say 'rise, pick up your mat and walk?'"

Several of my apostles knelt to the ground, recognizing what was coming.

I squeezed the lame man's hand and felt a warmth run through us that beaded perspiration across my brow. "And so that you all may know that the son of Man has authority to forgive sins ..." I peered directly into the cripple's longing eyes. "I say to you, get up.

Pick up your pallet and go home."

The man gasped once as if stung by something unseen—sensation and motor responses igniting down his lower extremities like dormant coals rekindled after an old fire has died. He rolled to a sitting position and grabbed his thighs, bursting into tears as he felt his hands on his legs for the first time.

Stunned babble erupted from the probing priests and some onlookers who had managed to scale the wall and now wedged their heads and shoulders into the window openings around the room.

The once-paralyzed man attempted to kneel, then grabbed my hand for support and stood on wobbling knees until we were nearly face to face. His awe-stricken gaze and moist eyes conveyed a gratitude no words could express.

"You will need some help on those legs until your strength returns," I smiled. "But return it shall."

As he raised his arms in joyful triumph to his rooftop brothers, I turned to the Pharisee who had labeled me a blasphemer. Instead of giving him a look of punitive satisfaction, I offered a supporting glance. I prayed that he too had been healed this day. The cripple's great faith had enabled physical restoration. But the kind of healing that truly changes lives is less tangible, yet more vital—the curing of the heart—the softening of hardened mindsets. This was the real miracle I hoped had transpired in Nicodemus' home.

*   *   *

Although I stayed in a small dwelling near Simon's house in Capernaum, I often spent the hours before midnight meditating on the crest of a steep hill while gazing down at the glowing torch lights from the distant pathways and residences below. This was one of those nights. I sat in the tall grass, enjoying the tranquilizing chorus of crickets that filled the air. Even in the weak light of a crescent moon, the visual contrasts were striking. The hillside, cloaked in darkness, reached down to the glimmer of Capernaum, its flickering glow abruptly snuffed to the south as the black vastness of the Galilean sea began. Only the uncountable myriad of stars indicated the horizon—lightless water touching a twinkling night sky.

My eyes suddenly pulled back from that distant line far away and refocused to a spot down the hill about fifty paces from my position. Silhouettes soon caught up with footsteps—two figures ascending the incline in my direction. I didn't move or attempt to hide. My apostles knew I frequented this hill at night, so I assumed two of them were approaching. As they came closer, I finally noticed the shape of John, but it wasn't until they were almost upon me that I recognized the other as Nicodemus. It had only been an hour or so since I left him. After the healing at his house, we had broken bread together and stayed to fix the roof through which the cripple had started his journey to freedom.

Nicodemus was an honorable man but placed too heavy an importance on what the council of Pharisees determined essential for a holy life. Privately, he sought a truth that transcended traditional thinking, but openly, he too often caved to the establishment's burdensome decrees, prohibitions and canons. When he wasn't constrained by the watchful eyes of his fellow scribes, he readily shed the confines of their limitations and hungered for a purer unconditional relationship with God. And where I now sat, far removed from any public assembly, on a deserted hilltop in the dead of night, Nicodemus actively sought it. I sensed his relief to have found me in this setting.

John motioned to Nicodemus, who was visibly out of breath from the climb. "I hope you don't mind, Master, that I have brought Nicodemus to your retreat." He paused to fill his own lungs with needed air. "But the good rabbi insisted I take him to you."

I stood up and smiled through the darkness. "Anyone willing to climb the face of this slope after sundown without torch or lantern should receive what he seeks."

"Thank you, teacher," said Nicodemus. "With all the commotion today, and all the people … and the signs you performed ..." He struggled to verbalize what was truly on his mind.

"This hilltop is flat and covers much ground," I interjected. "Let us walk while we talk."

He nodded and relaxed.

I patted his back and invited them both to accompany me. "You are a wise man, Nicodemus. Try not to let the waves from others toss your ship from focusing on the light."

"You speak much of the light," he said. "It is evident God put you on this earth to do great things and to teach many people. No one could do the signs you do unless Yahweh was with him."

Through the darkness, I beckoned him to speak from his heart.

He welcomed this gentle encouragement and proceeded, "The kingdom of which you speak, the kingdom of God … The thoughts you pronounce are so eloquent, as if you have actually seen it."

John edged in the conversation with an impulsive defense. "Do you doubt the Master has?"

Nicodemus hesitated. "I'm not doubting anything. After today, I don't know what to think, which is why I'm here now, I suppose."

"I was a guest in your house for much of the day," I reminded. "Is there a question you forgot to ask that has brought you deep into the night, or is it just the solitude of these surroundings?"

He wavered no longer. "I want to see the kingdom of God. What must I do to understand it as you do?"

John glanced over for my reaction to this overtly direct request. His own demeanor indicated he was sincerely pleased to be present as it was asked.

I kept my eyes forward and spoke as much to the darkness as to the two men on either side of me. "Unless one is born again, he cannot see the kingdom of God."

While John pondered this silently to himself, Nicodemus voiced his confusion without reflection. "How is that possible? How can someone be born again if they are already here? Surely they cannot reenter the womb to reemerge."

It consistently amazed me that despite the soul having more life than the body, the human mind too often operated purely from a material perspective. Only through finding and releasing the love and power of the Spirit could one ever hope to precipitate divine revelation. "That which is born of the flesh is flesh, and that which is born of the spirit is spirit," I simply stated. "You are focusing too much on the former. Unless someone is reborn of water and the Spirit, they cannot enter the kingdom of God."

Nicodemus tried digesting my words and walked several paces in silence before sighing, "How can these things be?"

His frustration was palpable. So many years of tradition and law as the crux of his belief; it would take a direct association to something familiar in order to spark an epiphany.

So to emphasize a very direct reference to myself and my heavenly Father, I stopped walking. Here upon this remote hilltop, shrouded by the blanket of night, hidden from humanity except for an ex-fisherman-turned-disciple and a befuddled religious cleric; it was here that I first directly conveyed the true substance of my Father's plan for mankind.

I glanced up at the sky and its North Star hanging boldly and brightly before us. I needed an allusion, a relevant reference they could understand and hopefully make a connection.

Then it came to me—the great Hebrew prophet and liberator whose raised staff rescued a lost nation—of course.

I remained focused on the radiant star above. "Listen to me and remember what I say to you. Just as Moses lifted up the serpent in the wilderness, so must the son of Man be lifted up, so that all might come to him and be saved." I lowered my eyes with intensity to indicate the profound depth of my next revelation. "For God so loved the world that he gave his only begotten son, that whoever believes in him shall not perish but have eternal life."

"You speak of the Messiah, teacher," Nicodemus breathed reverently. "Is he to come soon? To judge the world?"

There I stood, right in their midst, and he could not recognize me. Miracle worker, prophet, spiritual leader and teacher. That was all he could see—or chose to see.

"The Father did not send the son to judge the world, but to save it," I simply replied. "Those who believe in him will avoid judgment. Those who do not have already been judged by avoiding the light and remaining in darkness."

Nicodemus seemed anxious. "You keep speaking as if this has already happened."

"You are a good scholar of Israel, Nicodemus, versed in the prophets—Moses, Isaiah, Elijah. You know their writings and lecture on their meanings, and yet you do not understand?"

Unsure how to respond, he tried reading my expression for any hint of implication.

John turned to look behind us, suddenly startled.

"What is it, John?" I asked.

He waited a moment, eyes fixed like an alarmed deer in the direction of movement through the grass. "People approach, Master."

Before I could follow his gaze, a voice resonated across the dark hilltop. "John! Jesus!" It was Andrew.

"Over here!" John shouted.

Two shadows slowly grew out of the gloom—the contours of Andrew and Simon moving briskly yet cautiously toward us. The brothers reached our position and as we welcomed them, Simon rested with hands on knees to catch his breath.

"Master, Andrew has news from Judea," he said.

Despite this admission, his brother did not appear as if he wanted to speak.

"What is it, Andrew?" I encouraged, always emboldening them to express their minds without fear or apprehension.

"It's John the Baptist," he finally uttered.

Knowing Andrew had been a disciple of John's, I understood his feelings for my cousin were nearly as strong as mine. "Go on."

He fidgeted restlessly before divulging, "He has been arrested … held in prison by King Herod."

He spoke of Herod Antipas, the Roman puppet of Galilee.

The name Herod had pierced my heart with great sorrow for decades. While I knew I was here for nothing less than the salvation of the world, I was also keenly aware that many precious baby boys had been slaughtered by this tyrant's father as a direct result of my birth. In a horrible act of jealous fear, determined to destroy any prophesized messiah, he personally ordered Roman soldiers to run their blades through all male infants under the age of two in the region of my birth. Only the empty soul of a monster who had murdered his wife and two of his own children could have given such a heinous decree to massacre so many innocent little lives.

And now his heir and namesake—a gluttonous, sanctimonious sultan of indulgence—held my cousin prisoner. "Under what charge?" I tentatively asked, still trying to reconcile the news that evil men had taken John away from his mission.

Andrew answered with simple logic. "For what John does best. Demanding repentance."

"Demanding repentance of Herod himself," finished Simon, unsure whether he believed it a courageous act of boldness or an incredibly stupid one.

"How did he even *get* an audience with Herod?" asked Nicodemus, more shocked at this conundrum than the fact that a Jew had told Roman authority to repent.

"Herod is a fanatic about the occult," Andrew explained. "Gods, messengers of gods, possible signs from messengers of gods; he's obsessed with it. He had been seeking John ever since word began to spread about him."

"And he told Herod to repent?" I curled my mouth in an unexpected grin, wishing I had been there to witness it.

Andrew continued, "John knew Herod had divorced his wife in favor of his brother's bride. So John, being John, condemned the act to his face … in public."

Young John beside us winced at the words. "What was he thinking?"

"Wait, there's more—a rumor that comes straight from a Roman soldier in Herod's regiment." Andrew leaned in to privately confide as if it were midday in the village square and not midnight on a secluded hilltop. "Herod is secretly visiting John in the dungeon to hear him speak. He's still fascinated by John's message. Can you believe that, Lord?"

"I can. My cousin has the charisma and fervor to hold the attention of even an egotistical ruler such as Antipas."

Simon folded his arms to think for a moment, then stated matter-of-factly, "The Baptist is bound to tell Herod of you, Master. And even if he doesn't, word will surely reach his ears soon."

"Yes, I suppose it will," I replied just as frankly. "But God knows the motivation of all people. Those who seek me in shallow attempts to see wonders and signs will not be fulfilled, whether they witness a mountain moved or see nothing at all. But those who seek the truth and the will of God in their lives will find true fulfillment, whether I physically touch them now or if they simply trust in my words a thousand years from now."

Without the scrutiny of his fellow Pharisees present, Nicodemus spoke from his heart. "How lucky and blessed we are to have you here and now, teacher. While I find your concepts hard to grasp at times, your words and deeds amaze me beyond expression."

"Surrender yourself even more, Nicodemus," I said, "and you will possess a strength in me that will further amaze you."

John mulled this oxymoron over in his head and paraphrased quietly, "Surrender to become strong."

"Yes," I confirmed. "So take some time to come to a hill like this at night, or to a rooftop at dawn, or to a lonely shore on the Sea of Galilee, and say to the Lord, 'Father, in your hands I place my life; to your will I entrust my soul.' Do this, and I promise, you will foster an inner strength greater than you could ever imagine. In your weakness, God's power works."

"Can it be that easy?" asked Nicodemus, skeptically hoping it could be.

I looked at them as if an underlying truth had been discovered. "Easy to say … extremely challenging to practice as a way of living."

We stood there quietly for several moments before turning and starting back over the plateau of grass. We walked in silence, allowing the crickets to retake the night with their ceaseless singing. The high moon told me it was late, as did my yawns. I hoped the news of John's arrest wouldn't interfere with a restful sleep. So I took my own advice. I placed my concerns into my Father's hands, knowing that John was there as well, regardless of where he lay his head this night.

And as a warm breeze rustled through the grass and bowed the field reverently to the star-filled heavens, we began our descent to Capernaum.

9

Cultivating Hope

WE HEADED NORTH.

Following the road to Phoenicia, we hiked along the natural valleys that climbed higher into hill country. The farther we journeyed, the more amazed I became at how fast word spread throughout the region. It didn't matter if we passed a few travelers on foot or entered a well-populated locality, the words 'Jesus of Nazareth' never met with indifference. Whether driven by curiosity or conviction, they came, pulling friends and family to see this traveler who preached hope, taught love and healed all those who sought him. They did not take time to find their sandals, tie up their animals or put away their tools. They dropped everything and came to me, clamoring to see my face, struggling to hear my words, even risking scrapes and bruises in their attempts to get close enough to grab my hands.

Their hope in me renewed my hope in them.

My heart leapt in joy as I watched the blind dance at seeing family for the first time. My spirit soared as the deaf rejoiced upon hearing their own voice. I wept in happiness with the seriously ill as they became pain free and received an unexpected second chance at life.

But it was when I observed their simple compassion for each other that I found myself inspired most. Strangers helped strangers make their way to me. The young and the strong carried the frail and the weak to my feet. Those blessed with the good things in life troubled themselves with those in trouble.

A lump came to my throat, realizing that my Father extended true miracles beyond the physical signs and healings I performed. The power of selfless love moved me to touch them all—to allow them to crowd around, close in and press upon me. My twelve did their best to keep some order, but at times their best efforts failed. The urgency of human hurts and hungers overwhelmed us all.

This was certainly the case as we neared the end of our return trip, descending from the Galilean highlands toward the valleys below. Morning gave way to afternoon, and the narrow mountain pass finally opened to some rolling foothills. Finding ourselves in a lush, far-reaching field, the thirteen of us spread out as we walked. The air, noticeably damper, alerted us that the Sea of Galilee was not far ahead.

That's when they appeared.

They emerged through the trees on the far side of the valley—gradually, steadily, seemingly without end—hundreds at first, then well over a thousand. We stopped. There was no need to go toward such a crowd. They were indeed heading for us.

Thomas articulated our thoughts. "How do they always seem to know where we are?"

"Because we're foolish enough to disclose our plans before moving on," answered Bartholomew, leaning on his walking stick and mentally preparing for the masses headed our way.

Philip agreed. "It only takes one to announce, 'Jesus is coming.'"

The multitude apparently saw and recognized us across the field, their pace to close the distance quickening.

"I must say whoever went ahead of us this time spread the news rather well," stated Simon the Zealot.

I smiled a moment at their tongue-in-cheek grumblings, but as the crowd drew nearer, we easily sensed the dire desperation in their faces. Many hobbled forward with crutches, while others were dragged upon stretchers or simply leaned on one another for support. Their struggle to find me had exhausted them. Some wore little more than rags.

Poor in pocket and poor in spirit. With no hope in their lives, they came seeking me.

I was their hope.

"Let us meet them," I said.

My faithful entourage did not hesitate to accompany me despite knowing the arduous task ahead. And sure enough, we were soon surrounded, engulfed by outstretched hands and cries for mercy. Although the crowd seemed endless, I tried holding each one by the face to gaze deep into their eyes and project the warmth of my love for them—from my Spirit to theirs. My disciples did their best to clear a circle around me as we shuffled person by person through the swarm of impoverished souls. It was no use. It was bedlam at best.

Then suddenly without warning, my knees buckled. No one physically struck me, but just as swiftly and uncontrollably, all my energy, all my strength was gone. I almost lost balance.

John saw me stumble first. "What is it, Lord?"

I faltered again, and Simon snatched my elbow. "Master, are you okay?"

"Someone touched me," was all I could manage.

He stared at me with bewildered astonishment. "We are being mobbed by a throng of thousands. They're all touching you."

I tried looking at every face around me, asking no one in particular, "Who touched me?"

Only blank stares replied. After repeating this question several times, my apostles perceived the increasing emotion in my voice and hastily moved to my aid.

"Who are we looking for?" James asked, ready to throw people in the air if necessary.

I had no real answer. "I'm not sure. Someone definitely touched me lightly from behind. Not even me, but the edge of my garment."

"Lord," he said—one word easily conveying obvious perplexity since so many hands were reaching and grabbing for me.

"Trust me," was all I needed to say.

James turned and shouted authoritatively, "Everybody, listen! Who just touched the Master's cloak?"

The voices quieted only slightly until Simon bellowed as well, "Spread out, all of you! Who grabbed the cloth of Jesus? Who?"

Like the Red Sea before Moses, the people finally parted, and silence for the first time fell over those closest to us. They stepped aside to reveal a small, kneeling woman huddled close to the ground. Sensing our attention, she peered up with fearful eyes and confessed, "I touched you, sir."

I moved closer. Then stooping down, I held her chin so that her eyes wouldn't leave mine. "You must have been nearly trampled getting to me, my child." I spoke softly to her frightened stare. "And yet your simple touch has affected me more than you can imagine."

Her lips trembled. "I have bled for more than ten years." Tears spilled over her weary eyes, and her hands moved to expose blood-stained rags near her lower abdomen and pelvis. "No one has been able to stop this condition. It leaves me so weak."

"But when you touched me?" I coaxed her to continue.

"I—I thought if I could just get my fingers to brush against your clothing … I would be cured."

As my strength returned, so did my smile. "And?"

She nodded, dropping the soiled rags to the ground. "I felt such a rush of warmth through me, such comfort from where I bled, I knew … I knew instantly that your power had saved me."

My fingers gently brushed her cheek as I corrected, "Your faith has made you well. Go in peace."

I stood and studied the faces before me. Wonder, fear, reverence, but mostly distress and anxiety were clearly embedded on them.

And unlike this brave woman, many did not crave a physical healing. I peered over the vast multitude gathered around—dismay, discouragement and despair stretching across the field.

Raising my hands, I indicated those around me to sit. "All of you! Please, sit down and listen to me!"

As they began moving to the ground, more could see me, so I continued gesturing to have them seated. "Sit all of you! Sit and listen!"

My apostles did the same, encouraging large groups to gather on the ground. Those nearest reclined first and triggered the rest of the colossal aggregation to follow. Like an expanding circular wave, all were promptly seated.

Silence suddenly swept across the plain, and with a vapory mist hovering above the tree line, nature provided a fitting spiritual sanctuary.

I began with my own feelings for them. "Your defeated, dejected faces break my heart! You carry the burden of so many troubles! So many of you feel that life is too difficult—that despite living according to the scriptures, you have been forsaken!"

Even my disciples were now seated, leaving me standing alone over a sea of bodies. I slowly turned and addressed them all. "I am here today to promise you otherwise! To assure each and every one of you that you have *not* been forsaken by your heavenly Father, and that you are considered blessed in the eyes of God!"

A dull murmur ascended into the damp air, a muttering that debated this possibility. Blessed? None of them considered themselves blessed. Many of them could hardly keep clothes on their backs and food in their stomachs. How could they be blessed when they felt so deprived, so overlooked, so alone and abandoned?

I understood their reaction and responded accordingly, describing both their blessings and their fruits. "Blessed are you who are poor in spirit! You have not been forgotten; the kingdom of heaven is yours!

Blessed are you who mourn! You *will* be comforted!

Blessed are the gentle and meek! You shall inherit the earth!

Blessed are you who hunger and thirst for righteousness! You *will* be satisfied!

Blessed are you who are merciful to others! God will surely be merciful to you!

Blessed are the pure in heart! You shall not be overlooked by God; you shall see him face to face!

Blessed are you who work for peace! You shall be called sons and daughters of the Most-High!"

There was no more muttering, no mumbles of contradiction. I seized the silence and gave them the encouragement they would need to take my message back to their towns and beyond. "And blessed are you when people insult you, persecute you and utter every kind of slander against you because of me! I tell you rejoice and be glad! For your reward in heaven will be great!"

For the first time since they had emerged from the trees, I noticed some smiles. Many were through tears, but smiles now increasingly transformed more of the faces before me. And for those who still sat rigidly bound with fear and anxiety, I offered a cure. "Whatever troubles come your way, whatever hardships weigh you down, let them go! My command to you today is this … do not be afraid! Stop worrying! Do not even fret over the necessities of food, or drink, or clothing! Is not life more important than food, and your body more important than clothing?"

I pointed to the sky. "Look at the birds! They do not plant or gather crops into barns, yet their heavenly Father feeds them!" My outstretched hands collectively acknowledged the crowd. "You are all worth so much more than birds!"

I motioned up the hill toward the mountain pass. "As we entered this great field today, we walked through a thatch of wildflowers! I marveled at their beauty! For not even Solomon, as rich as he was, had vestments as magnificent as one of those blossoms! But how can they be so magnificent if they do not spin or sew cloth?"

I allowed the question to penetrate their troubled hearts. "It is

God who clothes the flowers of the field, flowers that are here today and gone tomorrow! Will he not be much more willing to clothe you—even you of little faith? Seek first the kingdom of God and his righteousness, and he will provide the things you need in life!"

Again I paused. A single crow in a distant tree offered the only verbal reply. I then finished my thoughts—my words also providing perspective for me. "So do not worry about tomorrow; it will take care of itself! Each day has enough troubles of its own! Why add to it by worrying about the next?"

And yes, I took these words to heart. Too many nights I lay awake, uncertain how the next would play out, wondering if I would gain the traction needed before my real opposition reared its head. I had suffered too many anxious forebodings about how this would ultimately end. If I were to dwell on that, I would be able to go no further. But by giving that undeniable dread to my Father, I could place him in control and thus keep to the mission at hand.

This decisive mindset—a confident, trusting surrender—was what I also wanted for those sitting around me ... to surrender their fears and worries to my Father ... and to me. Our love for them reached beyond human understanding. We would never forget them as long as their focus in life remained on us.

And the focus these people had on me this day was unmistakable. It took some time for the crowds to disperse and start heading back. They finally thinned enough for my apostles and I to regroup and head down the valley as well. My words had also lifted my friends' spirits. Feeling blessed and cared for by God put a certain spring in their step, regardless of how difficult the path. I prayed that my Father's plan for us included some food and rest before another flock of searchers found us.

Just before making it to the trees, a man I recognized but whose name I could not place spotted us and ran over. The anguish in his eyes surpassed any I had seen that day, which I wouldn't have thought possible. His clothing was hardly meager, and he seemed physically well, yet his countenance conveyed fear bordering on panic.

"Jesus," he wheezed, not waiting to catch his breath. "I have been looking for you all day."

"I know you from somewhere," I replied, hoping to calm him down and place a name with his familiar face.

"Yes, teacher," he nodded. "I am Jairus, an official at the synagogue." He did not pause for my response. "Please, I implore you, come with me to my house. My twelve-year-old daughter, my only daughter, is very sick … she is dying." He wrung his hands nervously as he spoke.

I grabbed his fingers and held them steady to show there was no need for fear. "Then we must go to her."

"Yes," he breathed, relieved that I would accompany him. "We must hurry though. Her condition deteriorates rapidly."

So we followed Jairus down toward Capernaum, heading east over the hills that led to town. Still at some distance from his dwelling, two men approached. The first walked purposefully up to us and grabbed Jairus by the arms.

"What is it, Eli?" Jairus asked, and before the man could speak, "I have found Jesus of Nazareth. He is here to lay his hands upon Rachel."

His friend did not respond with words. He looked at him with a gaze of sympathy that conveyed the worst.

"He is here to help her," Jairus repeated, denying the silent message before him.

Eli continued to hold his arms steady and languidly shook his head.

Jairus refused to accept the inevitable. "No. No, she must hold on just a little longer—long enough to see Jesus."

The second man now reached out and grabbed his shoulder. His voice was but a whisper. "She's gone, Jairus. Do not trouble the teacher any longer."

Jairus began to tremble. He shifted his attention to me as fear and panic returned to his face.

Although his two friends held him firmly for support, it was my confident, loving eyes that kept him from collapsing. "Do not be afraid," I said. "Have faith."

I then turned to Eli. "Where is she?"

"In the back room of the house."

"Show me."

His companion angled away from Jairus, hoping only I might hear him. "It is too late, teacher. The girl passed close to an hour ago."

"Show me," I simply repeated.

Again I saw the bewildered stare of one astonished by the unexpected God. But perplexity soon gave way to compliance, and they hesitantly led us down toward the residence. All was quiet until we drew near and could hear the sobbing from inside. A man stationed at the doorway, tasked with allowing entry only to close friends and relatives, saw Jairus and immediately gave him a supportive embrace. Jairus was in shock and hardly acknowledged.

"We are here to see Rachel," I announced.

The man scrutinized our large group. "The house is full of mourners. We cannot take any more now. Let Jairus see his daughter alone."

Jairus finally snapped out of his daze. "No. I want Jesus and the others to come with me."

While he didn't wish to argue with his afflicted friend, the man responded, "If all these enter, Jairus, I fear your wife cannot take any more in her state."

I motioned to the three closest by my side. "Simon, James, John; we shall go in. The rest of you wait here."

And so the four of us followed a disheartened Jairus into his house. Once inside, the love for this young girl quickly became apparent. So many gatherers, men and women, all grieving for their loss and the void now realized by her silent absence. It was always hard to watch anyone mourn the death of a loved one, but to behold those lamenting over the untimely death of a child was overwhelming.

When Jairus' wife saw him, she ran to his arms, buried her face in his chest and wailed, "She's gone! Our baby's gone!"

Jairus couldn't contain himself any longer and also broke down.

No one intervened or really moved at all, content to give them the time and space to hold each other and weep together. Perhaps I should have done the same, but I could not bear their sorrow.

I anxiously inspected the crowded room, over the heads of the many mourners until I found what I was searching for. A single linen curtain hung over a doorway dividing what was surely a smaller chamber off the main room. I gestured for my three disciples to follow and headed for the shrouded entrance. Jairus caught sight of us and pulled his wife, still sobbing, in our direction.

I gingerly lifted the linen divider, and we entered the small room. Inside, a single narrow window provided just enough light to see the reason for this day's great tribulation. A female servant knelt at the head of a small straw bed. She carefully draped a sheer, nearly transparent sheet over the face of a motionless girl and tucked it neatly under her head.

At the sight of her daughter's covered face, Jairus' wife burst into uncontrollable tears.

I looked at the woman stooping by the bedside and asked straightforwardly, "Why do you cover this girl's face?"

She hesitated, not wanting to state the obvious in front of the deceased's parents. But she answered quietly, "The child has left us, sir."

It was now I who appeared perplexed for all to see. "If you are implying she has died, I can assure you she has not."

"My only daughter is dead," sobbed Jairus' wife. "I rocked her tightly to my own breast with no breath upon my skin—no heartbeat against mine." Her tears flowed freely at hearing her own words.

"She is not dead," I reiterated. "She is sleeping."

The servant woman managed a sarcastic snicker. "I have hardly left this room since she fell ill, sir. I can attest to you that our dear Rachel is gone. Please let us grieve in peace."

I turned to Jairus and grabbed him squarely by the shoulder, quickening my breath as if ready to perform a strenuous task. I held his hopeless eyes with mine and asked intently between inhales of air, "Do you believe, Jairus?"

Though feeble, he did not flounder. "I do."

I closed my eyes and raised my face to the ceiling. I can sense that he truly believes, Father, I prayed. His belief in our power of life over death needs to fill his heart and this room. Free his faith to enable our will for this child.

I opened my eyes and returned them to Jairus. "Do you believe?" I said again, this time more fervently.

"I do believe."

"Do you believe because of what you have heard *of* me or *from* me?" I pressed my knuckles into his chest. "Do you believe from *here*, Jairus? What do you believe? What is it that you believe?"

"Stop tormenting my husband," cried his wife.

The linen divider swung open, and two men barged in. "What is going on in here?" one sternly asked.

But Jairus waved them all off and grabbed my wrist. "I believe in *you*, Jesus of Nazareth! I believe you have the power of good behind all that you do. And I especially believe God will do whatever you ask of him."

A faint whimper from behind me suddenly silenced him. John, to my left, clasped a hand over his mouth to keep a sob of joy from escaping, as he knew immediately from where the soft moan had come.

Another peaceful sigh emanated from beneath the sheet, causing the servant woman to fall back against the wall in shock.

"Rachel!" screamed Jairus' wife. She rushed to her daughter's side and gently pulled the covering from her head. Although still slightly pale, the girl peered up at me with two beautiful brown eyes.

"Get up, my child," I said to her.

She immediately sat up into her mother's embrace.

I looked to the servant woman who was now crying as well. "Fetch her something to eat," I suggested. "She is probably hungry."

Turning to Jairus, I could see he wanted nothing more than to hold his awakened child. Instead, he grabbed my cloak and asked through a tear-soaked beard, "What can I do to repay you, Jesus? How can I ever thank you for bringing my daughter back to us?"

I too reached out and held him steady before me. "I tell you the truth, Jairus … your faith in me has returned her to you."

He gazed at me with astonishment, then nodded, tears falling from his eyes.

"Go to her," I said. "She is well."

As he joyfully bent down to once again hug and be hugged by his most precious blessing, I turned to those who stood in the doorway and addressed their dumbfounded stares. "Tell no one of what you saw here today."

I glanced back at Simon, John and James. They too were stunned and speechless.

"Let's go," I whispered.

The houseful of mourners now surged toward the back room to see the unimaginable, allowing my disciples and I to slip discreetly outside and rejoin the others.

We stood there a moment and let our hearts fill with the welcome sound of rejoicing from within the house. I lifted my chin to the waning afternoon sky, rain clouds continuing to gather, and thanked my heavenly Father that the storm over this house had been quieted.

I smiled at my friends. We agreed, without sharing a word, that it had certainly been a long, productive day … a very blessed day.

10

Five-Thousand

IT WAS AN UNTAINTED TWILIGHT—no clouds to obscure the crimson skies from casting a blazing glow across the Sea of Galilee. With the sun gradually slipping beneath the hills, stars began revealing themselves in the eastern sky, highlighting the darkening aura of the dying dusk. I stood at the stone wall overlooking the main port of Capernaum, a perfect place to enjoy such a sunset, but I noticed none of it. Terrible news had reached my ears less than an hour before from two of my cousin's disciples. They had come to bring me and Andrew the agonizing report.

John the Baptist was dead.

Since learning of his imprisonment, Andrew had held hope that because Herod was at least partly sensitive to Jewish tradition and quite enamored with John's oratory, he would keep him alive and perhaps one day set him free. We all had hoped Herod might refrain from executing him if for no other reason than to avoid divine retribution for perhaps killing a true prophet of God.

And it may very well have worked out that way if it had not been for Herod's shallow pride. The account that came back was that his stepdaughter, a voluptuous girl of sixteen, had performed a veil dance for his majesty and other male dinner guests, a dance that left few veils clinging to her waist by the final stroke of the harp. Those lusting after the tantalizing dancer were no ordinary banquet guests. Far from it. Imperial officials visiting Herod's post from Rome and other wealthy constituents had come to feast and be appropriately entertained.

In an impulsive act of pretentious gratitude, vanity and ego, and most certainly impassioned by copious quaffs of wine, Herod promised the girl, in front of everyone, anything she desired, up to and including half his kingdom. He had been fairly certain, even in his drunken state, that she would request something less meaningful to him and more so to a teenage girl.

He did not, however, expect her to run to her mother for advice. Still insulted and humiliated from John's public denouncement of her scandalous union with Herod, her instructions to her daughter were precise and exacting. And thus the ruler of Galilee, despite his avowed allegiance to obey nobody but Caesar, acquiesced to the horribly ruthless request of a young woman. He had John beheaded—the prophet's trophy head presented to her on a silver plate.

With an experienced executioner wielding the sword, decapitation was a veritably quick way to be dispatched. I actually thanked my heavenly Father that the misguided girl wasn't told to request something more barbaric. Yet the thought of my pious cousin's severed head desecrated as fanciful favor to Herod's wife for her vengeful satisfaction, turned my stomach.

I needed time to think. I longed for some quiet space to clear my head where nobody could find me.

I needed to be alone.

Having told my apostles to meet me in Bethsaida the following day, I wandered down to the main harbor hoping to find a small rowboat on which to take refuge for the night. A few of the local fishermen preparing for a late excursion noticed me sauntering about the docks.

"Teacher, what brings you down here at this hour?" one asked.

I hesitated, then simply stated, "Herod has slain John the Baptist."

Another fisherman overheard and asked sorrowfully, "The Baptist is dead?"

I wasn't sure if I had nodded or not. "Would one of you be so kind as to loan me a small vessel for this evening?"

Still mulling over the news, he did not answer until his partner nudged him. "Jacob, Jesus needs a boat."

"Oh," he quickly came around. "Yes, of course. Any of these over here are easily manageable by one person."

"Thank you," I replied. "I am just heading over to Bethsaida and shall have it returned tomorrow."

He sensed my somber mood and nodded reverently. "No rush. Keep it as long as you need it."

I carefully pushed off from the pier and rowed on the gentle currents to where I could more easily navigate the shoreline. I waited until I had drifted past the flickering glow of Capernaum before dropping my small anchor.

The world finally seemed still and quiet. No crowds, no questions, no demands, no protests—just me and my Father.

At last.

I nestled into the stern of the small craft. Other than the faint ripples of water lapping lazily against the boat, silence commanded my surroundings.

I closed my eyes, took a deep breath and invoked my heavenly Father. We have taken a foothold, I reflected to his presence. Our message of faith is making an impact. Our declaration of love is being received. So many of those who had lost their way are now treating others as they would want to be treated. They are grasping the context that placing their neighbors' needs before their own pleases you so much more than any animal sacrifice they might offer. They leave my company with such hope. How it must bring you great joy to see this ... and oh what joy that gives me.

But I am also keenly aware that those in authority, the Pharisees and Sadducees, regard me more as a threat than as a beacon of hope. I hear it in their carefully worded questions and in their incessant probing of my profound, challenging and merciful interpretation of the Law ... and you. Although they have yet to directly ask who I am, I know they mean to. They want to trap me in a blasphemous remark. They do not want the truth. They do not seek the truth. It saddens my heart that these influential spiritual leaders mislead so many with egotistical hypocrisy. They say they are most concerned with respecting, preserving and obeying their sacred Law while maintaining King David's legacy, when in fact they are more worried about their own self-importance, doctrinal standing and economic status.

I wish I didn't intimidate them. But this is how they are, and so this is how it must be. I have accepted that they will ultimately seek to eliminate my threat by crushing me, and will assuredly look to Rome for support. And Rome will not hesitate to carry out their intentions.

I rested my face against my knees and shuddered as I continued to pray. Father, I am fully mindful that they will not take me swiftly with the sword. I know that to save this world from great suffering, I must suffer greatly. I must fulfill the prophecy and promise that God himself is willing to submit to humiliation, torture and death in our desire to win back humanity.

My cousin's mortality, Father, only heightens my awareness of how brief and fragile human life is, and why death is so feared. My anxieties are no different from any man's. I do not wish to die. But my divinity guides and propels me forward—teaching all how to live by example—including laying down my life to ensure eternal life in my name.

Strength, Father, grant me strength as I stand firm in the truth, so that those who seek the truth can hear my voice. Through our

Spirit, I thank and praise you for everything, never forgetting you are near to me and that we are one.

I opened my eyes. The night hung nearly as dark as my eyelids. I felt at peace. Praying to my Father—being with him and confiding in him—always eased my stress. With a calmed heart, I rested my head against a cushion and followed the clear, gently rocking sky. Being alone like this at last, out on the open water under the stars, restored my tranquility and refreshed my soul. And although I tried to stay awake and savor this rare respite, I fell quickly asleep.

*   *   *

The sun announced a new day with its first rays over the horizon, and the Sea of Galilee turned from shadow to shining almost as rapidly as a lantern lighting a room. The early sparkle teased my face, but I remained lying in the boat for some time, wishing I could gently float there all day. I knew, however, that my disciples would be waiting for me by the road to Bethsaida. So after thanking and praising my Father for the night's rest and the opportunities of this day, I pulled anchor and began rowing east, again following the shore. I kept my eyes open for the tributaries of the Jordan that would signify Bethsaida to the north.

I did not need to find them. Instead, where the river usually met the lake, now stood hundreds of people. This surprisingly large crowd faced the water, tracking the solitary boat drifting by. As they became aware it was me at the helm, they began pointing at my position. Many shouted and called my name, beckoning for me to row inland. Before I could consider the number that awaited me, I noticed my apostles standing together and waving to get my attention. Seeing them, I felt at ease. The surrounding multitude must have started with a few small groups recognizing my twelve on route to Bethsaida. Quickly concluding that I would eventually meet up with them, others hurriedly joined. I would now once again need my friends' assistance ministering to all those who searched for, and had unquestionably found me.

So much for my secluded retreat. I took a long, deep breath of the quiet morning air and carefully turned my boat toward shore. Approaching closer to land, I caught sight of some Pharisees standing to the left of the crowd, along with other religious scribes whose robes signified the even more conservative sect of Sadducees ... and from Judea no less. Only one reason made sense for such a long journey. Their governing body, the Sanhedrin, had dispatched them to Galilee to find me and report back. They were here on a fact-finding mission to decide if I was truly a rebel—a false prophet who would need to be dealt with—or simply a delusional fool whose support would inevitably fade out. Despite detailed information they must have already received from Jew and gentile alike, the prospect of possibly finding a true savior from God teaching in Galilee was not even something to speculate. A carpenter from Nazareth? I sensed their contempt from across the water.

I guided my vessel to within a stone's throw of shore but instead of drifting it forward upon the silt, I stood and planted my oar into the water as a makeshift anchor. Holding it steady, I surveyed the suddenly silent crowd, every eye upon me.

"Good morning!" I simply shouted.

They answered with a warm, animated ovation.

"Tell me," I called, "what brings you to the banks of this great lake this morning?"

"Have you come to save Israel, Jesus?" someone bellowed.

The question startled me, and I instinctively glanced at the Pharisees and Sadducees to gauge their reaction. Cold stares in the direction of the shout affirmed their antipathy to the notion of Israel's restoration coming from the likes of a poorly dressed peasant standing in a rowboat. But before I could even compose a response, I was saved by another, more meaningful inquiry.

"How can we attain the kingdom of God?"

"Now there's a good question!" I responded loudly. "And how nice it would be if I could simply instruct you all to 'do this' or 'do that' in order to gain the keys to the kingdom of heaven! But achieving everlasting life is not merely a checklist of behavior or a conformity to liturgical customs! No one can cling to salvation by clinging to their lineage!"

I didn't dare glance at the scribes to my left. I knew their eyes were boring a hole through me.

After a short pause, I continued. "Many of you have come from the fields this morning, taking time from your crops to seek inspiration! So what I tell you today is that the answer you seek is much like a farmer indeed—a farmer who set out one morning to sow some seed! As he flung the seed about, some of it fell along the path where birds quickly came and ate it! Some scattered on rocky ground, allowing plants to sprout, but without depth of soil they soon withered and died under the sun's heat! Still more seed fell among the weeds and thorns which choked the seedlings as they tried to grow!"

I scanned the crowd as I spoke. Although unsure where I was going with this, they related well to the allegory. "But some seed did land on good soil," I brightened. "This seed took root and yielded a crop of thirty ... sixty ... no ... even a hundred-fold!"

To fully grasp its meaning, they would need time to digest this parable, which was fine. If nothing else, they were enraptured with the relevant storytelling. It was a new form of teaching for them, and they took to it earnestly.

"But what about the occupation of our holy land?" another boldly shouted, bringing the topic of the morning back to Israel. "Will God ever deliver us?"

"Yes, Jesus, when might we be free from such callous control and oppressive taxation?"

The religious scribes now seemed pleased that the question about Roman rule had again been raised. They were anxious to trap me regardless of my answer. Any response would portray me as either seditious to the sovereign empire or apathetic to the prolonged plight of my own people.

Or so they thought.

"Let me answer by offering you a second story about a farmer!" I twisted my arm around the oar to keep my boat steady. "One who made sure his grain fell upon fertile earth! But later, while he and his workers were sleeping, an enemy came and sowed weeds and other tares among the good seed! When the wheat began to sprout, the high weeds grew intermingled with it! The laborers came to the landowner and said, 'Sir, an enemy must have planted these weeds; shall we try to pull them up?' But he said to them, 'No! For while you are yanking up the weeds, you may also uproot some of the wheat! Allow both to grow together! When harvest comes, gather up the weeds, bind them in bundles and throw them in the fire! Then gather the wheat and place it in my barn!'"

Most understood this parable right away. They comprehended the symbolism. They recognized that the free will of evil doers has always been permitted by God. To take away the freedom of the corrupt would mean taking away the freedom of the righteous as well. Both must be allowed to work out in the world. But in the end, upon harvest, true justice will transpire for both the good and the wicked. While this didn't diminish their longing for political deliverance now, it reinforced and vindicated those who had the patience to endure.

My apostles started moving along the bank in my direction, so I pressed back on the oar and sent my boat forward into the sand. James and Simon met me first and helped me out of the vessel. It felt good to have my feet back on dry land, and the greeting from everyone gathered on shore was warm and welcoming. But as I walked further up the embankment, those on my left suddenly moved aside so that the Sadducees and Pharisees could preempt their way over to me. I did not avoid their advance or retreat into the folds of the crowd, but stood my ground as they approached.

The lead Sadducee wasted no time issuing me a direct question. "Rabbi," he called, moving closer and quieting the crowd, "why do you speak to us in parables when teaching about the kingdom of heaven?"

I couldn't help but focus on the man's vestments. His cloth mantle was fringed in dozens of perfect tassels, his robe clearly woven from the finest material and the stole that hung low around his neck stitched with patterns worthy of royalty. For most of my fellow Jews, this *was* royalty. Those around us hushed upon their approach out of practiced reverence. These interpreters of the Law, who commanded the highest seats in the synagogues and lived off temple taxes and tithes, could expel a common Jew from their house of worship forever with nothing more than an extemporaneous injunction. They also had the power to hand down a judgment of death simply by manipulating the Laws of Moses to suit their needs.

I hardly felt threatened by this sudden inquiry into my teaching style, so I answered calmly and precisely. "I illustrate with parables because those who are open to the truth will find meaning in my words, while those who are filled with pride will not. Too many of you look but do not see—listen but do not hear or understand." I paused a moment, then glanced at the ground and muttered half to myself, "For even if I spoke explicitly on the secrets of these matters, many would not believe."

Another portlier scribe pushed his way forward and kept the interrogation going. "Several spoke of Rome today, teacher. Tell us your view. Should we pay the Roman tax or not?"

Did he really think I believed he actually cared one way or the other? I could read his true intent easier than I could identify the scorn on his tongue. Another trap. Say yes, and I enrage the masses around me by justifying the burdensome tariffs that raped these people's livelihoods. Say no, and they have hundreds of eyewitnesses who could attest to my statement of sedition against Rome.

My answer was neither, catching him off guard. "Show me the coin used to pay the Roman tax."

His brow furrowed. "Rabbi?"

"A Roman coin," I said more specifically. "Surely you have one in your purse. Let me see it."

Unsure where this was heading, he turned to the blank stares of his fellow scribes before reaching under his vestments and producing a silver coin. He hesitated a moment but then stepped over and handed it to me.

I gave it a glimpse, flipped it in my fingers several times and passed it back to him. He looked at me completely confounded.

"Whose image is on the head of that coin?" I asked, loud enough so all could hear.

He knew very well whose head was stamped into the metal but glanced down at the currency resting in his palm before returning his gaze to me and shrugging matter-of-factly. "Caesar's."

"Then I would give to Caesar what is Caesar's," I replied, and gently patted my chest to signify the human heart as I concluded, "And give to God what is God's."

The coin slipped from his hand, but he was too astonished to notice. There was nothing he could say, nothing he could argue—no words of rebuke to render. I had stunned him and his entire group to silence.

Rather than risk further humbling the elite, I smiled and regarded the crowd as a whole. "It is a most pleasant day in Galilee today. Let us head north."

And so we did. But rather than overrun Bethsaida with such a large following, we proceeded northwest, over the hills and tree-lined valleys that stretched between the river Jordan and the road to Caesarea Philippi. Where convenient, we stopped and rested. I continued teaching them in parables, offering insights into how my Father's eternal world related to this one, and more importantly, the wisdom of how they could relate to my Father. I also spoke of my cousin John, paying tribute to his works now that he was gone. I wanted everyone to understand that he had been so much more than a prophet—that John was the one the *prophets* had spoken of when they foretold a great messenger coming to prepare the way of the Lord.

This of course prompted many to ask if I indeed was the one John spoke about—if I was the Anointed one. To this I paused at first … then, inviting their spirits, simply responded, "Come to me, all you who are troubled and weary. I will give you rest. For my yoke is easy and my burden is light. And in me, you *will* find rest for your souls."

And come to me they did. The hundreds that earlier met me at the water's edge had now easily doubled, and even more joined from Bethsaida and Chorazin as we passed between the two villages. When the sun finally began slipping from its perch, there must have been well over five-thousand people gathered on the hillside where we pitched ourselves for a final rest.

My apostles and I climbed to the crest of the hill to assess in awe the size of the multitude assembled before us.

Bartholomew smiled nervously. "Dare I say not even the gladiators of Rome draw such crowds."

"You've done it, Master," said Thaddeus, peering out over the masses. "I do believe you've pulled every man, woman and child from northern Galilee."

Matthew didn't doubt it, simply asking, "What are we to do with all these people?"

Judas shielded his eyes from the sun's glare that now directly hit the slope. "There are too many. And it's getting late. We need to send them back, or they might not reach their homes by nightfall."

"We've come a long way with these people," said Philip. "I fear some won't make the return journey without food."

I decided to join the conversation. "So give them some food."

Sure enough, all twelve heads turned, as if I had lost my mind.

"Feed all these people, Lord?" spoke Thomas, trying to mask an incredulous tone. "With what?"

I looked to young John who often carried our provisions in a sack across his back. "I believe John has our food."

Completely puzzled, John glanced from me to the others, more than somewhat amiss.

"What rations do we have, John?" I asked.

He uneasily eyed the sackcloth that held our food. "We thought we were just going to Bethsaida today. Just our group."

"So what do we have … that we can share?" I spoke as if there were five people on the hill below us, not five-thousand.

John wavered. "Um, four or five loaves of bread maybe. And a couple dried fish."

"Very good," I said softly.

"Very good?" Simon restlessly ran his thick fingers through his thick hair. "The catch we hauled the day I met you, Lord, would hardly feed this crowd."

I stared over the multitude for a moment before turning my eyes purposefully upon my twelve friends. "James and John, stay here with me. The rest of you go down and get the people to sit. Tell them they must eat something before heading home."

Matthew sighed nervously as if he were being sent empty-handed into a lions' den. "What shall we tell them they are going to—"

"Matthew," I interrupted, looking at each of them, aware they were all thinking the same.

He nodded hesitantly. "I know, Master. Faith and trust."

I returned his nod with an approving smile. "Go then."

The ten obeyed and descended the gradual slope to where the first cluster of people gathered. As they began announcing that food was to be distributed, I sat down and opened the cloth that held the five loaves and two fish. I broke one of the loaves in half so I could divide the rations evenly and placed them on two separate pieces of material. James and John sat down next to me.

I then looked up to heaven and held open my hands. "Father, we thank you for this day and for this food that you provide. May it nourish all your children here. They have ventured far with us, and so we offer up these meager rations to your will. In thanks and praise for all your gifts … Amen."

I folded the cloth over the food and gave them to James and John. "Bring these to the first group of people. Tell them to take what they need, and pass it along to others."

My two friends, who had seen me turn water into wine and witnessed me raise a child from the snares of death, gawked at me with disbelief.

"Jesus …" James began, but caught himself.

"Yes, James?"

He closed his eyes and corrected his thoughts. "Faith and trust," he whispered.

John lowered his head as well. "Faith and trust," he echoed.

They reluctantly stood, and with two and half loaves of bread and a single salted fish wrapped neatly in each of their hands, made their way to the first group of people now sitting patiently in the grass. They handed over the food, gave the instructions to partake and pass along, then turned and looked back up at me with hardly confident faces.

I was already heading toward them. Upon reaching their position, John updated, "We delivered the food, Lord."

"Good. Here come Simon and the others." I then pointed farther down the hill. "Do you see that group of people there to the right? Those who were selling baskets earlier?"

"Yes," James replied, shielding his eyes in that direction.

"Tell them we wish to use some of their baskets to collect the leftover food."

"Leftover food?" The startled rise in his voice was priceless.

"Yes, leftovers," I reiterated. "We should let nothing go to waste."

James looked to John for his reaction, but his brother's eyes were fixed on neither of us. He was frozen, staring wide-eyed over the crowd. James followed his gaze and nearly lost his footing. Groups of people five or six deep into the thick of the multitude were holding up their arms and passing sheets full of bread and fish to waiting hands. Each time a new group took from the bounty, even more food seemed to weigh the linen down.

James turned to me with a trembling lip and eyes that begged forgiveness. He put his hands on my shoulders and whispered with full conviction, "All we need is faith and trust in you, Lord."

I smiled warmly. "Find it, and you will search no more."

He stared into my eyes, knowing he had indeed found it, enthralled and somewhat entranced by my unflinching compassion. John's tugging finally pulled him away, and the two scampered down to meet the others and obtain the baskets from the weavers.

As I watched the abundant amounts of fish and bread move farther into the crowd, I thanked my Father. Thousands of followers, disciples from far and wide, even my closest apostles—and yet none of them could fathom the significance of this very moment. Just as their ancestors ate manna from heaven while lost in the desert, those upon this hill today, adrift in their own different ways, were now doing the same—feeding on bread provided by the bread of life. Soon ... all too soon, I would offer my body as the real bread from heaven so that future generations can experience me just as closely. No ... even more closely than these five-thousand.

The sun continued its late-afternoon plunge to the horizon, and with most now having had their fill, groups leisurely began heading home, some toward the Jordan, others in the direction of Bethsaida. As they dispersed, my twelve strolled through the lingering flock, picking up the bread and fish left behind. It proved quite a task. By the time they hauled their baskets to the crest of the hill where I waited, dusk had settled in.

They stood before me, physically tired and mentally over-whelmed.

"Twelve baskets," I counted aloud.

Simon lowered his to the ground. It brimmed with bread crusts and chunks of dried fish. He genuflected behind it and bowed his head in my direction. "Forgive me for doubting you, Lord. As always, I kneel humbled before you."

The others did the same, each bending to a knee behind their basket of collected food. As I watched this show of contrite respect, I realized in my heart that these were not just friends before me. They were my brothers. Still too stubborn at times to readily allow faith and trust to guide them, I nonetheless cherished them like my own.

"You each deserve a good meal," I said. "Let us eat well this evening and thank God for this meaningful day we have spent together."

I glanced up to welcome a breeze through my hair. It reminded me how tired I was, and how I longed to spend a restful night upon this very hill. "I hope you all were not upset I left last night. With the death of my cousin, I needed some time alone to clear my head."

"We understand, Master," said Andrew. "We're just glad you're back."

"And know with conviction," I replied to their equally tired faces, "there is nowhere I would rather be than with you twelve. My brothers."

We shared a filling meal that night—plenty of bread, salted carp heated over a fire, even some wine that Matthew and Bartholomew made sure we were never in short supply. Frequent breezes swept comfortably across the hilltops, cleansing the heat from the day and relaxing us all. And despite our exhaustion and the trees behind us rustling peacefully in the air, we talked deep into the night.

Thaddeus was the first to seek better understanding. "Master, explain to us the first parable you spoke of this morning—the farmer sowing seed."

"I was wondering if that might come back for discussion," I said. "It takes a bit of insight to grasp, but it is all right there."

"The sower represents Yahweh," perked John, hoping to demonstrate his own discernment. "Just as in the second parable, right Lord?"

Reclining next to him, Thomas nudged him playfully. "I dare say most of us concluded at least that much."

"Listen, all of you," I acknowledged, sitting up to speak more easily. "In this case, it is more important what the seed symbolizes. The seed is the word of God. Those who do not pay attention have the meaning quickly snatched away by Satan, like the birds devouring the grain from the path. Others may receive the word gladly at first, but do not allow it to take root. This is the seed sown upon rocky earth. As soon as hardships arise in life, they lose faith and wither away. And the seed thrown among the thorns? These are people who receive the word of God but allow other emotions and desires like greed and anger to choke it from their hearts, killing it." I peered through the darkness and was glad to see all twelve sitting up and leaning eagerly toward my voice.

"But where the seed was thrown on good soil," I continued, "these are the souls who hear the word of God, bring it deep into their hearts and allow it to take root. Once the word is rooted in their hearts, they become rooted in the will of God. There they can never be overcome. These are the ones who will bear great fruit in life— thirty, sixty, even a hundred-fold."

Only the tranquil whispering of the trees kept the night from sheer silence.

Philip's voice broke the stillness around us. "I do believe that is the most profound thing I have ever heard."

"And you will tell it many times, Philip," I stated without hesitation. "As my apostles, you will each profess and explain my words throughout the nations. You shall sow the word of God into many hearts once I am gone."

Sitting next to me, Simon turned his head abruptly in my direction. "Once you're gone? What do you mean?"

I smiled and placed a reassuring hand on his shoulder. I then looked at them all. "I will explain everything in due time. Tonight, there are no worries. Let us get some sleep. Tomorrow we head further north toward Caesarea Philippi."

11

My Rock and the Power of Forgiveness

FARMERS AND MERCHANTS often fought for space where the northern roads to Caesarea Philippi and Damascus intersected. It served as a well-known supply stop for travelers continuing on through rather isolated country in either direction. Makeshift markets offered produce from the fertile southern plains to those journeying north—our group included. We were not, however, interested in the trinkets, charms or other pagan pendants and idols peddled to ward off evil spirits on the lonely road ahead. Allaying fear through superstition was certainly profitable for many a perverse trader.

With fresh fruits, water and other rations now in our satchels, we embarked on the long, winding, jaggedly beautiful path north. We kept our eyes to the cliffs and plateaus, both to keep alert for falling rocks, as well as to enjoy the wild grasses, flowers and shrubs that somehow found a way to flourish along the rocky heights. While the northwestern, Roman-engineered road toward Damascus was considerably more level and mostly paved with smooth stone, it hardly offered the rich scenery as the route we traveled. Despite its challenging, uneven features, we arrived at our destination in just under two days.

Carved into the foothills of Mount Hermon, Caesarea Philippi had been named in Caesar Augustus' honor by Herod the Great's son Philip. The city was a mishmash of Greek and Roman cultures practicing a variety of pagan worship. A monolithic natural rock wall stood as a temple to the gods with dozens of life-size sculptures chiseled into the stone. We were all captivated by the precision and creativity of the artists, melding pagan icons into the majesty of the towering, uneven precipice. But as Jews, we were also somewhat taken aback by what the mighty façade signified and facilitated—the worship of false deities.

We did not stay there long. Having proclaimed the good news of the kingdom of God for quite a while, I felt my apostles needed a few days with just me—an opportunity to relate to them personally, rather than within the company of hundreds, if not thousands of others. So after nearly a full day spent in this motley, overcrowded nerve center, which included a refreshing stop at the popular natural springs, we withdrew to the outskirts of town. Away from the noise, activity and worldly cares of this polytheistic city of rock, we slipped into the night, built a comforting fire in a secluded ravine and sought the unique solace that only comes from fellowship with the closest of friends.

"So," I said, taking advantage of a lull in the campfire conversation, "you have all been with me for quite some time now. You have heard my words and have witnessed many amazing events. You have ventured bravely into the multitudes, listening to them as closely as they have been listening to me. I am sure you have heard both praise of my message and skepticism as well. Some have approved of what we are doing, and some have condemned it."

"It is the intensity of both that attests to your impact, Lord," said Simon.

Matthew nodded. "Yes, those who love you, truly love you. And those who don't ..."

"Really, really don't," finished John, sparking some laughter, including my own.

"But they all flock to you," Thomas added. "Whether they adore or abhor your message, very little keeps them away from it."

"What are they saying?" I asked. "Who do they say that I am?"

"Most haven't a clue," said Judas, breaking and tossing sticks into the fire.

Andrew smiled. "Would you believe some think you're John the Baptist?" He paused and reflected a moment on his departed friend and mentor. "Which might not be so surprising. Descriptions of you both could be rather similar."

"I've heard even more remarkable speculations," added James. "One group says you must be Elijah come back from the dead."

"Elijah?" Thaddeus snickered at the idea. "I know the scriptures. Elijah's words, as amazing as they were, were never as expressive or meaningful as yours, Jesus."

"Well that's what some of them think," James confirmed.

Bartholomew acknowledged decisively through the light of the fire, "A prophet for sure. Whether one of the greats who has returned or a new charismatic one for this age, most believe they are witnessing a prophet—a very blessed and gifted prophet."

The others nodded in silence as the cracking embers echoed off the chasm rocks.

I thought about this a moment. So many people searching with such hope, yet unable to slow down and open up enough to really hear, learn and welcome … the truth. Not unlike the chiseled pagan gods we saw, carved into stone by those craving unity and harmony, but unwilling to let their fears down and allow authentic peace inside.

Would even these twelve closest to me here, who I sincerely felt had accepted God's revelation into their hearts, show the boldness and courage to express it aloud? And so I calmly asked, "And what about you?"

They raised their eyes, each somewhat caught off guard.

My question was soft but direct. "Who do you all say that I am?"

As the fire snapped a few more orange cinders into the night, I watched my friends shift uneasily in their positions. Each had reflections to express but seemed reluctant to display their deepest thoughts in front of the others.

Young John tried. "We call you Lord, and Master."

"Yes, you do. But why? Why do you refer to me as Lord?"

Their eyes meandered from one to another, each hoping someone else would chance a response or risk a remark that might be critiqued or even rejected.

Only Simon's eyes remained on the fire, as if he were alone. They never wavered from the flames. When he spoke, his voice was decisive and steadfast. "You are the Messiah ... The Christ ... The son of the living God."

Although sitting perfectly still, I had to catch my breath. Such jubilant acclamation consumed my heart—pure elation that this first sincere declaration of my divinity had not come from me, but from one who had fully surrendered to the truth and was bold enough to proclaim it. This stubborn, often short-tempered fisherman, who hardly let me into his boat upon our meeting, had just professed the Trinity's embodiment on the earth.

"Blessed are you, Simon son of Jonah. For this was not revealed to you by flesh and blood, but by my Father in heaven." I suddenly recalled that towering rock façade in town, a devotion built to inspire pagan superstitions. Simon's faith would now inspire many to me. "From now on, I shall no longer call you Simon. You shall be called Peter, *my* rock. And upon this rock I will build my Church, and not even the gates of hell shall prevail against it."

I could see immediately there was no jealousy within the group or resentment that Simon had bravely and frankly revealed his true heart about me. They were happy and proud for their friend, and even more thrilled that I had confirmed his proclamation.

While I certainly endorsed Peter's inspired revelation, I also cautioned them. "Listen to me, all of you. What Peter has said tonight will indeed be revealed to all the world—by you and by many others. But that time has not yet come. Many things must happen first, in accordance with the scriptures. These I will disclose to you when the time is right. Until then, the joy of Peter's perfect testimony must remain contained in your hearts. Tell no one of this … yet."

They nodded obediently, understanding the great significance of what had transpired in this natural grotto off the path to a pagan village. Andrew was the first to move over and hug his brother around the shoulders, honored that I had chosen his own kin as the bedrock, the foundation of the kingdom of God on earth. Then the others followed. They all gathered around Simon to welcome him now as Peter … their new elevated peer.

Simon did not normally smile much, but Peter now beamed from ear-to-ear. Seeing him smile like this broke a wide grin across my own face. I gazed up to where the fire's smoke disappeared into the black sky and directed my joy toward the heavens. Thank you, Father, I quietly offered. Oh perfect night. Our oneness has been confessed, impeccably revealed by one of your own, through no compulsory interaction on our part.

We now have our first sincere believers in our love for them.

* * *

Most of my apostles had never traveled the long route south out of Syria across the Bashan highlands toward the city of Golan. Nor had I for that matter. We were pleasantly surprised to find ourselves journeying through some of the most scenic countryside in the region. The rolling hills that rose and fell between small villages provided sweeping landscapes bordered by the largest oak and eucalyptus trees I had ever seen. Shepherds and their flocks, goats and cattle, all sought respite from the sun under their grand canopies.

Every crest of every bluff brought us to another magnificent valley vista. Sometimes we rested long enough to watch a few clouds maneuver their shadows across the grassy, often rocky basins below.

Occasionally we'd point out particular features we found personally stunning, but usually we just sat and gazed, allowing the scenery to stimulate private thoughts—thoughts that relaxed each of us in our own way.

As we crossed one such valley along a waist-high wall that penned a herd of grazing sheep, I listened intently to the engaged conversation several paces in front of me. My companions must have assumed they were out of earshot or did not realize how their voices carried along this hollow. Their tone was not argumentative but clearly sounded like a disagreement. Having accepted Peter's revelation about me, my followers now wondered how each of them fit into my mission. What may have started as a benign conversation, however, suddenly degenerated into a discussion of relative importance—who was more essential or valuable to the group. Seniority by age, time spent with me, knowledge of the scriptures, even former lifestyles and professions entered their frivolous sparring.

It was time to interject.

"Men of Galilee," I called.

They turned, startled and suddenly silent. I managed a smile as I approached, but my eyes betrayed discouragement.

James the less spoke first. "You overheard us, didn't you, Lord?"

I answered softly with raised eyebrows. "I hear more than you think."

"Naturally," smiled Bartholomew.

We resumed walking, and I waited a few moments before speaking to make sure I had the right words for my thoughts. "Worrying about status and influence will only lead to frustration and envy," I began. "It is true that the kings of this world rule over the people, and they themselves have those who hold power over them. But this is not how it should be with you … or anyone. Whoever wants to be the greatest, should make himself the servant of all."

Their surprised faces compelled me to reiterate. "You heard correctly. Those who want to be first, should put themselves last. For the last shall be first in the kingdom of heaven, and the first shall be last."

While they understood these plain words, they had trouble accepting the paradoxes. So I emphasized, "Just as the son of Man did not come to be served, but to serve, and to lay down his life for the ransom of many."

They now recognized that I referred to myself when speaking this way. But not wanting to dwell on this dire prediction, I pointed to two small children up the hill helping their father shepherd a few sheep down the slope. "See those two children? At five or six years-old, they have no real significance outside of their immediate family. They have no money, own no land, have no real education and possess few skills. Yet I tell you the truth, unless you become like them—innocent, honest, pure, obedient, humble … you will be lost." I moved my eyes from the hill back to my friends before referencing their prior argument. "Whoever humbles themselves as a child, is considered the greatest in the kingdom of heaven."

Matthew, who walked a few steps ahead, contemplated his past faults and failings and boldly asked, "What about someone who was lost for such a long time? How does he know God will accept him back?"

I grabbed his shoulders from behind with both hands, a warm gesture that signaled I already had. "What do you think? If a shepherd has a hundred sheep and loses one of them, does he not leave the other ninety-nine to go search for the one that is lost? And if he finds it, does he not rejoice more over that one than over the ninety-nine that had not gone astray? Trust me when I say your Father in heaven is the same way concerning his lost children. No matter how deeply sin may have pulled them from his divine will, he rejoices and gladly receives them back into the fold when they repent and seek forgiveness."

Matthew nodded with a smile that came from hearing exactly what he needed to hear, but Thomas pressed the issue. "God will readily forgive *anyone?*"

Infinite mercy was a hard concept for people to grasp. It was difficult for anyone who knew the devastating effects of evil in the world. "Let's say there was a wealthy man who had two sons," I said, deciding to use storytelling to analogize the magnitude of God's grace. "The younger one demanded that his father divide their inheritance so that he could take his share and leave. So the father complied. And with that, the younger son went off to a distant country where he spent several years living a shameful, decadent lifestyle, squandering away all his wealth. As his money dried up, so did the land in that country when a terrible famine hit. Impoverished and hungry, he finally found work tending pigs. But he was often reduced to fighting the swine for the husks they ate just to keep his own stomach full. He recalled how his father's hired hands always had plenty to eat, and yet here he was, a former heir to that estate, wrestling pigs to keep from starving."

"He thinks that now," said Thomas. "He should have considered that when he was throwing his father's money away so selfishly."

Philip agreed. "A bit late for regrets and contrition."

"One would think," I simply acknowledged. "The son knew he had no one to blame but himself. He knew he had no right to ask his father for forgiveness, nor should he receive it. But he decided to return nonetheless and ask his father to consider hiring him as a common laborer. Although it would be shameful working for the family he had rejected, at least he would have food and water."

"So he went back?" asked Simon the Zealot.

"He did," I said. "He set off for his father's estate. When he was still some distance from the house, his father saw him and rushed to his side, embracing him tightly. The son told him that he was unworthy to be called his son and hoped he could work as a hired hand."

"What did the father say?" asked John before I could catch a breath between sentences.

"I know what mine would have said," muttered Bartholomew.

"Well ... this father quickly turned to his servants." I turned abruptly myself, as if acting the part. "He told them to fetch the best robe and put it on his son—to put a fine ring on his finger and new sandals on his feet. Then he ordered to have the fatted calf butchered and prepared for a feast."

"You're not serious?" injected Judas.

"I am. He even called his neighbors to join the celebration—to rejoice that his son, who was once dead, had come back to life ... who had been lost for so long, was now found."

They all took a moment to digest the overwhelming and extraordinary mercy of the patriarch in this tale.

Andrew finally inquired, "What about the older son—the one who didn't betray his father?"

"Good question, Andrew," I said before re-asking it. "Yes, what about the older son? You can surely imagine *his* thoughts. When he came in from the fields that evening and saw the lavish party for his brother's return, he wouldn't even go inside. So his father came out to him. Clearly unsettled, he reminded his father that he had always been there for him, loyal and trustworthy, doing what he asked. And yet this brother of his, who devoured his wealth on prostitutes and easy living, gets a banquet celebration when he comes crawling back."

"Can you blame him for feeling that way?" asked James.

I shook my head with a benevolent smile, just like the man in my story might have to his older son. "The father simply replied to his eldest, 'Yes, you have always been with me, and everything I have is yours. But we *must* celebrate. I had lost a child. I thought he was gone forever, but he has come home to me. He has humbled himself, and I *will* be merciful.'"

Again, I allowed them time to ponder this all-important message that nothing, not even serious sin, can separate the love of God from his children and the unfathomable depth and power of his mercy.

Peter had remained silent through most of this, listening intently. He now spoke. "It will take a strong heart and a powerful love for us to forgive in the same way. But also patience. How many times should we forgive the same transgressor?" He lightheartedly grabbed his brother Andrew and continued, "Suppose my brother here insults, lies or even steals from me seven times."

Andrew feigned bewilderment. "Are you sure you don't have that the other way around?"

Peter tussled his hair as any older brother might. "I'm just making a point. What do you say, Lord? Should I forgive someone who has sinned against me seven times?"

I gazed upward as if giving the matter serious contemplation. "No," I finally answered. "You should not forgive him seven times."

Peter and Andrew glanced at each other, then at the others.

"So how many times should he forgive me?" swallowed Andrew, now playing along with his brother's proposition.

I looked at them all and could sense that each was guessing to himself … Three times? Four times? Twice?

I ended the conversation succinctly. "Seventy times seven times."

Suddenly, I was walking alone—all twelve of my apostles had stopped. I turned back to address their befuddled faces. "What, too few? ... Too many?"

No one answered. My directive was plain enough, but I clarified, "Take note, I did not say to tolerate the sin. You and others must help those trying to repent and reform their lives. But I tell you the truth, if you forgive as many times as you are asked, how much more your Father in heaven will forgive your own routinely sinful nature."

Peter finally muttered a mere fragment of what he had said earlier. "Powerful love."

"Yes," I agreed. "God calls us to live in powerful love with each other … to be merciful just as he is merciful."

We continued onward toward the populated Golan settlements. Once there, I maintained this essential theme of enduring forgiveness and mercy, preaching it in their synagogues. Those who gathered in these places of worship all too often and all too easily condemned others while excusing themselves. They needed to hear about the true power of forgiveness and its role as a fundamental pillar of love. Others, whose feelings of unworthiness kept them far from the sanctuary, readily clung to this new hope of God's perpetual mercy on their lives. My message to them was simple—it is never too late, or too soon, to lift your chin to the heavens and ask God for his grace and forgiveness. And the Lord, who is indeed all powerful, never fails to grant boundless mercy upon those who come to him with sincere hearts.

For those realizing their need for repentance, it was a welcome message. For others who had been seriously hurt by wicked words and deeds, it was a tough conviction to accept. A man with only four fingers on his left hand approached me. His tale was indeed horrifying. Bandits had attacked him years ago, not far from his own house. Unable to remove a tarnished silver ring, they cut his finger off to get it.

"So tell me," he challenged, bitterness still chilling his voice, "are you saying I should forgive them too?"

I held my eyes to his and tried pacifying their indelible anger and resentment. "Yes," I replied softly. "You should forgive them too. You should forgive them as much for your own good as for theirs."

He gawked at me like I had suggested climbing a mountain on hands and knees. "Would you be willing to do the same, Jesus? Forgive people who crush you to the ground, take everything you have—who literally cut your flesh to the bone?"

I lowered my eyes.

Could I really forgive such focused hate? Forgive torture? Forgive murder—up to and including my own?

"Yes," I finally acknowledged, looking back at him definitively. "I will forgive. Even to those who might cut my flesh to the bone."

12

Taming Tempests

WE STOOD ATOP the last great hill of the Gadara highlands, along the village of Umm Qais' northwest wall, and gazed across the valley to the Sea of Galilee's southern shores. How welcome a sight. While we had enjoyed our journey through the Golan territories, it was good to finally see the great body of water we all knew so well. Only a short walk remained to where we could hopefully find passage across the lake to Tiberias or Magdala.

I glanced at my apostles who returned similar satisfied smiles, knowing our final destination was clearly in view. We were all fatigued from our travels. The sight of flat blue water halfway to the horizon invigorated us from where we stood.

"Never thought that lake would look so inviting," said Peter.

"Let's not waste time then," John urged. "We're practically there."

Needing no further motivation, we started down the expansive face of the hill. As we neared the bottom, the day grew more overcast. Gray clouds slowly invaded the hilltop countryside—a somber sky that suddenly accentuated the dreariness of our new surroundings. Makeshift stone walls extruded from the base of the hillside, framing various sized doorways and crawlspaces. Heavy planks or large stones secured many of the openings.

These were the tombs of Gadara, a place for the dead built into the foundation of the mount overlooking the final bluffs to the Sea of Galilee. The murky skies now brewing above us strengthened the already foreboding nature of this location.

We walked in silence, partly in respect for this valley of the deceased, and partly from everyone's innate childhood phobias about death. We moved so quietly in fact, only the soft crunching of our sandals on the grit and gravel disturbed the eerie calm along this path among the tombs.

But then we heard something else. A groan—a deep guttural moan from somewhere within the darkened chambers. The hairs on my neck stood at attention.

We all stopped.

"Did you just hear that?" croaked Thaddeus.

"I heard it," Philip breathed. "Tell me that didn't come from inside…"

We stood perfectly still, waiting and wondering if we had truly heard a human grunt or if it might have just been distant thunder.

We did not have to wonder long. A distinct, cold, strident cry bellowed from one of the unobstructed doorways leading into blackness.

John seized my arm in fear. "Lord, you didn't …?"

"No," I assured. "I have not called any of these souls forward."

Another shout echoed from the open grave, louder still, accompanied by the crack of rocks smashing against the walls. Our hearts and feet collectively jumped.

Judas raised his walking stick like a fighter's staff and shook it toward the tomb's entrance. "Who goes there?" he called. "Show yourself!"

None of us could have expected his command would be so quickly and vehemently obeyed. A mountain of a man in his early twenties leapt from the shadows of the crypt, completely naked and covered in cuts and bruises. Tangled hair and grime partially hid his battered, contorted face. Metal shackles cuffed his wrists, the chains of which hung broken, allowing full freedom of motion. Most alarming, however, were the large rocks clutched in his filthy hands. His arms flailed about, whipping the manacle chains dangerously through the air.

The beast, and he surely resembled more beast than man, threw back his head and howled a prolonged wail that reverberated through the tombs. The stone vaults echoed back his cry as if an army of monsters had invaded the valley. He took a menacing step toward us and roared in garbled, hardly coherent words, "Who dares pass this way?"

To our amazement, he then smacked one of the rocks against his head, opening a gash on his already injured face.

"He's a madman!" James blurted.

"He can't take all of us," muttered Bartholomew, bringing his staff to bear and twirling it once with practiced efficiency.

The wild thing ferociously barked again as if we were absolutely no threat, then smashed the two rocks together, reducing them to small stones.

"I'm not so sure of that," said Thomas. He eased a step back. "This possessed freak seems to have the strength of ten men."

Although my heart beat as rapidly as theirs, I tentatively maneuvered to the front of our group. "I believe you are right, Thomas," I said cautiously. "Evil spirits control him."

This did little to alleviate anyone's anxiety, mine included. But remembering that God's Spirit overcomes all evil, I took a few steps forward.

"Lord, what are you doing?" asked John, right on my heels.

I motioned him back. "Stay there, John."

The deranged man shrieked in anger, raised his hands and flung the few stones he still had in our direction. We spun our shoulders and covered our heads as they painfully bounced off our backs.

"Let's get out of here," pleaded Andrew. "Before he really goes berserk."

I carefully rotated around to face our antagonist. Furrowing my brow, I advanced.

His head shook furiously, and the chains around his wrists hissed through the air. "Come closer! See what happens when you try to shackle me!" Spit flung from his lips. "Come closer! See what happens!"

I was not deterred. As the gap closed between us, we both raised our arms as if truly about to engage in combat. It was my voice that suddenly halted his motion. "Spirits, be still!"

Like a rodent encountering a cobra, that hulk of a man leapt to a halt. I held my hands authoritatively high and moved closer. His arms also remained raised but now in a defensive stance.

"You?" he spewed. "What business do you have with us, Jesus, son of the Most-High?"

My apostles gasped upon hearing this lunatic vent my name and reference my sanctity.

Affixing my eyes to his, I glared him down. "How many of you are in there, torturing this poor soul?"

Another stammering eruption of shouts and flails preceded a response. "Our name is Legion; there are so many!"

Goosebumps scattered up my arm. I hardly heard Peter's voice behind me. "Master, be careful."

I invoked my heavenly Father for encouragement. You, Father, have given me, and those who believe in me, the power to subdue any demon of the evil one—whether a single malignant spirit—or hundreds.

I pointed a commanding finger at him and shuffled dangerously within his reach. "Come out of this man, all you unclean spirits!"

Violent twitches and convulsions shook drool from his beard. "No," it wheezed in anguish. "Do not cast us out. We have nowhere to go!"

"You have tormented this man long enough! Come out!" I summoned.

"Where?!" His husky voice sounded as if it came from dozens of throats. "Where shall we go?"

"That is not my concern!" I fired back.

A further tantrum ensued. This naked, squalid vestige of a human being stomped, swung and pulled at his hair in agony. He then dropped to one knee and pointed across the valley while screaming, "The swine!"

We all turned to look. Sure enough, far across the wide valley on a plateau leading directly to the sea, grazed a large herd of pigs. Several men effectively kept them together as they rooted the meadow for food.

I wanted these terrible beings out of this man at once. And since I certainly didn't want them attempting to seek haven among my friends, I conceded.

"To the swine then!" I ordered. "Release this man, now!"

He arched his back and hurled forth a final, futile cry to the otherwise silent tombs. He then collapsed to the ground and lay motionless, as if dead. Like a final crack of thunder that rolls across the sky after a storm, that last woeful bellow left the burial grounds of Gadara quiet.

All was calm … for the moment. As my apostles moved cautiously closer to my position, we heard the distant, menacing shrill of the pigs. Our heads lifted from the inert man at our feet to the herd of hogs over yonder. They were in a frenzy. What were once orderly, tame animals, were now wildly gyrating monsters. They ran. They kicked. They bit. They trampled. And all the while they squealed incessantly. Their miserable screeching carried across the valley like a plague of locusts.

"Dear God," Andrew whispered.

The three men tending the pigs tried for only a few moments to control the chaotic bedlam. Fearing for their safety, they wisely abandoned their charges and ran, heading in our direction. The pigs regrouped and seemed to be running together as well, in a determined stampede. But they were moving headlong in the opposite direction—directly for the cliff. They did not slow or change course. The entire herd, numbering nearly a hundred, plummeted over the precipice in a rapid, unhesitating wave of motion.

They were gone.

As we stood facing the now empty field in utter shock, we suddenly heard a soft moan. I looked down to the spent figure at my sandals. He was moving. We helped him up and over to a large rock on which to sit.

"John, give me a cloak," I said.

He quickly handed me one, which I draped over the filthy, aching body of this young man who had been ravaged for so long. His head finally lifted to behold my eyes. "Who are you?" he asked—voice still raspy but thankfully projecting the stable tone and inflections of a man in his right mind.

Peter answered before I could. "You have been saved by Jesus of Nazareth."

A warm, surprised gleam came to his eye. "Jesus? The one everyone talks about?"

I nodded and wiped some of the blood from his cheek with an edge of the cloth.

We offered him some food and water just as the pig herders arrived, out of breath from crossing the valley but still excited.

"Did you see what happened to our pigs?" one clamored. "They went crazy!"

"We saw," replied Matthew. "Evil spirits."

"What did you say?" asked another.

John restated, "Your pigs were demonized, man. They were overrun with spirits."

The three looked at us in bewilderment. "Who are you people?" inquired the first. "And what are you doing among the tombs?"

"We have come from the Golan territories," I answered, "and are seeking passage north across the sea."

"Well you best not stay here," he provoked. "You mention evil spirits; there is a madman loose among these graves. The villagers have chained him several times, but he keeps breaking away and hiding here."

We tried to appear concerned but couldn't help smiling.

"He tells the truth," voiced his partner. "This barbarian will kill you if he gets the chance."

Instead of offering words, we simply moved aside so they could see the cloaked man sitting behind us on the stone.

All three jolted in surprise. One even took a preventative step back. "That's him!"

"He's okay," said James. "He's okay now."

"Impossible," he murmured, gaping in awe at the relaxed figure sitting before them.

The young man pulled aside some of the twisted hair from his face, and despite plenty of dirt and some dried blood still caking his skin, his calm visage exuded tranquility. He looked to the three herdsmen and nodded in my direction. "This is Jesus of Nazareth. He has driven many infernal spirits from within me. I can assure you that I am clean."

Although his body remained covered in thick dust, they all knew what he meant by clean.

One of them now stared at me with even more wonderment than having witnessed the possessed man at peace. "You commanded evil spirits to flee from this maniac?"

"And into your swine," reminded Thaddeus, as if they would ever forget.

"Yes, into our swine," he muttered, still eyeing me for a hint of deceit or trickery.

I candidly replied, "I did. And as you can see, this man is no maniac."

His partner leaned in to scrutinize us with a sneer. "You and your black magic are not wanted here."

"Black magic?" Philip took offense. "Do you know who you're talking to?"

"Not worth it, Philip," I said. I then regarded our three visitors.

"As I mentioned, we are simply seeking passage across the lake. To Magdala if possible."

"Don't care how you get there," replied the herdsman. "Your witchery destroyed our whole herd. Best you leave before others arrive to run *you* off the cliff."

"And with that we'll be going," said Peter, motioning us to start moving.

The man spit at our feet, nodded for his two cohorts to follow and started back across the valley.

We prepared to continue onward toward the sea ourselves when the young man stood from the rock, cinched his cloak and grabbed my shoulder. I turned to him as he pleaded, "Take me with you."

I looked at him warmly, so glad to see stability in his eyes. "Go back to town. Dress your wounds and show your family that you are well again. Tell them, and all those in the Decapolis, what the Lord has done for you."

He reluctantly nodded. "I will never forget you, Jesus of Nazareth."

I smiled at my apostles and then at our new friend. "Nor shall we forget you."

We gave him an extra pair of sandals and made sure he was sturdy enough to make his return trip before sending him on his way.

We then regrouped and restarted for a hopefully much more routine hike to the shore. And it thankfully was. After making it to the water's edge, we took a revitalizing dip before continuing onward, trailing the coastline toward the Jordan. Without the direct, oppressive heat of an uninhibited sun, we kept our walk at a brisk pace. There were no significant towns at the lake's southern edge which allowed us to move onward without interruption. This also meant, however, that hardly any boats were moored along the shoreline. As day waned, I questioned whether we might need to build camp near the mouth of the river if we couldn't find a worthy sea farer heading north. But our luck turned, and we finally came upon a merchant ship preparing for an evening sail to Tiberias. It was a moderate-sized vessel, and the small crew was eager to have the extra hands to help load crates and assist with the rigging.

As we walked on board and pulled up the boarding plank to get underway, Peter confided, "The clouds have been ominous all day, Lord."

I looked westward and carefully considered what might be brewing over the horizon before turning to my friend. "You are a good seaman, Peter. We shall keep an eye to the sky and hopefully pull into Tiberias ahead of any rough weather."

He agreed, trusting that if I wasn't worrying, neither should he.

"Besides," I said, "I always sleep well on the open water."

And I did. Upon learning who I was, the commander of the ship insisted I take his hammock below deck to grab a few hours rest. The berth wasn't much as sleeping quarters go—two or three small cots strung up among the crates—but it was all I needed. Lying there and listening through the boards to my apostles reminisce about their sea days, coupled with the ship's gently creaking timbers, comforted me. I drifted off, thinking about how far we had come in my mission since Satan's desert temptation.

Suddenly, I was dreaming, caught in that human realm of ultimate subliminal surrender—that mysterious subconscious state in which the human brain rests and recollects itself. It was here in this perfectly uncontrolled frame of mind that I found myself unexpectedly at home. My real home. A warm light caressed me with amazing clarity and kaleidoscopic colors more beautiful than any prism could produce. I was in my Father's presence. Only our kingdom could bestow a sense of serenity and peace so vivid and boundless. Wisps of spiritual fellowship fluttered by, the gentle genuflections of my angels honoring me as I moved freely through the resplendence. I was truly in my sanctuary ... my throne ... my refuge ... Home.

My Father, in his providence, spoke to me—not in words, for words were not needed here, but in the plane of our sacred harmony. He reassured me that the supernatural unity we shared could never be broken, but also reminded that our saving promise to humanity required humbling myself to endure every aspect of human tribulation, trial and pain. To become flesh was not enough; it was essential to personally experience and share the very worst of what the mind and body can suffer in this world. This included a terrible torment that often surpassed physical agony, namely, the harrowing sense of divine separation due to original sin. The kingdom of heaven's very nature had always been, and always would be, the ubiquitous and constant presence of God's care, affection and shelter. Earth, however, while designed and created by the hand of God, was most certainly not the kingdom of heaven. It was still a garden of sorts, but hapless humanity was now all too painfully aware of its pervasive evil, no longer encouraged by the similar awareness of its Creator's omnipresence. And while I was indeed bringing the light of our divine existence into the world and to the people of this day, I too needed to share in their temporary separation from sacred, transcendent safety and protection. As a living example of a suffering servant to all, I was to redeem them from their senseless selfishness and show them how to love each other as their Father loves them ... until they are reunited with him in endless salvation.

For the moment, I felt totally disconnected from the physical world, deep within this dreamscape with its glimpses of home and the celestial fulfillment of my Father. But dreams do not last, and this one did not either. A loud bang of thunder ripped my mind from its euphoria, my eyes opening to surrounding darkness. Something, or someone, shook me vigorously. The ship lunged to one side, and I nearly rolled onto Peter who had been trying to wake me. He was soaking wet.

"Peter, what is it?" I said, resetting my bearings as heavy, wind-whipped rain roared around our boat.

Night had fallen. How long had I been asleep?

"The storm has hit, Master!" he cried through the water spraying down to us from above deck.

I regained my footing and steadied myself against the hammock's beam. Shouts from above were hardly discernable over the howling wind and the ship's squawking hull as it was tossed about. Trying desperately to keep balance, we scrambled up to the main deck. Almost instantly an enormous wave came over the starboard side and rudely knocked us both to the planks. The vessel's navigator clung to the wheel, frantically trying to steer into the waves to keep from capsizing.

I barely got to my feet before Simon the Zealot was thrown into me. Realizing who it was, he seized my saturated robe and shouted, "Lord, where have you been? Do you not care that we are about to perish?"

"Jesus, what are we to do?" yelled Matthew through the drenching water and deafening wind.

I held tightly to the rigging as another wave came over the side. What a day it had been indeed—attacked by a demon-possessed goliath, threatened by irate pig herders and now caught in the middle of a ferocious storm in the black of night on open water. My followers were obviously at wits' end—drained and exhausted by a day full of peril and uncertainty.

But I was with them. They had *me* in their presence. Not just the knowledge of me, or even the spiritual me; they actually had the physical son of God in their midst. True Emmanuel. How was I to get them to someday convince others to have faith and courage during times of strife, to motivate those who would never see me, if they themselves had such trouble now?

A flash of lightning split the darkness with a nearly instantaneous explosion of thunder—a powerful proclamation that we had penetrated the storm's center. I shut my eyes to mentally distance myself from the thrashing wind and rain and the desperate shouts of those fearing for their lives. I thrust myself into deep communication—reaching out to the angels who had just escorted me to my Father's presence within my dream. I beckoned them to exert the full strength and might of God from my hands, to force one of the most uncontrollable forces of nature to obey a single command.

I lifted my free hand high in the air and braved the sting of wind-swept rain pelting my skin. I prepared to overcome this physical tempest in the same manner I had bested the spiritual one earlier in the day. In fact, I shouted the same injunction to the storm that I had dictated to the legion of spirits.

"Be still!" I yelled so loudly my voice cracked.

All heads turned to my attention.

The crest of the monstrous wave below us did not rock forward with the flow of the currents but dropped straight down as if sucked to the sea's floor. Our vessel fell vertically with it, smacking against the now flattened water with a jolt that nearly dropped us to our knees. The rain stopped just as suddenly in a final torrent—the sky emptying itself in one last biting spray. As the final drops splashed upon the deck, we realized there was no wind—no sound at all except for everyone's rapid breathing.

Dead calm.

Only the faint dripping of water off the boat into the placated sea broke the otherwise complete silence. My apostles looked at me, too tired for astonishment, but with grateful, reverent eyes.

I did not need to raise my voice to be heard across the vessel. "Why such fear? Why were you afraid, oh you of little faith?" My consoling tone indicated I was not displeased and that all was under control. Each of them collapsed where they were, content to just sit and rest their backs and heads against something that was stable. They could have fallen asleep anywhere at this point.

The ship's commander steadied himself against the wooden transom amidships. One hand still clutched the wheel to his thank-fully-still-intact vessel. He turned to his first mate whose eyes remained locked in terror, more aghast by how swiftly the storm had ended than by the gale itself. "Who is this man?" he whispered to him. "That even the wind and sea obey him."

There was no answer. As well-traveled merchants, they had undoubtedly over the years encountered the hoaxes and tricks of many grifters and charlatans. Immediately taming and quieting an intense storm at sea, however, was no illusion or sleight of hand. They recognized what had happened. They had witnessed an incredible event beyond natural explanation ... a miracle. And this understanding held them spellbound.

The skipper breathed to himself, "Who is this Jesus of Nazareth?"

I smiled comfortingly at his partner crouched in the darkness, expressing that all was okay—that the peace of God now enveloped their boat. He finally acknowledged my reassurance with a nervous smile of his own.

The dissipating clouds gradually opened for moonlight to bathe the water. The storm had created a misty haze just above the surface that soon glowed a lustrous blue as the moonshine filtered through it. I rested my chin on the deck rail to fully relax and appreciate this wondrous sight.

A gentle breeze crept in from the south. I considered suggesting we re-hoist the sails so we could make it into Tiberias by dawn, but I quickly thought better of it. There probably wasn't a soul on the ship still awake. As I reclined myself, watching the turquoise mist creep across the water and around our vessel, I realized I was in no particular rush to reach any port.

Bobbing adrift on this suddenly beautiful night, after such a trial-ridden day, seemed like a pretty good idea.

13

Marvelous Mary

TIBERIAS HAD BEEN BUILT and named by Herod Antipas as a tribute to the former Roman general and current emperor who now spent most of his days in self-exile, pursuing a life of debauchery atop the cliffs of Capri. The massive stone walls and towers of his namesake city rose majestically from the sea, fortifying seventeen natural hot springs, numerous dwellings and several synagogues. Its farmlands and vineyards stretched clear to Mount Arbel. It was no wonder that Tiberias had become the most significant hub on the Sea of Galilee. Many in the region now actually referred to the great body of water on which it thrived as Lake Tiberias. It not only served as a key trading center, but also as the official capital of Herod's northern territory, and ironically enough, populated mostly by Jews. In fact, so many of them came to call Tiberias home, Antipas began requiring non-Jews from Galilee and other parts of his domains to relocate there in an attempt to better balance its ethnicity.

I remembered well around my twentieth birthday first visiting the relatively new city with my father, Joseph. Back then it was little more than a resort destination and spa for the Romans. Now it was a flourishing metropolis—one where I found equal amounts of acceptance and rejection of my message. For each crowd that eagerly received my words, there were also those who after hearing them, at best urged me and my entourage to leave town … and at worst, wanted me stoned. Nevertheless, it became a fruitful place to preach and teach, so we typically stayed until a disruptive incident or two pushed us onward.

This particular time in Tiberias we enjoyed several days of rather peaceful campaigning for the reign of God. There was a high-ranking Pharisee in town named Simon, a leader in the local synagogue, but one who refused to live within the borders of Tiberias. In Herod's rush to build the great city, he had erected portions directly on sacred burial grounds without first excavating the dead. To the priestliest caste of Jew, this made the city ritually unclean and a place they would never choose to live or own property. So Simon the Pharisee built his home a considerable walk north on a tree-lined plot of land near the sea, roughly equidistant between Tiberias and Magdala. Visitors to this private residence, bordered by palm trees and surf, easily understood why he didn't mind the trek from either town.

Simon invited me and my apostles to dine at his house, along with guests that included other ranking Sadducees and Pharisees. Although I couldn't begin to imagine what rhetorical questions or topics they planned to challenge me with, we graciously accepted.

It was a Sabbath afternoon, and after attending the synagogue in Tiberias, we joined Simon the Pharisee for the walk north toward his home. We passed hardly a soul until reaching a small grassy dune overlooking his property. He stopped abruptly and stared with confusion and consternation down at his house. Intermingled with the palmetto trees and clogging the only clear path to his dwelling, congregated a throng of at least a hundred.

"Who are all these people?" he wondered, slapping his face in dismay. Not waiting for an answer, he quickly added, "How did they know we were coming?"

John offered a simple grin. "Welcome to our world."

If Simon hadn't seen a few of his fellow Pharisees in front of the crowd motioning him forward, I do believe he might well have turned back. But he didn't. We followed him down the gradual embankment, his head shaking in annoyance, toward the strangers on his land. He reached for a colleague's outstretched arm and asked, "Seth, where did all these people come from?"

His friend could all but shrug as he cleared people out of the way for us to walk. "Tiberias, Magdala ... for all I know down from Tabgha. Somehow they caught wind *he* was coming." His hand indicated me while waving us through. My apostles ducked their heads and followed close behind, squeezing through the intrusive crowd now reaching for me.

I wanted to stop, to sit with these people who had persevered enough to find me in this secluded location, but I had promised Simon I would dine with him this day. So as we whisked through the congestion, I pledged to return later. I kissed a few hands, stroked a few faces and was suddenly ushered inside. The door promptly closed behind us.

Simon led us to the main chamber of his home. It was a large room with varying-sized rectangular windows that surely allowed ample amounts of moisture in on windswept rainy days. Today, however, the sea breezes simply carried hints of Jasmine through the lofty apertures, casting columns of sunlight and fragrances upon a long, well-set table, draped with a finely woven cloth. Fresh cut flowers garnished the entire length of its center.

I hardly noticed any of these plush appointments—my attention suddenly focused on the Sadducees standing politely on the opposite side, obviously waiting for me. Their stolid, unreadable faces betrayed neither thought nor feeling. I felt cornered, as if I had taken a wrong turn onto a dead-end path.

"Jesus," one of them said cordially enough, "so good of you to come."

"Yes, rabbi, please join us," another offered, unsuccessfully masking a patronizing tone with a hint of respect.

I turned to Simon the Pharisee. We stood in *his* house, yet these religious leaders spoke as if the room belonged to them. Simon smiled uneasily and motioned for me to sit. I looked at the others in the room before accepting the assigned place at a table surrounded by priests, scribes and clerics. I gestured to my apostles, encouraging them to sit as well.

We reclined at the table as two servants appeared with trays of raisins, grapes, some mild cheeses and goblets of wine. As they placed the first course before us, a Pharisee commented, "We apologize, teacher, that so many ne'er-do-wells outside discovered your visit here on this Sabbath."

Simon the Pharisee rolled his eyes. "I can only imagine the state of my yard tomorrow."

I popped a grape in my mouth and shifted to face our host. "Simon," I said, roaming my eyes around the ornately dressed table, "all of you. For every dinner like this you prepare for friends, relatives and close neighbors, why not also plan one where you invite the poor, the crippled, the downtrodden … the ne'er-do-wells."

Their stares questioned whether I was being literal or simply trying to make a point. So I continued, "Why not invite those outside to come inside? For they are the ones who cannot repay you by inviting you back. By welcoming them, and expecting nothing in return, you will be blessed."

A Sadducee directly across the table challenged my explicitness. "I think we appreciate your principles here, Jesus, but you yourself wouldn't just call strangers off the street into your home. Would you?"

To fully reveal the truth, here and now, would surely get me tossed from this room, if not dragged to the sea and drowned. To suggest that many of the strangers outside would ultimately sit at higher places of honor at my Father's banquet, would not go over very well.

I decided on a subtler response—a parable. "A wealthy man once prepared a dinner much like this. When all was ready, he sent his servants to summon those invited. One of the guests, however, suddenly claimed to have land which needed tending, and wished to be excused. Another replied that his new oxen required training on the yoke, and also declined the invitation. Still another reported he had just gotten married and was much too busy with his bride to attend."

The Sadducee who had questioned me nibbled on some cheese, trying hard to discern any hidden comparisons I might be making about him. He and his fellow scribes knew well my reputation for this.

I took a sip of wine and allowed them to briefly linger on the first half of my tale. I sensed their minds at work as they searched for cryptic connections somewhere in my words. Continuing, I spoke directly to the base of my wine chalice and avoided their eyes. "When the servants returned to their master with this news, he became angry. He told them to go out into the streets of the city and invite the poor, the lame, the blind, and anyone else who wished to attend his banquet. For my house, he insisted, will be filled, even if those originally invited never sit at my table."

Silence now held *this* table. I feared for a moment these priests and religious leaders might interpret the story a little too well and too quickly. Thankfully, the main course suddenly came out, a welcome distraction to defuse the tension. Plates of lamb, freshly baked bread and bowls of olives passed around the table, and soon everyone seemed re-engaged and ready for the next topic.

"Tell us, Jesus," probed one of the elder Sadducees, "for someone who speaks much of the kingdom of heaven, what are your views on how best to inherit it?"

I dipped a torn piece of bread in some seasoned olive oil. "That's quite a question."

"We understand you are quite the teacher," came the straightforward reply.

Keep this light and transparent, I told myself. No use getting into a doctrinal disagreement with the devout, especially when they are not here to learn but to trip me up. In fact, I reasoned, maybe it's best if I allow *him* to answer. So I asked, "What is written in the Law? How does it read to you?"

Clearly frustrated I had dodged the question, he was much too proud to ask it again and appear unsure of hallowed Law. He shifted his eyes to his auxiliary members in an outward display of irritation before replying, "That is easy. You shall love the Lord your God with all your heart, with all your soul and with all your mind. And you shall love your neighbor as yourself." His words were unwavering; his chin held high, confident and ready to go on the offensive if I contradicted him in any way or proposed a varying viewpoint.

I surprised him by doing no such thing. The wind died from his sails as I curtly yet completely agreed with him. "You are correct. Do as you say, and you will live."

He eased back, noticeably discouraged that an opportunity to criticize me had been missed. After all, how was he to argue or ridicule my ideas if I agreed with him? And with that, I thought this particular topic might be over as well.

I thought wrong. The unfulfilled Sadducee suddenly leaned forward, folded his hands on the table and spoke as if it were just the two of us across from each other. "And who is my neighbor?"

Everyone veered their eyes to me, anxious for my reaction.

A descriptive narrative was in order, in hopes to again lure him into answering his own question. "A man was going down from Jerusalem to Jericho when he was attacked by robbers. They stripped him, beat him and left him for dead."

My words somewhat startled and certainly puzzled most of the table. I had been asked a specific question as to what 'neighbor' signified in the eyes of God, and here I was launching into a scenario about bandits and violence. The only ones who expected such a response were my apostles, who were now routinely accustomed to these impromptu parables and stories.

I paused to allow the mental image of this victim clinging to life to clearly and concretely settle in their minds. "Not long afterward, a priest was going down that road. He saw the wounded man lying on the ground ... but passed by on the other side. Likewise a Levite came by, but minding his own business, he also moved to the other side of the road and continued on."

A few murmurs escaped around the room. I had just indicated that a man of the cloth and a member of the Hebrew tribe of Levi blatantly disregarded a stranger in need. Preposterous. Who was next to ignore the dying man, the High Priest himself?

"Finally a Samaritan came along the path," I continued softly.

The mutterings rose in pitch. I might as well have said a Roman tax collector came by. Ever since the centuries-old division between the two kingdoms of Israel began, deep-seated prejudice had spawned hatred among Jews and Samaritans. Their political, religious and family disunity spread contention and ill will to this day.

Surely a Samaritan would also show apathy toward the man in need.

I cleared my throat and prepared myself. "When he came upon the man lying half dead by the roadside, he was filled with pity. He rolled him over, poured oil on his wounds and bandaged them. He then lifted him onto his own animal and took him to an inn where he looked after him that night. The next morning, he retrieved two silver coins and gave them to the innkeeper with instructions to take care of the man. And whatever is spent beyond this, he promised, I will repay on my return trip."

For the moment, despite lamb cooked to perfection and olives that were ripe and plump, no one was eating. While everyone surely assumed I had spun this tale from my head, they now whispered and grumbled among themselves at the implausibility of these imagined events.

I ended their babbling with a firm voice to the one who had put me to the test. "So I ask you … which of these three travelers was a good neighbor to the man in need?"

Avoiding such a conclusive query would have proven my point even more than stating the obvious—which he did. "The one who showed him mercy, of course."

I smiled, neatly closing the issue. "Go then, and do the same."

Surprisingly, this simple summation was enough to dissuade further attempts to stump me or lead me into a theological quagmire. The room returned to the dinner at hand. We ate and drank and discussed less complex matters of faith and scripture. After finishing the meal and pushing ourselves back from the table to recline more comfortably, a sudden commotion arose from the front room.

We could somewhat distinguish the protests of Simon's servants and family, but their voices were soon overtaken by the forceful, determined demands of a single woman. Her shouts grew louder as their endeavors to keep her from entering the house were undoubtedly failing.

"Don't touch me!" we heard. "I must see him! I know he's here; I must see him!"

Simon the Pharisee stood from the table, as did a few others. He moved toward the archway leading from the room when they suddenly appeared. A woman clad in attractive but dirty clothing fought her way to our dining area. She was quickly restrained by Simon's son and two servants. Her wavy dark hair, further tussled from struggling, simply added to her beauty. Her eyes were swollen from crying, and in her hand, she clutched a smooth, cream-colored alabaster jar.

"What is the meaning of this intrusion?" demanded Simon.

Before anyone could answer, she spoke, projecting just as much authority and even more emotion. "Where is Jesus? Which one of you is Jesus?"

The power in her voice stilled the room to silence. One of the servants hesitantly informed his superior, "She was with the others outside. We tried to keep her out, but—"

"But she overcame the three of you," finished Simon with a disapproving glare.

"Show this woman to the door at once," scoffed one of the Sadducees.

Still seated, I despondently lowered my head. Had they not digested a word I said?

"Jesus?" she cried in a last effort to find me.

The servants struggled to pull her back, but I called out, "Wait!"

Everybody froze. I focused my attention solely on this assertive woman held firmly before us.

We locked eyes. Her brow lifted above her tangled hairline as my encouraging gaze revealed that she had succeeded in her quest.

"I am Jesus, the one you seek," I said. Then to those holding her, "Let her go."

Their grasp loosened only slightly around her arms and shoulders, but she wiggled free and came for me. Even before falling at my feet, she was in tears, ripping the cork from the alabaster jar. She pulled my bare feet toward her and began emptying the contents of the jar onto them. Undiluted perfume, the raw essential oils of pure nard, cascaded onto my feet and between my toes. The aroma of natural lavender rose into the air with a scent so sweet and seraphic, it entranced everyone in the room. Her fingers rubbed the rare oils into my rough skin, delightfully soothing my feet.

As I watched with tender amazement, Judas, sitting to my left and knowing well about the finer things in life, altruistically interjected, "Lord, that is pure nard oil. This jar could have been sold for a considerable amount of money and given to the poor. And yet she is coating your feet with it." He was flabbergasted by what seemed to him an utter waste of a valuable commodity.

I didn't move my eyes from her caring massage. "Let her be. I have truly never seen such devotion. You will always have the poor with you, and you can help them whenever you want. But I will not always be with you."

Setting aside the now empty jar, she continued rubbing the perfumed ointment into my skin. Her sobs continued as well, tears dripping onto my feet and mixing with the oil. Her lips lowered to one foot and gently kissed it while drying my skin with the wavy locks of her hair. She then kissed the other foot several quick times, as lovingly as if it were a lost child she had finally found.

I was utterly amazed, overwhelmed at her genuine affection and adoration.

Her close, intimate ministering somehow instantly opened my mind to the many hardships this woman had gone through, both as a child and a young woman. I saw the many sins she had committed, mainly the wanton selling of her most pure temple—her body. There was also so much rage. The frenzied temper this now peaceful flower was capable of unleashing stole a breath from my lips. Many in the neighboring towns of Tiberias and Magdala, especially the men who had purchased her wares, now did all they could to avoid the mere sight of her. There was no denying she had caused much discord and disunity in the region.

Her name effortlessly coalesced in my mind. *Mary, from Magdala.*

A hushed whisper from somewhere behind me audibly made it apparent that Mary's reputation preceded her. A Pharisee leaned over to our host and muttered, "If this Jesus were truly a prophet, he would know the kind of woman who is touching him."

I wanted nothing more than to focus solely on the reverence of this penitent daughter caressing my feet with her hair. But this was also an opportunity to open some eyes to her perfect act of repentance.

While I didn't know who exactly made the remark, I addressed Simon the Pharisee specifically, knowing all would listen. "Simon, I have something to ask you."

He was startled by my voice since I still had my back to him. "Yes, teacher, what is it?"

"If a person owes a moneylender fifty denarii, and another owes one hundred, yet neither can pay, which of them is more grateful to the lender if he erases both their debts?"

I couldn't see Simon's face, but his hesitation hinted he wasn't pleased about being put on the spot. And while the answer seemed obvious, he paused to make sure there wasn't a deeper question here. "I suppose the one who was forgiven the greater debt," he finally replied.

"You have answered correctly," I nodded, still gazing down at Mary. "Do you see this woman here? You and I walked together all the way from Tiberias, and yet upon entering your house, you gave me no water for my feet. She, however, has washed my feet with her tears and has not stopped kissing them. You did not anoint my head with oil as an honored guest, yet she has rubbed pure perfume into my feet and ankles." I finally raised my eyes to the room and glanced around at the faces before me. "And so I tell you all … this woman can rejoice today because her considerable debts have been erased."

Whispers of shock, murmurs of astonishment, even gasps of outrage leapt from the table. I didn't care. My attention returned to her. She now rested her forehead upon my feet, signifying total devotion.

Reaching down with both hands, I lifted her face to a more upright position so our eyes could meet once again. "Mary," I said.

New tears escaped at hearing her name, not so much because I knew it, but because she had never heard it spoken with real love.

My words that followed released full sobs of joy. "Your sins are forgiven."

From the corner of my eye, I saw a Sadducee stand abruptly. "How dare you blaspheme in here!" he scolded loudly. "Who are you to forgive sins?"

I glanced up and into the gaze of Peter and James, nervousness in their eyes. Things were going south here rapidly. I carefully turned and confronted the table; faces of shock and anger seized me.

Simon the Pharisee tried softly imparting an awkward explanation. "Only God can forgive sins, rabbi."

"I tell you the truth," I directed to them all. "This woman's faith has saved her today. Moreover, the Father judges no one but has entrusted all judgment to the son, so that all may honor the son just as they honor the Father. Whoever does not honor the son, does not honor the Father who sent him."

"What in the name of the Father is he talking about?" asked a baffled Pharisee.

"Your words do not puzzle me," reprimanded the provoked Sadducee. "You should be stoned for claiming equality to God!"

"I heard as well," spoke another. "Sent from the Father? Entrusted to judge? What possesses you to say such things?"

"He's unfit to be in your house, Simon," muttered still another, shaking his head in disgust.

I finally stood and looked to my apostles with a gesture they were all too ready for—let's get out of here. I grabbed Mary's hands and helped her to her feet. "Come with us," I invited.

"Yes," she breathed.

That was the last straw. Not only had I profanely presumed a divine role with the Almighty, I had now accepted someone regarded as no more than a common whore to join my following. In a brusque single bound, the Sadducee hiked up his robe and vaulted over the table at me. "Out!" he yelled as he sprang forward.

My apostles shielded us with proficient readiness and moved us from the room while the infuriated scribe attempted to assault me. Most of the other guests impulsively joined his push on the huddle, not all of them attempting to land blows but clearly trying to get me and my entourage out of Simon the Pharisee's house as quickly as possible. I held Mary around the shoulders and protected her head as we fumbled through the stone foyer, nearly falling as a single mass of bodies out the door. It was hardly the way I had envisioned our dinner reception concluding, but it was definitely over.

Luckily, we were greeted by the hundred or so people still waiting for me outside. They surrounded us, overjoyed I had finally come out to them. The Sadducee stood in the doorway, flanked by his other scribes.

"You will not get away with this, Jesus of Nazareth," he seethed. "Your own words condemn you."

For the moment I felt safe, hemmed in by so many others, but a fearful chill shuddered my shoulders. It was beginning. My opposition was increasing. The establishment's enraged antagonism against me had begun. I knew someday soon, all too soon, there would be more than a handful of them waiting to pounce—a time when the crowds would also turn against me—a time when even these twelve would abandon my side.

But for now I was hardly alone. The large group pushed closer, and a man suffering from edema presented his badly swollen hand to me. "Jesus," he moaned, "my hand is in such agony."

Before I could acknowledge him, the Sadducee shouted from the doorway, "So you've been entrusted by God to heal too? Is that where your power to cure comes from, our almighty Creator? Tell us, Jesus, would God have you heal these people on the Sabbath? Would he command you to blatantly disregard his sacred Law to cure the sick, cast out demons ... mend a hand?"

By continuing this offensive to trap me in blasphemous words and deeds, he was only shaming himself. But so be it. I motioned everyone a few steps back to afford me space in which to work and speak. I then looked around and raised my voice for every ear. "What do you all say to that challenge? Is it lawful to heal on the Sabbath, or not?"

No answer came. Only silence. Those who had come from afar

earnestly hoped that I would but were unwilling to speak against the teachers of the Law who were still close-by.

I shifted my attention to the doorway of the house, to those leveling their disapproval at me. "Let me ask you this. Which one of you on the Sabbath wouldn't help one of your sheep or ox if it fell into a ditch? Which one of you wouldn't release a common dog from the thickets if you saw its leg caught on the Sabbath?" My logic paralyzed them. "So please tell me, is not a human being more valuable than a sheep, or an ox, or a dog? You question whether healing on the Sabbath is allowed under God's Law. *My* question for you, is how can it not be *demanded* by God to help your fellow man on the Sabbath?"

I could practically feel the Sadducee's heat from where I stood. His blood was boiling.

But he of course had no answer for me.

I turned to the man with the inflamed extremity. "Stretch out your hand."

He looked at me, both fear and hope breaking across his face. He did as he was told, a trusting response that proved sufficient for my mercy. As his fingers gingerly stretched out before me, the swelling dissipated and the pain faded away. He lifted his hand in front of his face, staring at it with jubilation and wonder, touching it with his other to indeed confirm that it was his own. He then dropped to his knees and embraced my legs.

Smiling, I placed my hands on his head to indicate that his display of thanks and piety pleased me as much as seeing his joy. I wanted to connect with everyone in just this way, even the stubborn authorities who judged and mocked my every move. I was here to be open and welcoming to all, and would continue as such to the end of the world. I wouldn't, however, force anyone to follow me. All must come willingly and with open hearts. My Father and I would never transgress free will. It is humanity's one true, private possession—the only thing that is sincerely theirs. Circumstances can influence and constrain it, but never dictate it. Nor would I.

I turned toward Simon the Pharisee's house, hoping the relentlessly harsh Sadducee might be somewhat softened by the elation and gratitude of this man, this child of God for whom I supposedly broke religious Law to make well on God's day of rest.

The doorway was empty. They had witnessed the healing and retreated hastily inside, defeated and exasperated. Although discouraging, it was better than seeing them come after me, ready to cast stones at my head. Still, I considered it best not to remain outside a house filled with fuming religious pundits. My welcome had long since passed.

We moved down near the water and strolled north a bit. I spent the rest of the day preaching and healing this group of persistent followers, of whom Mary from Magdala proved the most resolute and attentive. She sat on a nearby rock at the water's edge with my disciples, listening with rapt attention as I evangelized the word of God. This woman who had been pulled in so many wrong directions most of her life, now easily surrendered herself to the light that would guide her forever. As I spoke, I found myself sneaking glances in her direction. The way she smiled at my voice, how she held her chin to the breeze so that her hair gently brushed her face, was captivating.

Suffice to say, I was quite enamored.

This was neither unnatural or unexpected. I was, after all, a man. I had human feelings. I possessed human desires. Many young women in the towns where my father Joseph and I sought work had caught my eye. I saw and appreciated the beauty of the female form, and even felt the raw urges that without the bonds of love in place, led many to lust and sin. Not surprisingly, because of my human nature, I often longed for intimacy—the companionship of a woman with whom to share everything. But I knew from the start that this uniquely blessed experience was not part of my calling. Marriage required fully giving oneself to another, to dedicate everything for love of spouse and family. While this was certainly a noble and grace-filled life, *my* unique mission on earth was to uncompromisingly devote *my* all, *my* sacrifice ... not for one woman, but for all of humanity.

So while I furtively admired Mary sitting radiantly upon that rock, it struck me that I had found a strong and effective disciple who would greatly help my ministry with a passionate voice, driven by a determined spirit ... but a person I could not pursue with the human aspirations of my human heart. And while this realization may have discouraged me for a moment or two, the faces yearning for care and attention before me easily refocused *my* attention to the essential reason I was so fully dedicated to my Father's work.

The eternal life of the world was at stake.

14

Awakenings

IT WAS OUT THERE NOW. I was no longer just a prophet speaking about the kingdom of heaven. Although I hadn't explicitly called myself the *son of God*, I surely implied it to a roomful of Pharisees and Sadducees. Moreover, I now consciously played with fire whenever speaking and acting as if I held authority over sacred Hebrew Law. But indeed fire was part of my mission—to ignite the sparks of change and renewal. While I had assuredly come to unite the nations, this did not include building universal solidarity among all people. Many would be at odds regarding me and my message, causing great division over my identity. This became more apparent as I clearly spoke the truth about who I was and from where I had come.

It was not long before Passover, so my disciples and I began leisurely making our way toward Jerusalem. I knew that my ultimate sacrifice would culminate there, and during the Passover season, but I was confident I had more work to do. The time had not yet come to lay down my life. Even so, after the confrontation at Simon the Pharisee's house, I more than expected some rather dicey encounters with the religious establishment once we arrived in the holy city.

Before heading south from Galilee, we made a stop at my

hometown of Nazareth. My mother was overjoyed to see me and delighted to cater to my apostles. She fully recognized all they had been through with me, but more importantly, all that lay ahead of us. She treated them as sons.

She especially took to Mary Magdala. While many thought it scandalous for a woman to travel with a band of men, my mother understood her true heart. The two talked for hours—Mary to Mary. My mother confided to her many of the blessings shared with me over the years. She disclosed quite plainly how she knew I was destined to change the world and save it from itself. Mary Magdala, of course, recounted in detail how she had already been saved from herself—how through my caring concern and forgiveness, she became a new person with a restored meaning for life.

My mother's compassion was both heartwarming and compelling as Mary described her darkest days—the bitterness, the deceit, the animosity for self and others, and a despair that fed on the absence of hope for good in her life. She confessed that her fear of God matched her anger with him. She resented and blamed him for all the horrors and hardships throughout her life. Her dread that God wanted her less and less petrified her daily. But then she heard about this Jesus. She learned about his miracles, about his preaching unconditional repentance and forgiveness, and about how he reconciled even the most wretched transgressors with God.

Mary broke down in front of my mother, smiling through tears before explaining how this new hope in finding me kept her from the desperate, final escape of suicide. Mom gently took her by the hands and assured her with loving eyes, "All who come to my son shall find new life."

Later that night as I stood alone in the small courtyard behind the house gazing up at the twinkling sky, I thought about how well she captured the essence of my mission in those few succinct words. *New life in my name.* Eternal life. A spiritual oneness with me and my Father that eclipses any need, want or desire.

I closed my eyes and took in a deep breath of the night air that pleasantly cooled Nazareth from the day's warmth. With eyes shut, my hearing sharpened, perceiving faint, distant sounds—a sudden breeze from around the corner, trees whispering over the hill, even the cadence of far-off voices too indistinct to discern words or gender. Although standing, my very relaxed state led me into prayer. As I often did, I implored my Father to grant patience while living and working with the many uncertainties of human existence. Despite my divinity's realization of many spiritual truths, my human mental constraints kept me ignorant about so much. How much time did I have left to complete our work? What obstacles and confrontations would each day bring? What were the specific events that would lead to my final days … my final hours? And could this human husk in which I had grown for thirty-two years, be able to carry me through such anguish and chaos?

As I waited for an encouraging thought or premonition, I suddenly felt familiar hands on the back of my shoulders. I opened my eyes and turned to see my mother step around me. I was surprised but glad to see her. "Still awake?" I quietly asked.

She put her arm through mine and rested her head on my shoulder, following my gaze into the dark sky. "I'll sleep when you sleep."

"I'm not sleeping much these days."

She sighed. "Me neither."

I looked pensively over. "I know what keeps me up after dark. Why are you so restless?"

Keeping her eyes intently upon the stars, she remained silent for so long, I thought an answer might not come.

A single word finally escaped. "Simeon."

I tried placing the name. "Who?"

"Simeon," she repeated softly but definitively. "I remember the day as if it were yesterday, and his words as if they had just reached my ears." She remained trance-like at the heavens.

"Who is Simeon, mother?"

She finally wrestled her full attention over to me. "A man we met in the temple just after you were born. We had come to fulfill our duty with a first-born son. Jerusalem was such a short journey from Bethlehem; we thought it would be the perfect place to present you to the Lord and provide our offering."

She stopped, unsure if she wanted to continue, but the interest in my eyes coaxed her onward. "Your father and I didn't know he was a mystic when he first approached. He was just a very old and gentle man who was thrilled to see such a beautiful newborn. But when he took you in his arms, he raised his eyes and uttered words that still give me goosebumps."

"What did he say?"

She glanced down, recalling words from so long ago. "He thanked God for allowing him to live long enough to see his own salvation. He called you a light of revelation for gentiles and a living glory for the people of Israel."

"He said that to you?" While not surprised, I was a little perplexed why she had never mentioned him.

Her eyes again lifted to mine. "There's more." She struggled whether to go on.

I urged her silently to continue.

"As he carefully handed you back to me, his eyes became so despondent, so suddenly forlorn, I feared he might collapse. But instead, he grabbed me lightly by the shoulder and warned me."

"Warned you? Of what?"

"He told me very directly that sorrow ... like a sword, would someday pierce my heart."

Silence reclaimed the night.

I looked away, not wanting to accept the terrible implication of his prediction, but the certain reality of it was nevertheless immediately evident to me. My mother would witness my suffering. She would be present during my passion and death. Although I rather expected even my friends to scatter, fearfully hiding while I endured my most grueling hours, I should have realized that my perfectly loyal and most blessed mother would steadfastly and courageously see it through ... and see it all. The one whose heart I could not bear to see broken, would experience first-hand the atrocity of my sacrifice for the world.

There were no words for me to offer right now. Nothing I could say would console her or lessen the burden of Simeon's words that had so painfully haunted her for decades. So I simply turned and held her in a gentle embrace. We stood there for several long moments, each understanding there was only one conviction—one principle, one commitment—that could, or would, get us both through the evil that ultimately awaited.

Love.

"I love you, mom," I whispered.

Her fingers tightened around my arms as her own breath replied, "I love you too, my son. So very much."

*   *   *

Instead of heading south toward Jerusalem by way of the Jordan pass, we decided to travel through the territory of Samaria. 'We' had suddenly grown from me and my twelve apostles to now include Mary Magdala and two other women she had recruited to our following—Salome and Joanna. When Peter learned that Joanna was the widow of a servant in Herod's court, he was visibly concerned, worried word might get back to Herod that Chuza's wife was now following a new 'king.' I assured him that Herod's operatives were not scouting the whereabouts of any deceased servant's widow. Besides, Joanna was genuine, gentle and absorbed in learning about me and the kingdom of heaven. Not to mention her former husband had amassed some wealth while serving Herod, which she had cleverly hidden away and now donated to our cause.

And so with ample provisions for the first leg of our journey, we set forth for Jerusalem. While most Jews naturally chose to bypass this more direct route through Samaria, we figured, and prayed, there would be no real trouble along our way. However, it wasn't long after we entered the Jezreel valley along the base of Mount Gilboa, that we came face to face with a danger none of us had expected.

The sun inched higher toward its peak, so it was not unusual to see people approaching with hood-like mantles covering their heads. But as they drew closer, we noticed their hands were also wrapped in cloth. They numbered about ten, shuffling toward us, shrouded in ragged garments.

Bartholomew made the connection first and halted us suddenly with raised arms. "Everyone back," he alarmed. "Lepers approach!"

We would have stopped less abruptly if he had yelled fire. More than a contagious affliction, leprosy was the sheer manifestation of suffering and torment. The infection scattered large, painful pustules and boils across the body and along the extremities—eventually eating away fingers, toes, hands, even arms and legs. If stricken, death could not come soon enough. Those with advanced leprosy aptly resembled the living-dead, yet it was not their striking and horrible appearance that shunned them from their communities. It was the raw fear of becoming one of them. Friends and family alike fled the presence of these poor afflicted souls; thus loneliness prevailed as one of the most distressing effects of the disease. Certain botanical oil treatments worked in rare cases, but to fully integrate back into society, Jewish Law required, direct from the book of Leviticus, to be examined by a priest and pronounced cured.

Here now before us stood an obvious group of banned lepers. Exiled from their homes and loved ones, these castaways aimlessly roamed the uninhabited countryside with nothing left for which to live but a mercifully early death.

Joanna and Salome retreated into John's arms, who would have normally welcomed the presence of a woman under each wing had it not been for this potentially dangerous and deadly circumstance.

Before any of us could react further, one of the lepers spoke, a faceless voice from the shadow of his head covering. "Stay away, all of you. Do not chance exposure to our curse."

My entire group took an obedient step backward.

I stepped forward.

Not long ago my apostles would have questioned my sanity for moving toward certain and significant risk. Not anymore. They had begun to trust in the peaceful knowledge that I was aware of all and in total control. But while my friends may not have been overly shocked at my advance, all ten of the deplorable figures I approached were clearly startled.

"Did you not hear?" croaked the one who had spoken, his words raspy and labored. "Do not even place your eyes upon us. Be gone."

I took a final step in their direction and lowered my head, disregarding his plea to avoid their faces. What met my gaze caused such a pang of sadness, I could not mask the heartache from my brow. The man's face was a mass of blisters and abscesses—his left eye nearly swollen shut from the puffy, discolored growths on his cheek. He had no nose. In the places where there should have been smooth skin, now swelled festering inflammations. Where a nose once completed his face, there was nothing.

My expression changed from sorrow to solace. "Do you know who I am?" I asked tenderly. "Who stands here before you?"

He and the others did not answer. They were too bewildered at how very brave or very stupid I must be to have come so close to them.

"I am Jesus."

These three simple words were all it took. Hope. They began to visibly shake with it.

One of the lepers, hunching humbly behind the first, raised his deformed hands in prayerful supplication. "Jesus … have pity on us."

Pity for these unfortunates came easy, but I had so much more than pity to offer them. I had love, absolution and ablution. Disease was a horrible thing—an all too common reality while living in an imperfect world as imperfect people. But my all-powerful love could overcome even the most chronic, debilitating and deadly infirmities.

I opened my arms and collectively expressed my command to all ten shadowy forms before me. "Go, all of you, and show yourselves to the priests."

While I couldn't see their eyes, I could sense their perplexity. In their condition, no priest in his right mind would clear them to return to any populace. They themselves wouldn't dare enter a town in the repulsive state they were in. But they did not contradict me. They did not scoff at my request. They simply nodded reverently in my direction, backed a few steps away, then sluggishly turned and wandered off in the direction from which they had come.

I turned to face my disciples, all visibly relieved now that the threat of contracting leprosy was departing.

"Did you cure them, Lord?" asked Salome, her petite voice thrilled with the prospect that she might have witnessed her first miracle.

Before I could respond, James gloriously took the words out of my mouth. "If they have faith, they will be cured."

I was stunned—speechless. Such incredible joy and pride filled my heart from this one, concise, fully transparent roll of the tongue. My apostles were learning. They were getting it. My words were now becoming theirs. Their preparation was progressing well.

I walked up to James and clutched his arms approvingly, then addressed them all. "Faith indeed. Faith that your Father in heaven wants the very best for you. Not that he will cure every ailment, or provide the richest of harvests, or command calm weather for travel, but faith that he yearns to bestow upon you his most special gift—

his own life; life that draws on itself … His own Holy Spirit."

"How do we receive his Spirit?" implored Philip. "Are we to just ask?"

"Yes!" I exclaimed excitedly, startling them all. "You ask. What father here on earth would give his son or daughter a snake or a scorpion if they asked him for an egg? We who are human know how to give our children good things—how much more your heavenly Father will give his very self to those who ask him." I looked at them lovingly and softened my voice, speaking as a friend among friends. "So I say to you … ask, and it will be given to you. Seek, and you shall find. Knock, and the door will be opened to you. For whoever asks of my Father with a sincere heart, receives. Whoever seeks him humbly, finds him. And whoever knocks upon his door with faith, gains entry."

Their faces expressed that my words were taking hold. Their eyes displayed a real desire to beseech God right now for his guiding Spirit, for his divine and peaceful presence. I did not need to explain, for they now fully grasped the amazing truth—that an unconditional craving for my Father's presence was enough to carry it into their hearts and souls. Their God was willing, and even eager, to take up residence within them—within everyone—until that triumphant day when they can take up residence under his roof in the mansion prepared for them in heaven.

We continued our trek along the base of Mount Gilboa, gradually moving deeper into the valleys of Samaria. The walk became most pleasant—an afternoon of meadows, fields and wildflowers. We stopped for some water and a quick lunch on a well-chosen slope tinged with pure white crocuses, when we suddenly saw a figure come into view across the plain. Peering over the grasses and sage from our position, we thought the man might be running naked since we could only see him from the torso up. As he moved hastily toward us, a garment soon came into view tied tightly around his waist. We glanced at one another curiously, wondering why he was running frantically in our direction. His gait and determined course for our specific location prompted us all to stand. Who was this?

"Just what we need, a crazy Samaritan," muttered Thomas but indicated no real alarm regarding this scantily dressed loner swiftly approaching.

"He seems mighty eager to get over here," said Thaddeus.

Before anyone could comment further, the man was upon us. He stopped a few paces from where we stood, breathing heavily. His eyes locked upon mine before stepping forward. He then dropped to his knees so hard and abruptly I thought for sure he must have bruised them. With hands raised over his head, he bellowed with all remaining breath, "Thank you, Jesus!"

Birds scattered from the brush, frightened by the loud, impassioned exultation.

Andrew came to my side. "Lord, who is this man?"

I didn't answer for a very simple reason. I didn't have one. I did not recognize this person kneeling before me.

He looked up into my eyes and squinted from the sun. "You do not remember me, yet we spoke earlier this very day."

Reality sent tingles up our arms. He continued, "I am one of the lepers. The one who begged you to have pity on us. On the way back to town, when we realized we had been cured, we stripped off our robes and rags, freeing our cleansed bodies for the first time in so long." He seemed to laugh and cry at the same time. All deformities were gone, restored with healthy tissue. Not even the smallest blemish remained on his body. His now handsome face lowered once again toward my feet. "All my praises belong to you, Jesus. Thank you for giving me back my body … my life."

There was sudden silence—the emotion of the moment constricting our throats. I reached down and gently offered my hand. He took it graciously and gradually stood with my assistance.

Once his eyes had returned to mine, I quietly asked, "There were ten of you who were cured, were there not?"

He hesitated before nodding slightly. "Yes. They too are so very happy. I'm sure they are just as grateful as I am and would—"

I raised a finger to politely quiet him but also to convey my thoughts before my words. "You alone have returned to give thanks. While it was faith that healed you, it is your thanks and praise that has gained you great favor with God."

He smiled, and I could only imagine how pleasant it must have been to do so without the painful lesions of leprosy eating his lips. I placed a hand on his neck and shoulder with my own expression of fulfillment. "Your joy is God's joy. Go now, and live for him every day."

The man took a deep breath, grabbed my hand from his shoulder and kissed it. He then bowed respectfully to my disciples, turned with a lighthearted pivot and literally danced across the field.

Matthew leaned on his walking stick and grinned at the bouncing figure moving away. "There goes one happy fellow."

"He dances for something too many too often do not appreciate," I said. "Life."

They silently agreed. Having just witnessed the restoration of health and life over the ravages of disfiguring disease and death, they more powerfully understood this blessed bliss.

What remained to teach them now was that God's gift of life matters above all else—that loving others is the most important duty—and that sacrificing life *for* love … the highest honor.

* * *

Across Samaria we traveled. The small villages nestled along hillsides that we either journeyed through or circumvented around each reminded me in different ways of my Nazareth. Beyond those humble towns, we continued south across the valleys and beneath the bluffs, closing our distance to Judea. These were well-spent days with my apostles. We talked and laughed together, shared secrets and songs, raised cups, broke bread and watched over each other as we slept. They were good days, probably some of the best I could recall. A favorite verse from Proverbs analogized how one person sharpens another just as iron sharpens iron. So very true. Friendship was so vital to sharpening oneself for life's trials and tribulations. Sustained camaraderie drew the strength to turn strangers and outsiders into brothers and sisters—to meld those from different walks of life into companions *for* life. We were no longer parts or pieces figuring how to fit together. We were united—a close-knit, caring group.

After spending a restful night in a comfortable hollow between Mounts Ebal and Gerizim, we descended further into a vast valley. At its far end, a sprawling village shimmered against the sky, creating a jagged horizon. We stopped a moment and shielded our eyes as we stared across the lowlands.

Joanna motioned across the plains. "Have we reached Sychar?"

"I believe we have," I replied.

"Sychar?" perked Thaddeus. "We must be close to the field Jacob gave his son Joseph."

Peter moved his eyes from the dwellings on the skyline back to our current position. "I think we're standing in it."

Thaddeus brightened again, realizing we were close to a holy landmark. "Then Jacob's well should be somewhere—"

"I see it!" John shouted excitedly and pointed off to the right, about halfway into the valley.

Sure enough, the historic well our patriarch Jacob constructed many generations ago was just a short stroll away. It rose above the grass and thickets as little more than a spacious hole enclosed by a nondescript stone wall, providing purpose without polish. Large slabs of chiseled rock and other crude masonry work served as benches and makeshift counters near the renowned cistern.

With no one in sight, we made our way directly toward it. If others had been gathered at the well, we still probably would have approached, but certainly more deliberately. We were Jews outside a Samaritan city, accessing a scarce and valued resource—a sacred site. We could not expect a warm welcome.

Upon reaching the well, we discovered a significant obstacle to retrieving its water. While plenty of rope coiled around the rocks, we could not find a single bucket or container to lower down.

Bartholomew nudged his old friend. "Philip, see if you can climb down there and fill our waterskins."

"Are you crazy?" he blurted before sensing the joke and quickly muttering, "Silly fool."

We all found this amusing, including Philip who couldn't repress a chuckle himself.

"Seriously, Lord," said Bartholomew, "should we wait here or head into town?"

His voice betrayed an eagerness to venture into Sychar. The others agreed with wistful faces. Our journey through the hills and valleys had been pleasant, but they now sought more human interaction, even from Samaritans.

"Why don't you all go into town," I suggested. "It will do you good. Buy what we need and meet me back here."

"You aren't coming with us?" asked John.

"I think I'll stay and rest," I decided. "Leave your waterskins with me. If villagers come, I will ask their help to fill them."

Mary glanced around the seemingly deserted area. "Are you sure you'll be okay?"

I smiled to her and nodded. "I'll be fine. What better place to meditate and rest than at the well of our ancestor Jacob. Jacob was later named Israel, so this truly is the 'land of Israel.'"

"I shall stay with you," said Peter.

I looked at my dear friend standing next to me. "Your brothers and sisters need you in town, Peter. Go and have some fun."

A telling grin reluctantly curled his lips. "If you insist."

So they left me with their nearly empty waterskins and headed off for Sychar. After watching them disappear into the village, I found a comfortable shady nook among some smoothly chiseled rocks and sat down to rest against the flat stonework. Although I had planned on quietly praying in this suddenly still and peaceful late morning, I unexpectedly drifted off to sleep.

I wasn't sure how long I had dosed, but it would have been longer had someone over at the well not awakened me. It was a woman. She stood alone, and for a quick moment from where I sat with the sun now positioned in my eyes, I thought it might have been Mary. Her hair was dark like Mary's, but as she slightly turned, I noticed she was a stranger. Her facial expression and overall mannerisms conveyed the apathy and dejection of one who was very lost—not physically, but spiritually. I sensed this spiritual longing simply because she herself was so painfully aware of it.

She apparently had no idea I was close-by as she busied herself feeding a rope through the handles of a very large clay jar.

I remained seated and spoke softly so I wouldn't startle her. "Could I trouble you for a drink?"

Startled nonetheless, she practically dropped her container and spun around.

"Do not be afraid," I assured, gradually standing. "I am just traveling through on my way to Jerusalem. My companions have gone into Sychar for food, and I was waiting here for some water."

She calmed a moment while carefully looking me over. Whether by accent or dialect, she pegged me immediately. "You are a Jew," she said. "I am a Samaritan ... and a woman no less. Why is it you ask *me* for a drink?"

"Because I am thirsty."

It was no longer my tongue's vernacular but my caring eyes that allayed her concern. She slowly returned to her task at the well. "I'm assuming those are your group's waterskins, which you'll also want filled."

I discreetly approached and sat at the edge of the stone basin where she fiddled with the rope. I then gently leaned over into her line of sight. "If you knew who it was that is asking you for a drink, you would be asking him for one, and he would give you *living* water."

"Is that so," she replied matter-of-factly. "You have nothing to draw water with and this well is deep. Where do you plan on getting this *living* water? Are you greater than our father Jacob who drank from this well himself?" She finished tying off the jug and finally brought her eyes to me.

I placed my hand upon hers. "Although you may fill this jar to the brim now, I can assure you that later you will become thirsty again. But whoever comes to me, will never thirst. The water I give becomes a living spring within them, welling up to eternal life."

Genuine curiosity with a touch of sarcasm prompted her reply. "Then by all means give me this water so that I may not thirst or have to keep coming to this well every day."

I kept my hand on hers and could feel her heartfelt longing for fulfillment, hardly masked by her satirical tone. Her personal struggles also became evident to me.

"Why don't you bring your husband back here with you," I said.

She lowered her eyes and softly removed her hand from under mine. "I have no husband."

"I know."

This direct acknowledgement brought her attention back. "You know? How would you know?"

To cushion my response, my face and voice conveyed hope and love. "You are brave for telling the truth. The fact is, you have had five husbands, and the man you are currently with is not your spouse."

If it hadn't been for the unmistakable compassion in my eyes, fear would have torn her away from me. But she held steady, resisting tears that began welling up. "I can see that you are a prophet," she said, trying to keep her composure. "Who are you?"

"I am Jesus of Nazareth."

"Nazareth," she contemplated. "That must be why you are headed to Jerusalem. Jews from both Galilee and Judea tell us we should worship God from Jerusalem, but our ancestors worshiped from these mountains."

I shook my head to convey a pointless argument. "It doesn't matter. The time is coming, and is already here, when worshipers will honor the Father in spirit and in truth, regardless of where they are. God is spirit and calls his followers to worship him in the spirit. This is why he is willing to give his Spirit to whoever asks of it … to you as well."

She grabbed my hand again, suddenly yearning for my touch. "I know that the Messiah, called the Christ, is coming soon. When he comes, he will explain everything to us."

I took her other hand and stood with her from the edge of the well. My tender, affectionate gaze prepared her for my words. "I … who am speaking to you now … am he."

Her expression held no cynicism or contempt, only awareness and recognition. It was as if she suddenly realized she had truly known me all her life. Tears finally spilled forth, and she collapsed into my arms. With her face pressed against my robe, her sorrowful sobs mixed with joyful cries at finding herself in my unconditional, loving embrace.

"I am a good person, you must believe me," she cried. "I have made too many unwise, shameful choices. I cannot deny or change that."

"Determine whom you will serve from this day forward," I said, gently stroking her hair, "and your past choices will not matter."

"How can they not matter?" she continued to weep.

"Give them to me. Trust in me … and your past will no longer burden you."

This passionate release, this sudden washing of her soul in my arms, brought new waves of tears. Still nuzzled in the crux of my elbow, she pledged to accompany me to town and proclaim me as the Messiah to all she knew. She then looked up and found a smile through moist eyes. "And I will make sure that you and your companions have plenty of water for the rest of your journey."

"My promise to you," I replied while wiping tears from her cheeks, "is that you will never thirst again."

She knew exactly what I meant. She fully understood that her physical need for water would continually return her to this well, but she would no longer thirst to fill her spiritual life. That abyss, created by sin, had been replaced by the peace and contentment of her repentance and my forgiveness. She, like so many now, had found salvation simply by accepting my personal invitation to reform her life and seek solace in my open arms.

When my disciples returned from Sychar, she helped fill our water containers before escorting us back to town to make good on her word. In a most efficient and enthusiastic manner, she gathered together what seemed like half the village to recount her experience at the well and publically profess her belief that I was the one, the long-awaited Messiah. Without her sincere testimony chronicling our discussion, I could never have gotten such a large Samaritan crowd to sit and listen to me speak. But she captivated them with her candor. She prepared them for me—enticed them with a curiosity and eagerness to hear my voice. And with their ears and hearts open … they believed. My profound, solemn words of eternal life were enabled by this woman's determination to bring me and my message to her people.

The kingdom of God would surely go forward from here. These Samaritans now had the foundation and the conviction to go forth— to bring their witness of God's love for them to other towns and families—to spread my saving testimony throughout the region.

We could never have imagined as we embarked from Galilee to Judea that we would have detoured for several days in a Samaritan village. So many new disciples were made, so many new friends.

But we soon had to bid our farewells and prepare our departure for Jerusalem. I dearly embraced this woman who had found new life, who I first encountered alone at Jacob's well. It was once again just she and I. We hugged a few moments in silence, then squeezing my shoulders tightly, she renewed her vow to bring my name and message to everyone she met. What a devoted disciple she would have made as part of our group, but I knew she had young children, and they needed her. I did not, however, want to say goodbye, so I simply lowered my head and quietly whispered a new name for her. "You are Photini," I sighed into her hair.

Photini—*the enlightened one.*

Thus my heavenly Father and I again bestowed true honor and esteem in distinct contrast to the way the world falsely exalted those who embraced its evils. This woman was not a prophet. She had no formal training in scripture. She did not belong to a wealthy or privileged class or society. Indeed, she was ordinary in every way, undistinguished and unexceptional by earthly standards. And yet the Son of Man had just conferred upon her the identity of 'enlightened.' The very breath of God brought this spiritually lost and misguided soul true respect and stature in an eternal kingdom.

That's all it took. It did not require the rarest advantages of royal lineage or sophisticated culture. It simply demanded an open heart. It implored an openness to the truth—a willingness to listen to and accept my words of reform and peace—that God the Father sent his only son into the world, and that through him, the path back to the Father is restored.

Those who understood—those who believed and lived this truth—would truly be enlightened and blessed by the power of God.

And streams of living water would flow from within them.

15

The Good Shepherd

WE MUST HAVE MADE AN IMPRESSION. Upon leaving the streets of Sychar early in the morning, the crowds that followed seemed to empty the village. Everyone wanted to accompany us at least to the outskirts of their homeland. Most simply walked in silence, enjoying a final morning with their new-found savior. Others urgently approached for a last-minute healing or scrambled to ask questions about the kingdom of heaven and the deliverance of Israel.

My apostles, well-fed and well-rested, kept close to me as usual. They now felt emboldened to answer some questions themselves ... to practice teaching salvation. My friends had learned from me more than the words of eternal life. They had also picked up the manner in which to proclaim it. With a message so strong, so consequential, so personally challenging, it was easy to upset or offend many if not spoken with an approachable calm and compassion. God's good news was not to come *down* to people, but to come *through* them. Life-changing ideas and beliefs best took hold when spoken from the heart rather than the mind.

Some distance from town, on our way into the valley leading toward Shiloh, Ephraim and ultimately Jerusalem, the crowds began to thin. Many hugged us goodbye before departing for home with a new purpose in their lives. A man about my age, healthy and strong, suddenly caught up to us. He startled us a bit as he burst into our group.

"Jesus, good teacher," he exclaimed, relieved to have found me, "before you go, please, I am a man who gives and follows direction well. If provided a map, I will get there; if handed instructions for a house, I will build it. I adhere to specific tasks with determination and commitment."

I glanced at Peter on the other side of him. He returned a slight shrug, as baffled as I by our new guest.

I smiled at this exuberant but somewhat perplexing fellow. "What is it you want, my friend? Just ask."

His eyes beamed as he prepared his thoughts. "You spoke magnificently about the kingdom of heaven, about eternal life, about overcoming evil here on earth so we can solidify our place with God forever." He paused for but an instant. "Tell me, specifically, what must I do to ensure this—to inherit this eternal life in paradise?"

Here was a typical analytical mind—hoping to find a clear-cut means to an end—a way to achieve an objective through some method or routine. "You know the commandments," I replied. "Worship God alone. Do not murder or steal. Do not covet what isn't yours or bring false witness against anyone. These have always been the ways to please your Father in heaven by loving and respecting others."

The light in his eyes remained bright. "Excellent, teacher," he said. "All these commandments I have kept. I have always held them sacred."

I almost nodded in approval. I was about to encourage him to continue to do as he always had.

But I stopped. I caught myself. Before responding further, I took a moment to better consider the man before me. I easily noticed his neatly trimmed beard, clean nails and callus-free fingers. His tunic was woven from fine cloth and the pouch around his shoulder crafted from supple hide. This was a man unaccustomed to arduous labor—one who most likely had others doing it for him. Perhaps he owned a large orchard or vineyard, or was a merchant of rare spices from the East. In any case, he lived well, and I suddenly realized the motivation behind his question. He had obviously obtained a comfortable lifestyle for himself in this world. What he wanted now were specific directives to ensure he was just as substantially set for the afterlife.

So where did his true priorities lie?

It was time to find out. "There is only one thing left for you to do. One thing to guarantee you will have treasures in heaven."

He could barely contain himself. "Tell me, Jesus, what is it?"

Before answering, I stared deeply into his eyes to convey both love and candidness. "Go … sell everything that you have and give the money to the poor. Then come; follow me."

The request hung in the air, driving an awkward silence into our conversation. If I had commanded him to eat a scorpion, he would have been less taken aback. The vigor in his face lost its vibrancy. The gleam in his eyes vanished. He had come to me convinced I held the key to everlasting life and the knowledge of how to obtain it, and yet his wealth on earth held a stronger grip upon his soul.

The challenge was too much. He reluctantly turned and allowed us to continue without him.

Peter glanced over his shoulder, then back to me and the others. "He obviously had a lot of money. Did you really think he would give it all up to join us?"

My eyebrows raised. "For salvation?"

He paused and nodded thoughtfully. "I guess those who have many things find it difficult to imagine life without them."

I sighed. "It is easier for a camel to fit through the eye of a needle than for someone who is rich to enter the kingdom of God."

My typically vocal group became suddenly reticent, their baffled expressions understandable.

John finally spoke softly, "Who then can be saved, if it is so hard?"

Not wanting them discouraged, I stopped walking to address them more directly. "Let there be no doubt, with mankind, salvation is impossible. But take heart. With God, all things are possible."

Their faces showed some relief but hoped I might clarify.

I simply tapped my heart and offered a familiar smile. "Focus on me—on my words—on my love. Put your hope in me alone, and God's mercy will be immeasurable."

Peter placed his arm around his brother Andrew and motioned to the whole group. "Lord, we have left everything to follow you."

"And I tell you the truth, anyone who leaves their former lives behind for me and for my message will receive a hundred times as much in the age to come." I turned my head toward Jerusalem before continuing, "And although challenges and persecutions lie ahead ... the gift of eternal life awaits."

Angel choruses may have harmoniously celebrated these statements in heaven, but from where we stood, we simply enjoyed a peaceful breeze sweeping in from the highlands, caressing our faces and cooling our necks.

We lingered a moment to quietly appreciate God's presence in these gentle gusts across the valley—a welcome and satisfying gift.

*   *   *

Jerusalem. To Jews, the name literally meant the foundation of peace. This was the City of David, the very capital where he reigned nearly a thousand years earlier, the site where he enshrined the most sacred ark of the covenant.

There was no holier place on earth.

Regardless from which direction the great city was approached or how many times a pilgrim had journeyed there, its magnificence never ceased to overwhelm. One could not help but wonder at the massive walls that surrounded and protected it. Whether from the Mount of Olives above, the Kidron Valley below, or from across the rolling hills out of Samaria from which we came, Jerusalem's size and splendor humbled even the most sophisticated Jew or gentile. It was especially dramatic approaching as we did from the north. The colossal temple columns dwarfed the thick perimeter walls, which themselves rose nearly ten men high.

Eager to enter the city, we headed toward one of the main gates at the corner of the northern wall. We joined a multitude of others completing their own journey to this holy destination, their excited chatter growing louder as we all moved closer to it.

My attention suddenly shifted to the edge of a sloping plateau outside the northwest border. Tall wooden beams protruded from the rocky mesa like branchless tree trunks or the first structural joists of a new building. But these pilings had not been driven into the ground to support future walls. They were there to support hanging human bodies. Before I could look away, I realized that this crest of barren hill was Golgotha, the Roman territorial execution site. With or without crosspieces affixed, those timbers were undoubtedly crucifixion posts.

On this particular day, the wood stood empty. But even when Rome wasn't executing its enemies, the beams were left in place to remind all who passed that the empire took extreme measures with extreme criminals. It did not swiftly execute traitors, rebels or murderers to simply rid them from society. A spear through the heart or saber across the neck would most efficiently carry out a sentence of capital punishment. Instead, for treasonous acts or crimes against the sovereignty, the Romans had mastered a terribly grotesque torture that only slowly resulted in death. Handed down from the barbaric Phoenicians and Assyrians, this painful and prolonged execution served as a spectacle to intimidate any who might challenge Roman rule. They would brutally nail a man to a wooden beam, then hoist him on display to hang in agony until he gradually suffocated under his own weight, his lungs eventually collapsing from trauma and exhaustion.

I forced my eyes to turn away as fierce foreboding quickened my breath. I tried focusing instead on the towering temple that stood tall just inside Jerusalem's walls—the exact site of Mount Zion. What profound irony! Jerusalem's temple, the largest and most sacred Jewish structure that housed the holiest of holy sanctuaries, was erected at the very spot upon Mount Zion where Abraham, in obedience to God's request, agreed to sacrifice his firstborn son. As Abraham drew his blade with tear-filled eyes, ready to slaughter his precious boy Isaac, my heavenly Father sent an angel to stop him. His willingness to unconditionally obey God's command had been noted and rewarded by his Creator. Sacrificing his son was not necessary. His committed will to do so had sufficed. To destroy sin and death forever, God now placed his own son here in the flesh—his own son to lead and to teach—to seal the new promise between God and man ... to be sacrificed atop Mount Zion so that Abraham's descendants, and all those of every lineage, culture and nation, might have the prospect of eternal life in his name.

I prayed silently to my Father ... Although I walk with breakable bones and fragile flesh, I know that we are one. My thoughts are your thoughts; my words are your words. Keep my mind clear and focused as I forever draw closer to that day when I will be called to fulfill the scriptures and stretch out my hands between heaven and earth.

I took a deep breath. To divert my attention from the impending horrors of Golgotha, I grabbed the shoulders of Peter and James and nodded passionately toward the imposing gate, which grew more massive with every step. We were now part of an even larger crowd anxious to enter the city for Passover.

*   *   *

It did not take long for word to spread. Jesus of Nazareth was in town. While Passover was the reason Jerusalem overflowed with pilgrims from Judea to Galilee to Phoenicia, it became clear that I was a major attraction. We did not intend to make a scene or cause commotion, but everywhere we went, crowds grew around us. The stories, reports and descriptions that had reached every province, gathered them to me, eager to see and hear for themselves.

They came hoping for verification.

They came longing for hope.

Of course, I was also very much under the hypercritical surveillance of many Pharisees and Sadducees, those who had come from afar, as well as those who called the holy city and its temple home. Within Jerusalem's walls, I could not speak, teach or heal without the Sanhedrin's vigilant scrutiny watching my every move. Although they could not stop me in my mission, their cynical and negative attitudes were quite discouraging. Soon after we arrived, I healed a poor man who had been blind from birth. My constant critics, having never given him a second glance while he begged daily on the temple steps, now descended on him like vultures. They interrogated him, his parents too, on the specifics of his interactions with me and how he had become healed. Despite standing before them outnumbered and browbeaten, he declared bravely from his heart that I must have been sent directly from God.

He was promptly expelled from the temple.

Upon hearing this, I refused to retreat to the back streets of the city or to the surrounding hills. They would not force me from my Father's house and from his people. And so I boldly took my message directly to the main temple courtyard where more than a thousand pilgrims packed the larger of two open-air quadrangles. I stood at its center with my apostles seated near me and looked out over the crowd. The temple priests and scribes paced about under the colonnade, fully disapproving of this situation but incapable of dispersing such a large gathering during holy season.

My focus remained on the faces that longed for my words. They were like sheep, yearning to hear their shepherd and be led to greener pastures.

What a perfect visual for this day.

"How many here know the difference between a true shepherd and a hired hand?" My voice echoed off the high wall separating us from the adjoining courtyard and temple. "It is quite simple! A hired hand does not own the sheep! When he sees a wolf coming, he abandons the sheep and runs! He flees because the sheep do not belong to him! It is not worth the risk to protect them!" I paused, building to the all-important parallel. "But the shepherd—he owns those sheep! They are his! He travels with them, watches over them and guides them through rough terrain to find fertile fields! When he calls to them, they instinctively follow because they know and trust his voice! They listen and follow wherever he leads! A good shepherd is willing to lay down his life for his sheep! He will care for them day and night—even if it means sacrificing himself!"

The stage was set. Using a context they all understood, I had established the framework for an apt analogy that would definitively explain myself to them. Their silent expressions professed an eagerness to hear more.

"I am the good shepherd! I know my sheep and they know me, just as the Father knows me and I know the Father!" I no longer regarded them as a gathered audience but moved my gaze directly to as many individual, captivated faces as possible. "Without hesitation I lay down my life for my sheep! No one takes my life from me, I offer it up of my own accord!"

Some of the religious hierarchy began advancing from the shadows of the portico and moving to the crowd's perimeter. They did not like where this was going.

Watching them circle the plaza, closing in like the predators that they were, did not intimidate me. On the contrary—I continued, even calling them out. "Those who do not enter the sheep's pen by way of the gate are thieves! The shepherd enters through the gate, and the sheep follow him because they know his voice! They will not follow a stranger; indeed they will run from a stranger's voice!"

The scribes started pushing their way annoyingly through the multitude.

"I am the good shepherd!" I called again. "I have other sheep from other fields, and I must gather them too, so there will be one flock with one shepherd!"

The stillness around me finally broke. My name shouted loudly, mostly in a praise-like cheer, some even crying, "Save us!" Other voices, however, lacked any accolade. One called out, "He is demon-possessed!"

A Pharisee who had shoved his way to the crowd's center shook his finger in my direction. "Why do you speak in symbolism and comparisons? If you are claiming to be the Messiah, tell us plainly!"

There were many direct answers I could have given, but his closed mind would never accept them. And it was not yet my time. My hour had not yet come. "Why tell you directly; would you believe?" I challenged over the ruckus. "My words and my works suffice! But you do not believe because you are not my sheep! My sheep listen to my voice! I know them and they follow me! No one will snatch them from me because my Father has given them to me!"

My decisive tone nearly silenced the air. I concluded my retort with an explicit and succinct claim to divine authority. "The Father and I are one!"

The crowd immediately erupted. Many threw their hands toward me, begging to be touched and shown the way to the Father. Others screamed, "Blasphemy!" and shook their fists.

One of the Sadducees elbowed some people out of the way and pushed closer. "You dare blaspheme on this sacred ground! You shall be stoned!"

The divided crowd argued and shouted as well. My apostles were quick to encircle me and swiftly move us toward the eastern gate—the nearest way out.

Two of the Sadducees reached our position and struggled to dislodge the arms that protected me. "Take him out and stone him!"

Such cowardice—instigating the mob to stone me. While the Romans usually looked the other way when Jews killed other Jews, especially for breaking religious laws, he knew it was technically illegal to put me to death without a Roman sentence. So he hoped he could incite my detractors enough to stone me outside the city walls without any individual clearly responsible.

He was only an arm's length away, but the emotional shouting in the square was deafening. I raised my voice over the din. "Tell me, for which of my deeds would you have me stoned?"

"For your words, not your deeds," he returned. "You are but a man, and yet have proclaimed to this whole crowd that you are God's equal!"

I struggled to keep balance while my apostles and others continued thrusting us toward the courtyard gate. "If you do not believe the Father and I are one because of what I say, then believe because of what I do! Believe in my actions so that you may come to understand that the Father is in me, and I am in the Father!"

His reply was all but drowned in a sea of contention as we pushed through the doorways onto Solomon's porch and the immeasurably spacious court of the gentiles. During any other week, we would have been no better off here, caught with nowhere to hide in such a flat, wide open area. But this was Passover week, and the hordes of people scattered across the plaza provided instant cover. We easily lost ourselves in the clusters of bodies moving in all directions.

The Sadducees and Pharisees would have to report back to the Sanhedrin that while I continued to aggravate and infuriate them by gathering greater numbers to myself, I somehow escaped their reach and control yet again … For now.

16

The Lamb of God

AS LARGE AND DEVELOPED as Jerusalem was, it was unable to provide food and shelter for the thousands of pilgrims descending upon the city during Passover. Those without personal connections or extra money for accommodations either camped outside the city walls or sought lodging in one of the nearby towns—Bethany to the east, Emmaus to the west or Bethlehem to the south.

Although there were some who still wanted to see me stoned and tossed into a shallow grave, others warmly welcomed us, offering a place to stay and even celebrate the Passover meal. Despite their generous offers, we left the holy city and headed east for the short walk to Bethany.

I was anxious to see my good friends Lazarus, Martha and Mary. I had known the three siblings nearly as long as I could remember. I first met them as a small boy while traveling to Jerusalem with my parents. Unable to find quarters within the city, we too had ventured over to Bethany. Hot and tired from our journey, we were grateful when a generous stranger invited us into his home for some water and food. It was there I met his children—Lazarus, who was just about my age, and his younger sisters, Martha and Mary. We hit it off immediately—playing games, trading stories, running through the surrounding hills, climbing trees and savoring the simplicity and freedom of childhood.

My parents also made good friends with the family, so Bethany became a traditional stop for us each year, spending a week or so with them at Passover.

During my teenage visits with Lazarus and his sisters, we especially enjoyed lying together on the hills above town just after sundown, talking under the stars, sharing our joys, challenges and dreams. Even then, they sensed I was destined to play a significant role in our futures. Their love and encouragement helped me immensely. As we developed into adulthood, however, their parents passed away and we saw each other less often. This made the times we did have together all the more special.

Now following the valley road toward the dwellings of Bethany that freckled the hillside, my excitement grew to see my dear friends. Lazarus and his sisters were active, leading members of the Essenes, unmarried and dedicated to the sick and impoverished in their area. They still lived in the same complex of houses from childhood.

I sent word we were coming and hoped that they were as thrilled as I at the prospect of seeing each other after such a long time, especially now that I was actually living the sacred vocation they had anticipated for me. I couldn't wait to introduce them to my apostles.

As we approached their residence, Martha noticed us from an open window and shouted my name. I smiled at the familiar voice. It had been too long. She and her sister scampered from the house and ran to me. Lazarus, who had been cutting wood around back, quickly caught up. When he reached me, I already had a sister under each arm. He grabbed my head and kissed my cheek.

"Jesus, I cannot believe it is finally you," he exclaimed, pretending to wipe some sweat from his eyes, but I could tell they were moist with tears. "You are all anyone talks about around here. We have missed you so."

I kissed the heads of Martha and Mary and nodded to my good friend. "You have been in my thoughts and prayers often. It is so good to see you again."

"How is your mother?" he asked.

"Doing well," I replied. "She sends her best, and promises to make the trip next season."

I then proudly turned to my full entourage. "Lazarus, Martha, Mary; I want you to meet my companions and followers … truly my brothers and sisters."

Without hesitation, they welcomed my disciples with open arms. We followed them into the large dwelling that I had come to know so well over many years, the one Lazarus still called home. They had cleared much of the main room in anticipation of our arrival, and it easily accommodated everyone. We spent a while catching up and reminiscing—recalling chapters from lives that seemed so distant, it was hard to believe we were discussing ourselves. The three of them then sat mesmerized as they listened to my disciples relate our amazing experiences over the last two years. For the most part, I simply sat and listened myself, quite impressed with how well they conveyed my message and gave witness to my works. More than simply recounting the details of memorable events, they emphasized their own personal insights and the inspirations gained from them.

Everyone was so engaged that before we knew it, late afternoon had arrived, and it was time to prepare the Passover meal. We gathered around and unwrapped the fresh lamb's meat slaughtered in the temple court that morning. Thousands of lambs, raised in the fields south of Jerusalem, were sacrificed atop a heavy stone altar in commemoration of our ancestors' exodus from Egypt. It had been the blood of the lambs that saved the Israelites from the angel of death as it prowled the ancient Egyptian city, laying waste and destroying all firstborn … but passing over those who obediently smeared the lamb's blood upon their door posts.

This blood wasn't just a mark of survival. It was a powerful symbol of freedom—God's promise to save them, sealed in blood.

Each year the lambs were slaughtered in the most holy communal area of Jerusalem's temple, accessible only to Jewish men, just steps away from the gigantic doors leading to the even more sacred and restricted main building. If this bloody ritual killing of so many lambs over such a short period of time were not such a significantly hallowed and religious tradition, it would have undoubtedly offended the sensibilities of many. Priests took shifts with the knives as men from far and wide brought their family's lambs forward to be sacrificed. The blood cascaded down from the altar, running in ripples across the stone floor and around people's feet. Rather than avoiding the blood, many welcomed contact with it. This strong symbol of God's continued relationship with his people gave them hope and strength to persevere in their own lives. This was their unblemished sacrifice to the Almighty—recalling, honoring and invoking his unbroken commitment to them.

While watching our lambs slaughtered that day, the prophecy of Isaiah came to mind—*He was led like a lamb to the slaughter*. God would soon establish a new covenant with mankind through a similar bloody sacrifice of a spotless victim. It would not be long now, perhaps another year, before he initiated this new relationship, not with one particular culture or nation, but with the world. And not through the blood of countless lambs.

Only one was needed. The son of God, truly the lamb of God, would be sacrificed for something so much greater than temporary, earthly freedom. This new and final sacrifice, sealed in God's own blood, would offer freedom from death ... the promise of everlasting life ... binding for eternity.

God had created mankind in his own image, bestowing the ultimate gift of a free will upon every soul, yet requiring obedience, humble hearts and acts of love toward one another in return. Instead, human weakness and imprudence soon gave way to self-love, pride, malice and disobedience. Try as they might at times to return to God, sin had overwhelmed them. A troubled, misguided race had lost itself too deeply to find a way back to its Creator.

This human impasse was why I had come into the world, why the Word spoke through flesh, blood and bone—to reconcile these lost children to their Father—to become a lamb that would rescue its flock. Showing them how to live was indeed part of my mission, but I had ultimately come to withstand the most destructive evil hell could bring against me. And instead of using divine omnipotence to fight it, I was to show true triumph by expressing love to the end. Although I shared full supremacy with my heavenly Father and our Spirit, my mission was to demonstrate absolute obedience to the Father through the strength of the Spirit. I had been called to display unconditional love when faced with utter hatred—to do for mankind what mankind could not do for itself ... make amends with God.

All souls would return to God through me.

The aroma of roasting lamb now filled the house as I spoke on the power of love. Many of my apostles moved about, assisting where they could in preparation for the feast, but Lazarus' sister Mary sat steadfast beside me. She listened intently, riveted to my words, focused as if no one else was in the room. I could barely finish answering one of her questions when two more came forth. She didn't seem to care what time it was or where she was 'supposed' to be. Right now, the surrounding activities could not distract her—there was only me. I remembered when we were young, how she had so revered both me and her older brother, as if we knew all there was to know and could accomplish anything. Nothing seemed to have changed. She didn't debate my words or challenge my ideas. She took everything to heart, open and eager to learn.

Suddenly through all the hubbub, Martha hurried past carrying a basket of unleavened bread. Upon seeing her sister sitting beside me oblivious to anything else, she stopped abruptly and hovered right behind my stool. I sensed her eyes boring over me at Mary.

I swiveled around and smiled. "Hi, Martha."

She wiped some perspiration from her brow and sighed. "Lord, does it matter that my sister has left me to do the work preparing for all these people? Tell her to chip in and do her part."

I calmly stood and gently took the basket from her hands, setting it on a shelf beside us. I broke a small piece of bread from one of the flat loaves and ripped it in two. Placing one in my mouth, I brought the other tenderly to Martha's lips. She reluctantly took it, and as she chewed, seemed to unwind just a bit.

I again smiled affectionately and rubbed her weary arms. "Martha, Martha ... you are so very good at doing so very much. But too many relatively small things have you worried and troubled. Only one activity is truly necessary today. Mary has chosen that, and I cannot take it away from her."

Martha eyed her sister somewhat enviously—the weight of her self-imposed role as hostess still distressing her.

"Martha," I said to bring her focus back to me, "what remains to be done?"

She paused a moment to collect her thoughts. "Lazarus is already cutting the meat, and I haven't yet prepared the apples. There is wine to pour and this bread to distribute."

James and Mary Magdala were near, so I motioned them over. "Mary, there are apples to cut in the other room, a large bushel. Could you and some of the others see to that task? And James, take this bread, divide it among the places and be sure all cups are filled with wine."

"Of course," replied Mary.

"Right away, Lord," nodded James.

I bowed in thanks and appreciation.

As they turned to set upon their tasks, I returned my attention to Martha who was quite bewildered at how efficiently her chores had been delegated. "You see," I said, gesturing to the bread carried off, "love conquers all, even the mundane burdens of everyday life."

A faint smile finally found its way to her lips.

"Now come," I persuaded and indicated a spot next to her sister. "Dinner will be ready soon. Join Mary here and enjoy some quality time with me."

I was pleased Martha was able to do so—to rest a little, mellow out and feel relaxed alongside me. While these times in which we lived were very strenuous and challenging indeed, those in this house could not help but take for granted the rarest of wonders and opportunities they possessed over all other generations. They had the Word made flesh in their very midst. If they truly grasped the importance and magnitude of this reality, all else would become instantly irrelevant. Young Mary, although asking many questions, somehow got that. I was all that mattered to her.

I hoped in my heart her example would be remembered.

*   *   *

It was our last day in Jerusalem. In the same way that disparate throngs had converged upon the city just days before, an equally pressing exodus now clogged the roads to leave. Thankfully, it seemed to be progressing peacefully. The melding of so many oppressed people under a pagan empire's tyrannical rule naturally increased the chance of civil disturbance. Roman authorities always became nervous whenever large, fervent crowds from conquered lands gathered together in one place. Despite Roman soldiers clearly having the advantage of weapons and armor, it was always unsettling for them to be so despised by potentially rebellious peasants rallying in this distant outpost of their occupied territories. During Passover, legions of soldiers were deployed from other provinces to project an intimidating show of force. Rome unhesitatingly condemned and crucified anyone inciting riot or rebellion, but certainly preferred preventing such extreme necessity. Even a failed insurgency often inflamed others to resist and dare to rise up as well.

This morning, however, seemed very untroubled—a mild and tranquil start to the day. My apostles and I decided to hang back and allow the congested routes to clear a bit before heading out of the city ourselves. We relaxed in the temple's large court of the gentiles, sitting up against the perimeter wall. Pilgrims still traversed the sprawling plaza, but the teeming bustle that packed this area in recent days had now departed. I closed my eyes and relished a few moments of peace. The sun was warm but not hot. The stones supporting our backs were still cool from the night air, and the impressive temple edifice towered directly before us across a mosaic sea of perfect masonry. I could not think of a better place to rest before beginning our journey north toward Galilee.

With my eyes gently shut, I half listened to my apostles talking quietly with each other, barely audible over the soft drone of voices mingling throughout the vast temple grounds. I didn't open my eyes until hearing Matthew's whisper beside me.

"Oh no, here they come again," he muttered.

This got my attention. Ever since our narrow escape several days ago, we were all on edge anywhere near the temple compound. I immediately saw the cause of Matthew's concern. A group of about twenty men, led by a handful of robed Pharisees, hurried across the square in our direction.

We remained seated and watched as one of them yanked a woman forward. Although clearly forced against her will, she did not resist. They obviously had a specific agenda for her with me, dragging her in my direction and knowing exactly where I was. How many temple scouts could the Sanhedrin have possibly assigned to patrol the labyrinth of buildings, chambers and courtyards to determine and report my whereabouts? Undoubtedly quite a few.

Thomas rocked forward and readied himself to stand. "We're sitting ducks against this wall, Lord."

I eased him back with a consoling gesture. "I do not believe they are coming to do us physical harm. At least not before trying to trap me in one of their petty ploys."

"It's too late to evade them now," said Peter. "Best to stay calm and ride this out."

We kept seated along the wall and allowed the Pharisees and their entourage to approach. Since I was on the end, they shoved the woman down next to me, so roughly she nearly hit the wall as she collapsed. Mary Magdala and Joanna gasped at the contempt with which they treated her.

I looked up at the brood before me with cold consternation.

"Adultery!" the lead Pharisee shouted, pointing to the crumpled form of the woman beside me.

Her body shook and crouched as close to the wall as she could, close enough to become part of it. She kept her head low and avoided all eyes, fear and shame balling her into a fetal position.

"Why do you bring her to me?" I asked the Pharisee.

"Because you claim to come from God, do you not, rabbi?" he disdained. "This woman was caught in the very act of committing adultery. According to our Law, such a sin is punishable by stoning."

I stared at him straight-faced, as if waiting for a point.

I didn't have to wait long. "So we bring her to you, oh wise shepherd. Tell us … should we stone her, as it is written … or not?"

For a moment I contemplated inquiring where the man might be if this woman had been caught committing adultery, as they claimed. But it wasn't worth it. Their motive was not to seek any kind of justice or atonement for sin. I had indeed sensed their motives from across the square. This was nothing more than a conniving trick to lure me into self-incrimination, regardless of my answer. If I advise them to leave her alone, I would disobey their Law—another indictment against me for heresy. Tell them to carry out the traditional sentence, and as a Jew, I would be ordering an execution within a city under Roman rule. That wouldn't do well for me either.

I lowered my head. A verse of Jeremiah came to mind. Based on its theme, I traced a few words with my finger into the gritty, sand-strewn ashlar floor—*Those who turn away from the Lord will be written in dust.*

"Do not avoid the issue!" a Pharisee barked at my preoccupation.

"Give us an answer!" shouted another. "Should this woman be condemned or not?"

I refused to feel pressured by these vipers, but I also wanted them dealt with appropriately. I leisurely lifted my head and straightened my back against the wall as if casually stretching in the morning light. My eyes finally reached the rigid stares of my duplicitous challengers. They anxiously waited, ready to vilify anything I might say.

I pensively tugged at my beard and delivered my judgement softly, though loud enough for them all to hear. "She has sinned indeed ... Therefore, it seems appropriate that whoever has *never* sinned, should cast the first stone at her."

I did not wait for their reaction but immediately returned my gaze to the ground and continued tracing Jeremiah with my finger into the temple floor—*All who forsake the Lord will be put to shame.*

Despite the busy buzz across the massive courtyard, the silence in our small corner of it was palpable. I did not raise my head again. I had said all I intended, or needed to say.

After several seemingly long moments, a set of footsteps turned and begrudgingly walked away. Then another followed. Then others. Someone's sandal angrily kicked dust in my direction before departing. Mutterings and expletives were sworn under breath.

Soon all was quiet again.

Had they all gone?

I tentatively raised my eyes. No one was there. I glanced at my apostles. Peter and Matthew nodded with triumphant grins.

I turned to my right. The woman was now sitting up and staring off into the square, still visibly shaken but greatly relieved her accusers had disappeared. She felt my eyes upon her and gradually looked over. She was clearly at a loss for words, so very thankful, but also embarrassed and distraught that her wrongdoing had caused such a public commotion.

"Where have they all gone?" I asked—a subtle, comforting reminder that she was not alone in sin. "Is there no one left to condemn you?"

Her soft voice implied penitence. "No one, sir."

I reached out and softly stroked her hair. "Then I do not condemn you either. Go ... and sin no more."

She held her eyes to mine, marveling that a stranger, of whom the Pharisees were undeniably jealous, could show such compassionate clemency. She made the correct conclusion in her heart. "You ... you are Jesus. The Nazarene."

She needed no reply to confirm her words. She had not asked a question.

Her head bowed, and even against the dull hum of activity around us, I heard her whisper, "Thank you, my Lord."

Collecting herself as best she could, she stood and began slowly walking away. Then, as if sudden thoughts stirred within her, as if abrupt reality opened her mind, she quickened her pace. Her walk turned to a jog, then accelerated to an all-out sprint, nearly tripping over her garment. It was not a haphazard dash; she was not fleeing from anything, or anyone. She was hurrying toward a particular goal—a definite destination. And she couldn't get there fast enough.

Peter watched her bolt through the crowd and glanced at me with perplexity. "What is *she* late for all of a sudden?"

I did not respond. My eyes followed her as she disappeared near the western gates, and I thanked my heavenly Father for placing the answer within my heart.

A contrite wife was running back to her husband.

17

Sheep Among Wolves

THIS NIGHT SKY wasn't just any sky. The moon, the stars, the breeze that moved scattered clouds off the water—it all hinted of home. Finally back in Capernaum, I sat fully relaxed on my small rooftop, grateful there was nowhere to travel in the morning. Star gazing on this night was especially pleasant after such a long journey, appreciating again the familiar comforts around me.

I was alone for the moment but wouldn't be for long. I had asked my apostles, just the twelve, to meet me here shortly. Having mentioned something exciting to discuss, a mission of sorts, I knew they wouldn't be late. It was time for them to put their knowledge into practice—to develop their skills at proclaiming the good news—to preach and heal in my name ... without me by their sides.

I came to realize more each day that while I was indeed the Alpha and the Omega, my days upon this earth were numbered. Those entrusted with my message must carry and deliver it to others, planting the life-giving seeds that would grow throughout the world for all generations.

It was time to challenge my ambassadors. They were ready. I knew they were. Following wherever I went and dedicating their

lives to my mission of salvation was no easy task. They were faithful, fully committed, seasoned disciples with passionate hearts and
emboldened spirits. They were well prepared—ready to share with
others their relationship with me in their own way—empowered to
work wonders in my name.

I suddenly heard my name. "Jesus! Lord!"

I moved to the edge and peered over. Peter, Andrew, James and
John were below. Farther down the path, the others approached as
well.

"The door is open," I called and motioned them to join me.

They entered my modest dwelling, and even with oil lamps to
guide their steps, I heard them bumping into a bench, some pottery
and each other. I chuckled like a child as I listened to my comrades
stumble their way up. The small hatch was already open, and Peter's
head was the first to appear. His face, lit dimly by a small lamp,
brightened further upon seeing me.

Soon they were all present and seated. Several sat cross-legged
or leaned against one another, and a few rested along the roof's mud-
brick border. A half dozen lamps radiated warm light upon their
hopeful faces. They knew I had something of importance to tell
them, and they were eager to hear it.

"My dear brothers," I began earnestly, "I cannot express how
pleased and gratified I am to have shared so much with you for so
long. You have learned well, and while there is still much to learn,
I could not be prouder of how far you have come. You call me
teacher, and rightly so, but I tell you that every apprentice when fully
trained will be equal to his teacher."

Peter regarded the faces around him before speaking on all their
behalf. "You are more than our teacher, Lord. You are Master and
Savior. We will follow you anywhere."

I smiled, staring for a moment into one of the small flames before raising my eyes again. "You have followed me well, but for the
next several weeks, I do not want you to follow. I want you to lead.

You are ready to guide others."

Their excited expressions confirmed my decision.

"I want you to go forth throughout Galilee," I said. "Many already recognize you as my disciples. Enter the surrounding towns and proclaim this message—*the kingdom of heaven is at hand*. In my name, I give you power to heal the sick and give sight to the blind. Lay hands on the lame so that they may walk. Drive out demons by your very command, for you now have authority over them."

I noticed some trembling fingers and eyes moistening with emotion.

My own eyes conveyed unwavering confidence in them. "I am sending you out like sheep among wolves, so be as shrewd as snakes and as innocent as doves. What I have told you in the dark, I want you to speak in the daylight. What I have confided to you in private, shout from the rooftops."

"Can we possibly do this without you, Lord?" asked Philip with nervous elation.

"Teach and heal in my name, Philip, and you *will* be doing it with me. That I promise you all." My plan of action for them was precise. "Do not concern yourselves with things most would worry about. Take nothing for the journey—no bread, no money—only the clothes on your back. Find people who will give you shelter and stay with them until you leave each town."

"What about opposition?" Thomas expressed softly. "We are bound to meet resistance."

I nodded definitively, acknowledging the inevitable. "That you shall. There will always be those who hate you in this world, but take heart; they have hated me first."

A few apprehensive grins broke through their hesitancy.

"If a village does not accept you, then leave that place and shake its dust from your sandals as testimony against them." I wanted to focus more on the positive, so I continued, "Those who do welcome you also welcome me, and by welcoming me, they welcome the one who sent me. Even if someone gives you a simple drink of water because you are my disciples, they will not be forgotten in heaven."

John was humble enough to verbalize his true sentiments, "I can hardly contain my excitement, and yet I'm petrified."

The others nodded, verifying their own mixed feelings.

"Do not be afraid," I smiled. "You carry in your hearts the words of everlasting life. Never fear those who can harm the body but cannot damage the soul."

This encouragement helped, but I sought to invigorate their spirits even more. I leaned forward and stretched my arm over the amber glow of the lamps. "Take my hand, all of you."

They shuffled closer, and one by one, reached in to form a web of arms dangling over the light. We were now huddled together, hand over hand.

I spoke just above a whisper. "Think back, each of you. Think back just a few years to your former lives." My eyebrows lifted with emotion. "Now look at yourselves. You are embarking on the most important mission for mankind—to spread the word of God to his chosen people and work wonders in my name." I glanced over at my rock. "Peter, remember the day we met. I told you to follow me and you would no longer be a fisherman, but a fisher of men."

A tear rolled down his cheek. "I remember, Lord."

"Now that promise comes to fruition. For all of you." I moved my eyes to each of them and placed my other hand on top of the pile, squeezing them firmly. "Go ... have a bountiful catch. Gather my Father's people."

*   *   *

It was a long month or so. My apostles travelled in pairs throughout Galilee. I kept mostly to the secluded hills north of Capernaum, praying and preparing myself for what lay ahead. I often spent the entire night in the wild, feeling closer to my Father from the hilltops and fields under the stars. Some evenings I ventured back into town and made my way to the docks where news usually arrived first. Numerous details reached my ears of healings in Tiberias, Sephoris, Bethsaida and others. I couldn't help but smile. Our Spirit was working powerfully with my comrades.

While they did not plan any specific itineraries, the twelve agreed to meet in Tiberias on the evening of the following full moon. They would sail back together to Capernaum where I would meet them.

The morning of their return, I could not sleep. Although the sun had yet to rise, I was much too anxious to see them and hear their stories than to allow myself decent rest. I finally gave up and walked down to the main pier. It was still dark, and the wind was picking up considerably. I pulled my mantle over my head. The full moon had begun to set, and its glow became muted, obscured behind thick, threatening clouds to the southwest—the direction from which my apostles would arrive. With such strong gusts, I figured they were making good time on the water. Unless of course the weather was worse farther out and they had lowered their sails.

I was restless. I wanted to see them. My Father in heaven placed a startling notion into my mind that thoroughly surprised me. I glanced up toward the night sky. "Really?" I questioned aloud.

Another stiff breeze blew the mantle from my head. I closed my eyes and concentrated on my Father's presence. He seemed to be coaxing me forward. Reminding myself never to resist his guidance, I opened my eyes and fervently walked to the end of the long jetty, squinting hard at the black horizon.

There it was … a boat. I didn't have to wonder whose. I tentatively checked behind me to make sure the wharf remained deserted. Aside from a scattering of early-bird gulls, the docks and their few moored vessels were empty. Again I looked to the heavens. Was my Father really suggesting the implausible?

His indisputable validation swelled within my divine heart.

I stepped forward off the pier.

Never had I done anything quite so seemingly senseless, and yet I stepped out with assured confidence. I trusted my heavenly Father so completely, I did not brace for the wet chill of water. I dropped solidly upon the sea. Not in it, or beneath its surface ... but on top of it. I stood on the water, feeling the windswept waves breaking over my feet.

While the depth here easily measured at least a man's height, my ankles were hardly getting wet. I glanced back at the lightless, barren docks before returning my attention to the distant boat bobbing on the gloomy horizon. My feet miraculously stood on the surface of the surf, and I smiled to the heavens in wondrous awe at the love and power that flowed between me and my Father.

I started walking. Away from the pier and out into open water I strolled upon the Sea of Galilee. My sandals sloshed along as if through large puddles rather than over a lake of ever-increasing depth. The wind continued to strengthen, spraying water at my legs. I reached down and folded the ends of my robe into the sash around my waist. I did not slow my pace but continued across the currents toward my apostles' boat which grew bigger as the intervening distance became less and less.

It was indeed daunting to experience the unforgiving sea like this—alone and on foot, with predawn mists obscuring the horizon and ominous black clouds rolling in. But I had unwavering faith in my Father and his powerful care for me.

Closing in on the ship, I observed figures moving about on deck. My excitement grew. Before I could imagine how my arrival in this manner might affect my friends, I heard one of them scream in fright, "A ghost! A ghost is on the water!"

The others cried out in terror and pointed in my direction.

"Brothers, do not be afraid!" I shouted through the wind. "It is only I!"

They instantly recognized my voice, sucking back their fear and silencing their cries.

I understood they could not see my face in the dark at this distance, so I continued toward them.

"If it is you, Lord," called Peter over the discord of air and sea, "tell me to come to you!"

I loudly acknowledged my hearty and spirited rock, "Come!"

The wind was too strong to hear voices onboard, but I could see them cautioning their friend and mentor. Although convinced it was really me beckoning off their bow, going overboard into the pitch-black swells of the sea still seemed insanely treacherous. But Peter was determined. He cinched the lower fringes of his garments into his belt and swung over the side. Andrew and James held him steady by the elbows, prepared to hoist him back if he started going under. As his sandals hit the turbulent surface, he teetered, but confidently shook loose the hands holding him against the boat. His eyes locked on me, watching me take a few steps closer. He did not sink, but stood atop the waves as if upon the sturdiest floorboards.

"Ha-Ha!" he cried in jubilation and raised his hands as if to say *Look at me, Lord.*

I waved him forward. "Come!"

Like a toddler focused on a parent while attempting first steps, Peter kept his arms outstretched and took a few tentative strides through the swirls and surges breaking at his legs. "I'm—I'm doing it!" he exclaimed, knees wobbling apprehensively as he staggered forward.

And like a parent who beams with pride at those very first steps, I stopped and encouraged his progress with voice and gesture.

He had almost reached me when a sudden gale whipped the sea into our faces, briefly shutting our eyes. Peter frantically wiped his face and glanced back at the churning chaos between him and the boat. He then looked down to where his feet should have been. They had sunk well below the surface. Focused now on his sudden failure to do the impossible, he forgot about me and panicked. He desperately lifted each foot above the waves, only to sink further into the maelstrom. The whitecaps now broke about his waist.

He let out a fearful cry and finally returned his gaze to me. "Lord, save me!"

He fought to escape the angry water as if from quicksand and lunged his hand toward me. I instantly grabbed it and pulled him up. His fingers gripped mine for dear life.

I tightly held his other arm to steady him. "Why did you doubt, Peter?" I asked over the wind's barrage.

He stared at me in a stunned daze, just glad to be safe within my arms. Water dripped from his beard as he stammered, "I'm sorry, Lord. I lost sight of you."

"You took your eyes off me when the wind picked up," I corrected. "If you had stayed focused on me, you wouldn't have sunk, no matter how bad the storm!"

He understood and nodded, the fear gone from his eyes. We stood toe to toe upon the water a few more moments before I locked elbows with him and motioned back to the boat. "Shall we?"

Admitting the obvious, he agreed. "I'm ready!"

Together, we marched through the wind-whipped water toward the waiting arms of our brothers. They helped Peter over the side, and as they pulled me up as well, I looked to the sky and silently requested a divine favor. Before my feet hit the deck, my appeal was granted. The wind abated and peace immediately descended upon the lake—sea and sky once again harmoniously at ease with each other.

Everyone recognized how the gathering storm was suddenly suppressed, yet none of them seemed astonished or even surprised. Their Master had come to them walking upon the water after they themselves had performed miracles all across Galilee simply by evoking his name. There was no uncertainty or doubt among them— no skepticism to confuse their minds.

The misty fog began evaporating from the eastern sky, and dawn's smoldering red glow slowly pushed up behind the black silhouette of distant hills.

I wondered if my apostles noticed the same joy in my eyes that now filled theirs.

"Welcome back," I simply said. "I didn't plan on startling you all so. I just couldn't wait to see you."

My arms opened to gladly receive them back.

I don't think I had ever been embraced so warmly.

*   *   *

With the boat finally secured to its berth, my apostles hurriedly disembarked, longing for the familiar streets of Capernaum, fresh food from the market and a good cleansing of clothes and body. Despite the murky dawn, the morning steadily brightened and cleared. I made my way along the stone wall that hugged the shore, in no particular rush, allowing the day to infuse me with the warmth and zest unique to a coastal sunrise.

I suddenly heard a familiar voice behind me.

"Master."

My head turned.

"Judas," I welcomed with a smile, "why are you not seeking a good breakfast with the others?"

"I will eat shortly, Lord," he said. "But my appetite lies elsewhere this morning."

I perceived the intensity on his brow, so I stopped and motioned to a spot along the wall where we could talk. "Tell me, what is on your mind?"

He did a cursory check of our surroundings to make sure we were alone, albeit the many people passing. Now I was truly intrigued.

"Master," he began with a low, confiding voice, "I cannot begin to describe how the last several weeks have affected me. Witnessing what can be accomplished by the very breath of your name has given me such hope and promise for the future of Israel."

"What is your hope for Israel?" I inquired.

He hesitated, making sure I wasn't asking one of my frequently leading and loaded questions. "Autonomy ... Freedom."

While I certainly agreed that human nature should always long for true liberty, motivations and expectations mattered most, so I asked another short question. "Freedom from what?"

"From Rome, of course," he replied, eyes excited with anticipation. "We know you are the one, Jesus—the Messiah—the king who will unite the nations and lead Israel out of bondage."

I turned my face to the sea and considered how best to convey approval of his hunger but not the ultimate priority of his specific goal. "Yes, I have come to liberate Israel, and the gentiles too. But, Judas, my power and glory differ substantially from the world's."

He didn't seem to hear my words or consider their importance and quickly continued, "Never have I seen so many willing to rise up and follow you, to sacrifice all. We are eyewitnesses to how the sea and sky, even life and death, obey your will. It is so very clear that Israel's future rests upon your authority." He paused to search my eyes before asking, "When, Lord, when will you come into your kingdom?"

I lowered my head, suddenly struck by such an aright question based on such wrong assumptions. "Soon," I simply answered.

A sigh of relief escaped his lips as he brushed back the hair from his face. "That is good to hear. I know I don't have to tell you that there are many prepared to advance on Jerusalem with you. I have heard of a man named Barabbas who plans rebellion against Rome. He's a fool to challenge them with a haphazard following. Only you can lead us to a peaceful liberation, one without shedding so much of our people's blood."

He was talking too fast for his own sense to keep up. I mellowed him with a gentle hand on his shoulder. "Judas ... you are a well-educated man with an undeniable heart for his country. I tell you, yes, I am indeed a rebel, but I have not come to lead that kind of rebellion."

His eyes probed mine with a tinge of disappointment. "But you are the Messiah. Our future king."

"No conqueror or political leader remains in power here forever," I said. "Rulers and their realms have come and gone since the dawn of man, and will continue to do so. I have come to fulfill the Law once and for all—to set mankind free from spiritual chains forever."

He turned his face seaward and shook his head tumultuously. He then calmly looked back to me and spoke hardly above a whisper. "Herod seeks you out, Master."

I snickered through my nose. "Not to hear my voice, I can assure you. He, like the Sanhedrin, are only concerned with signs and symbols that can be twisted to justify themselves."

"But we cannot deny the fact that both seek your destruction ... and ours."

I languidly nodded. "Their foolish quest for illusory, momentary dominance has blinded them. Their concept of power is not based on love, and therefore is doomed, no matter whom they eliminate from this world."

"So then what's next?" He turned to me in earnest. "Where do we go from here?"

As I always do when met with discernable angst, I smiled to allay his fear. "He who ponders the past and worries about the future forgets who and where he is."

He remained silent, digesting my words.

"You, Judas, are my friend ... here ... in the present ... with me. Disturbing yourself with fantasies of future events will only bring stress and distraction from the most important here and now."

His head sank again. "Keeping tomorrow from my mind is difficult, Lord."

I nodded and gave him a nudge. "Don't I know it."

We regarded each other a few moments, each trying to figure the other out. I then squinted at the sun's position. "The best figs and dates will be gone from the market soon. Get some food. Regain your strength. Take the day to unwind and relax a little. You deserve it."

He grabbed the back of my neck and held it tenderly. "You know how much I love you, Lord. There's just so much I don't understand."

"If you love me, Judas, trust me."

He reaffirmed his loyalty with a bow and a smile. He then stepped back, turned and headed toward town.

As I watched him go, something deeply troubled me, and I wasn't sure why. I looked out over the water, trying to identify this sudden, visceral despondency within me. I sought my heavenly Father for anything that might aid my awareness of how best to do his will, which is to say, *I prayed.* My faithful searching suddenly discovered my own divine insights—*do not fish for the future.* Continue with the mission at hand. Accept the holy reality of the here and now. Specific life mysteries will unfold themselves in due course. Acceptance with thanks and praise suffices.

Uncertainty, however, naturally provoked fear, another significant human weakness with which I had to cope. Each day presented a labyrinth of unknowns that tested the trust and courage of every person, and most assuredly of me as well.

I thanked my Father, realizing that his care for me included my ignorance to certain details and particulars, not to confuse or distress, but to protect me. I knew a time was coming when I would need to completely submit myself to the evils of evil men. But the sufferings of that day must not corrupt and destroy today.

Tomorrow's obscurity was a welcome veil for my human mind.

18

The Bread of Life

THE SYNAGOGUE IN CAPERNAUM wasn't big enough for Sabbath crowds anymore. Jews from across the region gathered to hear me teach, so I stood on the long porch outside the main entrance. The multitude poured out before me—expectant groups clustered together along the steps and spilling down into the street, clogging any passage in either direction. My apostles positioned themselves close beside me as usual. Also as expected, Pharisees from throughout Galilee infiltrated the crowd. Nicodemus was there too, a secret follower of mine now, though he remained one of the local scribes in Capernaum.

His fellow Pharisees predictably asked shallow questions to challenge me on scripture and their sacred Law, but Nicodemus inquired honestly from his heart, speaking for the common people around him. "Teacher, what is the will of God for us?" he called from the veranda's corner step. "What does he want of us?"

I acknowledged him with a sincere nod before addressing the crowd. "God wants simply this—believe in the one he sent!"

Immediately another Pharisee challenged me. "We are all aware of your mighty works, rabbi! But what sign can you give so that we may see and believe you are from God? Moses provided his people with bread that came down from heaven!"

Indeed, a beautiful passage, I thought—when all hope is lost, hope in divine providence.

It gave me pause. With this example of manna from heaven and bread's symbolic link to life now inadvertently in their minds, had the time come to announce the perpetual gift I was preparing for the world? I knew beyond any doubt that no one, not even my own dear apostles, would understand this impending legacy from words alone. But this confrontational challenge had reminded everyone here of the heavenly bread my Father freely showered on their ancestors.

When would a better opportunity occur?

"I tell you the truth," I declared loudly, "it is not Moses, but my Father who gives you the true bread from heaven! God's bread gives life to the world!"

Someone shouted from the base of the steps, "Give us this bread, Jesus!"

There was no holding it in. "I am the bread of life! Whoever comes to me will never go hungry, and whoever believes in me will never be thirsty! I have come down from heaven to do the will of the one who sent me! And my Father's will is that everyone who looks for the son and believes in him shall have eternal life, and will be raised up on the last day!"

One of the Pharisees objected, projecting his voice to the crowd while addressing me. "Do not try to fool us, Jesus of Nazareth, son of Joseph the carpenter! We know where you are from! How can you claim to have come down from heaven?"

I briefly glanced at him before directing my reply to the people. "I say again, so hear me well; I am the bread of life! Your ancestors ate manna in the desert, and yet they died! But those who eat the true bread of life will never die! I am the living bread that comes down from heaven! This bread is my flesh, which I give for the life of the world!"

Not surprisingly, an uproar of contention erupted from the congregation and grew in turbulent waves, but I could only discern the exclamations from those closest to me.

"What is he talking about?"

"How can he give us his flesh to eat?"

"Is this another one of his complicated parables?"

Neither parable nor figure of speech; my words literally described God's perfect proposition for people to trust him enough to partake of their savior. Despite the intensifying turmoil of the confounded mob, I emphasized the specifics of this gift. "Listen to me and mark my words; unless you eat the flesh of the Son of Man and drink his blood, you have no life in you! For my flesh is real food and my blood is real drink! Whoever eats my flesh and drinks my blood remains in me, and I in them!"

Shock and confusion intensified. No one in the crowd remained silent. Most shared their consternation loudly with each other, some unleashing their astonishment directly at me.

"Have you lost your mind, Jesus?"

"You can't mean what you say, teacher!"

A Pharisee pointed at me and bellowed, "Do you all hear this? This so-called prophet tells us to eat his flesh! Are the sons and daughters of Abraham cannibals?!"

I glanced over at Nicodemus who tried mustering a supportive expression despite his own incredulity. He then bowed his head and slipped down the far end of the steps.

Many of the people also began leaving, shaking their heads and waving their hands, as if they'd finally had enough.

I could have wept at their departure, but I was in no way sorry I said it. I knew they were not prepared to absorb and accept my words, but it needed to be exclaimed as testimony to future events, to validate the offering my Father and I were prepared to hand down to future generations.

I turned and walked into the empty synagogue. There were no

column torches or lamps burning. The only light to guide my steps filtered downward through side-alcove windows, casting hazy rays between the limestone pillars. I sauntered through the main chamber while listening to the gradually quieting commotion outside. My virtually inaudible footsteps and shallow breathing somehow echoed distinctly in my head, accentuating my solitude.

Aware of the surrounding silence, I suddenly felt the presence of others.

I glanced behind me, startled to see all twelve of my apostles quietly approaching. They stopped as I turned to face them. Huddled there in the dust-speckled light, they sought the only leader they had come to trust. Undeterred by their own confusion and perplexity, they were still with me.

I nodded in the direction of the door and softly asked, "Do any of you wish to leave me now too?"

They remained stunned for a moment but one-by-one shook their heads.

Peter spoke, "To whom would we go, Lord? You have the words of everlasting life. Even if those words puzzle us sometimes."

I walked over and placed my hands on his and Bartholomew's shoulders, addressing them all. "It's okay to be puzzled. You're not meant to understand everything now. Have patience. It will not be long before you gain true wisdom concerning these paradoxes."

John's face looked as sincere as I had ever seen and his words just as devout. "We are prepared to go with you anywhere, Lord, whether we understand or not."

His loyalty sang to my heart, but his innocent naiveté also slightly stung. I stared off into the synagogue's somber dark recesses, wrestling with my emotions.

"A time is coming," I murmured, "when you will look for me but will not find me. For where I am going you cannot come."

"Where are you going, Lord?" asked James, following my eyes into the shadows.

I slowly returned my attention to them, and although still some-what distraught, I responded, "Do not let your hearts be troubled. While you cannot immediately go where I am going, you know the way to where I will go."

Thomas eagerly sought clarification. "We don't know where you are going; how can we know the way?"

"I am the way, the truth and the life," I replied definitively. "No one comes to the Father except through me. If you know me, you know my Father as well. You know him and have seen him."

Philip grabbed my arm like a child longing for something. "Show us the Father, Lord. That will be enough for us."

I smiled and tried breaking their one-dimensional thinking by placing my forefinger and thumb together in front of my face. "Listen to my words, Philip—all of you. Anyone who has seen and believes in me, has seen and believes in the Father. I am in the Father, and the Father is in me."

They considered intently this divine revelation in silence and gradually understood my meaning. Their renewed expressions no longer simply reflected respect for a holy visionary or even deference to a sacred emissary sent from the Almighty. They now regarded me with all the wonder and amazement of suddenly staring directly at the Almighty himself. Simon the Zealot even reached out and touched my cheek, running his fingers down my beard, fulfilling an abrupt urge to literally touch the face of God.

What a profound moment—this perfect connection between me and my faithful friends. I knew that someday all of creation would look upon me with reverence, but I also realized that the hatred of selfish men would first hide and disfigure my peaceful, caring countenance. The awareness of my divinity would shatter, and my sheep would scatter. All would seem lost—ruined—*God's mission foiled.*

Which is why I so passionately proclaimed my flesh as the bread come down from heaven. This very flesh upon my face they now cherished, I would soon offer up to be beaten and spit upon. I would allow it torn from my back and pierced with iron spikes. My human body and precious blood were indeed sent from heaven to rescue the world—to suffer and die as a ransom for all—then to revitalize back as a sign of enduring hope. I shall gather the nations with my body, as my body. *God's mission triumphant.*

*   *   *

The next few weeks I chose to teach in the hills. Those who flocked to me there were more interested in learning than protesting. My full entourage, including Mary Magdala and the other women, joined me as I headed northwest of Capernaum, seeking the Galilean highlands to escape the incessant harassment of the Pharisees and Sadducees. And escape we did, at least for a while. Reports also reached us that Herod continued his search for me—an over-superstitious ruler intrigued by any claim of godly power.

Our travels, however, did not keep the crowds away. They knew and understood God's *real* power to heal. Despite the ever-spreading accounts of my recent controversial assertions, they came from everywhere to see and hear for themselves. We kept to no specific agenda or schedule and detoured through several new villages and territories before making it back to Capernaum.

A large gathering met us in a field not far from town, bringing their sick and crippled—all seeking hope and healing. They sought restoration and rejuvenation of their souls as much as their bodies. I touched and healed them all. I answered their questions and spoke to their hearts. What struck me and my apostles most was that so many of their inquiries now presumed my divinity.

"Jesus, how will you choose who comes into glory with you?"

My disciples and I exchanged a quick glance, a bit surprised at the unexpected question.

It was a teachable moment. At the very least, it offered the opportunity to contrast the typical misconceptions of grandiose deeds with what truly pleases God. "When the Son of Man comes in his glory," I began, "he will separate everyone as a shepherd separates sheep from goats! He will invite his sheep to enter his kingdom because when he was hungry, they gave him food; when thirsty, they gave him drink; when naked, they clothed him; and when a stranger, they invited him in! And if they should ask him, 'When, Lord, did we see you hungry and feed you, or thirsty and give you water? When did we clothe you or invite you into our homes?' He will answer them, 'Whenever you did it for the very least of my brothers and sisters, you did it for me!'"

As was usually the case with my spontaneous narratives, the crowd gave me their undivided attention, making sure they heard and digested every word.

I continued, "But then he will say to the others, 'Depart from me, you who are apathetic! You gave me no food when I was hungry or water for my thirst! You provided me no clothing when I was naked, and when I was alone and a stranger, you ignored me!' They will surely cry out, 'When, Lord, did we ever see you hungry and deny you food, or thirsty and deny you drink? When did we see you naked and not clothe you, or neglect you when you were alone?' The Son of Man will reply, 'Whenever you refused to help even the least of my brothers and sisters, you refused to help me!'"

This was not a hard concept to fathom, but I could see some bewilderment in the eyes of those convinced salvation was strictly a matter of faith in God.

"If you think you can gain the kingdom of heaven simply by adhering to temple observances and pious prayer, think again!" I warned. "For if you claim to love God but do not show love to others, you are a hypocrite! That beggar in the street, the widow who weeps alone, the barefoot child with bleeding feet—God is in them! To deny them is to deny God!"

Before any in the crowd could respond, I concluded with simple instruction. "Do unto others as you would have them do unto you!"

The love and hope that sprang from my words touched the multitude within the deepest recesses of their hearts. I sensed their earnest ambition to go forth and begin living their lives for others … and for me.

They soon started dispersing and heading for their respective villages. My disciples and I followed, cutting across the sloping hillsides back toward Capernaum. Our conversation turned more general—the evening's meal for one and where to eat it together.

We weaved through a vineyard or two, crossed the tracts of land bordering town and finally entered the main road running south through Capernaum. News of our day traveled faster than our legs. Even those who had rejected me just weeks before, now welcomed us back, some with guarded smiles, but others with warm, decisive embraces. It was a bitter-sweet reception. While it was good not to feel the disapproving scorn from so many eyes, it deeply saddened me that these fickle people had either reconsidered their shallow convictions, or to conform with peers, appear as if they had.

I accepted humanity for what it was and forgave them.

As the crossroads and buildings grew closer together, we approached a centurion unusually far from where most patrolled the main square or harbor area. Roman officers certainly frequented a well-populated town such as Capernaum, but this one did not wear his helmet, carry a blade or even project the rigid authority of an occupying infantry. He stood uneasily, somewhat out of the way against a side-street wall.

Nevertheless, a Roman officer held imperial power over us, so we respectfully made our way by, quietly avoiding eye contact.

You can imagine our surprise when he called to us. "Jesus?"

We swiftly turned, wide-eyed with alarm. It suddenly seemed apparent that this centurion had hidden away, specifically waiting for me. He had probably spent the morning making inquiries, gathering intelligence as an effective officer would, and determining the direction of our approach. A variety of thoughts flustered us, the most disturbing suggested that Herod's arm had finally reached us. They had surrounded Capernaum and were closing in.

I steadily reasoned, however, that service to Rome had not brought him to me. The way he spoke my name—not with a stern or commanding voice, but in a softer, more lenient tone—allayed my apprehension. His greeting lacked the strict delivery of a military officer. Its uncertain hesitancy conveyed a humble need.

I tried overlooking his Roman regalia so it wouldn't daunt my reaction. "I am Jesus," I admitted boldly. "Why do you seek me?"

He stepped forward and lowered his head, assessing how best to verbalize his purpose. He began with what was likely a rehearsed response. "My servant lies at home sick and suffering terribly. He has served me faithfully and well for a long time. I fear greatly we may lose him."

My disciples remained silent. Quite a scenario presented itself. A Roman soldier, an officer in the controlling army that so often abused its power, now lowered himself to ask assistance from a Jew. All eyes were upon me.

I stepped over to the man and regarded him genuinely—not as a Jew to a gentile or a commoner to a dignitary. We quietly beheld each other unpretentiously as human to human. It always discouraged me that so many people allowed differences in culture, creed and ancestry to create vast chasms between one another. Regardless of how glaringly at odds they often felt, their inherent similarities far outweighed any incidental differences. An amazing common thread bound all of mankind—the distinction to be called children of God—not mortal enemies like animals of varying species. How I wished everyone could gaze into the eyes of someone they deemed so different, and just for a moment see themselves staring back.

So rather than assessing a potentially adversarial Roman centurion, I simply searched for a connection with my fellow man—appraising thoughts and feelings through the vulnerable self-exposure of direct eye contact. Strip away everything else, and there within the eyes that see, one could also see deep within.

"You care a lot for this servant," I said, re-expressing what I already knew and hoping he'd further articulate his motive for taking the time and trouble to find me.

"I do," he replied. "But his service is not what I hold dear. Any attendant can provide labor. This young man has done far more than work beside me for many years. He has grown with me. We have spent much time together. Neither kith nor kin refer to him as a mere servant. He shows compassion for my family, and they for him." He paused, the impact of his own words touching his heart. "He is like a son to me."

Such profound sincerity. It broke the barriers of our differences even further. We no longer saw a Roman officer standing before us. We saw a family man—a sympathetic and thoughtful employer. We saw someone capable of a love that stripped him of his weapon, and against code and custom, led him on a back-alley quest of Capernaum to place his faith and hope in a peasant Jew from Nazareth.

My response was simple and sincere as well. "I will go with you to him."

I was not prepared for what came next.

"No," he said. "I am not worthy and do not deserve to have you come under my roof. But I, like you, am a man of authority. I issue orders to those under my jurisdiction, and they obey. So I know that whatever command you give, it will be carried out." He glanced down for only a moment before looking back at me. "Just say the word, Jesus, and my servant will be healed."

I turned to my disciples who were just as visibly in awe. Then slowly shaking my head in blissful astonishment, I said, "Truly I tell you, I have not found anyone in Israel with such great a faith as this man here."

This foreigner—this centurion—this oppressing soldier of Caesar, with his gentle and humble demeanor, demonstrated the future that I prayed for all. Such blessed hope filled my heart that I almost broke down. Instead, I reached out, and going against all Hebrew code and custom, touched a Roman officer. I took hold of a man's shoulder considered unclean by our traditional standards.

"Go," I told him. "It will be done for you as you believed it would."

The solace in his eyes clearly expressed the trust that his servant would not die.

We both stood staring in wonder at each other. Our mutual admiration and gratitude made me acutely aware of the great contrast between mankind's marvels and my own fascinations. It all boiled down to witnessing with our very eyes the things that we could not accomplish by ourselves.

The sick became healed, the lame walked and the deaf heard. These were the miracles that astounded the masses and sent them dancing and singing. Their hearts leapt with joy at participating in the naturally impossible. They could not give sight to the blind through their own power. They could not restructure bone, cure disease or overcome evil spirits. So when they saw these phenomena unfolding before them, they marveled.

The centurion returned home joyful.

For me, I directly experienced what I could neither create nor control—faith—the faith of a creature with a free will of its own. I expelled demons from souls and raised the dead to life, and while faith was indeed a gift from my Father, it was not mine to give. It was up to each individual to accept or deny the presence of God in their heart—to let go and let me in.

And whenever I saw this unfold before me, I marveled. And like the centurion, I returned home joyful.

19

Repentance, Mercy and What Lies Ahead

TIME MOVED TOO FAST.

It was uncontrollable—a perpetual, constant state of motion and change that propelled all creation from a point of formation to an eventual and inevitable moment of destruction. Although established and started by God, not until my mother's submission to his plan did I actually experience time and its effects. Time inexorably chips away at every human life, mine included. Undeniable and unyielding, the unique tempo of this universe drives and paces everything in it. Heaven has no days—no months—no years. God exists without beginning and without end, and since God never changes, time simply has no place in heaven. No yesterdays to harbor regrets. No tomorrows to feed worry. God's timeless, ever-present love and protection defines and sustains paradise.

Here, however, no amount of money, prestige or earthly power can push time faster or pull it slower. Time knows no prejudice and bows to no ruler. As a youngster, I had the common perception that the months and years moved forward at a snail's pace. Everything in the past seemed recent and the future's uncertainties so remote, they did not require attention.

But now the cadence of time felt accelerated, moving faster and faster like water flowing from a deep bed into shallower rapids. Weeks ago seemed like days—months like weeks.

My days were flying by, and I could not slow them down.

Our busy schedule clearly explained much of this feeling. Whether taking day trips to Bethsaida or Tabgha, or longer journeys throughout Galilee and around its lake, we hardly had any down-time. Those with whom we traveled continued to swell in number—from my apostles and a growing circle of women, to other villagers who tagged along between towns within their respective territories.

During the day, I taught and healed at the synagogues, in mead-ows and on hillsides. At sundown, we usually welcomed shelter with newly-formed acquaintances, speaking to their friends and family by lantern. All the while, we added to our group those who accepted my words of life.

We found ourselves one evening at a house on the outskirts of Magdala, Mary's hometown. Dusk polished the sky with an ever-darkening burgundy as night crept in. I leaned under a wooden trellis thick with flowering vines and oil lamps that hung from the foliage to softly illuminate my space. More lamps dotted the courtyard where twenty or so people huddled close to talk, easing a long day into a peaceful night.

I relished these more intimate gatherings. Accustomed to deal-ing with hundreds, if not thousands of others, we definitely consid-ered a group like this a cozy bunch. It offered the convenience of conversing without a raised voice and the opportunity to connect more personally with each of them.

The tiny lamp flames flickered in the dark, just bright enough to lighten the inquisitive faces before me, and the soft breezes off the lake funneled the floral scents down from the vines. Despite having been on my feet for much of the day, our serene surroundings soothed and relaxed me as I spoke. "I challenge all of you to go beyond the commandments," I said. "Yes, it is written that you shall not commit murder, and those who do will fall under God's judgment. But I say to you now, whoever shows anger to another is also subject to judgment. Rage and resentment offend God. While you may not physically kill, your words can truly poison. Too many of you overly concern yourselves with making sure not to eat what the Law considers unclean. It is not, however, what goes into the mouth that defiles someone, but what comes out. Your words reveal your heart. So if while preparing an offering to the Lord, you remember an unresolved argument with your neighbor, go first and reconcile yourself with them. Settle the situation. Work to restore peace. Then come and offer your gift on the altar."

As I paused for reflection, only the chirping crickets and tree frogs replied. Several people turned to one another above their glimmering lamps—each recalling a time tempers had gotten the best of them—each regretting that they neglected to remedy their actions. Their shared looks of forgiveness and implicit absolution warmed my heart.

I then confronted them with an even more challenging proclamation. "You have heard it said, 'an eye for an eye and a tooth for a tooth.' But I tell you, do not lash back at those who hurt or speak against you. If someone slaps your right cheek, turn your left to them as well. Love's strength when confronted with anger and hate will overcome both. If someone demands your robe, also offer them your tunic. Give to those who ask, and pray for those who are unjust."

A few quietly discussed this startling call to active restraint. Someone unexpectedly asked, "Where do you get all of this, Jesus? From whom do your insights and wisdom come? You preach with such natural authority, not like any of the priests or scribes."

The essentials did not lie in the origin of my words but in accepting and acting upon them. I considered for a moment how best to illustrate this in a memorable way. "Those who hear my words but do not live them daily are like a man who built his house on sand. The rains came, the winds blew and the house was destroyed.

But those who hear my voice and put my words into practice are like another who built his house upon rock. The rains came and the winds blew, but the house did not fall, because it was set upon a firm foundation."

The implication was simple. Many would hear my voice, but those who ignored the sense and substance of my message would not gain entry to my kingdom. This was troublesome for even me to dwell upon. The thought of losing *any* of my children hurt deeply. So I determinately decided that I must more passionately emphasize the importance of turning to me and focusing on God's will above all else. I must underscore the profound merciful care that calls even the worst sinners to repent, regardless of how long or how far they have wandered astray.

I must sharpen my message to these key points.

I had to. The sands of time were running … and time was running out.

*   *   *

"They should not even be in here!" shouted the Pharisee, eyes narrowly fixed on me but arms gesturing broadly at many around me.

We gathered in Tiberias' main synagogue. The massive hall was packed. We had come south from Magdala, spreading a precise message of repentance, mercy and reconciliation. Those who longed most for its hope and promise had followed us from the poorer outlying areas into this great coastal city.

I knew exactly at whom he leveled his derogatory tone, but he had no qualms explicitly clarifying for all to hear. "Tax collectors, prostitutes, drunkards—this is a sacred temple, and yet you bring the likes of these in here! You yourself, rabbi, say that only the righteous shall inherit the kingdom of God, but look, you now lead these sinners into a holy place of worship."

I stood by the polished colonnade that supported the broad ceiling and glanced first with tenderness and respect at those he degraded. Surely they now felt like leaving quickly by the nearest exit.

I then took a few steps further into the large room so that all could see me. My temporary silence may have implied that I either accepted the indictment or felt indifferent to it, but I was simply preparing a meaningful response. After collecting my thoughts, I finally proclaimed to the hushed congregation, "Two men went up to the temple to pray. One was a Pharisee, the other a tax collector." It now became clear I was responding directly to the accusation. "The Pharisee stood in the center of the synagogue and prayed, 'God, I thank you that I am a decent and honorable man. I thank you that I am not like that tax collector. I fast twice a week and donate a tenth of my earnings to the temple.'" I paused, sweeping my eyes over the crowded floor. "But the tax collector, he stood at a distance and would not even raise his eyes to heaven. Instead, he pounded his chest and cried, 'Dear Lord, have mercy on me, a sinner!'"

I did not turn to observe the Pharisee's reaction but could see the tightened faces of his associates in their prestigious seats up front. "I tell you that this man went away in a closer relationship with God than the other."

I considered pushing it further, to indicate that many of those labeled a sinner here had as much, if not more, a right to be under God's roof as those adorned in the external dignity of clerical garb. Recognizing, however, that several of these scribes had been at Simon the Pharisee's house when pandemonium broke out over my acceptance of Mary Magdala, I decided not to press it.

For the moment, the Pharisee who had brazenly slandered the penitent in my group made no immediate retort. But another stood and pointed toward me, or toward us; I wasn't sure which. "That's it?" he clamored. "They spend a lifetime in disgraceful behavior, then suddenly decide to follow you and all is made right by them?"

As before, I did not immediately respond. I let the erroneous question of fairness register throughout the chamber. The sudden silence focused all attention on me. When I did speak, I once again expressed myself with a parable, and once again delivered it to the entire room. "The kingdom of heaven is like a landowner who went out early one morning to hire workers for his vineyard. He agreed to pay them a full denarius for the day's wage. Later in the morning he saw others looking for work, so he also sent them to his vineyard. He went out again about noon and then later, doing the same thing. When evening approached, he found still others standing idle around the marketplace. They sought work, so he sent them along to his vineyard. At sunset, the landowner said to his foreman, 'Call the workers and pay them their wages, beginning with the last ones hired.' Those hired late in the day came and each received a full denarius. So when it came time to pay those hired first, they expected a much greater compensation. But they too each received a denarius. They began to grumble, saying, 'How can this be? These others only put in one hour, and yet have been paid the same as us. They barely had time to break a sweat! How can they receive the same amount?' The landowner answered them, 'I have treated you fairly. I paid you well. I paid you what we agreed upon. I certainly have the right to spend my money as I wish and have decided to pay the others the same. Do you resent them because I am generous? Should I temper my generosity because of your resentment? Do I work for you, or did you work for me? Who owns this vineyard? Who indeed is in charge here, you or me?'"

All eyes moved to the Pharisees, most understanding the correlation between them and the workers hired first in my story.

I lowered my voice as I looked at my new friends who had repented from their ways to follow me. "I have professed on many occasions and do so again today; the last will be first and the first will be last."

A generously merciful God. This is what I hoped everyone took home with them. A God so accepting and bountiful that it was never too late on life's sundial to seek and work the vineyard. *Come!* my Father called them through me. It is not too late. Come!

*   *   *

My Father had something planned. Something big. Although unclear on the specifics, I was aware of three things. First, he would reveal something amazing to a select few, chosen by me. Second, he wanted to open a final window into my divinity before evil could launch its own invasion. And third, most importantly, this revelation would make manifest in every aspect, the kingdom of heaven on earth.

It also indicated that my hour of suffering approached. What once seemed safely off in the distance, now drew disturbingly close. I did not wish to dwell on the natural concerns—the precise details of when, and where, and how. But these disquieting uncertainties invariably penetrated and infected my human mind, giving me such anxiety at times that my knees felt unable to support my weight. I often had to sit and compel myself to take deep breaths and reaffirm that my loving Father was in control. I focused on my purpose—on my mission—on performing as the perfect agent of his will. With closed eyes, I silently repeated, 'All is fine. All goes as he plans … I can do this. I *will* do this.'

I would persevere to fulfill my destiny.

A part of me desperately longed for a few more years. Another wished it could be over tomorrow. Regardless, it loomed soon enough.

Mary Magdala and the other women easily found lodging in Tiberias. While my apostles and I could have done the same, we preferred a night's rest outside town where we could converse privately and avoid the crowds that repeatedly sought us well after sundown.

The night felt like any other to my brothers. Hidden deep in a valley of tall grass, our fire provided warmth, light and a stimulus for conversation. For a while, congenial debates and idle chatter rose with the sparks into the black sky. I was unusually quiet, reserved in my thoughts as the fire danced hypnotically.

A lull finally fell upon their discussion, and Andrew observed aloud, "Lord, why are you so quiet tonight? Are you tired?"

That was an understatement. I was physically exhausted from the long day, as well as emotionally drained and spent. "I am tired, Andrew, yes," I said. "But my heart is also restless."

Peter, sitting next to me, looked at me thoughtfully. "What is it? What's troubling you?"

I waited a moment, deciding how much they were ready to hear. They had come so far with me; they deserved the straightforward truth. I hoped it might also lift some of my burden to share this with them.

My thoughts continued to tussle, but I eventually vocalized my reality. "Soon the Son of Man shall fall into the hands of evil men."

Their fidgeting stopped. Their breathing may have too.

I gazed into the fire and held nothing back. "He will be rejected by the elders, the chief priests and the teachers of the Law. They will hand him over to be condemned. He will be mocked … beaten … put to death."

I did not have to shift my focus from the flames to perceive the shock and dismay welling in their eyes.

"But on the third day," I said, regaining my resolve, "he will be raised to life."

No one spoke as each struggled to digest these unsettling predictions. My eyes remained on the fire's soothing, haphazard rhythms.

Judas reluctantly cut the reticence. "Put to death? You can't mean that, Lord."

I finally glanced up and attempted to convey conviction despite my own angst. "Don't you see? There is no greater love than to lay down your life for your friends. These things must happen this way for the salvation of the world. We will go to Jerusalem, where I will suffer greatly—to make everything new again."

Peter spoke, more boldly than I had ever heard him. "God forbid this, Lord. We will protect you. We have managed this long; we will see that you are kept safe at all cost."

For a moment my mind agreed, silently acclaiming, *Yes*! Peter and the others could indeed help me stay undetected for a longer period—whisk me away to safety somewhere farther north perhaps. But I quickly recognized this as nothing more than the enemy trying to get inside my head. I shut my eyes and muttered aloud, "Away from me, Satan."

When I opened them, it was evident that everyone, especially Peter, assumed my reference to the evil one had been directed at my good friend. I certainly did not want this. I grabbed Peter lovingly by his shoulder and held him firmly. "Your heart is in the right place, Peter, but your words are dangerous to me. You are thinking from a human point of view, not from God's point of view."

His eyes tried hard to understand. "I only want what's best for you," he said discreetly, still troubled that I had attributed his inherent concern to Satan, not to mention the whole idea of me being beaten and killed.

I wanted all of them to understand, for themselves and for those they would teach in years to come, that to truly find God they must lose themselves completely for him—for me. Shed everything, risk everything, forsake everything. Only from this perceived ultimate human weakness can God's infinite strength transcend and overcome.

So I said to them, "Whoever wants to be my disciple must deny themselves, take up their crosses and follow me. For whoever becomes distracted with life, will lose it. But whoever loses their life for me, will save it. What good will it be for someone to gain the whole world but forfeit his soul?"

Only the fire whispered back, revealing faces still in shock but trying to regain composure through my words.

"Think of a rich man blessed with such a bountiful harvest that he has no place to store it all," I said to help craft a visual. "He preoccupies himself with constantly growing and amassing more and more. He even tears down his barns to build bigger ones. He figures this will suffice to keep him content and happy for many years. But God said to him, 'You fool, this very night, your life will be demanded of you.'"

The straightforward message hit home for them. No one knows the time or the place. Life should be lived as if every day were the last, giving oneself completely over to God.

Thomas rested his chin in his hands and sighed almost matter-of-factly. "Then we go to Jerusalem."

Thaddeus tossed a blade of grass into the flames and nodded. "Jerusalem."

Andrew and John followed in synch. "Jerusalem."

One by one they all said it, even Judas—though I sensed he harbored a strong ambition that our trip would ignite a revolt against Rome rather than my death. I think in the back of all their minds they clung to the hope that what was spoken here by the fire would not actually come to pass. Despite trusting my every word, the thought of God's own son falling victim to evil forces seemed unfathomable—beyond their understanding. They couldn't fully grasp a love so total, a caring so complete, that my own suffering and death would wash away sin, reconciling man to God.

Peter wavered a moment before staring deep into my eyes and finally relenting ... "Jerusalem."

I smiled warmly at all of them, touched by their personal courage and continued commitment to me, even after explaining that in no uncertain terms, a deathtrap awaited us. I would help them through this but knew that nothing could fully prepare them for what lay ahead.

I recalled my Father's forthcoming revelation intended for a few of these very souls and closed our discussion with words of hope. "I tell you the truth, there are some of you here tonight who will not taste death before witnessing the kingdom of God."

As ambiguous and vague as that statement may have sounded, I did not say it to reveal vast inner secrets or future visions. I said it simply to drop a seed of promise and anticipation. That was all. My friends needed as much rest as I, which would prove difficult if their minds were too troubled with forebodings of torment and martyr-dom. I didn't realize myself at the time, that this glimpse into God's glory for some of them would not come in a matter of weeks—but days.

20

Transfigured

MOUNT TABOR WAS HARDLY A MOUNTAIN but surely more than a hill. Like a single blemish on smooth skin, the rounded butte rose from the vast valleys south of Tiberias and west from the Sea of Galilee. Stout and steep, it proved an arduous climb even by the most gradual ascent through the weathered grass and scattered trees. Those who ambitiously challenged its more unstable rocky slopes, definitely withstood an adventure.

I had not planned on climbing it. We intended to only spend a night or two with some sharecroppers who tilled the nearby land—a short stop before continuing to Nazareth to get my mother and embark on our journey to Jerusalem for Passover.

For now, I had simply decided on a midnight walk alone through the wheat fields. In the silence of those seemingly endless rows of grain, I prayed intensely to my Father, stopping to absorb the night's pure beauty. The moonlight bathed the swaying heads of wheat, and a mellow breeze rustled the crop in waves that casually rippled across the entire plain. Such treasures to behold. So much I didn't want to take for granted, here or anywhere … a sunrise waking over the water, the music of sparrows bringing a tree to life in an otherwise silent meadow, this wheat field's warm glow transforming the cool shine from the moon. I prayed for guidance, strength and peace. I would need an abundance of each to accomplish what awaited me.

I later reclined by the field and slept. When I awoke a few hours later, I had distinctly received the desired wisdom and foresight, but for the moment, neither the strength nor peace. Nevertheless, I trusted they would come.

I returned to the farmhands' dwelling at the base of Mount Tabor with a heavy heart. My apostles slept soundly, the sun still a good hour from peeking over the distant horizon. I knelt next to Judas and wept—bitterly but silently. His motivations were now so clear, so very vivid. His own desires and selfish expectations overshadowed his true love and trust in me. Upon arriving in Jerusalem, he would pose an easy target for the Sanhedrin. They would lure him with false promises, seduce him with lies and convince him to hand me over. I felt the urge to retch but only wept away the nausea. Betrayed by one of my very own sheep. It blindsided me.

I struggled to my feet.

And Peter. My rock? I looked at the shape of my sleeping friend. He snored peacefully on a bed of hay under a warm blanket. This brother of mine, the first to declare from his heart that I was the son of God, who just a few nights ago swore to protect me to the end— would soon deny that he even knew me or had ever met me. What level of turmoil and panic would lead to such denials? New tears rolled into my beard, partly in expectation of my own abandonment, but mostly for Peter. How deeply his denial of me would ultimately hurt *him*, guilt poisoning his heart. He would need a significantly positive experience to assuage his regret and remorse. To keep shame from crushing him, it would take a stronger memory than that of his sin.

Now was the time for that experience. My Father pulled me from within.

I reached down and gently shook his shoulder. "Wake up, Peter."

He rolled over and gazed groggily up at me, acclimating himself to his whereabouts. "What is it?" he asked through the fog of half-sleep.

"Get up," I whispered. "Grab James and John, take some food and meet me outside."

He did not question but sat up and rubbed his eyes.

On my way to the door, I noticed Matthew beginning to stir in the corner. As he awoke, I bent down to him. "I am taking Peter, James and John up the mountain this morning. Tell the others we shall return later."

He did not question my words either. "Yes, Lord."

Within minutes, the four of us stood at the pasture's edge, stretching ourselves awake and passing around the water jug. We ate some bread, a few figs and even shared a honeycomb, all while looking toward the steep southern face of Mount Tabor. It loomed defiantly as a black mass in the predawn glow just now reddening the eastern heavens.

James wiped the water from his lips. "How far up are we going?"

I did not move my eyes from the silhouetted peak. "As far as it takes."

"Takes for what?" asked John. "What will we do up there?"

I glanced at them as if the answer was obvious. "Pray."

I started walking toward the base of the massive hillside. James ripped a final crust of bread and stuffed it in his mouth before following Peter and John in my footsteps.

We climbed for almost an hour in near-silence, watching the breathtaking sunrise creep around our ridge. Its beauty held our tongues nearly as much as the exertion necessary to make progress up the sharp incline. The morning sun coaxed sheets of vapor off the lake that gradually encircled the mountain and clouded most of the valley below from our view.

As we neared the summit, I stopped at a jumble of waist-high rocks. We agreed without words that we should stop and rest. I took a needed swig from my waterskin and turned to my brothers. "Wait here. I am going just a few paces further to pray."

James and John dropped to the wild grasses and rested their backs against the sunny side of the rocks.

Peter moved beside me. "Shall we join you soon?"

The foggy mist continued to rise, and a small rainbow glistened up ahead. I turned to him. "Soon. Pray here for guidance and strength."

He acknowledged with a nod, sat against a rock and uncorked his own waterskin.

I moved upward toward the rainbow. As I approached, the colors faded from the evaporating moisture. The spectrum then gradually reappeared, somehow circling me in a nebula of vibrant hues, swirling ever-closer until they shimmered about my waist and arms. I closed my eyes and dropped to my knees, realizing my heavenly Father was present. The colorful mist moved higher. It now swam in a halo around my head as sweet floral scents filled the air. The vivid vapors coalesced and fused into a single dazzle of phosphorescent white. Its intensity grew and yet my eyes opened and relaxed. The resplendence brightened around my entire body. I heard less and less of the world around me—only the startled, frightened shouts of my three apostles, who now undoubtedly saw this spectacle around me.

I slowly stood, precipitating two other figures to emerge. Two magnificent leaders from Israel's storied past stepped gracefully from my light and into the surrounding haze. Moses and the great prophet Elijah both faced me, appearing no older than I. These two vivaciously youthful men greeted me as if welcoming a king returning from a foreign land. They extended their arms to receive me with praise and honor.

Completely absorbed in this moment, I could hardly hear James shout behind me, sounding more like a distant echo, "Who are these men, Lord?"

I couldn't answer right away but delighted in the awareness that they too were fully experiencing this with me.

Moses, cloaked in white with a royal crimson shawl over one shoulder, looked at my apostles, then back to me. "My Lord," he said, "your deliverance of this world will soon far surpass my deliverance of our people. The time draws near. Just as it was *your* Spirit that gave me the courage and perseverance to lead a nation from an oppressive empire, how very much more that same Spirit will see you through this perfect, undeniable sacrifice."

I bowed my head, gesturing great thanks. His words invigorated and reinforced my resolve. I then turned to the eyes of Elijah, a face much younger than when he walked the earth prophesying Yahweh's works and turning kings and kingdoms away from false gods.

He could hardly contain his emotion, exclaiming, "And God so promised me, *'Behold, I will send Elijah before that great and dreadful day of the Lord.'*"

I stared deeply into those vivid brown eyes. "That day approaches."

He managed a compassionate smile and proudly reaffirmed his loyalty. "Here I am."

What a perfect way for my Father to demonstrate his divine support of my mission. Both the messenger of the Law and the greatest of the prophets collapsing centuries and overcoming time to stand here with me this day. As living witnesses to God's power, they testified to my role in the inevitable success of the great plan of salvation.

I turned, hoping Peter, James and John were still close-by and experiencing this glorious encounter. They knelt reverently behind me, full of fear and wonderment but with faces held high so as not to miss a single moment.

The brilliant streams of light hovered and drifted among us, as if angels themselves frolicked on the hillside.

"Stand, my friends," I beckoned.

They hastened to their feet, refusing to move their eyes from us.

"Do you know who these men are?" I asked while motioning to the two beside me.

Peter demonstrated how profoundly he was paying attention. "Could it be, Lord, that they are truly Moses and Elijah?"

I stepped forward and indicated the figure to my right as the very man whose arms had carried the ten commandments down from another mountain centuries ago. And on my left, the most influential prophet to come out of Israel. I said to Peter, "Your eyes do not deceive. Heaven has touched this mountain today so that you may see how the Law and the prophets all point to the Messiah's fulfillment."

These three ex-fishermen were experiencing a vision that even the most holy temple scribes could only dream of witnessing. It obviously and clearly overwhelmed them.

Moses and Elijah addressed some final words of encouragement to me, each expressing a gamut of feelings—from love and adoration to empathy and sorrow. The bright haze began to close over them again, but Peter was not ready for them to go so soon.

"Lord, it is good that we are here!" he exclaimed, hoping to slow the disappearance of his Hebrew heroes. "We can build shelters for the three of you, right here upon Mount Tabor!" His delirious admiration blurred his sensibility.

Suddenly, a sweeping cloud covered the entire mountain, hiding the sun and enshrouding us in a thick fog. The haze enveloped us so swiftly that my apostles had difficulty maintaining their balance. Loud, prolonged thunder rumbled overhead and echoed around us. Then that familiar deep voice I had heard after my baptism in the Jordan boomed with a resonance that seemed to speak from all directions, *'This is my son, whom I have sent. Listen to him.'*

This acute, ubiquitous intonation dropped the three of them back to their knees. In fear, awe and reverence they collapsed, faces to the ground, not daring to look upward. Only after several minutes did the cloud gradually dissipate and sunlight gently brighten across their closed eyelids. Otherwise, they would have likely remained prostrate and cowering all day. But as the warm rays reached their position, they opened their eyes to see the mist slowly vanishing and clarity once again returning to the mountainside. They each cautiously but deliberately turned to me, not sure what to expect.

I stood alone, no more than five or six paces from them.

They looked about, hoping that some vestige of the spectacular vision may have lingered, but no sign remained. Their apprehensive eyes tentatively examined their surroundings.

I approached and gently spoke the words they needed to hear most. "Do not be afraid. I am here."

They immediately stood to seek sanctuary in my open embrace. For several long moments we huddled there, the four of us clustered together, confirming for each other and appreciating this most blessed event.

John finally inquired softly, "Was that a dream? I feel like I just woke from the most incredible dream."

Peter opened his mouth, but his voice hesitated as he struggled to put his own experience into words. "Moses and Elijah, they materialized right … right out of the light … stepping from the light that surrounded you."

"That was no dream," said James, wiping a few tears with his wrist. "That was real. I'll never forget it as long as I live."

I tightened my arms around their collective shoulders. "How privileged you are indeed to have experienced this today. But for now, keep it here upon the mountain. Do not tell others what you have seen until the Son of Man has been raised from the dead."

They agreed with modest nods, hushed tongues and pensive eyes.

We descended the mammoth hillside in greater silence than on our way up. As we carefully negotiated the steep downward slope, I snuck periodic glances at my three friends. They were each in their own world, deeply engrossed in private thought. So absorbed in fact, I almost thought that if a stampede of wild boars came at us from the trees, none of them would notice. But that was understandable. They had much to ponder and digest. These close brothers of mine had spent several years traveling with me, their faith testifying to my divinity. But now they had received a first-hand experience of my glory. Although they could not fully comprehend it at this point, they possessed a better understanding of the anointed Messiah's divine nature than any other living person. They were eyewitnesses to my majesty.

Transfigured into such a profound vision, I had precisely symbolized that the Law and the prophets both acknowledged and adored a new hope for humanity. The time had come for me to fulfill the Law and the prophecies in scripture. These three men walking beside me had received upon this mountainside the rarest of gifts. With their own eyes they had seen the veil over my divinity lifted, if only for a few minutes. To the extent that humans can, they now grasped my splendor as the undeniable king of kings—honored and praised by two of the most revered men in the history of their race.

These realizations flabbergasted them but hopefully helped in their understanding of me and my mission. I knew it would provide strength and perseverance for the rest of their lives, but I was also painfully aware that even this amazing vision would not completely protect them from what now lay so close at hand.

Gehenna was ready for battle. Evil prepared to unleash its fury at me and test my sheep beyond their limits. For a time at least, the inspiration from what they witnessed on this hillside would succumb to the worst of human emotions—fear. Dread and dismay sent too many running from God like panicked prey whenever danger arose. And danger surely loomed for my inner circle. Undoubtedly, fear would soon break trust ... test love ... challenge loyalty. Temporarily, even faith would fail.

Only one thing could defeat this fear.

Hope.

True hope could come from but one source. An eternal God ... A risen savior.

21

And the Dead Shall Rise to Life

OUR CARAVAN MOVED SOUTH out of Nazareth. I turned to glance back at the rambling pattern of buildings that made up my home town. So many times I had looked upon my village from this very path, but now the scene struck me differently. It all seemed more vivid ... more venerated. The green, rugged hills gracefully cradled the closely-knit dwellings before rising up to touch the sky—a sky so big and so blue that even the largest clouds appeared lost above the horizon.

I knew I would never see this place or its appealing beauty again. I would leave Nazareth this time for the last time. I finally pulled my eyes away and over to my mother walking beside me. She noticed my pensive stare and immediately understood my meditative frame of mind. Neither of us needed words. She simply put her arm through mine, rested her head on my shoulder and walked with me.

Our travels through these southern reaches of Galilee were a far cry from my excursion three years earlier to be baptized by my cousin John. I had made that journey alone, a scarcely known carpenter from Nazareth. Today, my name was well recognized throughout every region, stretching far north beyond Damascus and south even into Egypt. I remembered walking these roads alone with nothing more than my own thoughts to keep me company. Now I enjoyed good company, surrounded by many committed disciples. Granted, most would have been making this pilgrimage to Jerusalem for Passover anyway, but an ever-increasing number now associated themselves with our entourage. My apostles, Mary Magdala, Joanna and Salome, even Nicodemus; they all set forth with me for this most holy trip—my final journey.

Nain was a town even smaller than Nazareth and just across the valley from it. With provisions well packed and our trip only just begun, we planned on passing through the modest village. As they always seem to do, however, circumstances would dictate otherwise.

We heard them before we could see them—sorrowful sounds thrusting their presence upon us, impossible to miss. Mournful cries and moans reverberated through the air like a melancholy harp's thickest strings. And although Nain was indeed small, a considerable crowd took to the central street, creating a solemn procession heading out of town. We came across this orderly cortege as we approached the unassuming village. Stepping out of their way, we watched them plod forward—bleak shadows pulling people along with them. Most wept openly. They lifted their heads to the heavens and beseeched God for some understanding, some rationale for their anguish. Even those who walked silently held blank, somber faces.

There were no doubts we had come upon a funeral procession. We also quickly inferred this was no routine requiem for an elderly soul called home after a long, fulfilled life. The people of this time, like all peoples of all times, understood the unpleasant but inevitable aspects of death and taxes, and rarely accepted either, expected or not. The more unforeseen the death, the deeper the void it carved into the hearts of those left behind, and sorrow seldom soothed.

The sorrow we witnessed leaving the streets of Nain penetrated like a cold rain. I shuddered at what tragedy might have caused this passionate outpouring. Perhaps a recently married spouse had died; maybe a child, or the long, much anticipated arrival of a baby, born dead. Only horrors like these could trigger and sustain the level of uncontrollable grief before us now.

I found myself reaching out and grabbing a passing man's arm. His gaze stared despondently through us. As I touched his elbow, he recovered the awareness of his surroundings and finally met my eyes.

"For whom do all these mourn?" I asked.

He reluctantly glanced over his shoulder. "We mourn for Aliza."

"Was she young?"

His eyes lowered. "We mourn for Aliza ... because she walks with us today. She walks to bury her son—her only child—a righteous young man." He bit his lip at the heartbreaking reality pushing everyone onward toward the graves. Before turning to rejoin them, he solemnly added, "She has lost her son only a month after burying her husband."

I immediately looked to my mother who was staring downcast into the passing crowd. Her soon-to-be similar reality tugged at my gut. Before long, my own widowed mother would lose her son as well. My head snapped around, and through moist eyes, I anxiously scanned the laggardly moving procession.

The raised wooden bier was not far away. Three men on each side carried the flat platform on their shoulders. The lifeless form of the deceased lay on top, wrapped in a burial sheet. It wasn't hard to distinguish his mother. She moved with the cadence of her son's pallbearers, requiring assistance to continue without collapsing from grief.

I moved briskly, nudging gently through the crowd. Those I brushed by turned to see who I was and where I was going. A few recognized me and called out, but I continued forward, determined to reach this widow.

I finally drew near to Aliza. She stopped walking at my approach, as did the men carrying her dead son. She looked at me with empty eyes, hollow from fatigue and hopelessness. Tears continued to flow over cheeks already stained with the salt of incessant crying.

I wasted no time grabbing her arms but held her even more steady with my sympathetic gaze. "Do not cry," I implored. "Your son lives."

She wasn't sure whether to take this as a kind indication that her son was now in a better place with God, or something more.

Someone behind me clamored, "Jesus, is that you?"

Upon hearing my name, the widow's fingers tightened around my sleeves. Her eyes widened just enough to ease her sorrowful squint.

Part of me didn't want to look away—my gentle focus restoring some hope. So I turned just enough to reach up and touch her son's wooden slab while addressing the men beneath it. "Lower the bier."

They returned silent, vacant stares.

Another shouted, "It is Jesus of Nazareth! Do as he says!"

The bearers moved together, grabbed the beams that rested on their shoulders, and in shaky unison, hoisted them up before controlling the bier's weight down to the ground.

Although many hoped for a miracle, the possibility of truly witnessing one—of actually seeing a dead body wake to life—petrified those around us. They cleared away to allow me ample space. Only the widow Aliza and a few pallbearers remained at my side.

I knelt to one knee and unwrapped the linen just enough to see the dead man's side. The strong aroma of spice filled my nostrils, his body heavily anointed for burial. Cold, colorless fingers lay against the wood, and I instinctively took his wax-like hand in mine. Those who saw this gasped, but I kept my grip. I looked to where the corpse's head lay covered in the diaphanous wrappings and spoke emphatically, as if the ears underneath could indeed hear. "Young man, I say to you, wake up!"

Silence swept through the street.

The crowd presumed my command insufficient—there was no movement upon the timbers. My heart raced, however, as several rigid fingers curled against mine under the cloth. I turned to Aliza, who now knelt directly next to me. "Unwrap your son's head," I urged.

She was anxious to obey, but seeing no change in him, she hesitated.

I nodded once to encourage her.

She held my eyes a moment longer. Her own finally acknowledged that she was prepared to act on trust.

She tentatively moved a quivering hand toward her son's concealed head when a strong puff of air ruffled the linen from underneath. She shrieked in alarm. The fingers around mine tightened against my knuckles as life surged back into him. Erratic breathing deepened and quickened like a man struggling to survive. Hearing her dead son gasp for air overjoyed her more than she could have possibly imagined.

"Samuel!" she cried, frantically fumbling to unravel the cloth from his face. It quickly fell away and his eyes opened, his mouth taking full, fresh lungfuls of air.

Stunned shrills from the crowd pierced the afternoon—startled discomposure at seeing a cadaver suddenly breathing. But their cries of shock swiftly morphed into elation, realizing this man was no longer a corpse, but Aliza's son come back to her.

The loudest cry sprang from the widow herself. She flung both arms around her bewildered son's shoulders as he attempted to sit, the burial shroud still tucked closely against his torso. He was near twenty years old and yet she rocked him like a small child, her head against his, sobbing in irrepressible joy.

Relatives and friends wasted little time approaching and joining their embrace. Before long, the hug grew four or five deep on all sides. Others simply stood and stared at me in disconcerted wonder.

Witnessing life infused back into the dead, even into a cherished one of their own, caused considerable shock and awe. Their minds churned, contemplating what sort of supernatural magic had happened before their eyes, or if the actual hand of God had restored a soul to its earthen vessel … and a beloved son back to his mother.

Most of them fully grasped that an indisputable act of God had overpowered death, which also imparted new life and hope into their own hearts. Their praise-filled acclamations were loud, no longer mournfully searching the sky for explanation, but extolling my Father's name with invigorated spirits. They rejoiced for their sister Aliza. They celebrated the wonder of seeing a miracle, of being present when the Almighty visibly reached from the spirit world into theirs.

They also understood it was *my* command that had worked this magnificent marvel—that personally bestowed this ultimate blessing to a distraught widow I'd known hardly a minute or two. I had expressed my will, and my Father responded—our Spirit delivering new life. How happy were those who now believed that placing their faith in my name was enough to experience daily miracles within their own lives. Not necessarily harnessing the power to pull back the dead, but just as surely to replenish life and vitality in themselves whenever worldly trials and struggles threatened to kill it.

Since no one on this earth escapes unscathed from pain, turmoil or tragedy, this facet of my mission and message held special meaning for all. The miraculous truth of this day, and every day, is that I am the pathway to joy. I am the *only* way to joy even in the darkest circumstance when no reason or possibility for happiness seems to exist. Those who come to me will find love in the midst of hate, hope when mired in worry, joy when consumed with sorrow.

The people of Nain did more than come to me that day. They refused to let me and my disciples go. So we stayed the night, adding many to our followers, and to those accompanying us to Jerusalem.

221

*　　*　　*

The great walls of Jericho encircled the city, their ancient, steadfast parapets rising imposingly above the road midway between Jerusalem and the Jordan river. With only a week to Passover, and now so close to the holy destination, severe overcrowding created tumultuous conditions throughout this neighboring city. Man and beast alike congested the narrow passageways and alleys, all moving concertedly in different directions. Weary travelers—fatigued and low on patience—poked, prodded, quibbled and swore at each other, all purportedly in support of a hallowed pilgrimage.

Finding a place for our entire group to eat and rest together proved impossible.

Night fell, and for the moment, only my apostles and I rested our legs and broke bread over broth on the first floor of a humble inn. Our thoughts and conversation centered on the week's journey. Details about my expected arrival in Jerusalem had developed with each passing day. So much anticipation. So many warnings. My contentious confrontations with the Sanhedrin last year now put them on high alert. Numerous new accounts of my activities over the last few months could only have deepened their disdain at the prospect of dealing with me again.

Not to mention the Romans. King Herod, who rarely missed a Passover trip to Jerusalem, still eagerly tried to find me. His resolve to determine my intentions grew, as did his desire to see one of the signs he had heard so much about.

My mind darted back and forth, running through a myriad of possible scenarios. The door to the inn suddenly swung open and scraped loudly against the stone floor. We all turned abruptly, on heightened alert ourselves.

My mother stood in the doorway with a man I recognized as a friend of Lazarus' from Bethany. Their concerned faces indicated something was wrong. They approached our table, and we lowered our bowls and wine goblets.

Mom placed her hand on the man's shoulder as a way of introduction. "Jesus, this is Benjamin, a good friend of Lazarus."

His solemn countenance only slightly improved at having found me.

"You have come from Bethany seeking me, Benjamin," I said, more assumption than intuition.

"I have," he replied and acknowledged my apostles with a respectful nod. "Martha and Mary sent me to find you."

"Is something wrong?" asked Peter, soaking his final piece of bread in chowder.

Benjamin's eyes indicated unsettling news before his mouth could confirm it. "Lazarus has fallen ill. Martha is caring for him, but he is not responding."

My apostles looked to me for a reaction, each knowing how close Lazarus was to me. My mother especially understood, having watched us grow up together.

I turned pensively back to the table and took a sip of wine. "This sickness will not end in death. It is for God's glory, so that the son of God may be glorified through it." I glanced back up at Benjamin. "Tell Martha and Mary I am on my way."

*　　*　　*

We came down through the olive trees. Their massive, twisted trunks stood like natural pillars supporting sage green canopies under which we walked. The sky was nearly cloudless, yet only speckles of sunlight completed their journey through the intertwined branches thick with leaves. We descended gradually, almost lazily, along this scenic grove, moving closer to the fringes of Bethany. The day seemed so peaceful, so perfectly tranquil, I fought hard not to imagine or presume how it would all change in the coming week. This day seemed without flaw. It felt untainted. On a late morning such as this, it felt as if I were truly walking in my kingdom with my subjects at my side.

But these appearances did not deceive me. I knew this was not my kingdom. I was far from it. This euphoric day would soon pass. Atrocities brewed. Yet somehow my step had renewed strength. My growing spiritual endurance, a gift from my Father, braced and fortified my habitually weak human nature.

Through the trees ahead, we noticed a group as large as ours ascending the slope toward us. Martha was leading the way.

Even before reaching us, the remorse in her eyes halted our advance. She rushed straight into my arms and sobbed as if it were just the two of us on the hillside. Words did not accompany her tears. Benjamin, who had journeyed ahead of us, stood by her side. His downcast face silently informed that we had arrived too late.

Amid Martha's cries, he sadly muttered the explicit, simple confirmation, "Lazarus is gone."

The statement stunned my apostles. They remembered my recent declaration that Lazarus' sickness would not end in death. Since it surely seemed apparent the man had died, they glanced at each other with suppressed surprise.

Martha finally drew her head back and looked dolefully up at me. "Lord, if you had been here, my brother would not have died. But I know that even now, God will do whatever you ask of him."

Such faith. Such a selfless heart. She did not reproach me, asking where I had been. She did not beg me to bring her brother back or grovel through desperate sobs to turn back time. She did not ask or suggest anything. Rather, Martha freely put the matter into my hands. She affirmed, perhaps without realizing it, the complete unity of my Father's will with mine—that whatever I asked, whatever I decided, would surely come to pass.

I swept her hair back and held her gently behind the ears. "Your brother shall rise again."

Unable to find a smile, Martha expressed her understanding of my words strictly from her religious heritage. "I know he will … in the resurrection on the last day."

Her articulation seized my heart, and since everyone gathered here heard this, I glanced up to address them all. "I am the resurrection and the life. Whoever believes in me will live, even though they die. And whoever lives by believing in me, will never die." I returned my eyes to Martha. "Do you believe this?"

"Yes," she replied. Then, with conviction strengthening her tone, "I believe you are the Messiah, the son of God who has come into the world."

While my disciples had already placed their faith in my divinity, Martha's statement astonished many who had come with her from Bethany. They undoubtedly knew of me and my works but had no immediate response to such an acknowledgement.

Movement through the trees caught my eye as others now ascended the hill. Martha's younger sister Mary led this second group, and upon seeing us, she too ran for the comfort of my arms.

Once there, her words profoundly mirrored her sister's. "If only you had been here, Jesus, Lazarus would still be with us." At the mention of her brother's name, she broke down and turned her head to weep.

Many of the others could no longer repress their own despair. They mourned the loss of Lazarus, but more so for Martha and Mary, suddenly without a beloved brother. I too felt tears welling in my eyes as I recalled a friend who was as much a brother to me. From boyhood to manhood, Lazarus had stood by me—always kind, forever compassionate, reliably gracious and gentle. On so many occasions he committed his unwavering support, humbly opening his mind and his home whenever I passed through.

And now he was gone.

I looked over this crowd that had grown to nearly fifty. News of my miracle in Nain a week ago would spread to Judea soon enough, but any sign or wonder performed here in Bethany, so close to Jerusalem, would reach every street in the holy city before Passover could even begin. Now was the time, and there was very little time left. I meant what I had said to my apostles in Jericho concerning Lazarus. The reason for his illness was not death, but for the glory of God and the glorification of God's son through it.

Mary Magdala and Joanna tried comforting the two sisters. Through fresh tears, Martha managed a sentimental smile toward me. "He held on as long as possible to see you, Jesus. The fever was just too strong." She covered her face in her hands and sobbed, "He loved you so much, Lord."

I whispered for them both not to cry, but my words had little effect since tears were also running down my cheeks. "Where have you laid him," I finally asked.

Gently whimpering, Mary took my hand and turned. "Come and see."

She led me through the olive trees and around the ridge. Everyone followed. Many of their comments, while muttered softly, reached my ears.

"I can see now how much he loved Lazarus," one said.

Another answered, "I saw him open the eyes of a blind man last year. Could he not have kept his own friend from dying?"

The hill sloped downward to an even steeper embankment. Thankfully, steps cut into the side allowed for a careful, final descent. We then walked along the base of the rocky façade where a half dozen or more tombs had been hewn. Large stones were rolled tightly across their narrow openings. I stood facing them. The crowd finished their way down the slope and spread out behind me.

Mary motioned to a sealed chamber near the center. "That is where my brother lies."

I fixed my gaze upon it and concentrated on nothing else. Although my dear friend's body lay in the dark recesses of this crypt, *he* wasn't really there at all. Lazarus had gone home. He was truly in a better place—an immeasurably better place—a place no one would ever wish to leave. I remembered one of Lazarus' steadfast traits—his enduring faith—his obedient surrender to divine will. He trusted and relied upon God, whom he knew possessed wisdom far beyond his own and who also wanted the best for him. So I felt confident he would understand what I was about to do. More than understand, he would embrace the eternal significance of this day, even if it meant postponing his share in the kingdom of God.

I inhaled and exhaled deeply, eyes riveted to the stone guarding the tomb. Those around me, believers and skeptics alike, had heard me proclaim that I was the resurrection and the life—that whoever believed in me would never die. As a concluding sign before accepting my own death, I wanted to establish that as the champion of life, I held complete power over death. In me, and through my name, while the uncertainties and pains of dying were unavoidable, there was no reason to *fear* death. In me, death did not end life. Death only transitioned from old life to new.

The great irony lay in the certitude that this promise for new life could only come through sacrificing my own. But first ... one final miracle ... one last request of my Father before fulfilling his request of me.

So with unflinching eyes on that grave, I delivered a terse, challenging instruction. "Take away the stone."

Dissension escalated, including from Martha who whispered, "He has been buried several days now, Lord. There will surely be a stench."

I turned to look lovingly upon her. "Did I not tell you that if you believe, you will see the glory of God?"

She responded with a repentant nod, then glanced to Peter and urged, "Please, do as he says."

Peter and a few other apostles did not delay. They hurried to the chest-high stone, chiseled from solid rock. With great effort, they leaned their combined weight against one side and gradually pushed it away from the tomb's entrance. Darkness concealed the threshold. My friends did not linger to peer inside, dispersing as soon as the stone was out of the way.

I took a few methodical steps toward the unobstructed sepulcher. The crowd had backed away to provide plenty of room during the grave opening but now closed in behind me and watched closely as I approached the entryway. I stopped and genuflected to one knee, rested a forearm on my leg and stared down at the ground. Speaking privately to my Father, I enunciated enough to be heard by many. "Heavenly Father, I thank you for hearing me. I know that you always hear my voice, but I say this now so that those here may believe you sent me."

My eyes closed. I asked my Father to allow this one last sign— this final mark of our union … of our dominion over natural laws … of our eternal, invincible love. Death has no jurisdiction where you and I dwell, I prayed silently and directly. Our Spirit breathes everlasting life. Come now and breathe life into this tomb as a profound prelude to that soon-to-be empty tomb which will break the bonds of death forever.

My eyes opened, suddenly probing the shallow den's pitch-black interior. Despite a reassuring peace filling my heart, my breathing quickened. I lifted my forearm from my knee and raised my palm into the air, a gesture that silenced any murmurs from the crowd.

To summon my Father's divine power within me, I could have expressed many deep, insightful concepts, but I best exhibited our authority with plain, straightforward mandates. And so I candidly commanded, "Lazarus, come out!"

This simple, explicit directive horrified many. They knew Lazarus had been dead for several days. They had prepared his body for burial. They had carried his corpse to this gravesite, placed it in its final resting place and secured the tomb. To hear me now call him forward as if he were no more than asleep, challenged their mental faculties. It unsettled their psyches. Several loud shrieks, a few trembling cries and a full chorus of gasps filled the air as something stirred in the darkness just beyond the tomb's shadowy portal.

Something was moving in there. We heard it. A distinct scuffle. And then …

Lazarus!

Fresh screams bounced off the steep rocks as everyone's innate fear of a walking mummy abruptly confronted that reality. A figure enveloped in burial cloth stumbled several steps from the blackness and collapsed just beyond the tomb, head still covered in linen wraps.

Martha and Mary cried their brother's name in unison, but like the others, this impossible event froze them in place. Sudden shock prevented all those around me from associating these writhing internment wrappings with a man who had worked and socialized with them for years. So I promptly and matter-of-factly called above the commotion, "Untie this man and set him free!"

My apostles, who had witnessed the dead restored to life on more than one occasion, hurried to where the burial shroud struggled with life. They lifted the figure to his knees and pulled the linens rapidly from his head. When Lazarus' face came into view, the surrounding hysteria transformed into cries of exultation and astonishment. All worry turned to wonder as they recognized their neighbor and brother, saw his chest heave up and down with air and beheld his open eyes.

I couldn't hide a broad smile myself, regarding my friend's familiar face. His gaze was understandably dazed and distant, but Lazarus was indeed back, the color already returning to his skin. I approached him, followed by scores of others now unafraid to do the same. James and John worked feverishly to untie the hand wrappings so he could move his arms freely.

Lazarus found my peaceful smile. His eyes recognized me and

conveyed a multitude of thoughts and feelings with a tender, child-like stare. I offered my own nonverbal gratitude, thanking him with a quiet nod for his willingness to return—to come back for me and for his sisters ... to come back for the world.

News traveled quickly. Some had already run back to Bethany, eager to spread the word of Lazarus' return from the grave. Others I imagined would carry these events straight to Jerusalem, to the inner sanctuaries of its temple and to members of the Sanhedrin who waited restlessly for any report, any rumor of my actions and where-abouts. While I longed in my heart that hearing these accounts might finally speak to the hearts of the Pharisees and Sadducees, I did not expect their conversion as a likely outcome. As more people turned to follow and praise me, the chief priests and scribes would surely redouble their efforts to silence them by silencing me.

My apostles finished helping Lazarus out of his burial garb and assisted him to stand on wobbly legs. As others moved to embrace and welcome him back, many chanted my name in a victory cry. Their chorus held Judas' face in a wanton gander of ambitious hunger. He viewed this event and the accompanying adulation as a sure sign for me to lead the revolt against Rome that he so deeply desired. It wouldn't be long before he felt fully justified to secretly help the Sanhedrin find me, forcing an encounter where my words and deeds might finally sway the Jewish leaders.

I reclosed my eyes. Dread washed through my mind and numbed my legs. Give me strength, Father, I prayed. My final hours are nearly upon me. I have almost reached the pinnacle of my existence in the flesh.

I only ask for the courage and perseverance to do your will.

22

A King's Welcome and Cleansing the Temple

THERE WAS NO GREATER VIEW of Jerusalem than from the Mount of Olives. The great city beckoned from across the Kidron valley. On a clear day, one could peer for miles over the oak, palm and juniper trees that surrounded the hillside olive orchards. Only from this ridge could the towering temple spires and ornate column caps be viewed from above. Looking down across the high wall of Solomon's Porch gave a unique, breathtaking perspective over such grand architecture.

I had been sitting upon this overlook since dawn, lost in the panoramic vista, watching the early crowds gather outside the northeastern gate. Such a colossal, fortified, bustling city … and yet I feared for its future. Whether divine discernment or simply an inner personal perception, tears came to my eyes as I looked out over the high walls stretching nearly to the horizon. This most holy of places would not survive much longer after I was gone, at least not in its present magnificence and grandeur.

Another few decades … perhaps.

I shuddered, closed my eyes and muttered aloud, "Days will come upon you, my poor Jerusalem, when your enemies will close in and leave no stone unturned. If only you had recognized salvation while it was in your midst."

I wiped the moisture from my eyes, only then noticing Peter and Matthew taking a seat next to me.

"Are you all right?" asked Peter, visibly concerned over my vaguely ominous words regarding the hallowed city below us.

Before I could respond, my name drifted faintly up from the valley, carried on the morning breeze. The distant crowds called for me, hoping I was somewhere within earshot.

"Can you hear them?" Matthew said nervously. "You have made zealots out of these people, Lord. They are waiting to usher you into your kingdom."

Peter glanced behind us. "Those from Bethany and Jericho will soon approach as well." He surrendered a reserved smile. "You will not make a quiet entry into Jerusalem today."

I gazed across the valley to the growing commotion. "No, I suppose not." I then paused before declaring, "Today, many scriptures begin to unfold."

Matthew leaned eagerly forward. "Tell us, Jesus, what should we do?"

The sun had now fully broken over the crest behind us and bathed those waiting at the mammoth gate in warm sunlight. Rather than enter their holy destination, they waited, hoping I might pass their way—that my smile, even my shadow might fall upon them. I nodded slowly but definitively, more to myself than to anyone else. Suddenly I knew.

"This is what I need you to do," I said to them. "Take the short walk back into Bethpage. As you enter, you will find a donkey. Untie it and bring it here."

Matthew hesitated. "Just take it? What if someone—"

"If anyone says something," I replied before he could ask, "tell them the Master needs it."

And so they went, needing no further explanation.

I sat and waited, preparing for the first of many prophetic writings to play out in the coming days. More than five hundred years had passed since Zechariah prophesized to this very nation—*rejoice, oh daughter Zion, for your king comes to you, righteous and victorious, lowly and riding on a donkey*. These predictions from Hebrew, transcribed into Greek and handed down through generations, would be fulfilled today.

The small town of Bethpage lay nestled just over the Mount of Olives' northern ridge. My companions returned swiftly with donkey in tow, and yet hundreds of pilgrims had now joined and surrounded me. Peter and Matthew pushed through the growing assembly, tugging the sluggish animal behind them. They continued to thrust forward until finding me standing with our friends.

Matthew chided Thomas, whom he saw first. "Think you could have brought any more?"

"Amazingly enough," Thomas replied, "I don't think there's a soul left in Bethany this morning."

"Apparently not," he muttered.

Bartholomew slapped the hide of the donkey and chuckled. "What's with this perverse beast?"

"Jesus requested it," Peter answered, insinuating no further motive needed.

Bartholomew and a few others glanced at me, a bit befuddled. What could I possibly want with a donkey?

I smiled at the irony that this humble animal's obedient service would someday be remembered, honored and even envied.

Judas smirked. "Tell us you're not planning on riding this donkey into Jerusalem, Lord. You should enter atop a stallion."

I took hold of the rope that held the dusty colt in place. "A stallion is ridden by one who conquers," I responded. "I have come to bestow perpetual peace, not incite war."

I could read their eyes though—all of them cognizant that these crowds, both here and below, did not really understand true peace.

They believed that peace in these times could only come through war.

"We shall guide this animal to the base of the mount," I said modestly, stroking its scruffy mane as if it *were* an Arabian foal and not a borrowed burro from a poor village. "From there I will ride it into Jerusalem, with each of you by my side."

"And half of Judea," added Thaddeus. It sounded less like an exaggeration as the multitude closed in.

We began our descent, leading the flocks who continued gathering from points east of Jerusalem. It did not take long for those clustered near the city gate to notice the surge coming down through the trees on the Mount of Olives. They started in our direction, moving on the assumption that only I could command so large a following.

The hillside gradually leveled off, and we entered the Kidron Valley just above the Garden of Gethsemane where these two throngs suddenly converged. Peter removed his outer robe and threw it over the donkey's back. As my apostles worked to keep the press of bodies from collapsing onto us, I swung myself onto the animal's back. He was a large burro and could easily handle my weight. Andrew, who now held the bridle, patted its head and slipped it morsels of food to keep it calm amidst the surrounding bedlam.

Harboring the loudest, deepest voice in our group, Peter pushed up the sleeves of his tunic and cupped his hands to shout, "Make way! Make way, I say! Jesus of Nazareth—Jesus our king, comes in the name of the Lord!"

The word 'king' linked with my name resonated in everyone's heart. A new king—a king of the people—a holy Jewish ruler *for* the Jews was heading toward the most holy Jewish city during the most holy time of year. Excited cheers and cries of hope erupted from the valley. The intense uproar must have turned every head inside the temple courts.

At this heralding of a new king, many before me began to bow and shout, "Hosanna!" and, "Blessed are you, Jesus, king of Israel!"

Their actions spoke even louder. Cloaks, robes and blankets billowed down across the path for us to walk. My apostles pushed forward, and Andrew pulled the donkey along the dusty road. Others simply tore palm fronds from the trees and swayed them through the air as they waited to place them before me, all the while shouting their joy and praising God.

Their ardent devotion understandably warmed my heart. I acknowledged them with a loving smile and reached to touch their outstretched hands. I heard but could not respond to all the cries and questions.

"Are you here to save Israel, Jesus?"

"Will you deliver us at Passover?"

"How many will you raise from the dead?"

The fresh news of Lazarus' awakening had truly kindled a fire and ignited a hope that fanned expectation. Unfortunately, worldly expectation too often leads to disappointment. It easily triggers impatience and over time fosters resentment. Throughout history, mankind had begrudged God for many unrealized expectations. Their naïve and irresponsible nature routinely blamed others, and most easily God, for unfortunate luck. Despite humanity's ignorance of my Father's motives and methods, people nevertheless repeatedly judged and convicted him. Only by self-surrendering to God; only by allowing my Father, and me, to set their course, could people overcome the pitfalls of angst and depression, of fear and regret.

Today, expectations ran high, and I received a sovereign's welcome. Excitement filled the air. My exhilarated apostles snuck glances at me as they worked breathlessly to control the sea of bodies and keep my donkey moving along the trail. I most certainly preferred this joyous, supportive crowd over an angry, hostile mob, but my friends found it somewhat daunting, especially from their perspective in the thick of the commotion. Thousands of palm branches fluttered and twirled through the air, knitting an abstract carpet of green onto the dry, dusty path.

We approached the city's entrance, but even with its mighty gateway open, the procession bottlenecked and halted our progress. A group of Pharisees ventured out with the masses to see what all this mayhem was about. They elbowed through the congestion that funneled toward the soaring arch. Around them, loud voices synchronized into a deafening chant, "Hosanna! Hosanna! Glory in the highest!" Arms and palm fronds waved in unison, honoring me.

Those ahead finally cleared the stone portal, so Andrew tugged at my donkey to restart its slow, methodical gait. More chants of 'Hosanna' echoed off the high walls as we reached the arch. One of the Pharisees pushed his way to my side and welcomed me with a shout. "Rabbi, rebuke these disorderly disciples of yours! This is getting out of hand!"

His words gave me great pause. In just a few days, these hymns of homage rising from the valley could, and would, turn into jeers of derision, hatred and condemnation. I would soon face many of these same faces again, their accolades capriciously and viciously morphed into demands for death. The unenlightened self-interest of many would drive my destruction as easily as the hunger for deliverance drove this jubilation.

But for now, for this brief time, these wildly enthusiastic escorts gladly received and glorified the son of God's presence. While evil bided its time, waiting to strike, generations to come would savor this temporary realization of heaven-on-earth.

My donkey meandered past the disgruntled Pharisee, and I turned my head to answer him over the loud intonations. "I tell you the truth, even if these people became silent, the stones themselves would start to sing!"

Astonishment, irritation, worry—I noticed all three in his eyes before I shifted to face forward again. The cool shadow of the archway enveloped us, and a few more leisurely strides from my animal carried me into Jerusalem.

"Jesus is here!"

"Welcome, Jesus!"

"Praise God you have come to us!"

I closed my eyes to fully appreciate these words. They fell like refreshing dew droplets upon a parched field. I felt a hand on my leg and looked to see Peter gripping my side with excitement. James walked proudly next to him, beaming to those who received us with open arms. John too strut happily forward, as a soldier strides when returning victorious from battle. All my apostles moved assuredly around me—my harrowing predictions far from their minds. Suffering? Death? How could it happen with so many clamoring to catch a glimpse of me—so many applauding my arrival?

The hearts of my brothers foresaw bright prospects. Their shared optimism both sustained and scarred my own heart. I enjoyed their raised spirits but also knew this euphoria left them vulnerable. The terrors and tribulations coming all too soon would undoubtedly catch them ill prepared, without the resolve and will to face and endure them.

The crowds continued guiding us forward along the northern wall of the temple mount and past the front steps of the Antonia Fortress, named after King Herod's good friend Marc Antony. The four imposing towers peaked as high as the temple itself, just outside its perimeter wall. A full battalion of deployed Roman soldiers resided within this fortress, some six hundred during Passover. Herod Antipas' palace bordered Jerusalem's western wall across town, but his regiment kept their headquarters here within the Antonia Fortress. Many indeed found themselves on duty at Herod's castle, keeping it especially well guarded now that the Roman prefect of Judea, Pontius Pilate, was also taking up residence for Passover week.

Pilate did not hide his dislike of Jerusalem or his assignment here and held almost as much disdain for his host, King Herod. He scoffed at the higher position of this lesser man. Herod, as an appointed ruler of a Roman province, held *royal status*, which Pilate did not. Pilate, a military officer, a *prefect*, governed the smaller, less-significant territory of Judea. This included Jerusalem, where Herod's father had built his spacious palace and magnificent temple. Pilate resented the onerous and nearly impossible responsibility of keeping order in this volatile, occupied domain, while the man who outranked him absorbed himself in leisure.

In every part of this city, civil instability and insurrection threatened to explode at any time. Like dry grass and kindling susceptible to a single spark, Jerusalem at Passover presented ideal conditions for triggering an event—a particular incident that might set Judea and all Jewish territories ablaze. It wouldn't take much to destabilize this region into chaos. And Pilate, not Herod, would be held accountable by Rome.

That particular something had now arrived, riding on a donkey.

* * *

The following day was Monday. It dawned clear and bright, ushering a new wave of travelers into Jerusalem as the city furthered its preparations for the Passover celebration. I spent my morning on the Mount of Olives praying, then returned to meet my apostles at the base of the temple mount's grand open staircase along its southwest corner. With hundreds of others, we climbed the sweeping stairway, platform by platform, to the royal colonnade.

A breathtaking portico stretched before us under polished-smooth columns—forty long by four wide—its soaring, coffered ceiling spanning perpetually overhead. We moved with the masses into this majestic atrium. From here, we should have easily headed north across the court of the gentiles to the main temple complex. Instead, a labyrinth of confusion captured us. A snarled congestion of pilgrims, merchants and animals cluttered every available space of this otherwise magnificent cloister.

"It's a jungle up here!" exclaimed James over the racket of a hundred heated exchanges.

His observation was appropriate. An irreverent jungle of greed and deceit played out as far as we could see. Fully aware that foreigners from every Roman territory had descended on Jerusalem for Passover, merchants fought for space to charge double, even triple the usual price for lambs, goats, birds and other sacrificial animals. But selling these creatures for exorbitant prices was only half the injustice. The most profitable pocket-lining came through mandatory currency exchanges, refusing to accept the most common coinage found in a traveler's purse—the Roman denarius. Claiming it was 'unclean' to pay the temple tax or purchase animal sacrifices with pagan coins, money changers kept busy collecting the denarii and issuing Tyrian shekels for all commerce within the temple grounds. They imposed and enjoyed steep commissions.

These greedy leeches especially targeted those who had no bargaining power, who had come from afar and needed to fulfill the customary rituals, regardless of cost. Thousands of these unfortunates fell to the mercy of these vendors and brokers who showed little leniency.

"Four shekels for a year-old lamb?" shouted an irate pilgrim. "I'd be crazy to pay two!"

Arguments ensued, coins clattered loudly and money begrudgingly changed hands.

We simply stood there dumbfounded, overcome by and lost in this overwhelming scene. It was hard to discern if we were standing in a holy, sacred place of worship, or at the vortex of an unruly contraband bazaar. It surely resembled the latter. Temple scribes and money changers hurried past without giving us a second glance. Pouches overstuffed with proceeds dangled from their arms. Others corralled sheep or hauled cages of pigeons and turtle doves, weaving in and out of the colonnade's stately columns. Scores of pilgrims, many with families in tow, shoved determinedly by us, or through us—their anxious faces consumed in the turmoil of finding the best currency exchange with enough left over to purchase their week's provisions.

A single day ... it had indeed been only one day. Just twenty-four hours ago, the focus surrounding these temple walls had rested on hope—hearts and minds centered on God's Anointed one entering their midst. Now, few looked in my direction long enough to recognize me. I stood there present and among them, steps away from their most holy place of worship, and I was all but ignored—overlooked for seemingly more important matters at hand.

How paradoxical! The lamb of God walked beside them in the flesh, and yet so many clamored to pay dearly for sacrificial animals while unscrupulous pirates preyed upon and exploited their ritual obligations to atone for sins.

Such noise. Such bedlam. I recalled from scripture how reverent builders had assembled Solomon's first temple here, sections formed and framed away from the construction site so that not even a hammer's noise would disturb the sacred silence. And now ... such shouting, arguing and bitter bartering profaned my Father's house.

Like a parent impulsively yanking a child's hand away from a flame, I moved swiftly to prevent further pain. I grabbed a bundle of leather chords left over from roping a pen of lambs and wrapped the strands tightly around my hand for a good grip. I then flung myself into the crowd so suddenly that only John noticed me.

"Lord, what are you doing?" He hardly got the words out of his mouth before I was gone.

I first kicked open the lamb's pen, startling them into a haphazard flight for freedom. Squealing and bleating, they darted under foot in all directions.

"Everyone, stop!" My voice boomed with power and intensity, as did my direct and forceful actions. I raised the leather straps in an arc around my head as if to strike. Those in front of me scattered, bringing me face to face with several money changers huddled over their table. I brought the improvised whips down hard on the wood, sending a sharp crack through the colonnade that silenced the area faster than any shout. The men behind the counter stumbled to their feet and hurriedly backed away.

"You have turned this temple into a market place!" I reproached loudly.

I gave them no time to respond. Seizing the table's edge, I overturned it to the floor with a fluid flip of my wrists. Stacks of coins and money scales clattered to the stone.

The packed portico afforded no running room, but many tried, succeeding mainly in toppling over each other. A bold merchant or two rashly lunged at me, but a few whistling swipes through the air with my chords promptly changed their minds.

"Why?" I yelled, then kicked the legs out from another money table and crashed its contents to the ground. The occupants protested vehemently as their neatly organized silver and copper currency scattered across the floor.

Pilgrims grappled for the rolling coins, heightening the chaos.

This did not stop me. I stormed from one area to another and grabbed the bamboo slats of a large bird cage. Pulling with my full weight, I capsized an entire stack of coops. They crashed heavily to the floor and splintered open. Pigeons and doves erupted from our feet, screeching and chirping as they soared to the high ceiling.

It took several moments for people to realize who was actually wreaking this havoc. Their shock and panic quickly turned to amazed bewilderment. While knocking over another table, I noticed a few of my apostles trying to reach me but stumbling into others fleeing my wrath.

A shepherd hastily swept two of his lambs out of the way as my whirling leather chords cleared a path. "Have you gone mad, Jesus?" he shouted, a fleecy animal clutched under each arm.

I made it to the edge of the colonnade and upended a final exchange counter. The open court of the gentiles stretched from here to the main temple complex, and many now approached from across the square to see what this commotion was about. I too swung back to face and examine the effects of my foray. Breathing heavily, I wiped some perspiration from my brow before issuing a succinct, authoritative indictment to explain my actions. "It is written that my house shall be called a house of prayer! But you have made it a den of thieves!"

A wave of tiredness hit me—more mental fatigue than physical. I had undoubtedly made my point, but would it sink in? Blank, puzzled stares gazed back at me. Merchants and money changers grumbled and cursed as they grabbed for their strewn property and accessories. Others stood or knelt frozen to the floor, perplexed by my uncharacteristic tempest.

Then *they* appeared, sauntering like wolves finally catching up with their quarry. A group of Sadducees, adorned in their grandiose best for Passover week, pushed through the converging swarm of inquisitive visitors. Their crown-like caps peaked from under softly woven mantles, and their finest robes and beaded stoles virtually flowed over the portico stones as they walked. They showed no interest in any of the surrounding disruption, instead affixing their attention forward, making cold eye contact only with me.

Still catching my breath, I watched them approach. The leather chords slipped from my hand.

They came to within several paces before stopping. Their hardened faces and narrowed brows held me in bitter contempt. At first their lips remained silent, allowing the muffled babble of scattered lambs and the outcry of infuriated traders to set the tone.

One of the nearby money changers held out a handful of denarii and shekels mixed together. "See what this prophet from Galilee has done, rabbi? This will take hours to sort through!"

The festooned priest did not turn to look. He needed no evidence or opinions to form his own attitude and judgment. "Prophet? A prophet who runs wild through our grand colonnade unleashing such mayhem—disrupting and damaging our temple?" He conclusively answered his own rhetorical question with a scornful shake of his head. His next seething inquiry, however, definitely sought a response from me. "Tell us, Jesus of Nazareth, what sign can you possibly perform that will prove your authority to do such things?"

I inhaled deeply to help slow my breathing. I then looked over at my apostles who had made it through my cluttered wake—to Judas who stood with anticipation, hoping I might take this opportunity to perform a great miracle in the presence of these cynical superior scribes. But my thoughts instead turned to my Father in heaven and how very close we were to completing this mission, one that would indeed culminate with the greatest of miracles. And so I decided to answer this Sadducee truthfully, albeit figuratively, through a profound contrast between the stone and mortar temple where we stood, and the flesh and blood temple that stood before them.

"Destroy this temple," I said clearly, "and in three days, I will raise it up again."

He couldn't respond at first over the startled murmurs breaking through the crowd. Holding up his hand, he waited for quiet before formally addressing my patently ludicrous ultimatum. "It took forty-six years to build this temple, and you claim you can raise it up again in three days?"

I did not answer. Silence confirmed my affirmation better than any spoken words. This only drew further mutterings from those around us.

Another Sadducee stepped forward. His voice choked with garbled revulsion. "You should be taken before the Sanhedrin for such fallacy!"

The lead priest again raised his hand, this time to calm his colleague, eyes never moving from mine. "And where pray-tell might you get the power needed to perform such an impossible feat? From God? Are you alleging before all gathered here that you could summon the Almighty's power to rebuild this temple in three days?" His question quivered with brewing impatience, but he remained controlled, having practiced well the art of keeping an expected composure. "Don't think I haven't heard the comments, whispers and suggestions that you are the Messiah, the long-awaited son of God." He paused before pointing a bony finger at me. "I want to hear it from your lips, teacher. I grow tired of rumors and hearsay. Tell us here and now. Are you claiming to be the Messiah? Are *you* the Christ?"

Utter blindness. Anger, jealousy, fear, spite—so many long-festering vices had created a cloud so thick around his heart, he could not see the truth, no matter how loudly he professed to want it. The divine reveals itself only to the pure, open and simple of heart. I refused to be provoked into wasting true words on deaf ears and a corrupt heart—one that would only pervert and subvert that truth.

I simply closed my eyes.

"Refuse to answer?" he clamored. "Did you not just call this temple *your* house? *Your* house?! This is God's temple! Are you implying that you and God are one in the same?"

Yes, I longed to shout. For someone who never hungered for the truth, he surely articulated it well. As I began to consider how best to resolve this dilemma, my Father provided a way.

"Jesus, Jesus!" leapt beautiful little voices.

I opened my eyes to several young hands tugging at my robe. Four, five, six—soon a dozen children encircled me, calling my name. I glanced up and noticed Mary Magdala and Martha standing against a stone column, encouraging a few more little ones my way. Where had they come from so suddenly? These two wonderfully clever women must have quickly rallied youngsters from Bethany, already here for the festivities, and sent them running for me. Both fully knew that neither man nor woman, only little angels such as these might divert the antagonism of the Sadducees.

I tried offering a smile to these contentious men while shrugging candidly as this charming distraction now edged me closer toward the crowd. I did not resist their eager hands guiding me away from the center of attention. I stroked a few of their heads and sidestepped along with them.

Groups of pilgrims, even a vendor or two, finally began chuckling at this unanticipated incident—such youthful innocents turning a tense situation into a humorous diversion.

The lead Sadducee, however, found no amusement and soberly shook his head. "Children may temporarily thwart your accountability for blasphemous remarks and disruptive actions today, Jesus, but you *will* be held accountable, I can assure you."

I refused to dwell on these hollow words. Instead, I returned my focus to my rescuers, to these remarkable children escorting me to where my disciples could take over and lead me away. Once safely back within the throngs of people, I picked up one of the smallest girls and rubbed noses with her before resting her in the crux of my arm and addressing them all. "Thank you, my precious cherubs," I exclaimed. "You have truly done the work of angels today."

We made it back to the grand staircase at the colonnade's southwest corner. From this spacious terrace, I gazed out over the sprawling, tightly-knit streets of Jerusalem, all the way to the tree-lined walls of Herod's palace in the distance. I leaned to either side and gave Mary Magdala and Martha a kiss on their cheeks. They looked at me with poignant, thoughtful expressions, somehow suspecting my time with them could not last much longer. It seemed their hearts grasped a reality with which even my twelve apostles had difficulty—that I was returning to my Father soon. Very soon.

Mary's eyelids fluttered delicately as a breeze swept around the stoa, whisking the curls from her face. "I don't want to lose you, Lord," she breathed on the passing air.

With a comforting smile, I quietly replied, "Whether I am in this world or not, you will never *lose me*. We are here for such a short time—all of us. I came from the Father and must now return. Following me from this world back to the Father is the only thing that should matter to anyone."

The words resounded within my head—*following me from this world back to the Father*. I painfully knew that few would follow me during *my* final steps back to the Father. But I suddenly suspected Mary Magdala would indeed do just that. I instinctively grabbed her hand and held it tightly in mine. "Don't leave me, Mary."

Our eyes glazed with moisture. So suddenly stricken with emotion, she couldn't even shake her head.

She slowly lifted my fingers to her lips and gently kissed them. Her soft voice released a faint, single word … "Never."

23

My Last Supper

WE SPENT OUR NIGHTS in Bethany away from Jerusalem's crowded streets, but this traditionally quiet village teemed with its own activity well into the evening. Less than an hour walk from the holy city, Bethany was a common destination for many weary pilgrims to camp. Their oil lamps and small fires dotted the hillsides like glimmering stars below the hidden horizon. Lively conversations mingled in the night air even after most of the village's dwellings went dark.

Despite comfortable accommodations in Lazarus' home, I slept in fits and starts. Too overwrought to sleep at times, I prayed for peace, and my Father helped settle me enough to rest. My appetite also began to wane, but I forced myself to eat. It was imperative to keep my strength.

Finding slumber and feigning hunger became particularly hard Tuesday morning as many spiritual and worldly concerns flooded my head. It was as if the rocks in a dam were breaking free, releasing a rush of revelation, a wave of wisdom that flowed from my divine soul into my brain. Now even obscure details stood stark and clear. I no longer sensed or guessed how things might unfold. I knew. The supernatural, shared omniscience with my Father burst forth. All was crystalline—especially the awareness that I would soon experience in the most profound way a fundamental human life characteristic. I knew that my ever-present Father was with me, and throughout me. That could never change. But here in the flesh and in this world, I also knew I must endure *all* its hardships, including having my personal hopes denied and accepting the agonizing perception of not feeling my Father's omnipresence when I needed it most. I must show through example that only faith can sustain the mind through such incomprehensible impressions.

After walking along the crest of the Mount of Olives, I leaned against a sturdy palm tree and looked desolately down over the temple buildings across the valley. A series of stone chambers bordered the southern courts of the Sanhedrin. While I somehow knew I would never see the inside of them myself, my breaking heart told me that Judas was there now. A small assembly of Sadducees and Pharisees surrounded him. These men, in direct contact with the High Priest, Joseph Caiaphas, would exploit him, mislead him, bribe him and ultimately play upon his greatest weakness—greed. His visceral, extreme self-reliance would now move me onto his own agenda. He sought more ambitiously to have *me* follow *his* path, rather than he mine. Turned from the light long enough, he was more easily seduced by the darkness.

While Caiaphas himself would waste little time with one of my disciples, he would undoubtedly push his scribes to spare no expense at finding a strategic opportunity to close in on me—preferably away from the crowds. Caiaphas, above all others on the council, cared little for the truth. He wished only to maintain his elevated role as High Priest through use and abuse of the Law and Jewish traditions.

My presence doubly threatened his status. If too many people continued putting their hope and trust in me, they would likely abandon his overly scrupulous interpretations of the Law. His functions would fade. His influence would weaken. A Messiah now would render his own prominence pointless.

The other potential consequence with me in Jerusalem was that while Caiaphas' contempt for Rome rivaled that of any Jew, he and Pontius Pilate had an understanding that he couldn't afford to violate. Despite the prefect's apathy toward elaborate Jewish rituals, the Roman governor himself appointed the High Priest as his deputy of sorts, one to help keep order over so many bothersome Hebrews. Caiaphas currently held this job, and if peace prevailed, Pilate would allow the Passover observances and ceremonies to continue throughout the week. This in no way implied a liking of the High Priest position or person, and Caiaphas knew that. Pilate would not hesitate to decree an end to the Passover celebration if disruptive protests or riots ensued and would certainly not waver to execute dissenters. Worse, if he even slightly suspected that Caiaphas had lost control of his own people, he would have him readily replaced.

The self-serving Caiaphas could not permit any chance of these possible outcomes. Reports of my actions in the temple yesterday must have further fueled his desire to terminate me. These mounting situations surely had him pacing the courts of his opulent home in the upper city, not far from Herod's more palatial royal residence. Caiaphas knew I had many disciples ... and nearly as many detractors. If he bided his time—if he simply stepped back and ignored me and my followers—he risked the continued strength of my ministry, threatening his all-important control. And if he waited too long to actively suppress my scope and significance, the resulting turmoil could incite the very civil upheaval that Pilate could not, and would not, tolerate. I was certain that to preserve his own power and to avoid any potential Roman consequences, Caiaphas would resolve to eliminate me now. He would hold nothing back to dispose of me quickly and completely, justified in his own mind to save Israel from collapse.

He had already put the wheels in motion. Passover began Friday at sundown. They would slaughter the sacrificial lambs early that day. Later, they would slaughter the lamb of God. My hour of suffering had come upon me. I would soon return the righteous back into the hands of my almighty Father, and despite my grasp of the impending horrors, all nations from here to the end of time would indeed remember it as a very good Friday.

*   *   *

The thirteen of us sat at my favorite spot on the Mount of Olives. On this late Thursday morning, my apostles kept close to me as we reclined on the hillside. We relaxed, cooled by the breezes whispering up from the valley. This final day before the Passover feast saw Jerusalem below vibrating with activity. The women in our group, including my mother, also prepared for the holiday, down there somewhere.

For a while we sat in silence and enjoyed the peace of a lazy morning away from the crowds. I allowed the surrounding tranquility to soothe our minds before speaking. "Tomorrow is Passover, but I wish to have a very special supper with you all this evening."

John answered without averting his gaze from Jerusalem's walls. "Every meal is special with you, Lord."

"Tonight is different," I replied, my voice hardly rising above the currents coming across the ridge. "Tonight we share a meal that I have waited to have with you for a long time. We will eat it together in a room I have secured in the city. Afterwards, we shall go to the Garden of Gethsemane to pray." I mentioned this destination for Judas' sake. He had been fidgety, fishing for a time and place he could lead the temple guards to apprehend me for an appearance with the Sanhedrin. I did not want dinner interrupted for many reasons. The Garden of Gethsemane, an olive grove with its cultivated pathways tucked snug into the valley, would offer an opportune place to confront me away from the city's congestion.

Andrew leaned back on his elbows, closed his eyes and lifted his face to the sun. "I'll be there."

"We'll all be there," agreed Peter. "Of course we will."

I waited a few moments before plainly professing, "The time has come when you will not see me for a while."

The statement hung in the air. Many of them glanced at each other, silently conveying, *There he goes again.*

I raised my voice an octave to clearly indicate I wasn't speaking to myself. "A woman giving birth experiences pain because her time to deliver has come. But when her baby is born, she forgets the anguish because the joy of having her child consumes her." I looked at their confused stares. "This is how it will be with you very soon. You will grieve for a time, but before long, joy will consume you."

They were unsure how to respond. Peter, not wanting the silence to drag and hoping none of his brothers would question my words, promptly asked, "Where is this room, Lord, that we may help prepare the meal?"

I squinted aimlessly off toward the horizon and reflected on the spacious upper room I'd finally come across the previous day. It had taken some time to find anything not already occupied or reserved. Nothing I checked into anywhere near the temple was vacant, but this second-floor chamber just inside Jerusalem's southwest section was not only still available, it would easily accommodate us all.

I thought of how best to articulate directions to Peter, then considered another idea. I had met a man who lived there, not the owner but a boarder—a deeply troubled individual. He had no wife, no children, no siblings to visit. He had some close friends but still felt extremely lonely, isolated and forgotten. Worst of all, he felt worthless. He felt meaningless to others and useless to God. I could see it in his eyes as I entered the building to look at the possible room upstairs. He had come from drawing water at the well, a task that only accentuated his solitude to anyone he met. Fetching water was a woman's task. Men tilled, fished or gathered food. Women fetched and carried the family's daily water supply. Seeing a man carrying a jug of water rather than just a waterskin could only mean one thing.

There was no woman in his life—no wife, no sisters, no close brothers with sisters. The need for water obviously forced these occasional unfortunates to parade their lonesome truth publicly to and from the well each day.

In about an hour, this man would go to draw his water as usual, considering himself empty and unimportant every step of the way.

Not today. Not ever again. While I did not know his name, I wanted this self-perceived insignificant soul remembered. *Everyone* is always loved and remembered by God, yet so many fail to grasp that they actualize and often *realize* God's will simply by offering their seemingly meager, day-to-day tasks in his name. This particular man, who desperately avoided eye contact during his treks from the city well, would have his walk today immortalized for eternity. I decided to include him directly in my preparations for establishing a new testament between God and mankind.

I brought my eyes back to Peter, who by now wondered if he was going to receive an answer. "Take John with you," I said to him, "and enter the city through the Gate of the Essenes. You will find a man carrying a jug of water. Introduce yourselves and follow him to where he is going. Once there, tell the owner of the house you have come to prepare a meal in the furnished room upstairs."

He nodded at the simple, direct instructions, fully aware that spotting a man carrying a water container would not be difficult.

Silence returned, and my companions settled back to their quiet savoring of this peaceful morning along the mount.

I took a deep breath, hoping to control the instinctive adrenaline that quickened my heart. Fate no longer approached. It was at my door. With each new task completed, with every unstoppable movement of the sun across the sky, my final hours drew closer. The time to enter my passion, to offer myself up for the salvation of the world was at hand.

Reality bit hard … my last supper was officially set.

* * *

Dusk descended on Jerusalem. Shadows from the western wall stretched farther over the city as the sun sank deeper behind the horizon. It was a blood-red sunset, painting the heavens afire. From the roof of the building where I was to eat dinner with my apostles, I watched the radiance slowly fade with the darkening sky. The day was coming to a close. My final evening was here, as were the final hours of the Mosaic testament between God and man. Tomorrow at this time, a new covenant would be sealed in flesh and blood. My flesh and blood.

The sun was so low now—just a crescent on the crest of that western wall—I could gaze directly upon it. I felt like a man kneeling in a barren, lifeless desert thirsting for his last drops of water, watching them dissolve into the sand. Imminent death beckoned. Darkness engulfed the sky and consumed my heart. My greatest act of love was all that remained. My teaching and healing were complete. My mission to spread the good news of God's love had been delivered. It was now time to authenticate that message with indisputable validation. For my brothers and sisters—for the human race that I cared so much for and chose to become one with—I now chose to be broken for them. I was prepared to take the weight of their sins upon my back—to endure their punishment for them.

This steadfast, absolute love is all that kept me from shaking as the sun went down.

I *love* you.

So much so, I discard my power and submit completely to the torments of evil to unequivocally demonstrate that love. My love for you is so infinite and so boundless, I consent to do on earth what I could not do from heaven ... die for you. I came in the flesh so that I could offer my flesh in death for *you*.

There is no greater love than this.

My apostles gathered inside. The room provided two sections—a large area near the door with sparse, unassuming furniture, and a smaller chamber set back for dining. Here, two short wooden tables were pushed together with mats and cushions placed around the perimeter. There were windows on each of the outer walls, but they were small with crisscrossed latticework. Since darkness had fallen, only faint, indistinct voices filtered through their slats. Tiny candles perched in wall niches, on window sills and across the table, providing a soft, warm glow to the room.

The table was set—the modest food prepared and waiting. Servings of diced cucumbers drizzled in olive oil separated bowls of olives, figs and grapes. In the center where the tables joined, a cloth covered basket of bread rested next to a jug of wine. Each plate already held a cooked portion of fish, filleted and sprinkled with chopped hyssop. We all stood around the adjoining tables, glancing at each other and at the food before us.

I nodded to Peter and John. "You have done well getting tonight ready."

John smiled. "You mentioned it was a special meal."

"I did." Then motioning them to sit, "Please, make yourselves comfortable and remove your sandals before we eat."

Hesitant with curiosity, they kicked off their sandals and sat on the cushions under the low-set table. I grabbed a towel from the shelf and tucked it into my sash before bringing a large bowl and container of water to where James sat. I knelt to one knee and looked into his eyes.

"What are you doing, Lord?" he asked, inferring but hardly understanding.

"I'm here to wash your feet," came my simple reply.

His bewildered stare matched those around the table.

"Your feet, James," I said softly, indicating he needed to move them closer for me to wash them.

He slowly turned and placed them at the bowl between us. All fell silent as they regarded this surprising spectacle. They each leaned forward or backward to more clearly see if I was actually going to wash the crusted dust from their friend's dirty feet.

I grabbed James' ankle and held it steady over the bowl. I then poured water from the jug onto his foot and wiped it dry with the cloth. I carefully did the same to his other. My brothers couldn't have been more astonished. Their teacher … their Lord … the son of God—down on his knees and cleansing the day's grit and grime off a pair of feet.

I then moved from James to Simon the Zealot. He felt just as awkward presenting his feet to me, as if to the lowest of servants, but he complied. I washed them thoroughly and then Thomas' and Andrew's too. Peter was next. His eyes conveyed more dismay than puzzlement.

"You're going to wash my feet too?" he asked contentiously. "You—my Lord and Master?"

I placed the bowl beside him. "You do not realize what I am doing now, but later you will understand."

He remained rigid, still uncomfortable with the fact that I was shuffling along the floor, touching and cleaning their feet. Urns of water were often placed by doorways for guests to cleanse their *own* feet, but to wash another's was considered demeaning at best. "No," he muttered, not wanting to disagree loudly. "You shall never wash my feet."

"If I do not wash your feet, Peter," I countered quietly, "you have no place with me."

His eyes locked with mine. He could see my sincerity, and the impact of my statement took hold of him.

He promptly brought his feet from under the table and placed one directly on my leg. "Then wash not just my feet, Lord, but my hands and head as well."

After cleaning and wiping Peter's feet dry, I continued with the others. When finished, I returned to my place at the table. "Take heart at what I have just done," I told them. "You call me Lord because that is who I am. Now that I, your Lord, have washed your feet, you must go and do the same. A new commandment I give to you tonight … Love one another, as I have loved you. By showing this love to all, everyone will know you are my disciples."

They nodded tentatively, wanting to grasp my words more than they did. And that was fine for now. They would understand so much more after my Holy Spirit was upon them … after enduring the fear and uncertainty of the coming hours.

I bowed my head to say the blessing, and they closed their eyes for grace. "Heavenly Father," I invoked, "bless this meal we are about to share. Strengthen us in body and spirit so that we may persevere to do your will. Keep us from falling into temptation, but if put to the test, guide us by your loving hand so that we may not falter." I let the words penetrate around the group before concluding definitively, "Amen."

And with that, the meal began. Passing and partaking of the food kept us in silence a few moments until Bartholomew mentioned frankly, "That rebel Barabbas and two others were arrested in an uprising this afternoon, out by the northern gate. A Roman guard was killed, another badly wounded."

James the less shook his head and snatched some grapes off the bunch. "Pray they just get the spear."

"A Roman soldier was slain," Philip reiterated, emphasizing the gravity of the offense. "They'll be crucified."

"What were they thinking; why lead a protest now?" wondered Thaddeus. "Even if no one gets killed, they'd be flogged to within an inch of their lives and tossed from the city. And for what?"

Judas set his cup down hard, the conversation striking a chord with his own hopes for a successful rebellion against Rome. "Barabbas leads a movement that while noble in cause, cannot win. Deliverance needs to come from above, just like our ancestors."

While I waited for the right opportunity to interject, John innocently asked, "Lord, you mentioned the time had come when we will not see you for a while. Where are you going? How can we come with you?"

The others nodded, hoping for a direct answer.

I swallowed, not wanting to explicitly convey that tomorrow I would likely hang from a cross between Barabbas and his cohorts.

"Where I am going, you cannot follow now. But you will follow later."

Peter, seated next to me, grabbed me lightly by the forearm. "Why can't I follow you now? I am prepared to go wherever you go. Don't you see that? I will lay down my life for you."

The look I returned was so somber, it nearly pushed him back. "Really, Peter? Will you really lay down your life for me?"

"Yes, Lord."

I hoped he couldn't read the true sadness in my eyes. "I tell you the truth … this very night, you will deny three times that you even know me."

My words drew a murmur from all at the table except Peter. He was too stunned to speak. "How … how can you say that?" he finally managed. "I would never disown you."

The others joined him, each pledging aloud their own commitment and devotion to me. I took another bite of fish, but my deep sorrow made chewing and swallowing almost impossible. "The shepherd will soon be struck down and his sheep will scatter," I said, trying to compose myself and not break down. "Dare I say even one of you will betray me."

They looked at one another, now all of them speechless. Judas had an olive halfway to his mouth when he stopped and turned to me. "Surely you don't mean me, Lord."

Denial. The evil one held him so tightly, Judas actually believed what he was about to do was not betrayal, but simply a needed catalyst in bringing me to power.

Satan was ready to delight in his moment of triumph, to revel in my physical destruction from this world. That fallen angel of so long ago, however, failed to understand that this very meal would cement my intimate relationship with so many souls, thus ultimately defeating him against *them*. Before he could begin to physically harm me, I would become physically and forever present to all who trust in me. Destroy me and remove me from this earth? Separate me from my children?

Never. I reached into the center of the table and brought the bread basket and wine flask over to me. I grabbed a rounded loaf from the top, broke it in two and handed the larger piece to Peter. "Each of you, take some of this bread and listen to me carefully."

Peter slowly obeyed. He tore a chunk from the side and then passed it to Andrew. Moving around the table, it divided quickly, now in each of our hands ... one loaf shared among many. I held my portion before my eyes and gazed at it more intently than one would ever look at a piece of bread. My brothers regarded theirs as well, wondering what was so special about baked dough.

"Take this and eat it," I said. "For this is my body, which is given up for the salvation of the world." I held it tightly in my fingers and glanced at them before continuing, "Whenever you gather to partake in this, do so in remembrance of me."

My hand went to my mouth, and I consumed it.

I had never seen them so apprehensive to eat something, but they did, some watching others before trustingly biting, chewing and swallowing their own.

I lifted the jug of wine and carefully poured a large goblet to the rim. Again, I positioned the cup steadily before me, beholding it as so much more than fermented grape nectar. I took a sip and handed the carved wooden grail to Peter. "Take this cup all of you and drink from it. This is my blood, which is poured out for the forgiveness of sins."

This declaration shocked and confused, even as they recalled my words from the Capernaum synagogue that my flesh was real food and my blood was real drink.

As the goblet made its way around the table, I vowed, "I will not drink from the fruit of the vine again until that day when I drink it with you in my Father's kingdom." I then added, "Remember me when you share this chalice."

Their faces now revealed an understanding that they were going to lose me in some way, at least for a while. Asking them to remember me implicitly indicated my impending absence.

"I want to tell you one more thing," I said, deliberately moving my benevolent, loving eyes to each of them—eyes that had provided such comfort through times of stress. "I want to tell you so much, but you could not bear it right now. Stick together, all of you. You are brothers, bound together in my name. Support and assist one another. Know that I will soon send the great helper to aid you. My Spirit will come over you. All that belongs to the Father is mine, and I will allow our Spirit to give you knowledge and courage you never thought possible."

Several of my apostles reached out for an arm or shoulder next to them, acknowledging each other as I spoke. Not really knowing what to make of my words, they took consolation in their steadfast companionship.

"Tomorrow is Passover," I continued. "Let us sing a portion of the Hallel this evening before we go."

The great Hallel was a common chanting of six Psalms, offering praise and thanksgiving to God. I needed in my heart to hear Psalm 116—*The snares of death entangled me; the anguish of the grave came upon me. I was overcome by distress and sorrow ... The Lord is gracious and righteous; our God is full of compassion. When I was struck down, he saved me.*

In the glimmer of the dancing flames that flickered around the room, we sang. No harp or flute—just our natural voices to God. How I wanted this moment to last—this final time alone with my friends. My heart had never been so torn, so filled with veneration and despair all at once.

But it was time. Destiny could be deferred no longer.

We blew out the candles, and left for the Garden of Gethsemane.

24

The Garden of Gethsemane

THE NEARLY FULL MOON dominated the sky, its white brilliance polishing much of the black night to a ghostly indigo. We easily crossed the Kidron Valley to the Mount of Olives without torches or lanterns. Several narrow paths branched off from the main road, crisscrossing through the trees and brush like serpents through a shadowy ravine. We chose a less-traveled passage along the valley's deepest depression and up toward the southern fringes of the Garden of Gethsemane.

Judas was no longer with us, having slipped away from the upper room before we left. His puppeteers awaited, already pulling his strings toward an inescapable fate.

I glanced above the approaching garden's many olive trees and up the hillside bathed in hazy moonlight. The first of many spiritual battles suddenly engaged my mind—the evil one striking first, pushing and urging me to run. *Safety awaits over the crest of the mountain*; I could almost hear that biting hiss of a voice, that guttural rasp I had last heard in the desert after my baptism. Satan's lies and false promises echoed in my head.

I grit my teeth and fought back these nefarious invitations, but fear and anguish consumed me. Sweat beaded my brow, and yet I shivered, anxiously clutching my fingers to keep them from trembling. How much longer? How much more waiting?

"What's wrong, Lord?" asked Thomas—the others also noticing my weighted anxiety.

I did not want this. These men would soon have to contend with enough panic and confusion. I did not want them overwhelmed at seeing me so profoundly distressed. But I also did not want to enter the garden alone. My three ex-fishermen stood near me—the trio who had witnessed my transfiguration upon Mount Tabor. They had seen me clothed in the glory of divine light. Could they now handle watching me prepare for my darkest hour?

"Peter, John, James … come with me into Gethsemane. The rest of you stay here under this juniper and keep watch. Remain attentive, and pray." I made fists to again keep my hands from shaking. "Pray that you will not fall into temptation. The spirit is willing but the flesh is weak."

Glassy-eyed stares and apprehensive nods reflected under the glow of the moon.

I looked to Peter beside me, tiredness in his eyes.

"Come," I said.

I reluctantly turned, and my three friends who had followed me through so much, now followed me through a break in the hedges and into the Garden of Gethsemane.

Its name literally translates, 'garden of the olive press.' A haphazard weave of sand and gravel walkways, each overgrown with weeds, snaked through the spacious orchard. Rows of olive trees whispered eerily on currents of air from across the valley. Their thick foliage stretched from tree to tree, allowing only pockets of moonlight to filter into the grove. I actually welcomed this darker environment—more securely secluded and less vulnerable than out in the open. Still, agitation seized and disoriented me. I paid little attention to where I was walking, or where we even were for that matter. My turmoil intensified at the growing expectation of being cornered, trapped … hunted by those who wanted me dead. These uncontrollable emotions sprang up, flushing my skin with heat—sweat soaking my neck.

We walked a bit further before I stopped again to survey our dark surroundings. The trees eclipsed a clear evening sky, yet I could still see visible concern on the faces of the men beside me. They noticed my aberrant heartache and were deeply troubled, unsure what tormented me to such a degree.

My despair was spreading to them.

"Lord, please tell us what's wrong," said Peter, almost pleadingly. "We are here for you. What can we do?"

I looked away, convinced I would break down if I tried to speak. Despite these dear friends standing with me for the moment—despite knowing my heavenly Father and blessed Spirit were present and within me, and our angelic multitudes close by, I suddenly felt so totally alone. This horrible sense of isolation nearly collapsed me. Empty and exposed, I felt increasingly separated from all semblance of earthly peace and love.

Once again Satan seized the opportunity to promote his heinous rebellion. Attacking from a different direction, he hinted and surmised that sinful humanity did not deserve my supreme sacrifice. All the hatred, malice, bigotry, perversion, deceit, greed—a perfect storm of outright antipathy toward others and apathy toward God stabbed at my mind. His cold, callous questions followed … Was it worth surrendering myself to such dreadful agony for so thoughtless and faithless a race? Would an act of love this epic be wasted on those who would only continue to sin and turn from God?

My fist went to the bridge of my nose, struggling to thrust these destructive thoughts from my brain. Before my companions could again voice their uneasiness over my appearance and behavior, I turned abruptly to them and said, "My soul is overwhelmed with sorrow to the point of death. Stay here and watch with me."

"Anything, Lord," replied James, his own voice quivering with remorse. "We will do whatever you say."

I motioned to the olive tree we were under, cloaked in darkness. "Stay and watch," I said again. "Pray."

They slowly sat in the grass against the enormously rugged trunk. I remained standing and turned to face a sudden gust of air that revived the rustling of branches through the garden. My eyes narrowed as I perceived the faint black outline of several large rocks at the base of a small slope, a natural grotto nestled between trees.

I started for it.

John leaned forward to rise, but Peter held him back, sensing I sought solitude to pray with my Father. He was right. With fear swelling to the verge of delirium, I staggered across the path, descended the grassy gradient and soon reached the hollow of rocks. My knees finally gave way. I sank to the ground and leaned forward, resting my elbows on a protrusion of stone. My hands clasped together, and I placed my forehead upon them.

I knew with certainty what loomed this very night. I had known for quite a while. Finally here at this precipice of unimaginable suffering, my humanity longed for my Father to find another way. Throughout my life on earth, I had always sought my Father's guidance with humble joy. Tonight, however, like so many afflicted souls every night, I prayed with desperate passion.

"Father," I invoked, squirming with anguish. "My heavenly Father, I know that all things are possible with you. My heart is burdened beyond words at what lies before me. Evil approaches even as I pray to you. No time remains—my hour has come. Only you can find a way. If it is possible … allow this cup to pass by me. I cannot bear to taste its poison." I peered reluctantly over my knuckles, up to the olive branches swaying spectrally in the distilled moonlight. My resolute whisper ascended with the breeze, "Your will though, not mine, be done."

It was the fragment of prayer I had taught so early in my ministry—*your kingdom shall come; your will shall be done.*

My Father's will is perfect. It shall be done.

My head lowered again, this time all the way to the cool, hard surface of the rock. I kept it there to sooth my hot forehead. Sweat continued dripping from my face as blood rapidly pulsed through my galloping heart ... blood that would soon be shed for the world.

I desperately needed to focus on the main objective—love. My all-encompassing love would see me through this passion, this torture of body and soul.

Love for God's purpose.

Love for my children.

Love for *you.*

I raised my head from the rock and warily stood. My own words came swimming back to me, my Father acutely reminding me of my own convictions. *No one takes my life from me. I give it up freely for the life of the world.*

Fear still gripped every fiber of my being, but my knees seemed stronger now. I looked up once more to the peaceful hints of luminescence twinkling through the tree canopies. Was this my last quiet view of all that was good on the earth? How I wished I could just close my eyes and stand there all night, chin tilted to the tranquil sky, listening to the sounds of silence, interrupted only by God's gentle breath upon my face. But it was time.

Now exerting the most arduous mental effort of my thirty-three years in the flesh, I forced myself to turn, to shift into the direction of a wicked, oncoming storm ... and start moving toward it. I didn't realize until I was nearly on top of my three apostles that they were asleep, each easily reclining against the olive tree's massive trunk. So much for keeping alert and praying.

I stood there a few moments, not sure what to do next—not wanting to do anything. The longings of my human mind struggled with the wisdom of divine intention, suppressing my ability to think clearly. I grappled with the desire to just will myself back to heaven, to avoid death entirely—especially so ghastly a demise. I *could* do it. I was Lord of both heaven and earth and could summon a regiment of celestial agents for protection and deliverance at any time. It would take but a single command. The power rested no further than my lips.

Nevertheless, I remained silent. I issued no summons—no intervention for my rescue. While a painless flight from this painful world simply waited for me to decree it, I instead sought refuge in my stronger determination to do the Father's will.

I would do this … to the end.

I first heard the voices at a distance through the trees. My other eight apostles had entered the garden and were scampering through the dark looking for me. Their muffled, indiscernible words sounded frantic.

I wiped the moisture from my brow and suppressed a last-minute urge to flee with a deep breath and a final nod to heaven. "See me through this, Father … My heart is ready." Then, turning to my sleeping brothers, I raised my voice. "Peter, James, John; could you not stay awake with me even for a while?"

They had only lightly dozed off, and Peter quickly came around, nearly leaping to a stand. "What is it, Lord?"

The other two awoke and stood as well.

"The hour has come," I announced, "for the son of Man to be delivered into evil hands."

Without a second thought, Peter swiped open his robe and unsheathed a sword. The blade was smaller than the Roman gladius but longer and more menacing than a dagger.

"Where did you get *that*?" blurted John.

"Don't ask," he replied. "I knew we might need it."

Before I could comment on the weapon, the others arrived, wide-eyed with fright and out of breath.

Bartholomew blurted between gasps, "Temple guards, Master.

About twenty-five … or more … approaching from the valley."

"Twenty-five?" exclaimed James, hardly believing what sounded to him an exaggeration.

"Or more," Bartholomew reiterated.

"They are well armed and carry torches," added Thomas. "And they are definitely seeking us out."

"How could they possibly know where we are?" asked Peter, skeptical how anyone could have assumed we'd be in an olive orchard after sundown. "Maybe they're just scouting the Mount of Olives for us."

Thomas shook his head in the darkness. "No. They are coming for Gethsemane. And moving fast."

"Then we must flee," said Peter. "Away from Jerusalem. Temple guards won't venture far from the city."

"Flee?" Philip argued. "They are practically here. We have nowhere to go!"

Peter pitched his sword into the grass. "Well I can't fend off twenty or thirty armed men with a single blade!" He felt useless with it.

Matthew tried allaying nerves by rationalizing. "There were no Roman soldiers as far as I could see. Perhaps we can—"

"What, Matthew?" Thomas interrupted. "Perhaps we can what? Reason with them, Jews to Jews?"

"Why would the Sadducees send so many?" he retorted.

"Brothers," I finally interjected, "don't you understand? Do you not remember my prophecies and teachings? What I said would inevitably happen has begun."

At hearing my words, their panicked quibbling ceased. I had come to know each of these faces so well. Their lives had shared so much with mine over the years. My heart broke as I realized this was our last moment together. I seized upon it to offer a profound goodbye. "Know that I love you," I said earnestly. "So much of me yearns to prolong our time together. But I must go. I must do what I was called to do since the moment sin entered the world."

John moved toward me as a child whose father prepares for a long journey. "You don't need to succumb to them, Lord. You have slipped away from their hostile hands before."

I wanted to respond, but the hourglass had run out.

"There they are!" The shout sliced coldly through the rustling trees. We all turned, startled. The glow from a dozen torches jostled in the garden's obscure gloom. Surprisingly, they could already see us. The moon's flickering, filtered light exposed shapes and objects rather easily. With the twelve of us together, they only needed to glimpse a few.

"They've seen us," croaked Thaddeus. "It's over."

Another stern command radiated from the approaching lights. "Stay where you are; do not move!"

As paralyzed prey, we kept rigid and still as our pursuers closed in.

"What do we do?" asked John nervously.

His appeal went unanswered. They were upon us. About ten torches now lit our area, bringing life to our shadows, twisting and undulating as the flames moved around us. Many had already drawn their swords. Unlike Roman blades crafted by an imperial armory to standard specifications, these were personal weapons of the temple guards, all unique in size, curvature and metal. Each wore a similar woven headpiece, a rawhide vest over his garment, and much like their Roman counterparts, leather straps from waist to knees.

They outnumbered us better than two to one, but moved with caution and uncertainty, as if waiting for something.

A figure then stepped from their midst, almost materializing out of nowhere. He came slowly forward, having hidden away from the torch lights until now. He sauntered toward me with his mantle far over his head and face hung low ... but we all knew who it was.

"Judas?" uttered James, completely aghast at seeing him appear from the center of this assemblage. "What are you ..." His voice trailed off as he and the others suddenly made the connection. The horror and disappointment that had crushed my heart over Judas' impending downfall now seized my apostles, numbing them with revulsion and rage. Their shock and despair immobilized them.

I now realized why the temple guards had not advanced further toward me. They did not know me by sight. Judas of course, did. He would need to give these men some sign, some gesture that would indicate me to them.

Everything moved in torturous slow motion. Judas approached until we were almost toe to toe before raising his face to mine. His eyes, hauntingly illuminated by a nearby torch, betrayed my betrayer. The energy, the animation, the life that had once given such character to my friend's countenance, was dead. Dull, empty eyes now met mine.

"Hail, rabbi," he said softly, then leaned up to gently kiss my cheek.

The first agonizing pang of my suffering pierced my heart.

"Judas," I whispered, "must you betray the son of Man with a kiss?"

He had no time to respond. I half heard Andrew scream, "No!" just as a tightened fist, reinforced by a sword handle, struck the back of my head and nearly knocked me unconscious. I staggered forward, only to receive another guard's solid punch to my left eye. Pain from both blows roared through my head, the skin under my eye swelling as another voice yelled, "Stop!"

It was Judas. He feebly grabbed for one of the sentries. "You promised you wouldn't hurt him!"

The man pushed him forcefully back, shoving him to the ground. "Your task is done!" he growled. "We'll take over from here."

The words were no sooner out of his mouth when two other guards pounced. One seized my right arm and pinned it violently behind me. I winced with a gasp and doubled over, a hard knee to my side knocking me back upright. As they wrenched my other arm to my back, Bartholomew and Thomas descended on Judas like animals.

"Traitor!" Bartholomew cried in rage. In three long years, I had never heard the man raise his voice. Now it may have carried clear to Jericho.

"How could you betray him?" shrieked Thomas, seizing Judas and shaking him furiously against the ground.

This only made matters worse.

"Arrest them all!" bellowed the lead sentinel.

Pandemonium erupted. Swords swung to the ready. Most of my apostles broke for the darkness of the surrounding trees. Bodies scattered in all directions. Three guards lunged at Thaddeus and Philip who knocked blindly into me, sending us all to the ground. One of them grabbed to pull Philip from his knees just as Peter struck. Swinging his sword in an arc intended to maim and not murder, he caught the man by the side of his head, the blade finding only his ear but severing it completely.

A bitter scream cut through the struggle. He rolled into a ball, clutching the bloodied side of his face.

Two others turned their swords on Peter who raised his again, this time in defense. "Leave us alone!" he shouted.

For the first time since the assault began, I found my voice. "Peter!" I yelled from the ground, held in place by no less than six arms. "Peter, put down your weapon! All who live by the sword will surely die by the sword."

Faced with the pointed tips of two threatening blades, Peter hesitated.

They yanked me roughly to my feet, and I addressed our attackers. "You have come to Gethsemane seeking *me* and have succeeded. You were given no orders to apprehend others." I paused, allowing this truth to penetrate. "Take me now. Take me alone."

One of those clutching my shoulder called to the two holding Peter at sword's length. "Forget him for now! See to Malchus!"

They only obeyed after seeing my friend's weapon lower to the ground.

They then moved to where Malchus writhed in the weeds. He had found his severed ear, moaning in pain and lamenting his disfiguring. They helped him to his feet, and one of the guards actually scolded him. "You're just a servant of the High Priest, Malchus. You shouldn't have even come with us tonight."

"Bring him here," I said.

They turned to me with shock and scorn. "Who are you to give orders, Nazarene?" one barked. "You're under arrest!"

Malchus approached anyway, clasping the mangled ear to his head. The bloodied cartilage shifted under his fingers.

"Your disciple has maimed me for life," he sniveled. "He should be arrested as well."

Although my left hand was painfully immobilized, I raised my right just enough to reach the wounded side of his face. And despite ringing in my own ears from the two punches to my head, I said to him, "Be healed."

The guards jerked me back.

Malchus lowered his hand with trembling fingers as his ear stayed in place. He touched it again, frozen in wonderment that it remained intact and fully reattached.

Most of the nearby guards hardly noticed this during all the commotion. One of my restrainers, however, saw the miraculously mended ear and derided at once, "The scribes are right; the devil's power resides in this Galilean! Chain him quickly!"

My only relief came from seeing the other sentries return from the darkness of the trees empty handed. My friends had swiftly dispersed without torches or weapons to slow them down. Even Peter had abandoned his sword and slunk into the night. He was not far though. Many of my brothers were finding various escape routes over the Mount of Olives toward Bethany to alert the women of our group, and my mother, to these tragic events.

The guards hastily produced an iron collar and savagely clamped it around my neck. They again pinned my arms to my back and secured them tightly with chains around my waist, linking to others fastened at my throat collar. They then tied several ropes to these couplings so that multiple guards could each yank me as they wished.

I stood there, bound and manacled like a wild beast, yet I did not struggle. They scoffed and insulted me, yet I did not retaliate.

Once they had shackled me enough to constrain a raging madman, one of them dangled a short length of chain before me and rhetorically asked, "You know how much money you lost my brother in the temple with your crazy overturning of tables?" He didn't wait for a response before furiously whipping the chain across my face, splitting skin and welting its oval markings into my temple and cheek. I sucked in a lungful of air to keep from crying out as fire leapt through my face.

"You'll pay, Nazarene," he hissed at my ear. "Oh, you'll pay."

By now their formation had regrouped, added tinder to their torches, and were ready to deliver their prisoner to the High Priest. They yanked forcefully upon the ropes. With both hands incapacitated, I stumbled heavily forward, hardly keeping my balance. Every few feet a brutal tug on a different rope jolted and twisted me without warning, cinching the chains tighter into my body. I did not stay on my feet long. On a particularly violent pull, I pitched forward, and with no arms to break my fall, slammed to the ground chest first. The chains gnawed at my ribs, and my face smacked hard against the sandy grit of the path. I tried shuffling to my knees but could not. They jerked the ropes again and heaved hard, dragging me across the trail. The dusty gravel scraped at my beard, and the iron collar dug into my throat. I could barely breathe.

I wanted to cry for help, to plead for them to stop, but I knew how futile it would be. As they pulled me like an animal carcass across the ground, I could hear their constant taunts.

"C'mon, prophet! We'll drag you the whole way if need be!"

"Get up!" one blurted. "You're keeping the Sanhedrin waiting!"

"You deaf?" another shouted. "Get up!"

They repeatedly yanked their ropes.

The metal bindings constricted painfully around my strangled torso and aching arms, and yet I finally fought to my knees and staggered back on my feet.

It seemed an eternity before we left Gethsemane and returned to the clarity of the open night. The barbarity of my captors, however, did not lessen as we followed the narrow valley floor that hugged Jerusalem's eastern wall. I desperately tried keeping pace so that the assaults to my body weren't so severe, but it was no use. This band of hired thugs started across a small wooden bridge spanning a gully wet with mud from previous rains, and they again vigorously yanked me forward. I fell hard but missed the platform completely. The ropes went taught over the side of the planks, jolting me in suspension before spinning me into the muck. Remarkably, my impact on the chains did not fracture my sternum. I lay motionless in the black mire, my battered face dripping with mud, heaving air and bits of marshy runoff into my mouth.

I only partially heard their conversation from the bridge.

"This wretch needs to stand trial. Caiaphas will not be pleased if we bring him to the tribunal unconscious."

"Or dead," one laughed.

"We can always shackle his arms in front—lead him by the wrists."

"Very well."

Several cursed and swore at having to step down into the muddy gulch. They grabbed me from either side and hauled me from the ditch. Once back on my feet, they released my arms from the small of my back and brought them around front. My elbows ached from being bent, twisted and clamped for so long.

While one of the sentries cuffed my wrists and tethered his rope to them, another ridiculed me with a sneer. "You got dirt all over your face, prophet." He then smashed a fist into my nose, snapping back my head and slinging mud from my beard. Warm blood coursed through my whiskers, over my lips and into my mouth. My eyes filled with water from the stinging blow.

How will I get through this, Father, I prayed. How will I endure?

The agonizing trek back to the holy city continued, my captors sustaining their contemptuous treatment of me with every step. It had already proven horrifically cruel, and yet I knew it would become so much worse. Isaiah's scripture passage foretelling what was to come filled my head. *He was pierced for our transgressions, crushed for our iniquities; the punishment that brought us peace was placed upon him, and by his wounds we are healed.*

Tonight's agony and the horrors that awaited would soon cleanse all sin-stained souls with my precious blood. This is what drove me onward despite a real need to simply collapse. After tomorrow, humanity would finally have a way out—no matter how awful or burdensome the sin.

I am the way to eternal forgiveness. I hoped that even Judas, my friend-turned-betrayer, would remember this complete and caring gift. I would forgive him—if he would only repent and come to me for it.

Little did I know, however, as I was yanked in chains through the dim Jerusalem streets toward the stately quarters of the High Priest, that Judas would hang from his own tree even before I hung from mine. Instead of seeking my love and mercy, his despair would choose a rope and a sturdy limb as a resolution.

Worse than betraying me … he would quit on me.

25

Sentenced by the Sanhedrin

THE HIGH PRIEST'S HOUSE in the upper city was not far from Herod's palace. Dwarfed in comparison to the Roman tetrarch's sprawling compound, Caiaphas regarded his own residence as a palace nonetheless. Archways and porticos divided four courtyards surrounding a large stone building. In addition to his home, the structure served as an ad hoc tribunal for the Sanhedrin—a place away from the temple to conduct more esoteric trials and proceedings. Despite accepted bylaws against assembling after dark, Caiaphas' house teemed with people, even at this late hour.

They expected me. Events happened quickly now. I was yanked viciously through the main arch and into the crowded front courtyard. My welcoming party included none of those who had sung my praises just four days ago. Instead, summonses and bribes had gone out, assembling the vilest derelicts and transients from the city and surrounding area. Since Jerusalem's pool of people was triple the size this week, finding those willing to lie for money and mistreat a foreign prophet was no difficult task.

Clusters of unscrupulous opportunists crowded the patio, many warming themselves by several large fire urns. The temple guards pulled me through the court toward the building's front doors as one loudly announced, "We've got him! The self-proclaimed king from Galilee has arrived!"

The ensuing insults and gibes stung like venom.

"Jesus, the Christ?" someone howled. "Looks and smells more like vermin!"

Another pushed his way up to me. "King my ass," he quipped and spit horridly in my face. "Worthless cretin," he then muttered, wiping excess spittle from his lips.

A third ruffian traipsed over from one of the fires. "So sorry, oh great one; we have no palm to place before you." He promptly flung a handful of smoldering soot and cinders into my eyes. "Hope that'll do!"

They cackled noisily, hurling more slanderous remarks my way. I stood silent, eyes closed, hoping my brimming tears would wash away the hot ash burning my corneas. I heard the door unlatch ahead of us and slightly opened my eyes. A group of Sadducees huddled in the vestibule. The orange glow from several torches silhouetted their figures in the entranceway.

As my ropes tugged forward, I turned my head. Through a stinging, watery blur, I caught sight of Peter standing by a fire. He had somehow made it into the courtyard. Even from this distance and with clouded vision, he appeared pale with fright and helplessness. My condition surely cut through his heart—observing his now disfigured Lord fully manacled—face bruised, bleeding, covered in dirt and grime.

His painful glimpse of me was mercifully short, for I was forced quickly into the building. Many of the more coherent, well-spoken vagrants were also hurried inside before the doors were closed and locked.

I was taken to the main tribunal, a large area with a high ceiling and three stone steps in the center dividing the room and stretching the width of the chamber. Although fully enclosed, wall torches and ceiling candelabras bathed the room with ample light. At the top of the steps, several rows of wooden benches hugged the walls in a wide arc. These were reserved for the Sanhedrin, mostly Sadducees from throughout Israel, but some Pharisees as well, including Nicodemus and another named Joseph of Arimathea. Like Nicodemus, Joseph of Arimathea was more inclined to learn *about* me *from* me, rather than simply mimicking the elders in a sweeping denouncement of my words and deeds. Sadly though, like his friend Nicodemus, Joseph rarely sought me in public, lest his association with me compromise his council status. And certainly promoting my teachings would prove even more damaging.

More than half of the full Sanhedrin gathered on this upper tier of the room, but only a few occupied their seats. They stood arguing and vehemently discussing my arrest. Below, the unruly mischief-makers from the courtyard now choked the assembly hall with chaos. The temple guards further incited the mob by thrusting me toward the steps—poking, shoving and kicking me forward.

At my approach, Annas, the former High Priest and father-in-law of Caiaphas, raised his hand high in the air and yelled loudly enough to still the room, "Council be seated! The blasphemer, Jesus of Nazareth, is here to stand trial!"

The room quieted. The Sanhedrin took their seats, and the riff-raff behind me finally settled down. I noticed Nicodemus' sympathetic stare from the bench, shock and sorrow welling tears in his eyes.

A door suddenly opened behind the assembly, and Caiaphas made his entrance. The High Priest, in full ceremonial vestments, ambled into the chamber. Handing his staff to a servant, he moved unhurriedly toward the crest of the steps. Unlike the priests' white linen stoles, his was embroidered in deep purple and scarlet. Twelve gemstones inlaid his breastplate, one for each tribe of Israel.

His presence projected authority. He swaggered ominously forward until he could defiantly stare down at me. Tightly bound between guards, my abject vulnerability was the complete antithesis of his pompous resplendency. Instead of noble, colorful vestments on my shoulders, I buckled under the weight of iron chains. Where he proudly wore rare stones of great value, I bore bruises and lacerations across my face, my hair caked in mud.

After allowing this stark contrast to absorb the room, Caiaphas addressed the temple guards on either side of me. "Bring him before us for questioning."

They cinched their ropes tighter and delivered me as instructed up the three stone steps. Several other guards followed to position directly behind me. The seated council muttered and whispered to one another, surely commenting on my appalling appearance.

Caiaphas paced before them. He shrewdly stroked his beard and scowled at me from head to toe. "Not so commanding, are you, standing in chains without your entourage around."

I was surprised to hear Nicodemus voice an objection from the back row. "This is not right. We should not be holding a proceeding like this at night. Where are the other council members?"

"Keep quiet!" shouted a Sadducee from across the tribunal. "The High Priest has the floor."

Caiaphas could not look Nicodemus in the eye. He responded while shifting among the Sanhedrin. "Recent accounts from neighboring towns, as well as right here in our temple, justify a swift hearing. If this were not so vital for the peace of our holy festival, dare I say for the peace of our nation, I would not have called it so hastily."

His wandering eyes returned to me. They were cold and calculating. "Jesus … raised in Nazareth, son of a carpenter … wanderer of Palestine. They say you are a king. May I ask from what lineage you are a descendant?"

I held my head respectfully upright but with downcast eyes. It mattered little where I had lived or that the carpenter who raised me from birth traced his lineage directly to King David. The question here was rhetorical, nothing but pretense for a confrontation under circumstances guaranteed to defeat me. I had no need or reason to respond.

"No answer?" he challenged, pacing again. "How about to the

charge of blasphemy then? Surely you have a defense for having claimed yourself as equal to God—even referring to yourself as God's own son!"

Rather than offer a reply, I silently prayed for him. I prayed for all in this room.

Caiaphas moved his hands to his hips and took a step back. "Still no answer? Even to defend your own words?"

Despite a badly swollen left eye, I lifted my gaze and answered hoarsely but audibly. "I have always spoken openly and never in secret. I have taught where we all gather—in the temple and throughout the synagogues. Why do you need my testimony? Ask those who have heard me. Surely they know what I have said."

The guard on my right backhanded me across the face so hard I fell to my knees. His knuckles raised yet another abrasion on my inflamed face. "Is that any way to answer the High Priest?" he yapped, hoisting me to my feet with a yank of the chains.

I tried catching my breath from the blow before calmly reacting to my assailant. "If I have uttered any deception, tell me what evil I have spoken. But if I have told the truth, why do you strike me?"

Caiaphas, somewhat nonplussed by my placid demeanor, hesitantly took a seat in his high-back chair at the center of the tribunal. "Yes," he agreed with a scornful nod. "Let us hear from those who have heard you in public."

He motioned evasively to Annas.

The former High Priest gestured for one of the paid witnesses to come forward. The man stepped up from behind me, paused as if trying to remember rehearsed lines, then pointed an implicating finger at me. "This man cures the sick on the Sabbath!" he blurted but quickly corrected, "He cures the sick *with the devil's help* on the Sabbath."

On cue, another came forward. "He claims God is his father and that the priests and scribes are all hypocrites!"

Offended murmurs droned uneasily through the Sanhedrin.

They were silenced by a loud voice deep from within the room.

"He has the audacity to forgive sins!"

"And yet he eats with pagans and travels with women of low morals!"

"He lets himself be called the son of God!" another shouted through the chamber.

At this, one of the Sadducees stood from his bench and expounded, "He *himself* claims he was sent by God!"

I kept my eyes to the floor, praying that God would not hold against *them* these taunting rants against *me*. I prayed that their condemnation of the truth in their own words would not finally condemn themselves.

It was now Joseph of Arimathea who spoke. "Who are these witnesses?" he exclaimed frantically. "Where is the proof of these charges?"

"I will give you proof!" a man from behind me snapped. He dared to climb the first step toward the council. "I am a Galilean myself. I heard this man claim in front of hundreds that he is the bread of life! He said if we do not eat his flesh and drink his blood, we have no life in us!"

Angered pandemonium erupted from this allegation. Profoundly disgusted, one of the guards slammed the butt of his palm into the side of my head, nearly knocking me down again.

"He's demon possessed!" came a shout.

"Some say he commanded evil spirits into a herd of pigs!"

"What kind of a king is that?"

"Listen to me!" Another Sadducee stepped forward from the first row, one who had approached me Monday in the temple. "My ears are also privy to this man's blasphemy. This very week he proclaimed that if the temple were destroyed, he himself could rebuild it in three days!"

Repugnant rumblings buzzed vociferously through the room, drowning any one voice.

Caiaphas rose from his chair and pushed past the elder. He stood once again before my shackled form, staring in mystified distaste at how detached I seemed. Without moving his eyes, he addressed the congregation with a resounding, "Silence!"

It took several moments for the chamber to settle down, but when it had, Caiaphas spoke as if it were just the two of us in the tribunal, though he made sure his voice carried for all to hear. "Have you nothing to say to these accusations? No response to even a single one?"

I spoke not a word but was thoroughly prepared to testify fully to the truth. I would not hide the Gospel even from this corrupt conclave that sought nothing less than my complete destruction.

The High Priest's arms opened wide, presenting me the full attention of his assembly. "I ask you now, Jesus of Nazareth, before this holy council ... are *you* the Messiah ... the son of the living God?"

Although uttered with guttural insolence, his question was direct and concise—acutely delivered. It warranted an answer just as genuine and to the point, one that would not simply be remembered tonight ... but forever.

My eyes lifted, and a tear slipped from each as I openly replied, "I am."

The room collectively gasped, but I did not hesitate continuing, "And you will see the son of Man sitting at the right hand of God, coming on the clouds of heaven."

The chamber again ruptured into bedlam. Caiaphas stumbled back as if my words cut him at the knees. He shook with rage, tempted to lash out, but instead grabbed his own garments by the neck and furiously tore them down his chest while screaming, "Blasphemy!"

I stood quietly as the clamor in the room escalated, thanking my heavenly Father for giving me the courage to persevere in the truth.

Caiaphas yelled to his council over the chaos, "We have no need of witnesses! We have heard him for ourselves! What is your sentence?"

In the same short, concise manner that I had answered the High

Priest, the Sanhedrin's reply was just as definitive. "Death!" several shouted at once.

"Condemn the blasphemer!" another cried.

Annas stepped forward, and although a man of some age, swung a fierce slap to my face. He then stepped back and spat at my chest.

The Sanhedrin were now on their feet, pointing and demanding to have me removed from the High Priest's sacred house. Many persisted and repeated their verdict with loud cries for my termination. They all but smothered the feeble protests from Nicodemus that this hearing was erroneous and should reconvene after Passover.

Caiaphas turned abruptly to the guards and again raised his voice above the uproar. "Take this sacrilegious pretender to the holding room! We will bring him before Pilate at dawn and make our case for execution!"

How he wished he could have simply commanded these men to drag me from the city and stone me—rid me from the earth even before sunrise. But during this most holy and volatile week in Jerusalem, and aware of how recognized my name was throughout the region, he had no choice but to adhere to law and protocol. Only the Romans could legally carry out a sentence of death.

This angered him beyond control. He stormed out, exiting through the same private door from which he entered.

The guards had their orders but did not rush to obey them. They turned me violently around and shoved me down the short flight of steps. My knees hit the hard stone, chains once again cutting into my body. The mob was quick to haul me back to my feet.

"King? *God?!*" one ridiculed before spitting vilely in my face.

Another hocked phlegm at me as well.

And another.

I closed my eyes to the saliva that clung to my whiskers and hair. Alone and despised, I stood surrounded by sheer hatred—unrestrained hostility and bitterness. But love sustained me. Love held my chin high as more spit found my face and beard. I will take these insults, I told my Father silently. I will endure this slander, this mockery, this repulsive discharge upon my holy face … for them. I will withstand all of this, and more … for them.

One of the guards noticed my closed eyes and punched me in the ear. "So you're the son of God? Tell us who hit you!"

His cohorts laughed loudly, inciting another to swing a painful blow to the other side of my head. "How about that time, Messiah? Who was that?"

The crowd closed in so they could better assert their contempt for my blasphemy with physical abuse. The sentries yanked my shackled wrists and pulled me through a horde of hands that hit, slapped, punched, and if unable to reach me, waved obscene gestures. It became impossible to land any blow on a part of my head that wasn't already swollen and sore from previous strikes.

These bodily ambushes and verbal assaults blanketed me so, I hardly noticed we had made it back outside. While reeling and recoiling from the kicks and buffets, I heard something that fully collapsed me to the courtyard floor.

A woman yelled angrily at someone from across the patio, "How can you deny being one of his disciples? We've seen you with him in the temple!"

I turned my weary head, and through the legs of my assailants, saw Peter struggling to break the grasp of several hands upon him. Shivers of betrayal chilled my skin as I watched and heard my dearest friend—my rock and my brother—push himself away and shout, "For the last time I'm telling you, I have never even heard of this Jesus!"

There it was. The first soul to declare from his own heart that I was the true son of God, now swore publicly that he knew nothing of me. I had tried preparing myself for this but was not ready for the flood of sorrow it caused, far surpassing even this enraged mob's savagery.

Peter tore himself from his accusers and turned to run. He only made it a few steps before stopping. Somehow our eyes met, locking through the congestion of those between us. I looked upon him with love—with eyes that might portray what I was unable to speak … Do not worry, Peter; even this will not break my love for you. I *do* forgive you.

I was dragged to my feet but not before noticing my disheartened apostle drop to his knees, burying his face in his hands and sobbing.

The guards finally pulled me away from the ferocity of the crowd. They whisked me through a back courtyard, empty and dark, over to another series of stone structures. We entered the first. It was pitch black inside. The lead guard lit a small torch that illuminated a narrow passage of descending steps. He motioned for all but one of his cohorts to turn back. "We'll take him to the holding cell. Go and disperse the crowd from Caiaphas' main square. Tell them we'll need more assistance at first light outside Herod's palace. Pilate will need convincing to condemn this blasphemer."

The two then jerked me down the cramped passage so roughly, I missed many of the stone steps, groaning as I painfully stumbled and fell upon them. At the bottom, a thick wooden door with a heavily latched bolt stood in our path. It was swiftly opened and I was yanked inside. The single torch insufficiently lit this dank subterranean chamber, making it hard to gauge how large it really was. And while I could never have escaped through the door even with my full strength, they refused to unshackle my wrists. I was thrown to the floor at the base of a crumbling column, their ropes tossed carelessly atop my back. One of them administered a heavy kick to my thigh before turning and exiting the cell with his companion.

I lay there crumpled on the cold floor and watched the torch's waning light slide across the stone pillar and disappear as the door swung shut with a thud, blackness overtaking the room once more. With my face and eyes so badly bruised, and without the slightest sliver of light penetrating this cave-like chamber, I could scarcely tell if my eyes were open.

My body ached—swollen with countless contusions. My head throbbed from so many jarring slaps and punches. Dirt, blood and spit hardened like crust to my face. And yet I took this moment to thank my Father for this short respite from my enemies.

The physical agony, the complete darkness, the daunting isolation—this is why I willfully succumbed to such hell on earth ... to save the world from an eternity of this. Humanity had fallen far enough away from God to never merit the warmth of his eternal light. Instead, they deserved to collectively waste away, alone and broken in blackness.

I was here to reclaim and retrieve them. Lying on this dungeon floor, muscles moaning with the slightest movement, I thought of the glorious irony in my sufferings. I was allowing the punishment, the very wrath of God warranted for mankind ... to befall on me, the son of God. Hopefully generations to come would comprehend their God as so loving, he endured his own wrath to save his children from it.

In the morning, they would take me before Pontius Pilate. It was not what Caiaphas wanted. His obligation for a pagan military officer to implement the Sanhedrin's verdict of death disgraced him and the council. But it was a necessary evil in his eyes. If nothing else, Rome would drive home the message to all that claiming to be a divine ruler would result in a horrifying execution.

The paradox of my heavenly Father's plan filled my heart with restored energy. Although I would surely lose my life in the coming hours ... in the coming days I would secure eternal life for the world. His plan is my mission—my purpose. I prayed for the fortitude to complete it.

26

Handed Over to Rome

FRIDAY'S DAWN ARRIVED crisp and clear, but its amber glow failed to penetrate my windowless chamber. I lay huddled on the floor, blanketed in nothing but musky darkness, wondering when the guards would return for me. I used the temporary silence to offer my morning prayers, beseeching strength and courage for what lay before me—this final day. Distant sounds tensed my anxiety, each creak or muffled voice a menacing threat that they were coming for me.

And of course, they did. The same two guards entered loudly and pulled me to my feet. Sudden motion after hours of cramped inactivity inflamed the pain of my bruises and injured muscles.

After dragging me up the steps, one forced a small clay flask to my mouth and poured a stream of much-needed water over my lips.

"Better drink up. The procurator might have a question or two for you," he grunted, dumping water over my nose and mouth as if I were an animal.

I gulped what I could.

Reinforcements soon came and took me from the High Priest's property into the streets heading north toward Herod's palace. The sun turned from orange to yellow, stabbing at eyes still unadjusted from a night in dungeon blackness.

Fast spreading news of my capture caused commotion in the streets. Many of my assailants from the previous night waited roadside to join the procession. Other people came to their windows or doorsteps, curious to see if it was really I who hobbled past in chains, beaten nearly beyond recognition.

A few voices cried out, "Jesus, is that you?"

"Where are you taking him?"

"What have you done to him?"

My detractors pushed through anyone in their way to keep pace with each of my stumbling steps.

"How'd you sleep, your highness?" one taunted next to me.

"The son of God is here to meet the Roman governor!"

"Pilate will be in no mood for a Nazarene!"

Their scoffing voices were little more than dissonance to me. My muscles agonized under the weight of my chains. Hunched over, I staggered painfully forward.

Even at this early hour, a full regiment of Roman soldiers secured the praetorium outside of Herod's palace. A massive common courtyard stretched from the compound's eastern wall to three adjacent buildings that completed the square. Each was a long, two-story structure trussed with a regal colonnade on both levels. The one directly across from the palace served as Pontius Pilate's state house. From here he lamented his time in Jerusalem—suppressing insurrections, commanding a level of respect for the empire throughout the city, and trying his best to avoid Herod, whose gaudy displays of intemperance nauseated him.

Caiaphas and several members of the Sanhedrin waited near the palace wall, visibly uncomfortable with a dozen Roman infantry at this end of the courtyard. The last thing they wanted on Passover morning was to mingle with pagan warriors—occupiers of their holy city. A message had already been taken to Pilate, asking for his judgment on a criminal condemned by their council.

Upon seeing our approach, Caiaphas motioned to the soldiers that the prisoner had arrived, and it was time to enter the praetorium. The temple guards were not allowed access to the square with weapons, so it took some time removing and checking swords before we could proceed. Once cleared, and now escorted by a contingent of soldiers, they pulled me even more abruptly across the large open forum. I lifted my head just enough to glimpse our surroundings. We moved toward the main building's portico where a shadowy stairway underneath ascended to a section free of any columns. Next to a single chair cut from marble at the balcony's edge stood the provincial prefect, Pontius Pilate. This somewhat portly figure about ten years my senior had donned the formal uniform of a Roman centurion, except for a helmet. A scarlet cape flowed over his shoulder and arm, attaching to a bronze breastplate. No less than four soldiers flanked him on either side.

A scowl tightened his face as he watched us advance toward the mezzanine where he waited. In addition to the temple guards leading me in chains and the five or six members of the Sanhedrin, a large group of slanderers slunk back, many too intimidated to step closer to Rome's local seat of power, Gabbatha.

The only one Pilate really recognized was Caiaphas. He immediately addressed him with blunt indignity. "Not only do you summon me at this early hour, Caiaphas, but you insist that I come out to *you*, lest you become defiled on this holy day of yours." He glanced at his fingertips as if his trimmed nails held more interest than anything the Sanhedrin had to say. "Not a great way to put me in a persuadable mood."

Caiaphas hated this meeting just as much, especially confronting the Roman prefect from this lower position. It only added to the contempt of his situation. "If this Jesus were not a criminal, Procurator, we would certainly not waste our time, or yours, handing him over to you."

Pilate's gaze returned, now shifting to me. His eyes narrowed disconcertingly at my haggard appearance. "Do you make it a habit of chastising your own criminals so severely before turning them over to the State?"

Before Caiaphas could answer, another Sadducee interjected, "This instigator has so riled the people, they have already sought their own justice upon him!"

"So go then," returned Pilate, "and judge him according to your own laws."

"Procurator," said Caiaphas with a condescending tone, "you know as well as I that we cannot pass a sentence of death."

"Death?" he astounded. "What could this demoralized miscreant have done to warrant death?"

I kept my eyes down, and just as I had the previous night while they bantered over my fate, I prayed for their souls.

Still enraged over my blasphemous words before his tribunal, Caiaphas failed to recall Pilate's disinterest for, and downright apathy toward, sacred Hebrew law, shouting, "He teaches false doctrines for one! And perverts our laws! He even claims to be the Messiah, the son of God!"

Pilate chuckled emphatically, only fueling Caiaphas' anger. This snickering from above, however, quickly reminded him how best to capture the Roman governor's full attention. He stepped forward, and with as much impact as he could muster, pointed accusingly back in my direction. "He travels throughout Judea calling himself the king of the Jews!"

It worked. Pilate's smug grin vanished. He stared down at Caiaphas a long moment before further dropping his eyes and muttering, "*Stercore* … this is the last thing I need today."

When he looked up, his shrewd, sarcastic smirk aptly implied that I certainly didn't appear threatening, let alone regal. He nevertheless motioned to the soldier standing beside us. "Bring him here."

For the first time since my arrest the previous night, the temple guards released me, now into the even more powerful hands of Rome. To those who had originally shackled me, I was nothing more than a profane blasphemer and a brazen threat to hallowed doctrine and tradition. To the Roman soldier who now pulled me up the portico steps, I was an ordinary Jew—not worth the chains that bound me.

The landing led to a private chamber off the main balcony, and as we reached the top, Pilate entered from the mezzanine. He eyeballed me with a furrowed brow, then turned to his centurion near the doorway. "I think I can handle myself alone with this prisoner. You two may go."

And just like that … I was alone with Pontius Pilate. I had heard the many stories about the prefect's ruthlessness, short temper, strict adherence to Roman law and errant superstitions. None of it mattered. To me, he was simply another lost child—another mortal too entangled in the world's false promises to notice his savior's presence.

He silently walked around me and frowned in puzzlement. Then coming to face me again, he shook his head, befuddled. "Well, you must be *something* special to have provoked the High Priest into such a jealous frenzy."

I discerned no question, so I remained silent.

He enjoyed seeing Caiaphas all worked up, but regardless, needed to make sure I was not a threat to Rome or to his hegemony over Judea.

"So … what say you then? Are you a king?"

My swollen eyes glanced up for the first time. "Are you asking this on your own, or because what others have told you about me?"

"You think I care what the Jews think?" he scoffed. "I am no Jew. It's your own people who have handed you over to me. What could you have possibly done to bring them here on their holiest day, demanding your execution? Claiming yourself a god? A king?"

It hurt to speak over an inflamed lip, but I answered softly, "My kingdom is not of this world. If it were, my subjects would have fought to prevent me from being handed over."

A smirk returned to Pilate's face. "Ah, so you *are* a king then."

This ambitious, power-hungry Roman officer could never understand the spiritual forces opposing each other in this very room. His concepts and perceptions of rulers and authority were limited by his very limited physical senses. But I responded, "It is you who calls me a king. The reason I was born, the reason I came into the world was to testify to the truth. Everyone who seeks the truth, hears my voice."

Pilate took a step closer to try and better ascertain my thoughts, but my peaceful expression amidst so many cuts and bruises dumbfounded him. "Truth? What *is* truth?"

I again lowered my eyes to the floor, subtly indicating that I had finished speaking.

He needed nothing further anyway. A contemplative nod and a decisive step back preceded his disclosure. "Anyone who can remain so calm and so reserved while so many are calling for his head, may very well be a god. But as long as you're not a god or a king in this territory, you won't be in *my* way."

He started to turn toward the doorway but hesitated. His eyes swung away, suspended in thought, as if he were suddenly alone in the room. "My wife had a dream last night about a prophet brought before me ... Troubled her deeply." He looked solemnly back at me and sighed. "Can't imagine why."

Then, walking past the centurion onto the balcony, he muttered, "Bring him out here with me."

The soldier approached, seized my arm and pulled me to a position beside Pilate under the colonnade. Pilate rested his forearm on the marble chair and gazed out over the praetorium. More peasants and scribes had entered the square, inciting another legion of Roman guards to take position around the courtyard's perimeter.

Pilate snuck one last disinterested glance at me before address-ing Caiaphas and his council. "I find no basis to charge this man."

Caiaphas defiantly retorted, "No basis? Procurator, he has se-duced the people! Made himself a king! We have witnesses to his witchcraft and magic; what more does the Governor need to pass a judgment of death?"

Irritated, Pilate folded his arms. The High Priest pushed the line questioning his wisdom and acumen. He countered by belittling him even more. "Is this not the prophet you welcomed into Jerusalem several days ago? And now you want him dead? Don't contest my rationale, Caiaphas. Your own Sanhedrin seems to be the fickle fac-tion here."

Caiaphas masked his agitation. He needed to press further but also knew if he insulted the prefect, this could all end very badly, even worse than having me simply set free. "*We* did not welcome him into Jerusalem. His misguided disciples, those under his curse honored his arrival. Which is precisely my point, Procurator. He has become the savior, the king, to a very large and dangerous sect. This Galilean threatens the very fabric of our peaceful lives."

"Galilean?" Pilate looked inquisitively over to me. "You're from Galilee?"

Receiving no answer, he queried the High Priest below. "He's a Galilean?"

Caiaphas wasn't sure where this was going. He glanced at his other council members, confused how to respond.

Pilate didn't give him a chance. "You're in luck, Caiaphas. Or should I say, I'm in luck. You don't need me, and I surely don't need to waste more of *my* time with you or this deluded nomad."

"What are you saying?" asked Caiaphas, suspicious of this un-expected turn.

"The ruler of Galilee probably awakens in the palace right be-hind you." Pilate took a step away from the marble chair. "Herod is here, and this Galilean falls under his jurisdiction."

Still unsure whether this helped matters, it now became painfully clear to Caiaphas that this whole ordeal was not going to solve itself as neatly as he had hoped. "Procurator, you can't be serious. While we hold much respect for—"

"Don't push it, Caiaphas. Protocol must be followed." With that, Pilate turned on the balls of his feet and ordered his centurion in a stern, yet satisfied voice, "Take him to Herod."

* * *

The palace of Herod Antipas extended just beyond the high wall near the praetorium's main entrance. From this side of the formidable façade, only the very tops of two majestic buildings rose higher than the stone parapets. Caiaphas became even more infuriated as the huge doors under the main arch opened and I was hurried through. He suddenly had to decide which was worse, defiling himself by entering a Roman palace on the most holy day of the year, or allowing me to slip from his sight, to hang back, unable to articulate the importance of my guilt to Herod.

His angry cry resonated in my head just before the doors shut him out. "He must be condemned!"

The soldiers yanked me down a set of steps as brutally as the temple guards had, then over a small bridge spanning a narrow moat that encircled the palace buildings. We moved swiftly along a cloister at the courtyard boundary and across a long patio busy with royal servants, officers and other soldiers. As we neared the main structure at the northern end of the forum, a palace guard turned to shout inside, "Alert Herod the prisoner is here!"

In concurrence with this announcement, one of the soldiers shoved me violently from behind, painfully snapping my neck and dropping me to the stone.

"Get up!" another shouted insolently. "Enter this hall with respect!"

Once on my feet, they pushed me again toward the doorway and then into the grand building. In my filthy, weakened state, they didn't lead me far into the palace foyer. Lavish carpets from the orient graced the floor between polished pillars of various stone and color. The soldiers halted before the first rug, not wanting to sully such fine textiles. Regardless, we didn't need to go further. A voice cut through this crowded, bustling concourse, approaching hurriedly from the back.

"Is it really him? Where ... where is he?" While gruff and boorish, the words sounded anxious—optimistically excited.

It was finally happening. For so long, King Herod had scoured the Galilean countryside in search of me. He had gathered reports and rumors throughout the land, even listening with intent to John the Baptist's own accounts before silencing him with the sword. Any news of my miraculous deeds further fueled his jealous curiosity to witness them with his own eyes. Although determined to counter any challenge to his power and control, he longed to be amazed even more.

In haste, he knocked over a young servant while hustling to reach our position in the grand foyer. At word of my arrival, he had impulsively thrown on a white tunic, trimmed in gold at the cuffs and waist. He now tussled with a lustrous, modestly-sized crown atop his head, trying to fit it straight as he walked. His beard was meticulously trimmed and cut short except for a single thin braid hanging from his chin.

Seeing the soldiers with my broken figure meekly between them, he immediately stopped. The gleam rapidly faded from his eyes.

"This ... this is not Jesus," he confidently stated.

"It is, your majesty," replied one of the guards. "Pilate found no judgment for death, but since he is a Galilean, the governor has decreed your verdict should rest."

"Under what charge?"

"The Sanhedrin accuse him of claiming to be a king—a son of

the gods."

"But of course!" Herod exclaimed, startling everyone. "Hasn't anyone heard the legends about this prophet? This Jesus? Why not a king? A king who heals the sick, gives sight to the blind, even raises the dead!" He paused, eyeing me with consternation, utterly shocked at my appearance—an absolute contrast to what he had envisioned. He pointed his full hand in my direction. "Is this any way to treat a king?"

Herod's cynicism stirred the soldiers to stammer for a response. He moved closer, shooing them backward so he could more easily approach and scrutinize me.

He then leaned tentatively forward, as if to confide. "Can we be direct with each other, you know, ruler to ruler?"

It didn't take long to conclude my eyes were not about to rise from the floor, so he stepped back, glanced at those around him, then back to me. "After so many months of wild stories and listening to the Baptist jabber incessantly from his cell about you, I must admit, I was expecting ... I don't know, a little more of an impressive first impression."

Signs and wonders. It was all he cared for. I could have easily accommodated his shallow wishes but had never performed a miraculous work for the sole purpose of convincing a skeptic. I never would. A dialogue with anyone so single-mindedly focused and fascinated by power would serve no purpose. He had no real interest in me, seeking only to be astonished. He had no desire to really know me or to be changed by that experience.

"I know well who you claim to be," said Herod, arrogantly grabbing a chalice from a nearby servant and enjoying several full swallows. He returned the cup before looking back at me, and with smiling eyes, proceeded insidiously, "The one whose birth was foretold. The one my father tried to keep from growing up into power."

Most of those in the room were unaware of the events to which he referred. And although I was all too aware, my chin remained down, refusing to look up.

Herod advanced again and waited a few moments. He tried discerning any hint of thought hidden within the dirt and blood caked on my swollen features. "I can see, despite your battered face, that you are about the right age. Trust me, I could easily accept and believe that my father failed, and that the heralded king slipped through his grasp—a king that wields divine power ... even that of the Hebrew God."

It was no longer just Herod's presence commanding silent respect from his subjects. His words held the room captivated, everyone eager to observe what might transpire as he baited me with condescending commendations.

Surrounded by many, I stood as if alone, in quiet prayer.

"This is your one chance," Herod coaxed. "I'm not demanding to see the sky open or feel an earthquake beneath my feet. But I need to see for myself, once and for all, that you are indeed the one foretold, the one of whom your people speak. Are you the one—the one John spoke of? Tell me. *Show* me!"

Silence answered him—a stillness so sudden and complete that faded voices drifted in from outside on the palace courtyard.

"Anything!" Herod stipulated. "Surely you can think of *something* to demonstrate your power. You've supposedly worked many wonders in front of multitudes. Don't deny us the same privilege. I command you!"

When I didn't respond, a soldier seized my chain at the collar and jerked back my head, forcing up my face. The iron dug into my throat. I struggled to breathe through my mouth since my nose was too inflamed to gasp for air.

"King Herod has commanded you to act, Jew!" spit the voice at my ear. "I suggest you oblige."

I offered nothing. The tightened chain wrenched open my eyes, but only faint, desperate wheezes escaped my split, distended lips.

Herod took a final step closer and leaned in again, contempt and pessimism now wavering behind his impatient stare. "Nothing? You finally have a noble audience with real power and authority, and you deliver … nothing?" His voice was restless and irritated.

The soldier holding me tightly would have killed me where I stood at a single command from his superior. But the tetrarch's attitude and objectives were ambiguous. No one would execute me unless specifically ordered to do so.

Not surprisingly, Herod's infamous pride took over. If he further lost composure, shouted more impassioned pleas for action or even angrily demanded my death, it might give the appearance of desperation. The last thing Herod wanted in a palace full of subjects and Roman soldiers was to appear frantic or frustrated—especially over so weak a prisoner. And if nothing else, my meek acceptance of his taunts had disqualified me as either king or god to him. Disappointed though he was that his expectations remained unsatisfied, preserving his dignity now took priority over further demands for a miracle.

So he laughed. He stepped back and laughed aloud, as if I were nothing more than a hapless jester in one of his royal entertainments. "Powerless fool," he snickered.

Always ready to please and appease their king, many servants chortled along with him in derogatory amusement.

Herod removed his crown in a subtle gesture that indicated I wasn't worth his own royal presence. "This buffoon isn't significant enough to implicate, let alone execute. Maybe the Sanhedrin sees him as a seditious king, but I think I've exposed him as a fraud."

He finally lost his scornful smile and narrowed his eyes at me. "I suggest you crawl back under whatever rock you came out from and stay there. You are banned from Jerusalem. If I ever so much as hear your name around Galilee or Judea, your fate will be far worse than the Baptist's."

His stern gaze quivered with intensity before finally turning to the soldier at my side. "Tell Pilate I concur with him. This wondrous Jesus has done nothing more than delay my breakfast."

And with that, my appearance with Herod Antipas was over. As promptly as he had entered with the hope of witnessing the miraculous, he now disappeared back into his natural, mundane and profane life. He had, in so many ways, missed his chance.

One of the soldiers nudged his partner. "What now?"

"We take this worthless Jew *back* to Pilate to be released," he replied. "But not before I teach him a thing or two about wasting valuable Roman time."

With a hard yank of the chain, he swung me around and dragged me like a stray mongrel toward the palace door. Once open, he violently flung me forward onto the patio square. I fell hard to the stone, inflaming my bruises and sending new throbs of pain through my already pounding head. One of them lifted me up only to better land a solid elbow to my jaw, rattling my teeth and dropping me back to the ground. Consciousness faded in and out. I hardly felt myself pulled to my feet again. An ominous shout brought me quickly around. "How high and mighty do you feel now?" the roar exploded in my ear. "This is what I think of Galileans who don't keep their place!"

The soldier seized the chain not far from my neck and vigorously shook it back and forth, brutally jostling my head—the iron clasp grinding abrasions and blisters into my neck. Pain and nausea drummed my eyes as if they might burst from their sockets. He finished his assault by shoving me backward and releasing the chain. I pitched to the stone tiles, rolling and writhing in agony. My tormented moans only increased their insults and harsh derisions. Two of them grabbed my manacles and awkwardly dragged my collapsed, exhausted body across the square. I desperately clutched the taught chain to keep the iron ligatures from cutting further into my neck and chest. What a spectacle this must have been—a throng of Roman guards hauling the beaten, nearly unconscious body of the man who just days before had ridden into Jerusalem amid cheers and swaying palm.

After they pulled me up the steps to the doors leading from the royal compound, I somehow regained my footing. The colossal portals opened, and waiting right where we had left them, stood Caiaphas and the other members of the Sanhedrin, now among many more ruffians, peasant Jews, and what seemed a third battalion of Roman guards.

Caiaphas approached and immediately demanded, "What was Herod's decree over this malefactor?"

The lead soldier sneered at him with almost as much repugnance as he had to me. "This Jesus isn't worth his time! He's sending him back to Pilate to have him banned from the city."

"Not acceptable!" bellowed Caiaphas, pounding the butt of his staff on the ground.

"Don't object to me, priest!" the soldier shouted back against the escalating noise of the crowd quarreling over my return. "*My* luxury is simply following orders of *real* authority. Now out of our way!"

To the gasp of many Jews, he pushed the High Priest aside and yanked me through the congestion back across the praetorium.

Caiaphas could not, and did not, give up. He and his fellow scribes followed close behind, trailing with them a now hectic mob. Roman guards shoved and shouted for this unruly procession to settle down but only added to the bedlam.

Not peace but division. I had warned my disciples that great division would arise concerning me. It seemed to culminate right here and now. Many argued for my release, especially those I had personally connected with. Others yelled vehemently that as a dangerous blasphemer who would bring down Israel, I must be terminated.

Despite Herod's agreement with the procurator's initial judgment, the chaos approaching his quarters would not please Pilate.

27

Condemned

WHEN PILATE HEARD the steadily increasing commotion, he stormed back onto the balcony with his centurion and several guards just a few steps behind. He stared in dismay at the tumultuous crowd advancing toward the judgment seat. Far beyond perturbed, he made no effort to hide his anger. This was the one day he had hoped might project a pretense of peace, a semblance of order throughout Jerusalem. Although he half expected the sporadic bleating of the slaughtered Passover lambs to keep him indoors and perhaps an inebriated dissident that his Roman soldiers would need to quickly quiet, he had, for the most part, presumed a peaceful, more reserved day.

This is not what unfolded before him. Mounting disorder stretched across the square, with me as the focal point. When the soldiers finally pulled me to a position under the portico's shade, Pilate's annoyed impatience abided no longer. "What is Herod's verdict?"

The soldier clutching my chains answered, "He accedes to yours, sir, and commands the Galilean banned from the city immediately!"

"So be it then!" Pilate proclaimed, alleviated and somewhat

shocked to hear Herod had so swiftly agreed with him. Perhaps the perfunctory potentate wasn't as senselessly thick-headed as usual today.

Pilate also reasoned that if the growing mob kept me in their charge much longer, they might well tear me apart before he could enforce Herod's decree. "Bring the delusional prophet up to me!"

Two of the soldiers ripped me from the rabble and rudely escorted me up the stairs, through the side chamber and onto the mezzanine. Pilate waited, looking at me as if he'd had quite enough. Angered frustration welled behind his eyes as he turned to the aggressive crowd.

"I hereby release this so-called king of the Jews and banish him from within the walls of Jerusalem!" Like fresh oil on existing flames, the prefect's voice ignited a fireball.

Jeers and hisses erupted. The Sanhedrin derisively shook their heads. Caiaphas stepped forward and shouted up at the Roman governor, "Outlawing this instigator from the city will do nothing! His following has already spread throughout the land; can you not see the danger in this, Procurator?"

"I see no danger in this passive prophesier!" Pilate retorted, motioning his hand at me without moving his eyes from below. "I find no cause to convict, and neither does King Herod!"

Two words then distinctly ascended from below—a vehement, wrathful demand from one of the scribes beside Caiaphas. "Crucify him!"

The cold cry chilled the sweat beading on my torn neck.

Embittered to near rage, Pilate shook his fist at the Sanhedrin. "I am crucifying three murderers today! Murder, sedition, treason; these are the crimes that warrant such an execution!"

"This Nazarene *has* committed treason!" yelled Caiaphas, his voice hoarse from shouting. "He has not only betrayed our sacred Law but also broken Roman law!"

Those around him loudly vented their anger and disdain, raising fists of their own.

"He deserves death!"

"Crucify him with the others!"

A few voices deeper in the crowd clamored for my release but were quickly suppressed by rioters pushing and shoving them back, regardless of man or woman.

Pilate gestured decisively to his front-line soldiers to close in and restore order. As they unsheathed their weapons and threatened the reckless mob, Pilate glared indignantly down at Caiaphas. "Perhaps *you* cannot control your people, Caiaphas, but Rome can! I will see to it that this traitor of yours never dares break Roman law. I shall have him flogged to demonstrate the empire's intolerance for rebellion, and *then* I will order him expelled from the city!"

He did not wait for the High Priest's response and refused to glance in my direction as he turned to his centurion and muttered, "Chastise this troublemaker severely so these Jews get off my back, but do *not* kill him. I will be damned if Caiaphas tells *me* how to judge a criminal in my court."

"It will be done," came the simple affirmative.

*   *   *

The long palace guardhouse lay on the north side of the praetorium across a much smaller open forum. The building served as the main station and quarters for Roman soldiers dispatched from the Antonia Fortress and assigned to Herod's compound. In the center of this modest courtyard stood a single stone pillar, no higher than an average man's reach. It supported no building, truss or arch. It had no structural purpose and featured no carvings or decorative sculpting. Only faint, rain-faded maroon streaks stained one side of the cracked masonry. Two large iron rings hung from the top on either side with strands of old rope tethered to each, swaying in the breeze now picking up around the palace grounds.

They yanked me across the guardhouse patio to stand before this stark, intimidating stone column. A few dozen people from the main square followed and spread out behind us. Most chose to stay in the praetorium. They didn't have the stomach to witness what was in store for me here. Several members of the Sanhedrin pushed through. Caiaphas, however, stayed behind, needing to further strategize how best to convince Pilate to have me executed—unless the soldiers heedlessly accomplished this in their barbaric ferocity.

Those assigned to carry out my sentence were not actually soldiers at all, or even Roman guards. While directly under Rome's command, the two grungy brutes who stepped from the guardhouse were callous criminals themselves, derelicts from the Egyptian territories, captured by Rome and forced into hard labor constructing aqueducts and public buildings. Roman authority tasked the vilest of these bandits to do the dirty work of flogging—the onerous, sordid filleting of a fellow human using inhuman instruments of torture.

I stood trembling before the blood-stained pillar, weakened and bruised from my previous beatings and also terrorized by what I must now endure. The two sadists approached the post, laughing and slurring their words as if already drunk at this hour of the morning. Their inebriation, however, did not impair their movements. It only riled them into a fierce frenzy that fueled their vulgar, coarse behavior. They menacingly flung their whips by the column while challenging each other on who could inflict the most pain without allowing me the comfort of dying.

My horrified gaze naturally focused on the scourges themselves. Each wooden handle anchored six braided ox-hide bands, all laced with sharpened metal shards, small iron hooks and bits of whittled bone. These bundles of cruelly woven thongs were not meant to simply welt or even cut into a criminal's back. They were designed to tear the flesh from the body.

As the pair of indentured beasts continued barking and quarreling with each other, two Roman soldiers brought forth the temple guard with the key to my shackles. They abusively removed them, allowing no time to savor freedom from the chains before wrenching my garment over my head and tearing off my sweat-stained tunic. They even ripped the sandals from my feet. With apathetic procedure and efficiency, they stripped me naked, save for a tightly wrapped linen cloth around my waist and loins.

Speaking not a word, the two soldiers seized my forearms and swung my hands up to the iron rings hanging from the column top. They produced new lengths of rope and fastened my already sore, red wrists to the metal hoops, hoisting me up until I was practically on my toes before cinching and tying off the cords. Now snug up against the pillar, my rapid, shallow breathing resounded in soft echoes on the cool stone. I hung there, exposed and defenseless, trying to keep balanced weight on my teetering feet.

As the two ruffians snatched their ghastly flagrums from the ground, I heard the ominous jingle of their metallic fragments behind me. They tested the whips through the air—the sickening whistle of the knotted leather chords chilling my bowels. They snorted, laughed and bantered with each other on who should enjoy delivering the first blow. I tucked my chin under my shoulder and rested my throbbing forehead against the pillar.

I thought of you. It not only gave me strength, it enabled me to thank my heavenly Father one more time for allowing me to suffer this impending horror … for you.

All of this for *you* … so that someday you may inherit my kingdom with me.

"Begin!" The soldier's command tensed every fiber of my aching body.

The first barbarian mechanically obeyed. His grunt channeled all energy through his arm as he swung the flogging tendrils fiercely across my upper back. Fire exploded over my shoulder as if glowing torch embers had scorched deep into my skin. No scream escaped my mouth, for no air could exhale to carry the sound. My breath sucked in so forcefully, my windpipe nearly collapsed. I wanted to scream, but couldn't. The pain was too intense.

The second thug wasted no time, his lash tearing a half dozen jagged canals into my opposite side. Again, pain roared through me as if on fire. A third, fourth and fifth blow quickly followed, ripping flesh from my middle and lower back. My bound hands stiffened under the ropes, but I could no longer feel my raw wrists gnawing against their bindings—the inferno across my back blocked all other sensations from my brain.

My torturers did not stand in one place. They took several steps into each stroke for maximum momentum before slicing their spiked tentacles across my body. The metal shards and fanged hooks tore me to pieces, whizzing into me at speeds only a whip can produce. My legs gave way. Now hanging by both wrists, I clenched my fingers on the iron rungs as the lashes literally cut to the bone. Several of the deadly chords enmeshed and tore muscle right from my ribs. I twisted and jerked in agony—my cries and moans reverberating in my ears as if they were someone else's. I begged my Father to see me through this.

But the beating continued. The monsters not only scourged my back to a bloodied pulp, they slashed their whips into my legs and across my arms, lacerating all my limbs. I tried securing a foothold under the blows, but the balls of my feet kept slipping in the growing pool of my own blood. On the heavier, most excruciating strokes, I lost consciousness, only to be jolted back as the next flagrum tore through me.

When they had thoroughly flogged me to ribbons, one of the heartless beasts spit my spattered blood from his lips. "I'm not finished with this one yet! Drop him to the ground."

The closest soldier hesitated. "Our orders forbid killing him. It's a wonder he's still breathing."

"Just drop him!" yelled the fiend, imploring more than demanding. "There's something I can't *figure* about this one. He can take more!"

I weakly coughed. I gagged. I shuddered while hanging limply from the column.

The soldiers muttered to one another before one finally decided, "Let the swine have their way with this Jew. It's Passover," he laughed jokingly.

The wisecrack resonated—soldiers and torturers chuckling loudly.

They grabbed rags so as not to bloody their hands and lifted my elbows to cut the ropes away from my wrists. I toppled to the ground, my shredded back twitching in the sticky puddles of blood.

I was too delirious to hear the soldier. "Have at it, boys."

The vicious thug wiped his brow. My blood smeared from his forearm across his sweaty head. "Never let it be said I wasn't thorough," he snarled.

The lash came without warning, shocking my brain awake. Leather, metal and bone sliced across my chest, tearing more of me away with it. Again they took turns thrashing their instruments of fury over, and over, and over again. I writhed helplessly as my chest, trunk, ribs, arms, legs were all slashed and gouged unmercifully. I might as well have been doused with oil and set ablaze. It would have been quicker.

A voice finally cut through the courtyard. "Enough!"

Pilate's centurion testily entered the square. Had his order echoed off the walls because I no longer struggled under the blows and appeared dead, or was there simply nothing left of me to scourge?

"Imbeciles!" he blurted. "Pilate's direct order was not to kill this man!"

Despite a faint, weakened groan bubbling through my lips, I truly resembled a bloodied corpse.

"He's not dead," informed a soldier. "Though not for lack of effort by these butchers."

The centurion pulled him aside but refused to lower his voice.

"These butchers are under *your* authority. Pilate said to chastise him severely, not massacre him. Now get what's left of this king back to the praetorium."

He turned and stormed from the almost empty square. Only a few of the initial curious onlookers had tolerated witnessing the horror of such a prolonged and ghastly beating. The members of the Sanhedrin had left as well, seeking Caiaphas with word that so relentless a scourging might ultimately serve their purpose—sending me to the grave.

As the soldiers pulled me up, I doubted there was any way I could possibly stand. My entire body seethed with pain. The centurion was right—this had not been a chastisement. It was lethal attack. So how was I still alive?

My feet came down, and through some miracle by my heavenly Father, my knees found the strength to support my weight. Stabbing flares fired through every nerve and fiber, overwhelming my brain with agony. I shivered in shock. The soldiers' voices registered only as distant echoes while my mind struggled to recover from such physical brutality.

"Don't put his filthy rags back on him," instigated one. "He's a king after all!"

He snatched a large scarlet cloak, a cape of fine Roman cloth, from under the guardhouse arch and haughtily walked it over to me. "A more fitting robe for royalty!" he exclaimed, draping the long crimson stole over my shoulders. Even this pleasant material tormented my countless open wounds. I winced and contorted as he tugged the cloth around my lacerated arms.

Another soldier retrieved a short wooden staff from under his belt and tilted up my chin with its ornately carved handle. "You forgot your scepter, your majesty."

When he removed it from under my jaw, my head drooped again.

"Mind your subjects, king!" he shouted and cracked the staff across my skull.

Pain clouded my vision and nearly dropped me back to the stone tiles. Dazed and dizzy, I staggered to the side, but a soldier's firm hand promptly steadied me.

"Take the scepter, you grubby king!" he commanded, seizing my wrist and thrusting the reed into my hand.

Somehow my fingers tightened enough around the wood to keep it from slipping to the ground. The strike to my head swirled waves of stupor behind my eyes, and I wobbled while trying to stay on my feet, blinking determinately to regain my bearings.

"One thing is missing!" came a nearby shout. A soldier stood by the western wall where a stretch of Euphorbia-milii hedge lined the guardhouse façade opposite the palace. Its bright red flowers and thorn-armored branches made it a favorite Roman plant and metaphor of power.

Using his sword to hack a few branches from the thicket of barbed twigs, and several folded rags to protect his fingers, he twisted and shaped a crudely woven bowl of briers. Admiring his work, he proudly raised the spiked entanglement to his cohorts as he approached. "A king's crown!" he announced.

One of them laughed. "That's a crown? Looks like a mesh of sticks and spurs to me."

"Like I said," retorted the soldier, "a shabby crown fit for a shameful king."

"Coronate the emperor!" callously called another.

The soldier with the bonnet of briers stepped over to me. I gazed dreadfully at the number and size of the thorns—a crowded cluster of spikes, some a full thumb's length, crisscrossing in all directions.

"Your majesty," he mocked and placed the makeshift crown atop my head. Still clutching the rags for protection, he pressed down on this entangled halo of thorns. The pointed barbs jabbed through my hair and pierced my scalp. I moaned in anguish as he leaned up to crush it further into me. Blood drizzled down my neck. It trickled behind my ears and over my brow.

The wooden reed slipped from my fingers and rattled to the stone. The soldier swiftly picked it up, then gripped both ends so he could ruthlessly force the thorny headdress deeper through my scalp. The twigs crunched under the force of the stick, driving the sturdy quills into my head. Blood now raced from dozens of puncture wounds, cascading over and into my eyes, even dripping into my mouth—my lips parted in a continuous rasping groan.

I wavered on the brink of collapse—a scarlet shawl dangling over my tattered shoulders and a crown of thorns enveloping my entire head. Could this savage charade for their amusement finally suffice?

While their physical abuse abated for the moment, their verbal derisions remained insatiable. They bowed overtly in front of my trembling, tortured form.

"At your service, your highness," one ridiculed, genuflecting with feigned respect.

"All hail, king of the Jews!" another shouted with laughter.

They berated, insulted and parodied my presence. In their incessant mockery, they failed to notice tears mixing with the blood streaming into my beard. It was not the unbearable torment, however, that triggered my tears. I wept for my abusers. They too were my children, laughing and sneering at God—a God who loves them unconditionally. Blinded with evil and driven by a free will weakened by habitual selfishness, sin's whittling indifference had left them more disoriented than I, even in my present state.

Although I posed a threat to no one, the soldiers would never return a criminal to Pilate unbound. So they shackled my wrists and led me away from the guardhouse, back into the praetorium. Each new step proved more excruciating than the last. My ragged gashes and gaping wounds twisted and tugged with every movement, and the thorns embedded in my head panged my scalp like angry hornets as my persecutors propelled me forward.

Surrounded by guards, I gruelingly ascended the portico stairs.

Raucous unrest vibrated from a now packed praetorium—my name bellowing near and echoing far, some screaming for my crucifixion, others begging for my release.

Inside the private chamber, Pilate barked at two officers of his personal detail. "No one else gets inside the forum!" he commanded. "If anyone tries, run them through with your blade. And get another detachment down there. It's bedlam!"

With affirmative nods and respectful fists to their chests, they were gone.

Pilate turned and suddenly caught sight of me standing among the soldiers. He nearly fell over backward. For the shortest, briefest of moments, I actually discerned pity in the eyes of this ruthless Roman commander. His hand went to his mouth, and his fingers tightened against his chin in utter dismay—distaste for what he saw.

He slowly approached and finally forced his eyes to the handful of soldiers around me. "You all just stand there while chaos is breaking loose outside my door? Move!"

They abandoned my side and hurried down the steps.

I was once again alone with Pontius Pilate and his centurion. The prefect stood quietly, grimacing at my condition, cringing at the thorns crushed into my forehead.

He eventually sighed in disgust, "You *had* to come to Jerusalem. You had to come *here* … *now*. You couldn't have just stayed in Galilee, preaching your contentious beliefs there. You had to come here."

Pain still fired through my body so intensely, I was unsure if he had asked a question.

He pointed toward the balcony arch. "Do you hear them out there?" His voice rose in frustration. "Caiaphas has half the courtyard demanding your execution. What have you to say to that?"

I shuddered uncontrollably, my body still in shock. I may have wanted to reply, but my mind couldn't assemble thoughts or my mouth articulate words.

Pilate paced, kneading fingertips into his temple. "Instead of tending to important affairs, I spend my morning dealing with an unruly mob and burning incense to the gods over you." He looked over at me. "Trying to figure out what I'm supposed to do! My wife suddenly has visions, now begging me not to kill you, and yet it will be *my* blood Caesar spills if I cannot maintain order in this rotten outpost of a province!"

Simply raising my eyes was a struggle. I said nothing. The shouting outside intensified as another regiment of soldiers pressed in on the crowd.

"Who *are* you?" Pilate implored, trying to ignore the heightened commotion. He shook his head at my grisly countenance and whispered half to himself, "Where do you come from?"

Again faced with silence, he gradually glanced at his centurion, hoping to get some cogitative assistance, but returned to my afflicted stare when he received none. "Have you no answer? Do you not realize I have the power to release you ... or to have you *crucified*?"

My lips parted, and shaky words finally came forth. "You would have no power over me if it were not given to you from above. Those who handed me over to you are therefore guilty of the greater sin."

This only confused and alienated Pilate more. It also alarmed him. Driven by superstitions, he tried reading between every line— seeking a symbol, a sign, a premonition that might shed light onto the course of action he should follow. Completely vexed at gaining no insights from either me or the gods he invoked, he motioned with exasperation to his centurion. "Bring him outside."

Pilate marched tempestuously from the room. The centurion grabbed the length of chain between my wrists and tugged me in the prefect's path.

Outside, the maelstrom escalated, especially as I came forward to stand at the balcony's edge. A sea of unrest stretched across the entire square. My gruesome appearance had little effect on many who angrily shouted for my condemnation, riled into a fury by the

Sanhedrin. Caiaphas and his scribes had used their time well, convincing much of the crowd that if allowed to live, I jeopardized the few freedoms they held under Roman occupation. Small pockets of my followers braved this hostility and raised their outstretched hands toward me, thoroughly aghast as I emerged into the sunlight, bleeding from head to foot.

Despite my swollen, blood-stained eyes, I suddenly saw her. A third of the way into the crowd, I met my mother's gaze. Her forlorn-look-turned-cry-of-anguish seized my heart. A face more pained than mine, she wailed in interminable sorrow, finally beholding her dear son consumed by such suffering and surrounded by so many enemies. I longed to comfort her, to tell her that my unimaginable torments were part of God's plan for the salvation of humanity. I think she somehow knew this, but the cold reality at seeing flesh of her flesh beaten and maltreated so harshly, overwhelmed her. She collapsed into John's arms. Young John, the only one of my twelve to stand beside her through this, supported her grieving body, and Mary Magdala as well.

I could read Mary's lips crying my name over and over.

Stay strong, Mary, I thought. I love you, and without hesitation do this for you.

My subtle connection with those I so profoundly loved abruptly ceased. Pilate grabbed my elbow still enveloped in the scarlet linen across my shoulders, and to showcase how well Rome humbled even the most tenacious rebel, he presented me to the multitude, exclaiming loudly, "Behold the man!"

"To the cross!" one of the scribes fired back.

A chorus of denunciations erupted from the crowd.

"Crucify him!" several shouted.

Pilate gestured at my thorny crown to emphasize the foolishness of such an execution and mocked them with regal mimicry. "You want me to crucify your king?"

Caiaphas shook his staff and dared to holler a near-blasphemous remark in return, but one he felt might resonate with this embittered governor of Rome. "We have no king but Caesar!"

"Crucify him!" came more shouts.

Several feeble cries shrieked over the din, "He is innocent! Jesus is innocent!"

Pilate stood between me and his marble judgment seat, watching the chaos unfold before us. He glanced momentarily to the adjoining building on our right, to a woman standing at the balcony. It was his wife, Claudia. He couldn't discern her expression from across the square, but her presence unnerved him nearly as much as the turbulent crowd.

Without turning his head, Pilate summoned his centurion. "Maximus!"

The officer hurried to his side. "Sir."

He shifted his eyes from his distraught, distant wife to the racket below as he confided to his head soldier, "Maximus, is there not an ancient custom at Passover where the procurator may release a prisoner to the people as a sign of mercy?"

The centurion fidgeted, caught off guard by the question. "I believe I have heard of such a custom, Excellency. I'm just not sure if or when it's been exercised."

"Never by me, I can assure you," snapped Pilate. "But we have three prisoners already condemned for crucifixion today, including that wild boar Barabbas who—"

"Killed a Roman soldier," finished the officer, delicately indicating the severity of such a crime.

Pilate finally turned to meet his gaze. "I am aware of his offense, Maximus. And that is precisely the point I want to exhibit before Caiaphas and these irrational Hebrews. I have already condemned the real conspirators, rebels and murderers. How can they argue that this maimed, half-dead Galilean represents a greater threat than a violent bandit like Barabbas?"

The centurion stared at him a moment, weighing his superior's words with his own abhorrence of Barabbas and everything about him.

Pilate nodded definitively, his mind made up. "Fetch Barabbas. Quickly."

Maximus reluctantly left to carry out the command.

Pilate managed an encouraging nod across the square to his wife.

She promptly turned and vanished into the second-floor quarters. He fully understood that her sudden cold shoulder, even from across the praetorium, signaled distress over his inaction. Pursing his lips, he stepped to the front of his judgment seat and raised both hands for silence.

Despite an emotional, argumentative throng of hundreds, the elevated arms of the Roman prefect instantly brought the roar down to a rumble over which he could be heard.

"Is today not your Passover?" Pilate called above the murmuring discord below. "And yet you labor and stew before me, obsessed with passing judgment on someone you claim is exceedingly dangerous to the peace of your people ..." He looked at me, hardly believing he was about to say this, "... and to the power of Rome."

"Anyone who claims to be God deserves death!" shouted a scribe.

"Silence!" commanded Pilate. "How pitiful that I must come to *you* on *your* holy day with a peace offering! Yet I do it to demonstrate the real threat to peace!"

The clamor increased again, so Pilate spoke quickly. "As is customary at Passover time, I will release one prisoner back to the people as a sign of my mercy, but more so to clearly expose reality!"

Since Herod's prison languished directly beneath the guardhouse, it wasn't long before the soldiers rattled up the portico steps dragging someone in chains. Pilate didn't pause or glance behind him.

"Two prisoners I present to you," he issued, raising his hand and again gesturing to my bloodied, slouched figure. "Jesus the Galilean, charged with claiming to be the king of the Jews ..."

Much of the mob did not wait for him to continue. They shouted their demands for my execution. By this time, the centurion returned with several soldiers, pulling a chain-bound Barabbas behind them. They entered the balcony from the governor's chamber and yanked him to the other side of Pilate's marble chair. It took four soldiers to hold him steady. He wrestled under his manacles, unsure what was happening.

It actually pleased Pilate that Barabbas did not appear meek or frightened, despite his conviction and sentence. The condemned killer angrily strained to shake himself free from his captors. His disheveled hair, much like a madman's, obstructed eyes gazing wildly over the crowd.

Those assembled closest to the mezzanine muttered and whispered to one another. Many recognized Barabbas and certainly identified with his cause against Rome, but also knew him as a rogue agitator, too often endangering his own people by wantonly provoking violent confrontations.

Caiaphas and the Sanhedrin were no less shocked to see this barbaric, self-pronounced revolutionist brought before them.

Pilate now raised his left hand and contemptuously presented the second prisoner. "And we have Barabbas! Guilty of treason, insurrection and cold-blooded murder." He paused, preparing to deliver his compelling logic. "Shall I release Jesus—your wounded, humiliated king? Or Barabbas—whose riotous, murderous acts have already condemned for crucifixion two other Jews."

"Release Dismas, the other prisoner!" came a pleading shout from below.

"No!" Pilate countered. "Your choices are here! Jesus the delusional? Or Barabbas ... inciter of riot, rebellion and the death of both Roman and Hebrew."

In a manner that could not help his cause, Barabbas squirmed and growled under his chains like a trapped animal.

Muddled chatter droned through the crowd. Pilate's ploy had given pause to many. Caiaphas was the first to utter a definitive shout back to the procurator. "Set Barabbas free! Jesus is the real traitor to Rome!"

"Crucify Jesus!" yelled another scribe.

Several detractors methodically followed. "Crucify the Nazarene!"

"Release Jesus!" cried a voice from the multitude. "He is the true prophet!"

"He's a blasphemer! Crucify him!"

The uproar again intensified.

"Release Barabbas! Barabbas!"

"Condemn Jesus! Crucify him!"

A wide-eyed Pilate gripped the back of his marble throne and shouted back, "I find no justification to condemn him! I have punished him sufficiently for his crime!"

His sensible, authoritative argument fell on deaf ears. The chants grew louder, more in unison. "Crucify him! Crucify him!"

Someone hollered through the noise, "Why do you just stand there, Jesus? Save yourself!"

I quietly gazed through blood and tears upon the crowd, praying to my Father to overlook the hatred hurled at me. It is Satan, Father. The evil one has plagued their hearts and minds. *Do not hold this against them,* I petitioned.

My heart broke as the desperate cries of my mother and Mary Magdala faded in and out of the bedlam. John grappled with a man who tried silencing them with annoyed shoves.

Other clashes ensued—the crammed mob now engaging in more than just verbal altercations. Pilate locked eyes with another centurion, motioning him to use force. The officer nodded and called for his guards to move in. They infiltrated the pandemonium, pulling quarrelers off each other, bludgeoning some with the butts of their swords and threatening others with their blades.

Caiaphas was nervous. He worried Pilate might explode and send his battalion throughout Jerusalem to put an end to the Passover festivities. In a last-ditch effort to convince the prefect, he utilized this escalating hostility as a precedent. "This is not what *we* want on our holy day!" he called up to Pilate's fractious glare. "We want peace! You want peace! *Caesar* wants peace! Not to condemn the Nazarene will only bring more of this!"

Pilate's eyelids quivered, as if a thousand competing concerns and consequences contested vigorously within his mind.

Caiaphas went for broke. "If you release Jesus, how can you call yourself a confidant of Caesar? Anyone who claims himself a king and causes such division speaks against Caesar and against his empire!"

The words were direct. They were not watered down or masked behind respectful, reverent babble. There were no innuendos. The argument was meant to shock … and it did. On any other given day, such words spoken to a Roman dignitary, even by the High Priest, would well have garnered swift retaliation. Instead, Pilate stood frozen, listening to the incessant chants rising from his praetorium.

"Crucify him!"

"Crucify him!"

"Crucify him!"

He looked at his centurion, Maximus, who returned a concerned stare at the prospect of Barabbas going free. Pilate curled his lip in revulsion as the chained prisoner grunted and motioned for his exoneration.

Lastly, Pilate swung his eyes to me. My broken figure trembled under the effects of a prolonged scourging and the horror of so many thorns nested in my head.

He closed his eyes, furrowing his brow at the ceaseless cries for my crucifixion and dreading an inevitable confrontation with his wife. After a long moment, he turned and nodded to Maximus. "Bring me my wash basin."

The centurion obeyed. He retrieved a large porcelain bowl of water from the governor's private chamber and returned to the balcony to find Pilate sitting in his marble judgment seat. Barabbas stood on his left, still held bound by the soldiers. I remained stoic to his right, staring vacantly into the contentious mob. I wasn't sure which pained me more, my innumerable, agonizing wounds or the cacophony of cries reaching my blood-soaked ears, demanding that I be nailed to a cross.

Maximus moved to his commander's side and held the basin within reach. Pilate did not glance over or even acknowledge his presence. His full attention remained narrowed on those turning his courtyard into chaos and his soldiers working frantically to keep a riot from spreading throughout the city.

Realizing he could never be heard over all this, he muttered to anyone nearby, "Sound the horn, before this square is filled with blood."

Maximus motioned to one of the soldiers who promptly retrieved a shofar, ornately carved from ram's horn. He leaned to the balcony's edge and blew the instrument long and loud. The two-toned blare resonated above the turmoil. Its startling peal through the air turned all heads to the source and quieted the boisterous crowd.

When the horn stopped, Pilate raised his hand to silence the final shouts. "I have made my decision!"

An anxious murmur ascended from the choked courtyard.

Pilate shifted to scoop some water from the basin, and while rinsing his hands and forearms, exclaimed loudly, "I wash my hands of this innocent man's blood! If executing this Galilean will bring peace to your Passover ..." He glanced at me before shaking the water from his fingers and looking back to the impatient mob. "Then let him be crucified."

The multitude thundered its response, and Caiaphas rested his forehead against his staff in exultant exhaustion.

Maximus leaned disquietly over to Pilate. "Sir, what of Barabbas? We can't just let him go."

Pilate's conciliatory eyes were hardly placating. "It is what it is, Maximus. Take the murdering mongrel and toss him from the city." He looked over to Barabbas, still bound tightly by the soldiers.

The rebel had stopped struggling. He now stared at me in horrified awe, finally noticing my ghastly presence.

Pilate observed his terror-stricken gaze. "Trust me. We shall not hear from Barabbas again."

My eyes closed. By accepting to become flesh, I had accepted the inevitable destruction of that flesh through death. Pontius Pilate had now officially sealed my fate. They would soon inscribe my sentence in a Roman ledger under his decree—execution by crucifixion. I shuddered, no longer from physical shock but from new waves of fear coursing through me on what was yet to come. My torment was hardly over.

I prayed for my mother. I prayed for Mary Magdala.

Since the dawn of time, I knew *this* time would come, this ultimate sacrifice of love. I am ready, Father, I prayed. I am ready to die for our children.

Two soldiers grabbed me abruptly from behind, reigniting pain through my tender wounds. They turned me around, and one seized the chain dangling from my wrists.

They led me from the praetorium … to be crucified.

28

Crucified

THEY TUGGED ON MY OLD GARMENT, back over my thorn-ridden head, and yet for the moment, I escaped. I shut my eyes and allowed the distinct scent of cypress to transport me to another place and time so removed and surreal to me now. Kneeling on the stone floor of the guardhouse square surrounded by Roman soldiers with a newly chiseled crossbeam by my side, my closed eyelids allowed a bittersweet deliverance.

That aroma of freshly cut wood brought me back to Joseph's workshop—to a distant Nazareth of memories—cutting timber, fitting joists, practicing our craft, talking, learning and laughing. Now immersed in such horrifying passion, I had constantly prayed to my heavenly Father for courage and stamina. But sudden thoughts of the father who taught me so much of earthly life, reassured me that I would again share his company in eternal paradise.

I love you, dad, I silently affirmed. Our time together seems worlds away. How I long for a simple day with you at the lathe. Yet here I am at the pinnacle of my objective, hoping and praying I can endure to see it through. May your spirit comfort mom in this great hour of suffering as she bears witness to my sacrifice. Just as I once confided fears and uncertainties to you as a boy, I easily reveal them to you now. Dread consumes my heart over my fate, yet I accept this cross with a certain serenity, fully aware of the loving symbol that it will become through the ages.

See you soon, dad.

Two soldiers lowered the center of the crossbeam onto my tattered shoulders, shattering my reverie. Its solid mass pressed the coarse fibers of my robe into the innumerable lacerations covering my upper back. My ears were so caked with blood, I hardly heard my own agonizing groan as they lashed ropes over the timber and around my chest, securing this wickedly heavy crosspiece to my battered body. Holding the beam in place, they then stretched my arms behind it so I could steady and balance the load. Its weight bore down upon me. Wounds reopened across my back, setting my shoulders ablaze. I gasped for breath under the burden and burn of the crushing cypress. The Romans preferred cypress crosses. Its spicy scent offset the stench of death.

"On your feet, king!" came a directed command.

They knew I could never lift this piling in my weakened state, so two of them hoisted up the ends of the crossbar, with me attached. Again, I marveled that my knees held. They trembled feverishly as I struggled to stabilize this heavy, awkward mass. Hunched over and dripping blood, I feared I might lose consciousness. A white wave of vertigo blurred my vision.

A soldier's shout cut through my fog. "On to Golgotha!"

I couldn't move. My knees shook under the burdensome weight, but my feet could not find the will or strength to step forward.

"Move!" yelled a stern voice from behind, quickly followed by the sharp blow of a knotted rope across my back and kidneys. The thick braids fell like fists against my body, inexorably intensifying the agony across my already torn, tender back.

Reflexes from the impact propelled me forward. My fingers dug into the wood to prevent it from shifting against my raw shoulders.

Each slight scrape of the timber further ruptured my wounds, drowning me in pain.

They guided me along the guardhouse, through an open passageway and out of the courtyard. No less than eight soldiers escorted me into the crowds, repelling the mob that spilled from the praetorium and congested the already busy Passover foot traffic.

They should have doubled the detail. The upper city's main artery overflowed with those emotionally riled over my sentence, whether for or against it. Seeing our slow merge into the street, cries erupted and bodies pressed even tighter.

"Here comes the blasphemer!"

"He'll never make it; look at him!"

"He deserves what he gets!"

"Jesus! Jesus, don't let them do this to you!"

"Save yourself from this!"

The front soldiers wielded their spears diagonally to push back the surging crowd. The guards on either side garishly shouted for the masses to keep their distance, and those bringing up the rear hollered obscenities while whipping their ropes and straps to keep me moving. The crossbeam jostled and bumped with every step, grinding my grated back and repeatedly knocking the thorns impaled in my head.

A cyclone of turbulence swirled around me—jeers, heckles and hisses … wailing and sobbing … soldiers shouting their commands and curses—yet I saw none of this. The timber's weight forced me so far over, all I beheld were my sore, swollen feet stumbling across the flat cobblestones.

We turned a corner, and several more detractors leaned in to hurl insults. The aggravated soldiers pushed them away, but one of them knocked me to the side as he did. I lost footing, and the wood finally gave way. My quivering arms tried to steady the beam, but its momentum overpowered. The left corner banged to the street, jolting my inflamed muscles. It then fell forward, still affixed to my shoulders, crushing me under its load and trapping me underneath. It shifted cruelly over my neck and crunched the spikes in my head. Blood oozed from my eyes and drooled from my mouth, which I opened to cry for help but only feeble groans and gags made it past my lips.

"Get him up!" ordered the officer in charge.

Disorder prevailed. They struggled to lift me upright while also constraining the surrounding mayhem. I could hardly reorient my catatonic gaze, let alone steady my stance under the oppressive weight. A guard squatted to readjust the ropes around my shoulders and the wood. He shouted to my face, "Try staying on your feet, your majesty!"

I tightened my hands around the back of the beam and heaved it into a more controllable position, gasping at the torturous tearing of lacerations underneath.

Another loud bark from a soldier, another swipe of a chord across my back, and we were slowly moving again. The street suddenly narrowed, and the congestion naturally worsened. Every few steps my body faltered under the crossbeam, but a soldier or two now yanked me back into a stable stance. We turned north, just a block from the Garden Gate exiting Jerusalem. More onlookers merged from adjoining streets, many stepping forward and yelling their admonishments. Others simply stopped in their tracks, stilled to silence at the sight of me staggering under the cross. Could this be Jesus, they questioned in disbelief—the great prophet and healer? Most could not bear to look, fearfully turning away. Women wept bitterly and covered children's eyes to shield them from such bloodshed.

Others heartlessly pressed as close as possible without engaging the guards and launched their salvos—spewing heated hatred from their tongues, spitting in my path, even throwing rubble from the street as I stumbled by. We approached the towering wall's open gateway when our procession again stopped short. Hundreds crowded the large stone portal, pushing and shoving to catch a glimpse of this once revered leader now condemned to crucifixion atop the aptly named 'place of the skull.'

There were too many. The soldiers shouted and waved their weapons to clear a path, but it was impossible to get everyone out of the way. We pushed forward nonetheless, arms and hands reaching in at me. The guards wrestled away as many as they could, but their numbers overwhelmed, and I was again knocked to the side. The left edge of the beam lurched once more to the ground, but this time I dropped to my raw, abraded knees to keep it from driving me forward under its massive bulk. I impulsively swung my head back in agony only to have the wood thump the thorns in my scalp.

Then, amid this intolerable torment and misery, her voice rang out. Its tender inflection, now punctuated with the shrill of anguish, finally made it to my side. "My son! My son!"

The crowds had formed living walls around the guards, but my mother somehow got through, collapsing where I knelt beneath the beam. While so many could not bear to cast their eyes upon me for long, she cupped her hand under my chin and brought her face directly to my battered, bleeding, disfigured profile. "I'm here!" she cried, distraught sobs choking her words. "I'm here!"

I turned my head to her voice, our terrors and emotional afflictions deeply shared. Her gaze ignored the gore and lovingly met my eyes. This woman who had cradled my infant body to keep it warm in a dark stable, who had kissed my scrapes as a small boy, who had sung me to sleep so many nights, now beheld her precious son as a victim of unrelenting torture, crushed under a chunk of tree to which he would soon be nailed upon.

"Jesus, please," she sobbed uncontrollably, "let me go through this for you. You are my son. You are my spotless son."

As the soldiers grabbed the crossbeam and leveled it, I opened my quivering lips to console and reassure her. "This is my choice,"

I gasped, wood shifting against my shoulders. "I will make all things new again."

The guards heaved upward and lifted me to my feet. My mother also stood, her hands pleading as she watched me quake with pain. "Take me with you," she cried again.

Sensing the soldiers were ready to push forward, I offered her a final compassionate glance. My words barely escaped under the weight of the wood. "Love ... will ... triumph."

A path through the soaring gateway finally cleared, and the guards advanced me with a hard lash of the rope. My mother's muffled tears caressed my ears before she became lost in the chaos.

And so it was. I had entered Jerusalem riding a foal, surrounded by hymns of praise and waving palm branches. I now exited under the weight of a crossbeam, besieged by rage, hatred and heartbreak.

Once outside the city walls, the crowd spread out, enabling more room to proceed toward the base of the hill—toward the barren bedrock of Golgotha.

Although it neared midday, I could not see the sun climbing higher. I did not notice the clouds rolling in from the west or the gradual incline rising before me. And while I had no idea how much further I had to go, I suddenly realized I would not make it. My mouth hung open, so parched I actually welcomed the blood continually dripping over my lips. Desperately dehydrated, weak from blood loss, mercilessly brutalized and laboring under a massive wooden beam ... my breaking point surely awaited only a few steps ahead. This distinctly human perception of recognizing inevitable failure so often carries as much deliverance as distress. It's an impulsive awareness that pervades the mind and soul—the undeniable realization that a full shutdown is imminent—that another step, whether literal or figurative, cannot be taken.

It is then, above all other times, one should surrender completely and directly to God. As fully human, I did not know *how* I would make it up the impending hill. I knew only that I could go no farther like this. The unbearable load across my shoulders sent waves of nauseating pain through my entire body. My arms were too fatigued to balance the weight. My back could no longer tolerate such a crippling strain. My legs shook to the point of collapse.

I give this cross to you, heavenly Father, I offered silently. This burden with which I can cope no longer, I place in your hands. Somehow, you will see me through to my destination.

And with that, my body fell. I dropped once again to my now skinless knees. The crossbeam plunged to the side and pulled me with it. Depleted of all endurance, I fully submitted, allowing the timber to continue forward. Its force drove my chest to the ground and knocked what little breath I had from my lungs. It wedged itself against my entangled crown of thorns, pinning my head sideways to the earth.

The shouts from the soldiers did nothing.

Their rope and chord strikes did nothing.

The taunts from the bystanders did nothing.

I was not getting up. I lay in a broken heap, wheezing like the critically wounded victim that I was.

Three of the guards hoisted up the beam. My limp arms slid off the wood, and my chest dangled against the ropes. It was obvious to everyone that I was totally spent. No amount of intimidation or punishment would get me back underway.

"Cut him loose!" shouted the officer.

"Loose?" countered a soldier.

"Cut him from this beam, or he'll die before he's crucified!"

"Then who'll carry the cross?"

"Just cut him loose!" he repeated, turning to scan the crowd.

Several sword slices severed my ropes and dropped me back to the ground. The heavy thud of the crossbar reverberated as they pitched it beside my disabled body.

The officer now moved among the onlookers. People backed and ducked away, knowing he sought an able body to help carry my cross. He motioned at several men who turned and slipped deeper into the crowd as if not noticing him.

"Come now!" he yelled. "Which one of you Jews is going to assist your crippled king?"

His comrades left me in the swirling dust to join him. Their commands and the accompanying protests briefly took attention away from me. Most of the young men pressed upon by the soldiers made it perfectly clear that it was unlawful for them to carry the cross of a condemned man. Even in the face of a menacing Roman blade, those threatened preferred the possible peril of a soldier's gladius over carrying another's crossbeam to Golgotha. With such chaos and disorder, and multiple Roman detachments already at the crucifixion site, no one seemed willing to chance the possible nightmare of crucifying the wrong man.

Help me, Father, I prayed. I do not seek deliverance from my destiny. I know this is your will ... and mine. But I lay here completely and thoroughly exhausted—shattered and drained of any energy to move—certainly incapable of carrying our cross of salvation. Assist me, Father ... as only you can.

Her delicate voice hardly penetrated my coagulated hair and clogged ears—so soft and meek, it was a wonder I heard it at all amidst the surrounding mayhem. "Jesus?"

I raised my bruised, punctured head to a young woman kneeling beside me. She shook with fear and dangled a damp white veil from both hands. My inflamed, blood-filled eyes gazed up to her warm, beautiful brown ones. Tears of compassion escaped over her cheeks as she presented the moist cloth to me.

All the confusion and clatter around us seemed to coalesce into a dull drone—my sole focus suddenly fixated on this wonderful woman's simple yet significant offering.

My trembling fingers reached out and took the end of the veil. Its cool texture invited me like an oasis. I tried to steady my hand so as not to drop the cloth on the dry, dusty ground and brought it to my bloodied face. Although pain pulsated from every nerve in my body, I sighed in relief. I pressed the veil to my swollen brow, my broken nose, my split lips. I allowed it to soak blood, sop sweat, absorb heat—bring a brief moment of solace to such interminable suffering.

I wanted to keep the damp, soothing folds of fabric forever against me, but I could hear the soldiers finally wrestling a man into their charge. I wiped my face and peered gratefully up at the woman before gradually passing the now soiled cloth back to her. Holding it open, she startlingly beheld the perfectly stained image of my face. No distaste or repulsion crossed her eyes. Instead, she gazed upon the linen as a priceless gift, bringing it to her own brow and weeping soundly.

"I shall remember your act of kindness forever," I whispered to her. "As will the world."

The world in fact would remember her as 'Veronica' because of my perfectly transferred image to her veil. *Vera icon*, meaning *true portrait*.

Commotion ensued as several soldiers grappled with someone close-by—a man who had not accompanied these crowds from Jerusalem but was journeying toward the city when fate brought him upon this death-march to Golgotha.

"Kneel down," ordered the officer. "You will take this criminal's cross upon your shoulders, and you will carry it to the mount with him."

Painfully aware he couldn't defy and elude armed Roman soldiers, the unfortunate traveler instead stated his case loud and clear to those around him. "Let it be known my name is Simon from Cyrene!" he called. "I have *not* been condemned by Rome! I am forced against my will to carry this cross!"

"Get down there next to the Nazarene!" bellowed the guard, shoving him to his knees beside me.

Simon of Cyrene's breathing quickened as he lamented his deplorable luck. He watched the crossbeam's shadow swing over his head and heard several in the crowd cry out my name. His eyes swiveled to where I laboriously struggled to my forearms and knees.

"You are Jesus?" he asked, but hardly expected an answer. "The one they call the Christ?"

Like so many, he had heard the accounts of my teachings and miracles, but to finally see me here, so beaten and dehumanized on the road to crucifixion, troubled him deeply. His lips trembled, but before he could gather his thoughts, the wooden beam lowered upon his shoulders. He grit his teeth and wrapped his arms around it.

A soldier bent down to inform with a scowl, "If you can't keep it steady up the hill, we'll tie you to it."

Simon managed a single nod, and with the soldier's assistance, he stood. He took a moment to adjust the cross and acclimate his legs to its weight. Two of the guards hoisted me up and dragged my debilitated body under the beam. Although they physically draped my arm around the wood and over Simon's shoulder, it was more to stabilize me against the crossbar than to have me assist in bearing its load.

Simon's face hung no more than a hand's length from mine. Our eyes silently regarded each other. I wondered if he could sense how much I thanked my heavenly Father for his presence and assistance. Even in my weakened, semi-conscious state, I read his thoughts … or sudden lack of them. His cares, plans, burdens, demands—all his life's daily concerns were no longer *of* concern. He was undividedly focused on and immersed in my suffering, amazed by the bewildering endearment in my eyes despite such horrifying agony. It instantly bore into him and took hold of his heart. He would never be the same. He would never again worry or obsess over the typically normal trials that had so unsettled him prior to our encounter. More than carry my cross now, Simon of Cyrene would live to serve me every day for the rest of his life.

With moist eyes, he mouthed, "I'm … sorry."

This short confession did not solely convey sympathy for my barbaric treatment. He apologized more for not finding me sooner. His penitence stemmed from living too caught up in life's mundane matters to have taken the time to learn more about me, seek me and walk with me earlier. He regretted not actively pursuing me—finding me only by chance.

Without hesitation, he now gratefully shouldered my cross.

I gently closed my eyes and clung to him as if to say, *You are here with me now, Simon of Cyrene. Walk with me.*

The soldiers ordered us onward, and the procession restarted. The logistical functions of my mind had by now shut down. My sense of time, surroundings, direction—they were long gone. A fever crept through my broken body, induced by relentless trauma and fatigue. My blistered feet scraped forward as I floundered next to Simon, trying to remain conscious. The weight of the wood, combined with me leaning and limping so close to him, visibly hampered his efforts to bear the crossbeam, but he grumbled not. Instead, he offered encouragement. In a sea of taunts and jeers from the soldiers and crowd, Simon's voice strengthened me.

"You can make this," he breathed softly. "I've got you."

It was all I could do to raise my thorn-encrusted head and acknowledge his words with a gratified gaze.

The barren hill finally leveled off.

"Just a little more," Simon urged. "Just a little more."

When the sun reached its peak in the sky, stifled behind thickening clouds, we reached Golgotha. I knew we had arrived by the agonizing screams. One criminal already hung from his cross. The other lay on the ground, soldiers nailing him to a beam.

The guards lifted the wood off Simon's back, and my hand slid from the timber onto his shoulder. I curled my fingers around his garment, my eyes acknowledging the magnitude of his role. And while it was I who wavered on unsteady legs, it was Simon who dropped to his knees. With hands clasped to the back of his head, he broke down and sobbed. He didn't want to leave my side. A soldier, however, suddenly grabbed him from behind and dragged him away. He had served Rome's purpose, and they now promptly discarded him.

The banging of wood against wood filled the air—my crossbeam solidly pounded into the main pillar mortise. This vertical support log, whittled flat on one side with a chiseled niche for the crossbar, lay by the hole in which it usually stood. One of the soldiers brought forth a wooden plaque bearing the charge for my crime. Inscribed in Latin, Hebrew and Greek were the words, *Jesus of Nazareth, King of the Jews*. They nailed this tablet just above the fitted crosspiece. My body convulsed at every alarming clank of mallet against nail.

This is it, Father, I invoked. A single command could still put an end to this unimaginable suffering. But my love for our children and for our plan to win back their love burns so passionately now within my divine heart. Here, upon this lifeless hill, atop this new altar, I submit myself—the lamb of God—to be sacrificed for the forgiveness of sins.

It was time to save the world.

A sudden jolt of pain clawed through my scalp as a soldier dislodged the embedded crown of thorns long enough for two others to yank my blood-soaked robe over my head. Ripped away from my shredded skin, the enmeshed fabric tore flesh from my lacerations. Again reduced to nothing but a loin cloth, I shivered not from exposure but from prolonged, repeated trauma.

"The plaque reads *King of the Jews*," chided the soldier. "Better keep your crown." He pressed the spiked headpiece back onto my head. Some thorns found previous wounds, while others created new punctures to my skin.

No shoves or shouts were needed to send me to the ground. My body finally succumbed to stress and injury. I fell. I wished I had fainted or blacked out, but anxiety-induced adrenaline kept me alert as they dragged me to the waiting cross. They flopped me upon the main log with all the care and attention of tossing a sack of feed into a trough. I did not resist their arms sliding me into position, the wood splintering my wounds. Surrounded by my executioners, I hardly heard the scattered voices of other soldiers keeping bystanders back. They would confine the crowds behind a secured perimeter until all crosses were erected.

A grieving woman crying my name drifted through the commotion. My mother? Mary Magdala?

The swarming, boisterous soldiers and the lingering wails from the already crucified victims drowned everything else. I again tensed in terror at the sudden vibration of hammer against nail as they secured a wooden pedestal to the beam for my feet. The Romans treated crucifixion as any engineering job—performed precisely with a process. Based on my height, they had carefully measured where to place my feet so that even when pierced with a nail, I'd be able to painfully support my weight, ensuring a slow death.

They then stretched my arms wide, dislocating my left shoulder, and quickly determined where my hands should go. Marked with quick notches to the wood, they bore starter holes, readying the timber to easily but tightly receive the nails that would drive through my wrists.

With preparations fully complete, they could now crucify me. A soldier pulled my hand to the waiting hole and clutched it firmly in place by my wrist. Two others held me down by my opposite arm. Another retrieved a mallet and a long iron spike. My chest heaved in dreadful anticipation of his obvious task. And although I held perfectly still, it was neither exhaustion nor the weight of the soldiers that kept me in place.

Love.

Love steadied me. My greatest expression of love for the world. Why would I resist? This was not surrender. God's commitment to humanity culminated now in this ultimate act of self-giving.

I felt the stinging stab of the nail gouging my sacred flesh as the soldier pressed it into the very base of my palm, centered where hand met wrist. His mallet raised. It seemed to hang in the air forever before rushing downward and connecting with the large nail head. This single hammer smash propelled the spike through my hand—driving through nerves, cartilage, carpal bones and into the wood of the crossbeam. The iron sliced my wrist's median nerve, roaring pain up my entire arm, exploding into my brain. I choked on the air that gasped and groaned from my lips. Three more pounds of the mallet shot waves of torment through my whole body.

They wasted no time wrenching my other hand over the wood, tugging my already pinioned wrist against the anchored spike. I clenched my jaw. Blood seethed through my teeth with every breath.

Again the hammer came down, and another nail fired into the bed of my palm and out the back of my wrist. Intolerable pain leapt through my arm, arching my back and thrusting the thorns further into my head. I hardly felt them over the screaming, searing nerves of my extremities.

In this insufferable state of mind-drilling torture, I could have easily howled for their immediate destruction. As it were, I did call loudly for my Father's powerful actions upon them. I made an urgent demand regarding those who nailed me to this beam, as well as on those who condemned me to this fate and handed me over to such extreme evil.

"Father, forgive them," I cried as they positioned my feet, one over the other against the pedestal. "They know not what they do!"

The cold sound of mallet against nail carried the crunch of iron into bone and the agonizing pain of tender feet impaled onto wood.

A long, guttural groan graveled my throat—fighting for air through such racking pain. "Hold this not against them," I prayed between broken gasps, now so well fastened to the cross, I could not even writhe. "They reject the cornerstone because they cannot see!"

Psalm one-eighteen came to pass without notice. *The stone the builders rejected has become the cornerstone.*

A soldier's voice rang out, "Raise the cross!"

Lying nailed and motionless upon my tree was unbearable enough. As it began to rise, my weight shifted from the lumber to the spikes, igniting a blaze of fire around my wrists and feet.

Several soldiers heaved on ropes tethered to each of the three cross caps, while a few more guided the bottom toward its fitted hole. The main beam angled higher, approaching its vertical, upright position. With skilled technique, they maneuvered the wooden base to the edge of the depression. Upon reaching its peak, it slammed into the recess and jolted me sharply upon the nails. The iron pressed and pinched whatever nerves were not already severed. The full weight of my upper body hung from my wrists—hands paralyzed, pain throbbing from my wounds. My mouth opened in anguish but no sound escaped. I could not exhale. This suspended position had elevated my ribcage, permitting only inhalation. Unable to expel air, each gasp got shorter and shorter. If my chest remained this extended, I would never again empty my lungs ... or take another breath.

My instinctive reflex to breathe kicked in, pushing down on my feet and hoisting my elbows up by my mounted wrists. This gratefully allowed me to exhale and take a breath, but the pain was excruciating. The unyielding nails crushed nerves against bone and ligaments against iron. Warm blood coursed down my arms and feet. My entire body quivered in agony. I only now realized my eyes were shut tight, sealed by such torturous misery.

I finally opened them. They focused and refocused to my new perspective, to this elevated panorama never recounted by others who had experienced it. I was crucified—nailed upon wooden beams and lifted on display atop a desolate hill between two criminals whose crosspieces nearly touched my own. While other shafts of timber stretched along the mount, the three bearing bodies today were grouped side by side so that the Romans could more easily contain the multitude.

Dark, ominous clouds continued unifying across the sky, rolling ever more rapidly in from the west, as if driven by unnatural forces.

I looked down on the slowly thinning crowd idling closer to the crosses. It was Passover after all, and many had turned back once the crosses were raised. My eyes found my mother and Mary Magdala. Their anguished cries easily reached my ears. John remained with my two Marys, trying his best to shield them from witnessing my horror too closely. They came forward anyway. My mother trembled constantly, muttering prayers for an end to my suffering and clutching her heart with new sobs each time her eyes lifted to my cadaverous figure.

Although pale and drained from crying herself, Mary Magdala stood radiantly. She watched with her own shattered heart as the first man to ever show her respect, give her hope, and love her unconditionally despite her sins ... hung waiting to die for those sins and for the sins of all. Her tear-blurred gaze, however, was not one of revulsion at such barbaric torture. She did not scrutinize my stripped, beaten, punctured body with aversion and abhorrence as most onlookers did. Instead, she beheld me with a devotion and gratitude reserved for the greatest of heroes. She could actually see through all the deceiving appearances. She beheld me not as broken and defeated, but as a champion. Although woefully wringing her hands at the sight of her Lord in such deplorable agony and on the brink of certain death, she knew somehow I was in control. Despite her limited understanding, she held faith in me.

And John. While my brothers had all run from the Sanhedrin's resolve to destroy my cause, John stood by me. His eyes had been locked in a stare of interminable shock and dismay ever since Pilate had presented me to the crowd. That fixed look of consternation finally broke as he emotionally succumbed to seeing his Master crucified. He buried his brow in the crux of his elbow and wept.

Remember my words, John, I wanted to tell him. The son of Man must suffer greatly at the hands of evil men for the forgiveness of sins. Take heart, my friend. The joy of God's triumph beckons. I will rely on you, among others, to write down all these events so that the world may never forget.

A man to John's left suddenly pointed up at me and shouted to those around him, "He saved others but cannot save himself! So much for delivering Israel!"

At this, one of the lingering members of the Sanhedrin swaggered by and scornfully raised his eyes. "Never mind rebuilding the temple in three days!" he called, more for the sake of others than for my ears. "Come down from that cross, and we will believe!"

John held my mother's head against his chest as more taunts and heckles indulged the scribe's insults, prompting him further.

"If you are the son of God, come down and verify yourself the king of Israel!" He then shook his head, spat at the base of my cross and moved on.

I took a breath and eased my weight off the biting nails. Another garbled shout flung in my direction, not from below this time but from the crossbeam to my right.

Gestas, a Barabbas henchman crucified for insurrection and murder, fumed at me amid his own agonizing curses. "You claim to be the Messiah! Save yourself and *us* from this suffering!" He winced, elevating himself enough to speak. "If you're the Anointed one, why do you just hang there and allow this? How can you let them ridicule you like that? Prove yourself! Do *something*!"

"Quiet!"

The cry came from my left, and despite torment pulling at every fiber, I turned my gaze to the other condemned man dying next to me—Dismas.

He shuddered and rebuked his cohort from two crosses over. "Have you no fear of God even in your last hour, Gestas? You and I have only ourselves to blame for this. We are paying the price for our deeds. But this man ... this man is innocent. He has done nothing wrong." He clenched his teeth and moaned in anguish while shifting his weight. He rolled his afflicted eyes to me, struggling to get the words out. "Jesus, remember me when you come into your kingdom."

The very foundation for my message of repentance hung beside me. No sin is too great for God's forgiveness, and no time is too late to seek it. I noticed the regret, the remorse, the honest contrition upon his brow. But most of all, I sensed his hope in me—his faith that a true kingdom awaited my followers.

I pressed down my feet and bore the wrenching pain against the spike to rise and regain my voice. I took a short breath, looked upon Dismas with loving assurance and hoarsely replied, "Truly I tell you, this very day, you shall be with me in paradise."

He rested his head back against the wood and closed his eyes. The promise of salvation and eternal life somehow overcame the throes of his present torture.

The sky grew murkier. A breeze crept in and shivered my exposed, traumatized body. I could hardly hold myself up against the nails. Agony and exhaustion prevented me from supporting my weight for more than a moment or two. Short breaths were all I could muster.

My mother's sobs again reached my ears from below. She was now directly beneath my cross with John still clutching her tightly around the shoulder. They stood no more than five or six steps from my pooling blood. My mother reached out, wanting to come forward, but John kept her in place. He knew the Roman guard stationed beside me would swiftly intervene.

She compelled her eyes to dreadfully climb the shredded, nailed, already rotting frame that was once her son. Her quivering hand lifted with her gaze to my face. "My son," she feebly wept, not expecting me to hear, though I did, "when will you allow this suffering to end?"

I wished I could have embraced her just one more time. As the mystical word of God, I existed before time began, and yet I had come into the flesh through the sacred womb of this most pure vessel … my mother. I chose her as my mother, and she would always hold that title. I love and respect her with all my human heart, and with all my divine heart.

And so shall the world.

But for now, her own heart broke with unbearable sorrow and loneliness. I thanked my Father for John's gallant reverence and care for her through my passion. I tightened my forearms under the pangs of the nails and pulled up just enough to address her. "Woman," I muttered, motioning my eyes ever so slightly over to John, "behold your son." Then, acknowledging my disciple, "John … behold your mother."

He nodded, wiping away his tears. He knew what I wanted and was more than willing to oblige. He would care for my mom as his own.

My head tilted sideways and gently rested on my dislocated shoulder so the thorns wouldn't knock the wood. My breathing became more labored.

Time dragged. I hung for what seemed an eternity, every unyielding moment arduously drawing into the next in varying degrees of throbbing misery. I felt my heart contracting slower and slower, struggling to pump what little blood remained. It no longer flowed or oozed from my wounds. My tongue was like worn leather—withered and parched.

Alone and dying. Perishing in the flesh.

So much pain.

Psalm twenty-two filled my head, and while its words ultimately sung the praises of a mighty, delivering God in times of trouble, I cried aloud its opening line, "My God, My God, why have you forsaken me?"

Some of those below, so seasoned in scripture, recognized this verse, remembering much of the litany that followed and how miraculously it coincided with these very events—*I am scorned by everyone, despised by the people. All who see me mock me. I am poured out like water and all my bones are out of joint. My heart has turned to wax. A pack of villains encircles me; they have pierced my hands and feet.*

These poignant meditations of King David were lost on the Romans and the less-devout curiosity seekers. They did not appreciate the implications of my cry. They missed its impact, regarding it superficially.

"Listen!" someone shouted. "He calls for God! Let's see if Elijah comes down to save him!"

Consciousness began to fade. My hearing drifted in and out. White blankets passed before my eyes. I tried swallowing, but my pasty, blood-caked mouth could not. I didn't consciously think the words, but somehow they escaped my arid lips. "I thirst."

The soldier by my cross heard my fragile appeal and gazed up. A moment of pity overcame his indifference. He glanced over to a bucket of cheap wine for the guards' indulgence. A large sponge floated inside for them to squeeze the wine into their mouths, ridding the need for bothersome skins or goblets. The guard hesitated, then took his spear and stabbed the saturated sponge. He raised it up high and pressed it against my chin. The sudden wetness startled me, but I instinctively opened my mouth at the dripping material shoved into my battered face.

The spear receded, and I closed my eyes.

There was nothing left of myself to give. My final moments were upon me.

I had stretched out my arms and had been lifted up to draw the entire world unto myself. My blood, completely poured out, had washed away all sin, rejoining the hands of mankind to the hands of God—a bond that would never again be broken. This one sacrifice initiated a new mutual commitment, a new testament, a new promise of salvation in my name.

It was complete.

Knowing I could not hold myself upright on the nails any longer, I proclaimed the conclusion. "It is finished." Tears ran down my face at the magnitude of this defining moment. My head swung back, thorns digging my scalp one more time. "Father!" I cried. "Into your hands … I commend my Spirit."

This final utterance expended my last bit of energy. I drew a paltry breath and relaxed my cramped muscles. My body sagged, extending my disjointed arms and raising the intercostal tissue between my ribs. I had breathed my last. My body slightly convulsed as nerve reflexes tried to move lifeless lungs.

Finally finished.

My head slumped forward, and a closing colorless wave blurred my vision, suddenly carrying all pain away with it.

I was gone.

29

Resurrected

I DID NOT FEEL THE EARTHQUAKE, but I saw it.

No longer in the flesh, I hovered outside my thoroughly ravaged remains, watching the crosses rattle in their mounts as the earth shook violently. Hysteria gripped the hill. Bystanders scattered. Soldiers fought to keep balance.

When the tremors abated, the skies tore open. The clouds looming low over Jerusalem and its surrounding hills suddenly ruptured. They abruptly burst into tears. The deluge spilled hard and silent—no lightning to ignite the gloom, no thunder to clap the air. The heavens poured out in heavy, voiceless grief.

The Roman officer made his decision impetuously and shouted through the downpour, "Prepare to vacate this post!" He motioned to several large wooden clubs in the stockpile of execution equipment. "Break the legs!"

The cool rain refreshed and reoriented the soldiers from the bewildering earthquake. Now very anxious to depart Golgotha's plateau, three of them snatched the heavy cudgels, each club brandishing a thick knob at one end. They determinedly approached the crosses, and with hefty, solid swings, slammed them into the legs of

Gestas and Dismas just below their knees. With feet firmly affixed to the pedestals, their legs could not absorb the blows, breaking instantly. Feeble gasps rushed from their lungs as their bodies fully collapsed against the nails. Unable to push back on fractured limbs, they quickly expired.

The third soldier approached my cross, and raising his club to strike at my legs, gazed up at my motionless corpse. He wiped his face to peer harder through the rain.

John stood just a few steps behind him and confirmed what the soldier suspected. "He is already dead."

The guard turned to look at him.

"You don't need to break his legs," said John. "He is clearly dead."

The soldier glanced again at my shattered frame. Rain flowed over my open wounds and sent canals of bloodied water cascading down my body. My head hung limp. The crown of thorns still gripped firmly to my skull despite the earthquake and steady sheets of rain sweeping against it.

'Clearly dead' was an understatement. He certainly preferred not to make the effort to break my legs, but duty required him to make sure I was dead before leaving this post. So he chose an easier and more conclusive option. He dropped the wooden club to the puddled ground and reclaimed his spear from against the back of the cross.

John promptly angled my mother away.

The guard thrust the lance deep into my side, slicing it upward between my ribs and into my vital organs. Instantly, blood and water spurt from my side, mixing with the dwindling rainfall and sprinkling across the soldier's face. He wiped it away and stared at his red-stained fingers. His hardened mind suddenly softened as he recalled and realized the importance of all that had happened—my words from the cross, the earthquake as I expired, the sudden torrent from above, my sacred blood now upon his face—it all spun together in rapid recognition.

The spear slipped from his other hand, and with trembling fingers, he muttered, "Surely this man was the son of God." Profound euphoria at such clear revelation wrestled with the horror of having participated in my destruction.

He stumbled away, weeping and clutching his now consecrated fingers to his face.

As the remaining soldiers worked to lower the crosses and yank the nails from the dead, the rain finally diminished to drizzle. Sinister clouds continued moving across the sky, reinforcing through the firmament above the sorrow on the ground below.

Now in Spirit, I watched it all. After extracting the nails from my wrists and feet and pulling me off my sacred cross, they allowed John, my mother and Mary Magdala to come forward.

My mother knelt and lifted my limp shoulders while John carefully removed the crown of thorns and tossed it aside. She gingerly slid a hand to the back of my neck and brought her eyes to my battered, lifeless stare. This day had seemingly drained her of all tears, but a new flood suddenly poured forth, dripping to her son's cold body. Lowering her head, she raised mine, then rested her face against my riddled forehead and sobbed. Her other arm clutched my shoulder and pulled me into an embrace, rocking me as if I were once again her small child. She delicately cradled my mangled corpse and sighed quietly through her tears, "My Jesus. My Jesus. My precious son."

John and Mary allowed her to grieve, gently crying themselves and rubbing her back as she swayed me in her arms.

It was time for me to depart. In less than three days, I would rebuild my temple as I had promised. But for now, I had someone— some*thing* to confront. While it may have seemed difficult to categorize this day as a *good* Friday, it was indeed a victory for both God *and* mankind. My single sacrifice now finalized the downfall of the prince of darkness—the evil one. I fully knew he would never give up until the end of time itself, yet he would hear my words today nonetheless. I was ready to proclaim in no uncertain terms that his persistent warfare, waged for his own selfish, wicked desires … was futile. Despite having driven my children, molded in my own likeness, to pierce my hands and feet, my willingness to submit to such suffering for their eternal salvation had completely sealed his eternal doom.

First, I needed to escort Dismas' soul to my glorious Kingdom. I would also bridge the great spiritual abyss that had kept all penitent righteous before him separated from full inclusion with my Father in paradise. By accepting death upon a cross, I had opened wide the gates of heaven to our faithful flock.

I then had a brief, determined message for Satan and his venomous spirits. How they would rue this day for eternity.

*   *   *

Nicodemus and Joseph of Arimathea had left the Sanhedrin that fateful Friday and boldly requested my body from Pontius Pilate. Unless family intervened, Rome simply tossed most crucified victims into mass, unmarked graves. Pilate, in no mood to deal with anything else concerning Jesus of Nazareth, granted my body turned over to these wary disciples of mine. Caiaphas protested of course, insisting that if those sympathetic to my cause buried me, followers might try stealing my body and claiming I had risen from the dead.

"Why does this man scare you so, even after he's gone?" Pilate had contentiously inquired. "Do you actually think this Jesus will have any real followers after what happened to him today?"

Still, he appeased Caiaphas by ordering a small detachment of guards to secure whatever tomb I occupied. He agreed to keep the burial place under watch only until travelers left Jerusalem the following week.

Like most Pharisees, Joseph of Arimathea was far from poor. Guilt-ridden for not having more earnestly protested my treatment before the Sanhedrin tribunal, he now did all he could to ensure my remains were cared for and prepared properly for burial. He even provided a newly cut tomb, reserved for him and his immediate family.

He and Nicodemus painstakingly anointed my tattered body with myrrh and aloes. They could not hold back regretful remorse as they dressed the countless gashes across my stiffening corpse. With sundown approaching, they decided to delay the final application of burial spices until after Passover. For now, they gently wrapped me in an expensive linen sheet and placed me on the first slab inside the tomb. Joseph had purchased this small tract of land north of the city because of the landscaped gardens surrounding the property. He had specifically chosen this serene hill for his family crypt.

They exited the burial chamber and saw three Roman soldiers approaching for the first shift guarding the gravesite.

The two scribes didn't dare ask for assistance sealing the tomb. They rolled up their tunics and pushed together, sliding the heavy stone over the entrance. The only interest of the otherwise apathetic soldiers was to ensure that my physical remains were accounted for before the stone slid into place.

Evening fell.

Darkness covered the land.

My flesh and bones lay interred in the even blacker darkness of a burial cave.

*   *   *

There is that moment at dawn when the sky burns vermilion, increasingly brighter, awaiting the first stab of true light to fire over the horizon and across the sky—that very instant when dawn becomes sunrise in a flash of vivid rays—day breaking, conquering night.

At this precise moment on Sunday morning, the greatest of all Sunday mornings, a light far brighter than the awakening sun over the Mount of Olives radiated from within my cave. As day broke across Jerusalem, a dazzling burst of brilliance exploded from innumerable filamentary beams, shooting forth from every particle of my lifeless body. For less than the blink of an eye, this pitch-black tomb flashed brighter than the sun itself, eternal life rushing into my cadaver.

My eyes opened to nothing but the burial cloth covering my face. My ears awoke to only two sounds, one from this world and one from another. I heard the coarse scraping of the stone opening the tomb's entrance, as well as the grating screech of Satan screaming in defeat.

I had returned.

Sunlight now streamed through the crypt's open portal and filtered through the linen fibers before my eyes. I sat up, swung my legs over the stone slab and swept the burial sheet away from my head and chest. My lungs sucked in a full breath of the morning air that drifted into the miraculously open tomb. I felt good, relaxed ... normal. The agony of my crucifixion seemed so long ago. I gazed down at my chest—smooth and spotless—free of any wounds or scars. I slowly touched my fingers to my face. No bruises, bumps or blood. My beard and hair were clean and fresh.

All who will someday receive their new bodies in heaven—this is how they will be. Regardless of earthly afflictions, deformities or disabilities, all will become new ... youthful yet mature ... perfect.

Lowering my hand, however, I noticed the pronounced hole through the base of my palm and wrist. There was no pain, not even to the touch, but the nail cavity was clearly there. I folded the crumpled sheet down my side. Not a single laceration, welt or mark from the flogger's whip remained on my body, yet the gash between my ribs from the Roman spear remained, again lacking any soreness or pain.

I smiled, knowing well why my Father kept these wounds visible. I am more than the risen Christ. I am the risen crucified Christ. Nails were driven through my hands and feet for the salvation of the world. My eternal body will forever display the victory marks of love's greatest sacrifice.

I glanced at the sunlight bathing the tomb's entrance and stood to face it. As stunningly as the stone had rolled open, a fresh robe, tunic and sandals now waited for me at the end of my burial cove. I put them on and moved toward the daylight. My fingers gripped the stone, and I ducked through the opening before stepping confidently into the morning. Dew glistened on the grasses, plants and flowers. Rising sunshine broke through the trees, glinting off palm and cascading through leaves. Although I indeed found myself back on earth, it truly felt like heaven on this most splendid of all mornings, this most glorified of days.

Only the panicked guards fleeing down the hill disrupted the sunrise's peaceful tranquility. A massive tombstone rolling open by itself had sent them frantically running. They dared not mention this to Pilate. Caiaphas would pay them well to keep quiet with assurance that the Roman governor would receive no report from the Sanhedrin either.

The impending cover-ups would be well executed.

They mattered not. My messengers lay in hiding, unaware that their fear and despair would soon transition into resolute joy and vocation.

*   *   *

I rested privately, a stone's throw from the tomb, meditating in a bed of landscaped shrubs along a short stretch of palm trees. Tucked neatly out of sight, I pulled my robe's mantle over my head to shield my face in shadow while I communed silently with my Father and our Spirit.

The hour remained early—the sun still too low to cast real heat. Two figures suddenly approached. Mary Magdala and Salome ascended the gradual hillside, carefully carrying jars of burial spices. They kept silent as they neared the guards' hastily abandoned camp. Smoldering cinders sent a thin stream of smoke into the morning air.

"Where are the soldiers?" Salome wondered aloud. "We were told to expect several."

Mary intently roamed her eyes, searching. "If they are not here, who will help us move the—" A sudden gasp silenced her.

Salome followed her gaze. "The tomb!"

Both stared in shock at my open burial cave. The chiseled round slab leaned against the rock, fully rolled away from the entrance. Although bleak and black, the unobstructed recess beckoned without any hesitating hint of death.

"Who opened it?" Salome questioned fearfully. "Could someone have taken the body?"

Mary's hand went to her mouth, a flustered daze quickening her heart.

Thinking they were alone, the two women looked at each other in alarm.

"Who would have opened the tomb this early?" Salome bemoaned again, the jar of spices nearly slipping from her fingers.

Mary bit her lower lip as a tear found her cheek. "We must tell Peter and the others. Quickly."

*   *   *

Shadows grew shorter across the gardens. Mary Magdala, Peter and John made their way hurriedly toward the open grave.

"There, you see?" pointed Mary, huffing up the gradual incline.

Their rush from Jerusalem had tired them, but John felt a sudden burst of energy at seeing the unsealed tomb ahead. He broke from Peter and Mary and sprinted the rest of the way. When he reached the opening, he stopped, momentarily frozen by hope and elation, ready to believe but frightened nonetheless. He bent down and peered into the darkness.

By now Peter had arrived and did not hesitate to enter the chamber. He ducked his head and stepped inside.

John followed.

The burial linens were where I had left them, folded upon the slab that held my body since Friday. Peter stared at the interment cloth tucked neatly on the corner of the stone and ran his fingers anxiously through his hair. He tried rationalizing that no body-thief would methodically fold a sheet that had covered a corpse.

"He's done it, Peter." John could hardly speak the words over the lump in his throat. "He has risen just like he said he would."

Peter looked at his good friend—his fellow apostle and fisherman. He offered a kind smile and reached out to grab his shoulder. "You were the brave one, John. You saw him scourged, crucified and lanced with a Roman spear. I want so much to believe." His eyes dropped. "I disowned my Lord. I must not forsake him again with my lack of faith."

"So you believe, Peter?"

He glanced back up as a single tear broke from his eye. "I do."

They exited the tomb to where Mary lingered, nervously staring into the distance, deep in thought. Her trance broke as they rejoined her. "He's gone, isn't he?"

"Yes," said John.

"Who would have taken him?" she beseeched. "Where could they have moved him?"

"We will figure this out," calmed Peter. "John and I will alert the others. You should find the women—"

"No," she interrupted. "What if whoever took him brings him back? What if Joseph and Nicodemus return? I will stay here."

Peter squinted into the sunlight and briefly surveyed the area before moving his eyes back to her. "Do as you wish. But don't be long." His eyebrows softened so his words wouldn't convey worry. "Just make sure you're not followed."

"You forget who you're talking to, Peter," she reminded. "I spent many years lurking in the shadows and evading others. I will not be followed."

They hugged her tightly, as brothers to a dear sister. They then turned and began the short trek back to Jerusalem.

Mary waited until they had moved from sight before bending over and stepping tentatively into the tomb. Something other than the chamber's macabre murkiness or the sight of folded burial linens caused her to back quickly out, mesmerized in both wonder and fright. She staggered a few steps backward and almost tripped before turning and regaining balance.

What had she seen? An angel?

Whatever she observed now roused a feeble cry from her lips. "Hello? Is anyone here?"

Sweeping her eyes high and low, she listened intently to the surrounding stillness. Only the leaves and palm whispered quietly back. A raven cawed from a nearby tree, adding to the abrupt, unforeseen eeriness she felt.

"Hello?" she called again. Fresh tears muffled her tone. "If someone is here, please show yourself."

I stood among the shrubs not twenty paces away beneath the swaying palm, head covered. My voice traveled just enough to reach her. "Woman, why are you crying?"

She swiftly turned and noticed my cloaked figure in the flickering shade. Although more than a little startled, she began walking decisively toward me. "Sir, are you the gardener here?"

"Who is it you are looking for?" I asked as she approached.

"Someone has taken Jesus of Nazareth from the tomb," she said. "Have you been here long? If you know where he is, please tell me."

I smiled, but she could not see. She was only a few steps away but did not recognize me under the shadow of my head covering.

The last she had seen of her Savior alive, I was disfigured and awash in blood—hanging on a cross.

The one standing before her now stood upright and strong. I knew it would take just one word from my lips for her to identify me.

"Mary."

I never saw eyes upon this earth light up so briskly and brightly. Joy rushed through her heart as she reached out her trembling hands. I pulled back my mantle to reveal my unblemished face and loving eyes.

"Master!" she cried, convinced for a moment heaven had swept her up. Quickly realizing she was still very much here, the inevitable swirled through her head and sent a warmth through her extremities that tingled her fingers. I had risen from the dead. No one took me from my tomb ... I walked from it. All the anguish and horror she had witnessed on Friday—conquered. She threw herself into my arms and sobbed with unimaginable bliss and bewilderment. She finally had me back.

But this was only partially true. I had undeniably come back, but this was not my final promised return. I would soon leave again and return to my Father in heaven. My final gift to the world awaited once I was gone—the Holy Spirit—endowed to whomever so opened their hearts to receive it. I knew Mary desired to keep me here forever in the flesh, but this was not the plan. My mission on earth was complete. She and my apostles, my mother and the other women from our group, indeed all my followers, would soon have to walk with me as all future generations must—holding me in the temple of their hearts until the day when they can physically walk with me in my Kingdom.

And so I said to her softly, "Do not cling to me, Mary, for I have not yet ascended to the Father. Go and tell my brothers that I have risen, and they will see me shortly. Tell them I must soon return to my Father ... and your Father. My God ... and your God."

I had spent my whole ministry calling upon my Father, even characterizing him as my God—a show of intimate oneness with the Creator. Through my death and resurrection, and by the impending baptism of the Holy Spirit, humanity could now have that same intimate relationship with the Almighty. Everything I have, I give my followers, including infinitely close harmony with a God who loves them enough to put on their flesh—coming into their midst for their salvation.

Mary leaned back and gazed into my eyes. The peace of my presence swept away any fear or uncertainty. I grabbed her hands and squeezed her fingers lovingly. She saw the nail marks in my wrists. It was truly I who held her in my grasp.

"Go," I said again, smiling and releasing her. "Announce the good news of this day to my friends."

30

I Am With You Always

THE SECOND FLOOR where my apostles and I had shared our last meal together was no longer simply a gathering place for food. It was now their sanctuary ... their hideout ... their prison. The door latch hadn't moved since Mary Magdala's departure. My eleven remaining brothers were left to contemplate her incredible report—that she had not only seen me alive, but had spoken with me.

Some sat. Others stood. A few paced. Surrounded by oil lamps and candles, they gathered in the larger area, leaving the smaller dining niche in shadow. Lost in these shadows, I sat, watching and listening in obscurity. I had not entered through the door. Although my arrival had gone unnoticed, I sat as physically present as any of them but remained unobserved in the darkness. They reasoned aloud back and forth with one another—their hopes and fears driving and tangling their thoughts.

"It sounds more than a little hallucinatory," said Thomas, standing up against the wall. "We have all come to love and cherish Mary as our own, but come on, seeing him in a garden outside his tomb? Doesn't that sound just a stretch fanciful?"

John lightly shook Peter from his private thoughts. "Remind him what we saw, Peter. Tell them again."

Seated and engrossed in personal reflection, Peter slowly raised his head to acknowledge his weary companions. "The tomb was open ... Nothing but burial cloth remained inside." He paused, then shrugged. "There is nothing else to tell."

"That's it?" Philip asked with open hands. "Our Master and Lord was slaughtered by Rome. The one who walked to us on water somehow allowed that to happen. John, you yourself described his wounds savagely stretching from head to foot." He hesitated, shuddering at the thought of such agony. "How could anyone come back from something like that?"

"Do you all hear yourselves?" James scornfully rebuked. He moved to the center of the room. "If any of *us* were crucified, than yes, that would have been the end. But we're talking about *Jesus*. We walked with him every day for more than three years. How many times did we see him raise others from the dead? Lazarus was in his tomb several days before Jesus called him back."

Peter now stood and more robustly joined the discussion. "I remember his words by the fire outside Tiberius. He told us that the elders would reject him—that he would be mocked, beaten and put to death. But that on the third day ... he would rise to life." He scanned their faces earnestly and eagerly. "We now know the first part to be true. Why is it so hard for us to believe the second?"

"Because it's too hard for me to come to terms with the first," said Bartholomew. "The man I entrusted with my soul has been crucified. My spirit feels like it has been crucified with him. I don't know where to go next."

"He is more than a *man*," Thaddeus interjected. "We all know that. He is the son of God, the Messiah. His thoughts and ways are so much more than ours."

"It's wishful fantasy," remarked Thomas again, shaking his head and refusing to allow false hope to abuse his spirit. "Have you ever seen a Roman flogging? Have you ever witnessed a crucifixion?"

The room lay silent at his biting words.

"I have," he continued. "Rome doesn't just execute; they butcher. They butchered our Lord! They scourged the flesh from his body then hammered him to a cross!"

John tried calming him down, "Thomas, we all know—"

"You *saw* him John!" he shouted back. "You above all should realize the finality of such an execution. I miss him as much as any of us, but until I probe the nail marks in his hands with my fingers, I will not believe."

Matthew screamed.

His terrified yell startled everyone to flinch, fumble or fall as they spun to follow his petrified stare. If they had turned to face a temple guard or Roman soldier, fight-or-flight reflexes would have instantly kicked in. Bedlam would have ensued.

Instead, they saw me. I calmly walked from the shadows, the candles and lamps illuminating my clean face and groomed beard.

Those not frozen in fear burst into tears. Others moaned in shock and awe.

I brought my hands delicately forward so as not to further startle them. "Peace be with you," I said softly, as if I had never left them.

"L-Lord," breathed Andrew, somehow finding his voice. "Is it really you, or are we seeing your Spirit?"

I smiled endearingly and took another step toward them. "Why are you all so troubled, and why does doubt fill your minds? Behold, it is I who stands before you." I reached out and steadied Andrew's shaking wrist. "Touch and see for yourself. A spirit does not have flesh and bones, which you can clearly see and feel that I do."

Trembling, they touched my arms, erupting into tears of joy as they felt the real me—their Lord ... their Master ... their life.

I then looked lovingly at Thomas and slowly rotated my hands to display the holes in my wrists. "Thomas, reach out your hands and put your fingers into my nail marks."

My steadfast friend and apostle broke down, sobbing quietly.

"Do not persist in your unbelief," I graciously told him, "but believe."

Thomas did not move his fingers toward my wrists. He dropped to his knees and muttered through his sobs, "My Lord and my God."

I gently consoled him with a hand on his head before glancing up at them all. "Because you see me, you have come to believe. Blessed are those who will not have seen me ... and will believe."

Their watery eyes conveyed so many emotions—elation, guilt, amazement, hope.

"Peace be with you," I offered again. "The Father sent me into this world to save it. And as the Father has sent me, so I now send you."

"Send us where, Lord?" asked Peter.

"Everywhere," I answered. "You will soon receive the Holy Spirit. You must go out into the world and proclaim to everyone that *I have risen.*" My eyes regarded them with compassion. "You are my first disciples ... my pioneers ... my holy ambassadors. The authority I gave you before, remains yours. If you forgive sins in my name, they are forgiven. If you hold them bound, they remain bound."

A flood of questions and uncertainties raced through their minds, overcome by the solace and wonder of my presence. It would be hard for them to discern and retain their critical missions at this awesome moment in time.

So to shift their thoughts away from future challenges, and to secure their hearts that the real me had truly returned, I simply smiled and said, "Do you have anything to eat?"

Bartholomew managed a chuckle, sounding somewhat like his genial self again. "Yes, Lord. We have some fish and bread. Enough to feed us all ... or perhaps five-thousand more."

Delighted and captivated beyond words, my friends welcomed me back with more embraces and tears of gladness.

As we ate, I couldn't help but think of the last time we broke bread together in this very room. So much had transpired in a matter of days. With my mission on earth now complete, my apostles were poised and positioned to get theirs underway. I reflected on my relatively short ministry. It had taken just three and a half years to forge a strong, pure foundation. The plans and materials for my Church rested in my everlasting words, my sacrament of bread and wine, my redemptive, sacrificial death … and most importantly, my victory over the grave.

Its builders sat at this table—the first of billions.

*   *   *

Widespread, outward proof of my resurrection would only diminish faith's true power, and yet profound testimony to it rested in my changed apostles. My gruesome, public execution had temporarily advanced the exact outcome sought by both Caiaphas and Pontius Pilate—an abrupt collapse of my following, and hence our mission. Roman crucifixion never failed to intimidate and deter supporters of the condemned. My death on the cross was no different. My very closest disciples—those who had lived my teaching, watched my miracles, experienced my glorious transfiguration—had all scattered. Even John hurried to hide after my death—a lost forlorn sheep without a shepherd. With windows shut, doors latched and voices hushed, they sheltered away, minimizing any risk of being recognized as one of mine.

If I had remained in the tomb, let there be no doubt, that would have been it … over. Perhaps some of my tenets and teachings would have survived for a while, but the name Jesus would have inevitably melded together with all the other notable prophets cut down by their adversaries when jealousies and prejudices arose. In similar circumstances, history never failed to repeat itself.

Today, however, dawned differently. An amazing rebirth defied all human understanding. I had reversed the finality of death into the hope of everlasting life. This single, all-encompassing event had transformed my apostles' overwhelming fears and perplexities into a courage and conviction that would lead them to lives of faithful evangelism ... as well as their own martyrdom. After all, could the reason for their tucked-away-terror-turned-bold-fearlessness really stem from a simple desire to save a dead man's legacy?

No. It would take much more to get them out of hiding. It would take a supernatural resurgence to see them walking the streets together again, strolling the temple square and traveling the countryside, chins held high. It would take a renewed, unwavering trust in a victorious God to move without fear, worry or doubt.

What freedom.

I waited until they had returned to Capernaum before appearing to them again. The northern fishing village somehow seemed foreign to my brothers now—their former everyday lives overcome by all that had happened over the Passover journey.

But they were home. The Sea of Galilee ushered in a quiet, cloudy morning. Only small patches of sunlight kissed the placid ripples of water. Always the fishermen—Peter, Andrew, James and John, along with Thomas and Philip, drifted gently in a borrowed boat about a hundred paces from shore. They floated in solitude east of town, away from the other fishing vessels farther out.

Peter sat in the stern, eyeing the four or five fish in their basket. "Not a very good haul, boys."

James tilted his head leisurely to the sky. "No, but it's nice just being out on the water again."

Each agreed with contemplative silence. Peter sighed, relaxed in thought, and began helping Andrew fold the net.

My shout from shore startled them. "Hey out there ... have you caught any fish?" Even if my head hadn't been covered and cloaked in shadow, they could not have recognized me at this distance.

Peter glanced again at their pittance of a catch.

John shrugged and asked quietly, "How much do you think we could get for five fish?"

"Four fish," corrected Philip. "I plan on eating one."

Peter raised his head to shore and shouted back, "No! We've caught nothing!"

"Throw your net off to the right!" I called through cupped hands. "You'll find some fish there!"

Thomas chuckled. "Wouldn't that be nice."

Peter and Andrew hardly heard their comrade's quip. Their eyes locked in anxious reminiscence.

"Could it be him?" whispered Andrew.

Although no glare hindered their concerted gaze toward shore, they could not identify my figure on the narrow beach.

"Throw the net," Peter commanded.

Andrew and John fumbled with the mesh, hardly bothering to unfold it before tossing it over the starboard side. Each man gasped in elation as a school of fish larger than the boat itself cascaded into the expanding net.

"It's him!" shouted John. He tugged at the taut netting, joy and excitement moistening his eyes. "It's the Lord!"

Peter wasted no time. He dove in and swam with head high so as not to lose sight of me. Upon reaching where he could stand, his strong frame waded the rest of the way to my waiting smile. We latched arms, his face dripping water and beaming exuberance.

"You have come to us again, Jesus," he breathed. "My heart rejoices!"

"Yes, I am here," I affirmed, hands still linked to his arms. "In the flesh."

His grasp tightened as if my sudden appearance was the greatest gift he could have received. "Stay with us today, Lord. We have longed for your return."

I smiled earnestly and motioned to a small fire I had started in a circle of stones. Bread loaves warmed over the embers. "Bring some of the fish you caught," I said. "We shall have breakfast together."

I had never seen Peter so happy. Like the leper who had watched his disease melt away, Peter felt reborn—no longer simply alive, but enlivened. He had to consciously pull his eyes from me to return and help his brothers drag the boat aground near shore. They left the net dangling in the water, still affixed to the hull, wriggling with fish.

How overjoyed they all were to see me again. We ate. We talked. We shared our minds and souls. They needed no further coaching or training. My presence stood as direct evidence—perfect validation of everything they had already learned. My company with them fulfilled the promise of my previous words and deeds. Now those words and deeds germinated inside them as seeds of everlasting life.

My other apostles soon joined us.

Later, as they doused the fire and readied the boat to return to the Capernaum docks, Peter and I stood watching from a grassy dune just beyond the beach. My eyes lifted to where the gray horizon met the water, and I asked thoughtfully, "Simon, son of Jonah, do you love me?"

Peter turned to my gaze, which remained upon the sea. He was startled to hear his former name, let alone such a question.

"Yes, Lord," he answered definitively. "You know that I love you."

"Feed my lambs," I replied.

Encouraged to hear this request and reassured that I still entrusted him to guide my followers, he returned his eyes to the water.

"Simon, son of Jonah," I repeated, "do you love me?"

My attention remained focused over the vast lake, and Peter once again looked at me with a troubled stare. His words were slow, yet conclusive. "Yes. Of course I love you."

"Take care of my sheep."

He paused for only a moment. "Lord, you are the son of the living God. I will do all you ask and more. I will—"

"Simon, son of Jonah," I interrupted, finally bringing my eyes to his. "Do you love me?"

If Peter hadn't suddenly understood my meaning and motivation, he may well have broken down. I had asked him to verify his love for me three times—the same number of times he had denied knowing me outside Caiaphas' house.

He now accepted my provocation and nodded humbly. "Lord, you know all things. You *know* that I love you."

I nodded myself and grabbed his shoulder. "Feed my sheep."

His eyes and lips whispered decisively, "Always."

I returned a poignant smile. "Peter, when you were younger, you did as you wanted to do, went where you wanted to go. But someday you will stretch out your hand and someone else will take you where you do not want to go."

His silence confirmed his faith in me. He questioned not what this meant, unaware it alluded to a similar fate as mine, but willing nonetheless. Newfound strength in my resurrection had transformed him.

"Follow me," I encouraged.

What better example of the human journey and its resulting spiritual growth than in my friend Peter. From a modest, ordinary place in life, I had called him. His credentials rested not in his personal abilities, daily wages, social status or political pull. He did not follow the lead of others but spoke from his own heart. To find the truth, he continually sought me. Wherever I went, he went, so that wherever I was, he was. Learning eagerly, he trusted my counsel and placed his confidence in *my* understanding rather than his own. But most importantly, when he failed—when he gave in to common fear and deceiving diversions—when he distracted himself from my presence, he did not wallow or despair in defeat. He overcame his remorse and used his contrition to surmount his regret … and run back to me.

Should I now strip him of his leadership and mission because of stumbling and missteps? By no means. Triumph climbs out of failure. Peter triumphed over his collapse by returning to me. All my brothers and sisters would soon triumph in unimaginable ways despite their natural failings. How? By living in relationship with me and making it their mission to share that relationship with others.

So with arms on each other's shoulders, Peter and I walked down to the beach. The clouds began breaking across the sky and allowing larger pockets of sunshine to brighten the expansive lake. My apostles waited for us at the water's edge. James and John finished folding the net and returned it to the boat.

"We are about to push out to sea, Lord," said James. "Will you come with us?"

I motioned to the net they had tucked neatly in the bow. "Where are all the fish?"

For a moment they stood silent, each waiting for another to respond.

"We let them go," Andrew finally answered. He snuck a quick smile to his older brother. "We are ready to be fishers of men."

The soft, steady ripples of the sea swirled around our feet, and I smiled back.

Victory.

*   *   *

A month passed. Time spent with my apostles further reinforced the reality of my physical presence. I had not returned as a spirit or as some dreamlike experience. My resurrection was not a vision— not a hallucination. I again walked side by side with them in the flesh. Mary Magdala often joined us, and others as well. My mother too.

On this particular evening, my eleven and I sat together along the short stone wall bordering the Garden of Gethsemane. I had asked them to return to Jerusalem. Beside this orchard of olive trees where I had prepared in anguish for my passion and death, I now sat renewed with my friends, preparing them for my final departure back to the Father. I would ascend from the Mount of Olives farther up this very hillside.

Tonight would be my final night.

The setting sun bathed us in scarlet warmth. Its direct rays slipped lazily behind Jerusalem's walls. I leaned back against the stone—Peter to my left and John on my right. The others huddled close-by.

"We sense that you will be leaving us soon, Lord," said Matthew. "Will we truly know where to begin when you are gone?"

"You will," I replied definitively. "Stay in Jerusalem and wait for the gift that I told you my Father has promised. In a few days, you will be baptized with the Holy Spirit. Then you shall bear witness to me here in Jerusalem, throughout all of Judea, Samaria and to the ends of the earth."

Peter rested his head against the stones, then moved slowly to my shoulder. "As long as there is breath in our bodies, we shall do your will."

I gazed over the Kidron valley to the high city wall eclipsing more sunlight with each passing moment. My will and the Father's had always been one. His dominion rested in me. My love for the world had opened the gates of heaven, and now these few before me would grow the roots for my Holy Church.

"All authority in heaven and on earth has been given to me," I affirmed. "Therefore, go and make disciples of all the nations, baptizing them in the name of the Father, and of the Son, and of the Holy Spirit. Teach them everything I have shown you."

I alone watched the fading glow over the temple mount. My brothers looked directly at me, savoring my presence to remember these final hours with me.

"Stay with us tonight, Lord," John beseeched. He eased his head upon my other shoulder. "You give us such strength and comfort."

I smiled lovingly at my dear friends, hoping my heart might speak to them before my words.

"Do not be afraid," I reassured. "Know that I will be with you always ... to the end of time."